ROSALIND LAKER

Claudine's Daughter

Pan Books

First published 1979 by Eyre Methuen Ltd

This edition published 2002 by Pan Books
an imprint of Pan Macmillan Ltd
Pan Macmillan, 20 New Wharf Road, London N1 9RR
Basingstoke and Oxford
Associated companies throughout the world
www.panmacmillan.com

ISBN 0 330 40057 6

A CIP catalogue record for this book is available from
the British Library.

Printed and bound in Great Britain by
Mackays of Chatham plc, Chatham, Kent

To F. W. and Margaret Jenkins

I

She stood fiercely and aggressively on the rocky mound, the black veil of her bonnet billowing out behind her, tendrils of her vivid hair whipping about her taut and angry face. Lucy di Castelloni was watching for the first locomotive on the newly-constructed railway line to come into sight, wanting to protest by her presence there against the speedy transport that had become more important than people's homes and livelihoods. In a landscape backed by cypress-covered hills and made up of small farms, a trail of destruction had been scythed these many months past to make a right of way for the iron tracks along which the train would pass on its way to Pistoja.

'There! It's coming!' she cried suddenly, pointing to a puff of smoke that seemed to have materialized out of the hills. The peasants there with her murmured amongst themselves. They could all hear it now, a distant vibrating rumble that was throwing out echoes. The sun caught the flash of polished brasswork and the smoke showed thicker, curling out across the countryside. The rumble of the train's approach increased, and a child at Lucy's skirts whimpered with fear. Swiftly she snatched him up and held him close, never taking her eyes from the iron monster that had come into view. It had a high, fluted chimney of narrow dimensions and was black with scarlet framing over the churning wheels, several carriages rattling along behind. Dear God! There were streamers and flags attached to the train, a rainbow flutter trailing out in its wake. Did it mean nothing that honest men had been left without work, women had been raped by the rough Sicilian labourers who had laid the tracks, and five children had been lost in a fall of earth when supporting timbers had given way? The district in which she lived had been hit harder than any other along the line.

In silence the little crowd on the mound watched as the locomotive drew level, the rush and roar of it assailing their eardrums. Only Lucy made any move, suddenly shaking her fist furiously at the train for all it represented of men's greed and inhumanity, but the smoke billowing from it enveloped her and those with her, causing them to be lost to sight from the train and from each other, their forms momentarily ghost-like until the air cleared and the train was gone.

Lucy remained staring after it, the child still clutched to her. It had been a sharp climb up to secure her viewpoint, but she had managed it, careless of having muddied the petticoat hems beneath her hooped skirt, her high-buttoned boots similarly soiled. On all sides the peasants who had gathered there with her began to disperse slowly and despondently, a few glancing towards the young woman in her widow's weeds who had done everything in her power to help them through a winter harder than any other in living memory. Not only had there been the destruction wrought by the building of the railway, but also the wind had never blown more icily from the snow-capped Apennines, never had there been more illness, more despair, or food more hard to come by. Selflessly she had given her time to the sick and the hungry whilst at the same time tending her elderly husband who had lain in a coma at the di Castelloni villa until a few days ago, when at long last life had left him.

The child was wriggling to be put down, all fear gone, and Lucy set him on his feet, letting him run down the slope. She followed him, and returned to the two-wheeled equipage that awaited her. As she drove herself away she wished she had been able to do more for the poor people who had suffered. The compensation for the destruction of property and the taking of necessary land had been paid by

6

the railway to the rich owners and not the tenants, who had had to shift for themselves.

She took the winding road at a good speed, realizing she had been absent from the villa longer than she had intended. The funeral had taken place only that morning, but it was no disrespect to Stefano that she had left his family to themselves and gone alone to see the train. Soon she had reached the tiered vineyards and the acres of lush olive groves that had belonged to the di Castellonis for generations, and afterwards she drove past the great spread of espaliered cherry and apple trees, cloudy with pink and white blossom. A final bend in the road brought her within sight of the villa, which had been there since Medici times, its russet roof showing amid the mimosa trees. She saw no one as she drove through the gardens, but when she alighted at the entrance she was met by a servant in a state of agitation.

'Everyone is waiting for you, Signora! The lawyer has arrived and the will cannot be read until you are present.'

'Oh, dear! Am I so late?' She sped up the wide stairs to reach her own suite of rooms, where she was greeted with a show of relief by Alina, her stout, middle-aged maid, who rushed about to get her changed out of her muddied garments into fresh petticoats and another black gown. Pins and combs were whipped from her hair, which was brushed under the maid's expert hands and re-dressed in the simple style she favoured. A newly-laundered handkerchief with lace trimming was fragrantly scented for her, a jet necklace slipped over her head, a black enamelled gold mourning brooch was refastened at her throat, and then she was ready. Taking a deep breath, she smoothed her tightly-laced waist with the heels of her hands and went downstairs to arrive at a more sedate pace in the saloon where the family awaited her. All the men rose to their feet, and at Stefano's desk the lawyer bowed to her.

She took her place in the great carved chair which had been placed in readiness for her as the widow of the head of the house, albeit she had been his third wife, a whim of his old age, and his many children and their marriage partners, seated in a semi-circle on either side of her as well as in a row behind, were all much older than she. The lawyer cleared his throat and began to read. His voice had a droning quality, and she was reminded of a bumble-bee.

She listened impassively, sitting young and still and straight-backed. If the others expected her to feel disappointment at the total absence of her name on the will, it showed how little they had come to know her since Stefano had made her a bride, for she was neither avaricious nor acquisitive and never had been. Let those who wanted his wealth receive it, and with her total goodwill. She had known his generous heart. It was enough for her.

Domenico, the eldest son, narrowed his thickly-lashed eyes as he glanced sideways at the young widow and congratulated himself on the fact that, although the marriage had been of five years duration, some quirk of advancing senility had made his father overlook the necessity of adding a codicil to make provision for her. Everything had been bequeathed to the rightful heir. It was all his: the mansion in Rome and this residence on the outskirts of Florence where all had gathered at the death-bed and stayed for the funeral; the palazzo on the Adriatic coast that had once been papal property; the vineyards; the estates; the greater part of the old man's fortune. More than that, there was a bonus in Lucy, born in Italy of English parentage, who had been delivered penniless and dependent into his charge by the very absence of her name on the will. It made his pulse quicken just to contemplate the power it gave him over her.

Not that she was beautiful or even comely in the conventional sense, nevertheless she had an arresting face, creamy-complexioned and well-shaped, with fine grey eyes, and her hair, which was an unusual red-gold, lay smooth as paint over her neat head from its middle parting and was drawn into a heavy, plaited coil at the nape of her neck. Her hands, graceful and with long fingers, were folded one above the other in the lap of her black silk dress, the skirt of which sprang out from gathers at her slender waist like the petals of a sooty rose. He had desired her from the moment he had first seen her at his father's side, and who would think, to look at her present composure, that she could turn into a spitting virago as she had done on the night of some amateur theatricals in the gardens when he had first attempted

8

to discover for himself the sweet secrets of her body that were being wasted on an old man?

'Don't touch me!' she had shrieked out on a shudder, her Italian flawless. 'I am your father's wife. I love him!'

Had he been less angry, his conceit less affronted, he would have laughed. Old Stefano had never been a handsome man, as was his elder son, and in old age he had been gross and ugly as a devil, with his florid complexion, pouched eyes and a stomach like a barrel. Yet there had been a certain *rapport* between the old man and the girl that resembled affection on both sides. At first she had been exotically dressed and bejewelled, to be flaunted by Stefano everywhere in Rome as a tribute to his lingering virility, but later, instead of leaving him to the care of the nurses as she could have done, she had fed him like a baby, performed the most menial and disgusting tasks, and sat with him by the hour. When he died she had dropped to her knees at the bedside, weeping over his veined hand which she held to her cheek, and long after the family had withdrawn with a feeling of relief that all was over, she had continued to kneel there in her grief, silent and alone.

'Go to her, Domenico.'

His wife's whisper startled him out of his reverie and he became aware that the long list of minor bequests had come to an end and the reading of the will was over. He rose from his chair, a broad, dapper man with every reason to be proud of his appearance, and after a courteous nod to the lawyer he took Lucy by the hand and raised her up from where she was sitting. As her skirts rustled with her movement, everybody else around her stood in respect. It was the last time they need give her the acknowledgement that had been due to her in the past, and each could afford to be magnanimous since none of them had been left out of the will. They bowed or curtsied according to sex as Domenico led her away, some who liked her giving a little smile, others unable to hide their gleam of satisfaction that nothing belonging to the di Castelloni family had been bequeathed to a foreigner.

He led her along the corridor where the windows gave views of the formal gardens and a stretch of almond trees and umbrella pines hid the distant, sienna-coloured roofs of Florence. Only when they reached the circular saloon of her apartments did he release her fingers.

'You will need a little. time on your own to gather your thoughts and adjust to your new level in life,' he said benignly but authoritatively as befitted his new attitude towards her. 'Naturally you must come downstairs to dine with the family at the appointed hour, although you will no longer take the place at table allotted to the wife of the head of the house.'

She had remained standing exactly where he had let go of her hand, which by chance was in the very centre of the gracious room with its green marble pillars and gilt furnishings, and she was sideways to him, her gaze directed ahead as if focused on some point far away beyond the glass doors that opened onto the balcony.

'I decided long ago what to do when this day came,' she said quietly.

'Do?' he repeated a trifle irritably, sensing rebellion. He meant to start as he intended to go on, and thus eventually to bend her to his will.

She turned to face him, her visage illumined as by some inner radiance. 'I'm going home.'

At first he thought she meant the convent where she had been reared almost from birth, and the protesting expostulation burst from him at the thought of such carnal loss to a man's world. 'No! You have no vocation to take the veil. I have heard you say as much yourself.'

Her brows, fine and singularly straight, lifted high. 'You misunderstand me. I'm going home to find the place where my father was born. To England.'

He was aghast. 'But Italy is your home. You were born in this country, and if there had not been an English nun at the convent you would never have learned one word of the English language.'

'I like to think that is why my mother left me at that particular convent.'

'It had nothing to do with it.' He knew all about her origins. The nuns had given Stefano a biographical report, and Domenico, who had long used a secretly duplicated key to gain access to his father's private papers, had read it with interest. 'She left you there simply because that convent was the nearest to the villa in which you were born and your father died,' he declared cruelly, having drawn his own conclusions on that point. 'It happened to be convenient and she was in haste to be rid of you and get back to England.'

'That's not true!' In childhood she had fed herself on dreams of her parents, that had been culled from Sister Alice's descriptions, comforting herself with images of her lovely, red-haired mother and her sick, fine-looking father who had come to Italy as so many did in a last hope of recovering his health in a climate kinder to consumptives than that of his homeland. 'My mother was distraught after my father died. Grief quite turned her head. She adored him so much that not once during those last months of his life did she set foot outside the villa grounds, wanting only to be with him. Had he lived they would have taken me back to England and I would have grown up at a place called Attwood Grange.'

'Instead of which she never wrote or contacted you, but gambled and frittered away everything she had, and when the money she had left for your keep at the convent had been used up the nuns kept you out of charity.' He was taunting and bitter, not sparing the full-breasted young woman for whom his whole body craved. 'She even sold the house you mentioned to one of her husband's distant cousins, who would want no meeting with you. When the nuns sought financial reimbursement from that quarter he wrote back that the late Lionel and Claudine Attwood had had no issue other than an infant stillborn in Italy at that time, and he added the caustic advice that the nuns should try their Popish tricks to extort money from others more gullible than a staunch Wesleyan.'

That denial of her existence came as a great shock to her. Her face blanched and even her lips lost their colour. She answered him in a choked voice. 'But I know that I'm Claudine's child. She had no need to lie to the nuns, and neither did they lie to me. It only confirms what I said about my mother having lost all reason through bereavement.'

'No papers were left by her. No proof at all of your identity. How can you be sure that you are not some other woman's offspring?'

She refused to let him break her and straightened her shoulders bravely. 'Sister Alice received me into her arms when my mother brought me to the convent. It is through her I know that I bear a striking resemblance to her, and that makes me very proud.'

'Hmm.' He was unimpressed. 'It's a pity that the abbess at the time of your taking in was too old and senile to have the wit to obtain detailed documentation or that Sister Alice did not leave a statement of witness before she died.'

'You seem to think I intend to make some belated claim upon the Attwood family, but that is not so. I had never thought to burden myself on the present owner of the Grange, but only to see the house, walk the paths that my father trod, and wander the district where he grew up.'

'That is as well, seeing that you would be labelled as an impostor from the start.' He was showing no mercy, wanting to see her flinch, but she disappointed him.

'I have planned all along to earn my own living.'

In his aggravation with her he switched to sarcasm. 'How? By scrubbing floors?'

Her gaze did not falter. 'If I must. I scrubbed floors at the convent. But I do not think it will come to that. I could teach music and Italian, put my hand to sewing, or better still, launch into something more adventurous. There is the skill at cards and the gaming tables that I learned from Stefano. Who is to say that I could not put that knowledge to some practical use?'

His patience went entirely. 'Let me hear no more of this nonsense. You cannot go to England. I will not allow it. As my father's widow you are entitled to be taken care of until the end of your days and you will remain in the family home where you belong. I will remind you that you are entirely without funds, and whatever allowance I choose to grant you will most certainly not go towards a fare to England.'

She was undeceived as to the true reason for his concern. Men had a way of looking at her that gave away their thoughts, and what Domenico desired had been known to her long before the time he had thrust his hateful, silky hands upon her flesh. She had no illusions about her claim to beauty, and yet wherever she went it was the same: the sharply-turned head followed by the open stare with its instant recognition of that indefinable lure over which she had no control, eyes deepening and darkening to burn into her with a message of their own, from which she had always turned away. Had she worn fancy gloves and a bell on her forehead like those that had adorned Florentine women of a certain calling in the past, she could not have been more certain of persistent male attention. 'I have some money and the jewels that Stefano gave me,' she answered him. 'I'm not quite destitute.'

His temper flew before her continued defiance. Nobody ever defied him. Nobody! His word was law in his household and over the lives of everyone whom he employed or used to gain his own ends. With his face congested he took a swift step towards her and grabbed at the jet necklace that she wore, wrenching it from her neck so that the string broke and the beads flew in all directions across the marble floor.

'You have nothing! You own nothing! Nothing that I do not allow you to keep!'

She stiffened, refusing to quail, but a sick fear of him churned her stomach. 'I shall leave for England tomorrow if I have to walk every step of the way and row myself across the English Channel.'

He almost struck her. His fists clenched at his sides and his whole frame shook from the strain of controlling himself. Lust had risen with his rage and all he could think of was that she was about to slip through his fingers without his having ever possessed her.

'You underestimate my power,' he warned in a deadly tone. 'The palazzo on the coast has many secret rooms. Who knows what they were used for in years gone by – meditation? Assignations? Incarceration?'

Her pupils dilated and the bones stood out on her face. 'You would not dare to shut me away! This is 1850 – not the dark ages.'

'And this is my domain where all is done exactly as I wish

13

it. You protest that your mother lost her reason through bereavement. All will be sad to hear that grief has had the same effect upon you.'

She almost fainted. Bitterly she regretted ever mentioning to him her intention of going home. She should have slipped away secretly, but now he would alert every servant, and with his ability to corrupt and bribe and crush whoever stood in his way politically and domestically, he would have no compunction in carrying out his threat. He would only need a false statement on a medical certificate, a closed carriage, and a retainer willing to keep his mouth shut and a ring of keys on his belt. The suffocating decadence of Italy was rising to cloak away the vision of freedom that had been hers for as long as she could remember, but she would not surrender to it. She would not.

'No!' She shook her head violently, drawing back from him. 'No!'

In spite of her denial, he had seen her terror and was certain he had broken her, which was as well, because his wife thought highly of the girl and would make a deal of trouble over any sudden disappearance, and there were others in the family who would probe and question and refuse to let the matter rest. His anger ebbed, and in triumph he advanced towards her and put his hands on her shoulders to run them sensually down her arms to her wrists.

'There need be no trouble between us,' he coaxed munificently. 'Let us forget all that has been said. Both of us are overwrought on this funeral day. You will find I can be as generous as my father with jewels and anything else you happen to fancy. Come, my dear –'

She hurled aside his light clasp, her whole face a mask of loathing. 'No! No! No! I tell you that you shall never have your way with me!'

She whirled about and dashed for the double doors through which they had entered the room, knowing she had only to reach some other members of the family to find at least two or three champions among them, but he was the swifter. Even as she reached the doors and jerked them open he flung his full weight forward and slammed them

14

closed. Thrusting her back with one sweep of his arm he turned the key.

For a matter of seconds they faced each other, he breathing quickly, her throat working as she saw in his face the awful purpose registered there. With a little moan she grabbed her bell-shaped skirt and swung it round as she bolted from him again, making this time for another door, but she never reached it. He seized her before she was halfway there, and even as she struggled he caught hold of the high neckline of her mourning dress, and in a searing tear of silk he stripped the garment from her, stifling her scream in the savagery of his mouth.

When it was all over he knew a sense of shame and a kind of incredulous dismay at his own actions. He got up from the floor where he had thrown her, inadvertently stepping on one of the jet-beads and crushing it, the tiny sound magnified by the stillness of the room. For a few moments he avoided looking at her, tidying his clothes and groaning inwardly at what he had done. Smoothing his hair back into place with the palms of his hands he did at last turn and look down at her where she lay in misery, her eyes tightly shut, her only movement having been to curl up like some little wounded animal and pull the rags of her garments over her. The awfulness of what he had done took on a new significance. What if she should take it into her head to denounce him to his wife and family? He did not dare to contemplate such a disaster, realizing he must go against everything he had resolved, and let Lucy go. Moreover, he must facilitate her departure with all haste while giving her no hint as to the reason behind it. He cleared his throat.

'You had better leave tonight,' he said hoarsely. 'Take whatever my father gave you. It is yours and I had no right to say otherwise, but I was prepared to use any means to stop you from going away. I will arrange for a carriage to be at your disposal, with outriders to ensure your safekeeping, and wherever you embark it shall be shipped to England, and there take you to your destination. I ask only that you stay in your apartments until the time of your departure and then go from this house without saying goodbye to anyone. I shall not offer you money, because you would only misconstrue the reason for it, but I will see that all travelling comforts are arranged and intermediate expenses paid for out of your late husband's personal account until you are settled.'

She made no sign that she had heard what he had said, only willing him to go, feeling that at any second she might start to scream hysterically and never be able to stop if he did not soon go from the room and leave her on her own. His footsteps clacked across to the double doors, then paused as he turned to look once more at her. Then the lock clicked and the doors opened and closed. The key, which he had removed as he went through, was reinserted the other side, the lock snapped again, and the key was withdrawn, leaving her safe from intruders. The carpet in the corridor outside swallowed up his going.

Slowly she sat up, drawing her legs under her, and her head drooped, her hair torn loose and covering one bare breast. She was chilled with shock and pain, dazed with horror, and physically nauseated by such intimate contact with a man who had always been odious to her. But out of it all was dawning a resolution never to be subject to the will or domination of another person ever again.

She reviewed her past with unusual bitterness. Her father, dear to her heart, had nevertheless been forced to desert her by dying, and her mother had been so lacking in maternal instinct that she had chosen to abandon her to the care of others and had cut away all bonds through a very denial of her existence. The nuns, kindly though some of them were, particularly Sister Alice who had taught her to speak her mother tongue, had tried from the start to subdue her inherent longing for freedom and independence. Failing to make her conform to their ways, they had married her off at the age of sixteen to a man old enough to be her grandfather, and now that same man's son had violated her most cruelly. But freedom was hers at last. Gradually and almost imperceptibly the wonder of it began to flow through her veins, reviving her spirits and her strength.

Her head lifted and she shook back vigorously the disorder of her hair. She was sure that only those who had never had freedom understood its true worth, a treasure to be guarded at all times and never to be lost again. Her chin took on a determined thrust that her father would have recognized as his own. In future she would be the one to rule the path she followed, and woe betide those who tried to cross her or thwart her in any way. She had been taught a hard lesson and she would never forget it, or else the cost could be the very liberation that she had waited so long to achieve.

She rose unsteadily to her feet, hampered by her torn clothing, and pulled the last shreds fiercely from her. The colour of black would ever remind her of this terrible day. She would never wear it again. Leaving the remnants lying on the floor, she stumbled naked through to her bedroom and into the adjoining marble bathroom to wash away through total immersion all trace of the past from her.

When darkness fell she left without a word of farewell to any but the servants who gathered outside to see her go, the grapevine of the lower quarters having spread the news of her departure. Some of the womenfolk were in tears and wiped their eyes with their apron corners, thinking that the new master had lost no time in issuing banishment, and knowing that many small kindnesses shown to them in the past had gone for ever under the new regime. As for the di Castelloni family, there were two or three with whom Lucy would have spoken had they come to see her go, but she had made no close friends among them, for even those who liked her had feared she would usurp them in Stefano's will. It struck her as slightly ludicrous that Domenico had ordered one of the most ornate travelling carriages to take her away, with the three postillions in charge of the six matched greys liveried in green and gold to match the luxurious equipage. With her she had Alina, who had always been respectful, loyal and willing, and although the prospect of a long journey to England did not appeal to her, she had considered it her duty to accompany her young mistress. Without doubt she had drawn her own conclusions about the torn garments she had gathered up and thrown away, but she had made no sign and had herself swept up all the scattered jet beads instead of summoning a lesser servant to do it.

Lucy's only regret in departing from Italy in such circumstances was that she had no chance to return again to the Adriatic coast and make a last visit to her father's tomb, which was situated in a churchyard quite near the villa where he had spent the last months of his life. The inscription was in English. *Here lies Lionel Attwood, beloved husband of Claudine, Lord of Attwood Grange, Easthampton, England. April 1796–May 1829. Rest in Peace.* The nuns had always allowed her to visit the tomb periodically with flowers to lay upon it, the convent being no distance away, and once in Sister Alice's company she had gone to the high gates of the villa and looked through at it, able to picture her father sitting in the sun on the terrace, looking out to sea at the passing fishing-boats, or smiling at her mother as she sat with him, reading aloud letters newly come from England. But the villa had been sold after his death and the people who lived in it had no interest in the convent, and so the opportunity to see the villa at closer hand never came her way.

It had been on those visits to the churchyard that Signor Stefano di Castelloni had taken notice of her. His neighbouring residence was palatial and set in vast grounds, and she had never imagined when she had first entered it after her marriage that one day his eldest son would threaten to incarcerate her in that very place, and with her husband's funeral barely over take from her the virginity that had still been hers.

'Are you all right, Signora? I have smelling-salts should you require them.' Alina was leaning towards her from the opposite seat of the carriage, her face showing concern in the dim light of the interior lamp.

Lucy stirred, realizing she had covered her eyes with one hand, her elbow leaning heavily upon the arm-rest. 'No, thank you. I am well.'

'Do you wish to sleep?'

Lucy nodded, and Alina sprang up to arrange cushions for her head and drape a soft travelling-rug over her as she let her shoes drop to the floor and lifted her feet onto the upholstered seat. Lying curled up she closed her eyes in an overwhelming weariness. Whether she would manage to sleep she did not know, but she hoped she would, because every minute of oblivion shortened the journey and brought her nearer home.

Had it been possible she would have travelled night and day without stopping, but there were the servants and the horses to consider, and with overnight stops it took several days before the carriage rolled down the hill to the harbour of Genoa, over flagstones that made the wheels jar and the hooves slither, rumbling through streets so narrow that pedestrians jumped into doorways to let it go by, past palazzi of black and white marble, and coming at last to the quayside. There Lucy learned that an English ship was due to sail that same evening, and before long she and the servants were aboard, the horses taken to stalls on a lower deck, while the carriage itself was lashed and secured aft with tarpaulins roped over it to protect it from the spray.

Accommodation for the passengers was well-appointed, and once under sail the seas were not unpleasantly choppy, although enough wind was embraced by the huge spread of canvas to maintain a swift, wave-slicing speed to the ship's bow that suited Lucy's fervent impatience for the voyage to be done. She stood at the rails when finally the gentle contours of England began to form out of the mist on the horizon, and she wept with joy at the sight of it.

2

As the carriage covered the last remaining miles from London to Easthampton in bleak March weather, Lucy looked out eagerly from side to side, wondering in which direction the Grange might lie and hoping to see a signpost somewhere, but although they passed several imposing mansions set back in spacious grounds, none was the late Lionel Attwood's home. But at least she was gathering an impression of the countryside that he had known and grown up in. Ever since they had crossed the county border and passed through a market town called Merrelton there had been thick woods and rich agricultural land protected by the slopes of the grassy Downs. In spite of all the signs of prosperity in the abodes of the landed gentry there was also abject poverty in the hovels and humble dwellings of those who laboured in the fields and scraped out their own meagre existence on smallholdings. Many people looked thin and hungry, and everywhere children ran barefoot and in rags.

When the outskirts of Easthampton came into sight it did seem that the poorer people were better housed and better clad, and she supposed that there was always work in the resort. Then almost at once the carriage was enclosed on either side by large residences with railings and gardens and an abundance of trees. When the road opened out she saw that the carriage had arrived at the centre of the resort, for a splendid house, set upon a hillock, commanded a view of the broad stretch of a flint-walled park, flanked by fine terraces, which stretched to the promenade that followed the seashore.

Even as she was observing everything, so was the carriage being noticed in its turn. Everywhere pedestrians were stopping to stare after it, and those in other vehicles or on horseback turned their heads in amazement. It had caused a minor sensation in London where she had stayed to see something of her country's capital and organize her modest finances at a bank with which Stefano had had dealings. She had been most courteously looked after and as soundly advised as if she had had a fortune to invest instead of the small sum at her disposal. The hotel at which she stayed had organized a booking for her at the Warwyck Hotel in Easthampton, informing her that it faced the sea at the eastern end of the promenade and offered the most commodious and comfortable accommodation. If she had come to England at the height of the summer season when the coastal resort was crammed with the well-to-do it would have proved difficult to obtain somewhere to stay with additional accommodation for a maid and six retainers, but since it was early in the year, plenty of room was available. She had been able to give the postillions some direction as to where the Warwyck Hotel was located from what she herself had been told.

Among those watching the Italian carriage approach were three young men, each with the easy, self-assured air that comes from wealth, good schooling and a solid family background. All were well-clad in warm top-coats, two with high-crowned grey bowlers and the third in a black stovepipe which accentuated his already considerable height. About to cross the road from the gentlemen's club from which they had emerged after partaking of a lengthy luncheon together, they remained on the pavement kerb for the carriage to pass, eyeing it incredulously. In a soft-hued English setting amid bare-branched trees that lined a road still gleaming from a slashing shower of rain, it looked bizarre with its abundance of gilt ornamentation, its brilliant sapphire bodywork and flashing wheels, its ornate hubs and harness; moreover, the Latin complexions of the postillions were patchy in the sharpness of an unfamiliar climate, their braided coats flapping in a brisk wind blowing off the sea.

'Good Lord!' exclaimed one of the watching trio expressively, giving his neighbouring companion a dig in the ribs with his elbow. 'What do you make of that monstrosity?'

The reply came with a wine-ripe chuckle. 'Such splendid vulgarity. Her Majesty don't own an equipage to beat it unless you count the Coronation Coach. Looks foreign to me. Those postillions are dagoes right enough. What do you say, Warwyck?'

They both looked towards their friend in the tall hat, but Richard Warwyck did not appear to have heard the question. He had glimpsed the occupant of the carriage and his gaze was fixed on her. Lucy, still bending forward to glance one way and then the other, happened to turn her head in his direction as her window came level with the three on the pavement, and she looked full into his alert, strong-boned face with its high brow and square chin, his light blue eyes holding hers. She was conscious of a curious sense of being drawn to him, but it was an asexual reaction, odd in the circumstances, and it was gone like the flare of a match instantly extinguished. She resisted the temptation to look back at him, but the image of his face remained with her as if briefly she had looked into a mirror and seen his visage instead of her own.

Richard waited until he had seen whether the carriage turned to the right or to the left when it reached the seafront, and only then did he swivel on his heel to make a comment and take leave of his companions. 'The new arrival is most probably bound for the Warwyck Hotel. In my father's temporary absence abroad it falls to me to greet all distinguished newcomers, so I'll bid you good day, my friends.' His eyes twinkled. 'There are those of us who have to work, don't y'know.'

Some good-natured repartee followed him as he set off in the wake of the carriage, the angle of his stovepipe not rakish, but at sufficient a tilt to show that in spite of the serious mien normal to him he could enjoy the lighter side of life to the full, and that included pretty women. In his long stride he matched exactly that of the parent he had mentioned as well as in height and build, the powerful strength of his shoulders due to his sparring in the ring at the local gymnasium as once his father had fought in the prize-ring; indeed, he had benefited in his childhood and adolescence from coaching given by an old man, Jem Pierce, who had been his father's trainer, but who had long since died in retirement. It would be difficult to say who had spoiled him most, old Jem in those early days or his father, and it had fallen to his mother, the calmest and most tender-hearted of women, to discipline him with a strictness held to for his own good whenever it was necessary. Whether he was as much the apple of her eye as his father's he doubted, for although she never showed favouritism, he always felt that his sister, Donna, came first with her, simply because Daniel Warwyck treated his only daughter with an inexplicable harshness, there being something about her that never failed to irritate or annoy him no matter how hard she tried to please. Richard had clashed with him in defence of Donna many a time, but at the age of nineteen she appeared to have become resigned at last to their father's indifference and kept out of his way as much as possible in the large mansion on the hillock overlooking the park, which was known as Easthampton House.

Reaching the steps of the Warwyck Hotel, Richard saw that the carriage had already deposited its passenger and pulled into the stables at the rear of the building. There were only two hotels in Easthampton, the reason being that many visitors preferred to bring their own servants and take a villa, a terrace house or other spacious apartments for the summer, but since his father owned the Warwyck Hotel and had half shares in the other, once called the George IV Hotel to honour the monarch in whose reign it had been built and now known simply as the Royal Hotel, he could have gone into either to greet the new arrival within the portals.

The glass doors were swung open at his approach and he went swiftly through the vestibule into the crimson-carpeted lobby with its flock wallpaper, forest of aspidistras and buttoned velvet upholstery. The young woman from the carriage was signing her name in the register, and waiting at a respectful distance from her was a short, dumpy lady's maid, laden with furs, hand-valise and a stout jewel-box. Richard went straight to a recessed door which brought him into an office at the rear of the reception desk. He removed his hat and top-coat, checked the neatness of hair, well-trimmed sideburns and knotted cravat in a wall mirror bearing the name of the hotel in opaque letters, and went through an archway to the desk. The young woman was putting the pen back in the inkwell. Before the clerk in attendance could make a move Richard twisted the book around to read her name, and saw that she had come from Florence in Italy.

Lucy, picking up the glove that she had removed and set aside before signing her name, suppressed a start at seeing him again. He must have come on winged heels from the place near the park where she had glimpsed him.

'Welcome to Easthampton, Mrs di Castelloni,' he said, his eyes hard on her. 'Are we to have the pleasure of your husband's company at a later date?'

'No, I am widowed,' she replied, not quite sure why she had given her status, there being no need, but with his stern, almost piercing look he had somehow compelled the information from her. Again she felt the strange rapport with him that she had experienced earlier, and was made uneasy by it. Had she believed in reincarnation she would have imagined that they had met and known each other in some previous existence.

'Allow me to introduce myself.' He lifted up the flap of the reception desk and came through to her. 'I am Richard Warwyck. Yes,' he added, seeing the immediate lift of her eyebrows, 'my father gave his name to this hotel, which he built together with most of Easthampton as you see it today.'

'How interesting,' she said politely but distantly.

'Is the resort to be honoured by your presence for any length of time?'

Somehow his question was not impertinent. She replied courteously. 'I'm thinking of residing at Easthampton, but I have made no decision yet. Now I would like to see my room.'

'Certainly.' He nodded to the clerk, who in turn handed

24

the key to a liveried porter. 'I trust you will let me be of assistance to you at any time.'

'Thank you.' She half-turned to follow the porter with the key, and then paused. 'Tell me, is Attwood Grange far from here?'

'Why, no. A couple of miles distant at the most.'

'In which direction does it lie?'

'Eastwards. If you came by the main road from Merrelton you would have passed a turning not far from a place called Radcliffe Hall.'

'Is the Attwood family in residence, do you suppose?'

'There is no family. The present owner is a bachelor. Perhaps you are thinking of his late uncle from whom he inherited the house last year. None of that gentleman's children survived childhood.'

'How very sad,' she said with all sincerity, thinking that ill fortune had dogged that particular owner of Attwood Grange as it had her own father. She hoped the present one would be spared such sorrows. 'What is the name of the new owner?'

'Timothy Attwood. At the present time he is in London, but he will be returning shortly and then the house will be opened up for him. Are you acquainted with some branch of the Attwoods perhaps?'

'None that Mr Timothy Attwood would know. It has been kind of you to impart so much information. Good day, Mr Warwyck.'

She moved away from him in a faint, wafting fragrance of some flower scent he did not recognize, but which pleasured his strongly-moulded nostrils. With her maid in tow and several porters following with her baggage, she ascended the wide staircase and disappeared round the bend of it to the floor above. He returned to the desk.

'For how long has the new guest booked her room?' he asked the clerk.

'She has taken it for two weeks, but said it is possible that she may require it for a longer period, her plans being uncertain. But the accommodation for the servants is for overnight only, and I gather they will make a start on the return journey to Italy in the morning.'

'Will they indeed?' Richard tapped his fingers thoughtfully on the desk's polished mahogany surface. His curiosity was sharply aroused by Lucy di Castelloni's interest in Attwood Grange and he was intrigued by an unmistakable aura of mystery around her. No, he was more than intrigued, much more. He knew it with every nerve and fibre of his being, all his senses thrown during that brief meeting with her.

When he had retrieved his hat and coat he left the hotel. The rest of the day was spent in the office of Daniel Warwyck and Son. Once a disused brewery had stood on the site now occupied by up-to-date premises, but that had been nearly a quarter of a century earlier, when Daniel Warwyck had utilized the building for workshops in the days when he had taken the biggest gamble of his life, buying up cheap land and creating with borrowed funds a resort for sea-bathing and other seaside pastimes out of a poverty-stricken fishing hamlet with nothing to commend it beyond a beautiful setting and safe beach free from dangerous currents. Out of it fortunes had been made by Daniel and those who backed him, and he still owned most of the property and the land for miles around. Richard, although he had only recently celebrated his twenty-first birthday, had a full control in the running of the business, having always possessed a sense of responsibility beyond his years. From early on he had shown the first signs of the business acumen that was a family trait, his Uncle Harry having made his first fortune when not much older than Richard was now. Although he had the greatest respect for his father's achievements in the past Richard resented Daniel's resistance to change, which resulted in many a verbal battle over the office desk. But the disagreements, however violent, were never malevolent; the filial ties were too strong, their affection for each other too deep. Invariably Richard would win his point, but there were times when the stubbornness of middle-age refused to bend to youth's eternal optimism, and the resulting impasse kept them at loggerheads for weeks. Richard had furthered several ideas of his own during his father's absence abroad, and knew full well there would be the devil to pay, but he was convinced that eventually his efforts would prove him right.

After he had dealt with correspondence and some other matters a clerk from the outer office showed in a fisherman, Bob Cooper, who was waiting to see him. In his early twenties, the fellow had the proud head, quick eyes and bull-neck of the fighter born, and could have gone far in the prize-ring, but nothing could divide him from the sea which his forebears had followed for generations before the Warwycks had come to Easthampton. He did occasionally take part in bouts held in the district, and Richard found him an able sparring partner in the ring, but that was as far as Bob had ever wanted to go into the realm of bare-knuckle fighting.

'Well, Bob? What did you want to see me about?' Richard asked, leaning back in his chair and idly turning a pencil from end to end on the blotter before him.

Bob had settled his big frame uneasily on the edge of the leather chair that had been offered him, and he sat ill at ease with his knees sticking out. 'It's about that triangular 'alf acre along the track at Denwin's Corner, Mr Warwyck. I've just found out that it belongs to your father. Somehow I always thought it must be part of the Attwood estate, seeing 'ow that's where the boundary runs to meet the Radcliffe woods 'alf a mile distant, but when I went to see the Attwood steward 'ee told me who was the owner.'

'So?'

Bob cleared his throat, taking his time getting to the point. 'It's not like your father to let anything 'ee owns fall into rack and ruin. That's what misled me. Not that the Attwood estate is in any disrepair, but with nobody living there for a long time before the present Mr Attwood inherited the place, I was that sure the land was 'is.'

Richard listened patiently. In a boat or in a ring Bob was swift enough, but expressing himself with words was a different matter. 'Yes?' he prompted, jogging the speaker along.

'I wants to rent it. I'm thinking of getting married soon and the cottage there would be real convenient.'

Richard showed his amazement. 'But it's completely

27

derelict. It's years since anybody has lived there, and the whole place is swampy and overgrown.'

Bob sat forward eagerly. 'It only needs the old ditches to be re-dug to drain the ground, and there's nothing wrong with the cottage walls. I reckon if I worked on it, 'ad the roof done and cleared the land, I could make it into good living quarters. You're a fair man, and I think I can count on you to make allowances for the cost of everything and all the time it'll take to put right.' He drew a deep breath. 'Will you let me 'ave the tenancy at a rent I can afford, with a chance to buy later on in life when my finances are in better order?'

It was not a decision that Richard could make without consideration and investigation, although on the surface he could see no reason why Bob's request should not be granted. If the man was willing to salvage something that was of no use to anybody else and make a viable proposition of it with some financial benefit to the Warwyck coffers, then encouragement should be given on all counts. After saying he would look into the matter, suggesting that Bob should call in again at the end of the week, he asked one more question.

'May I ask the name of the lady whom you are to wed?'

Bob paused with his hand on the door-knob to depart. 'I can't ask 'er till this business of the cottage is settled, but between these four walls it's Meg Linden I've a mind to marry, sir.'

Meg. Like a flick-book he had had as a child, which had a picture on each page that simulated movement when turned quickly enough, images of Meg flashed through Richard's mind. Youth and softness and a laughing face. Meg. The memories vanished as quickly as they had come.

'An excellent choice. She'll be a good wife, I'm sure.' He gave a nod of dismissal. 'Good day to you, Bob.'

A few minutes later Richard also left the office and took a gig from the premises to drive to the outskirts of the resort where the Warwyck brick and tile industries gave work to a large number of men in the vicinity of Easthampton and supplied markets far beyond the boundaries of Sussex both in England and overseas. He went on his daily tour of in-

28

spection, examined a new batch of finished tiles, had a few words with a foreman in the pug mill where men were shovelling clay under the rollers, and when everything was to his satisfaction he left again, well aware that behind him there were sighs of relief at his departure. He had earned the reputation of being a keen taskmaster, nothing escaping his sharp eyes, but he could also be fair and just and liked to think he handled the labour force better than his father had ever done. There were plenty of tales from the old days of Daniel Warwyck taking off his coat and settling a dispute with prize-ring methods; one incident had become legend when he had routed a local bathing-machine proprietor and a band of thugs and hoodlums who had ranged against him and his workmen to stop them taking shingle from the beach for building purposes. The Warwyck bathing-machines used during the summer originated from that day, when Daniel had set up in opposition and finally driven his rival out of business.

As he drove towards Easthampton House, Richard concentrated his thoughts fully on Lucy di Castelloni again, not that she had been far from his mind for a single moment since they had parted company. He decided she had been a widow long enough to be out of mourning unless, a cheering thought, the marriage had been unhappy enough for her to dispense quickly with black apparel. After all, her age could be little different from his own, twenty or twenty-one at the most. He tried to analyse her features as he remembered them, but found himself bedazzled by an impression of luminous eyes in a pale visage, and a red, moist mouth.

From the pavement an acquaintance greeted him and Richard, forced out of his reverie, saluted in return with a nod and raised whip, but it was an automatic reaction, and Lucy was still with him as the horse trotted around the north end of Ring Park and through the wrought-iron gates to take the loops of the drive that wound itself up to the forecourt of Easthampton House. The entire slope of the hillock that the drive traversed was laid to lawn without a single tree, for when Daniel Warwyck had built the house he had wanted nothing to block the panoramic view of the park, the sea, and the spread of the whole resort both eastwards and westwards around the curve of the bay, and thus it had remained to the present day. Richard, although he had his own establishment in apartments on the top-floor of a house in another part of town, had moved back into his childhood home for the duration of his parents' absence, in order that Donna should not be alone in a houseful of servants with no other company. It curtailed the freedom of his movements hardly at all, and since he and Donna had always got on well together it was no hardship to fulfil his mother's request and take up residence once again in the rooms that had been his own since early adolescence, the windows looking northwards above the trees at the rear of the house to vistas of the woodland and the Downs where he liked to walk and wander, to ride alone or to hounds with the local hunt.

Donna, re-reading a letter by the fire in the Green Drawing-room, heard her brother come into the house. When he entered the room she looked up and drew her Paisley shawl closer about her shoulders against the cold sea air that hung about him. She was a composed, graceful girl, neat in hands, clothes and figure. Her eyes, a deeper blue than her brother's, enhanced a triangular face framed by shining hair of a similar fairness to his, but hers had a tendency to curl, which made it easy for her to wear it in fashionable ringlets over each ear. The smile with which she greeted him was tilted and seemingly quizzical due to only one dimple ever being brought into play by it.

'A letter from Mamma has come with the afternoon post,' she said, indicating the sheets of closely written paper that she held. 'She and Father are visiting in Pennsylvania at the present time. Apparently there is a big fight being staged in one of the towns there that he wants to see.' She gave her head a shake, making the ringlets swing. 'You would think he had had enough of the prize-ring after all he went through in his youth, and yet a championship bout draws him still. But you would like to read it for yourself.' She held it out to him, but he put up a palm to show he was not ready for that, grinning away to himself as he stood with feet apart and his back to the fire, full of his own information that he was waiting to impart.

'I'll read it later.' He rocked on his heels in his sense of well-being. 'Something of utmost importance happened today.'

She lowered the letter to her lap and sat back in her chair, her smile widening as it reflected his. 'Well? What is it? Don't tell me you have heard that the Queen and Prince Albert are bringing the royal children to Easthampton when summer comes?'

He gave a laugh, jerking up his chin. 'Better than that. Oh dear, yes. Much better.'

She was incredulously amused. 'Whatever can it be?'

He looked at her for a moment, his eyes closing briefly at the wonder of what he had to impart, and made his announcement. 'Today I met the woman I'm going to marry.'

She sat as though stunned, her mouth opening slightly in her surprise. Dismay afflicted her and yet she knew she should have been pleased. He was as dear to her as any brother could be and she wanted him to have all the happiness he deserved, but inexplicably she was filled with dread. It was the same awful feeling that came to her at the sound of her father's tread, when she knew that once again trouble loomed. She found her voice and it came out faintly.

'Who is she? Where did you meet her?'

Briefly he told her, and in a way there was little to tell beyond the momentous decision he had made, but he walked about as he talked as if excitement had aroused a restlessness in him that he could not suppress. Donna was amazed. Richard of the sober judgement, the keen intelligence, the logical intellect, had fallen head over heels in love with some young woman with a foreign surname about whom he knew nothing, except that she had drawn him to her with a magnetism that had made him like a man possessed. Donna continued to have qualms.

'I should like to meet her,' she said genuinely, but not for the reason he supposed.

'That is exactly what I want you to do, Donna,' he exclaimed enthusiastically. 'It is absolutely essential that as Lucy and I become better acquainted she should understand that my intentions towards her are completely honourable.' He seized a chair and swung it round to straddle the seat, resting his folded arms on the back of it. 'I suggest that in a few days you invite her here. Tea first, perhaps, or morning chocolate. Nothing must be rushed or anything said or done to run the slightest risk of causing her offence and preventing my wooing of her.'

'You know I'll do whatever you think best.'

For the moment he was hardly listening, his face rapt. 'I'll give a dinner party in her honour, with plenty of good company and amiable conversation. We'll include three or four of the newly-married couples whom we know best, as well as your old school-friend, Anna Edenfield, and her betrothed.'

'I'll make a list. Shall we say a dozen guests in all?'

'Yes, that is exactly right. Thank God everything is running well at the brickyard and everywhere else at the moment. It will give me some freedom in which to court the lady.'

He did not add that it was highly convenient that their parents were away as well, but Donna concluded that for herself. Their father was inclined to make demands on Richard's leisure-time, thinking nothing of calling him to a business consultation at some late hour if in the mood for talk. It was only fair that her brother should have no harassment at this particular time. Again she wondered what it was about the widow that made her stand out from the many young women with whom he dallied and flirted with never a hint of serious intent, no matter how persistently he was pursued, a common enough occurrence. In a whisper once overheard and not intended for her ears she knew that he had had a mistress or two, but that was his own private affair and nothing to do with her or anyone else, provided scandal was avoided.

'I think I'll call on Mrs di Castelloni at the hotel,' she decided aloud. 'If I write she would most likely refuse an invitation from a total stranger, but once I have made myself known to her and we have talked I should imagine she would accept.'

'Bravo! I was certain that you would go the best way about it.'

There was so much she wanted to say to him, but how could one caution a fully grown man able to shoulder the entire responsibility of a complex business company in their father's absence and who was more than experienced in the ways of the world? 'I have never seen you like this before about anyone,' she said weakly, exasperated with herself for not being able to express her concern for him in suitably tactful phrases.

He laughed again, but gently. 'I've never been like this before. I took one look at her and somehow I knew we belonged to each other.' His voice dropped a note on a volume of tenderness. 'When I spoke to her in the hotel it was as if she filled my whole heart with herself.'

'Oh, Richard.' She was deeply moved, the glint of tears showing in her eyes on the wave of emotion that engulfed her. They had always been close, but it was the first time he had disclosed such personal feelings to her. Wisely she refrained from expressing the hope that Lucy di Castelloni would prove worthy of such a love as Richard would show her, and raised her hand in a sweeping little gesture of aid. 'I will do everything in my power to help you in this matter.'

'I knew I could rely on you.' He got up from the chair and went back to the fireplace where he leaned an arm on the mantel as he gazed down into the flames, speaking more to himself than to his sister. 'I mean to have Lucy di Castelloni.' His face was set inexorably and the firelight played along the tight line of the bony jaw. 'Nothing on this earth shall stand between us. Today I glimpsed Destiny in a bond never to be broken.'

The burning logs spat and crackled, sending golden stars up the chimney. Donna could find nothing to say, choked by misgivings she could neither define nor understand. A page from the letter on her lap slid from her silken lap to the floor, but she did not notice it until he, catching the flutter out of the corner of his eye, bent to pick it up for her. She took it from him.

'If I arrange the dinner party to coincide with the end of the month, do you think Timothy Attwood might be back at the Grange by then?' She was not looking at him as she pressed the crease of the returned page between her finger and thumb with concentrated deliberation.

'I have no idea. Why?'

'Since your lady expressed interest in the Grange, it would be a nice compliment to her if we included the owner among our guests.' She looked up at him and saw he was smiling at her, undeceived by her carefully guarded tone.

'And nice for you too. Eh, Donna?'

Her cheeks coloured up and she gave a nod that was almost shy. 'I'll not deny that, although I've no notion whether he would feel the same.'

'Why shouldn't he? Didn't you tell me that you have been corresponding since he left?'

'Only occasionally.' Hastily. Wanting no false impression to be given. 'I have simply been keeping him informed on Toby's condition and progress.' She was referring to a stray mongrel which she and Timothy had rescued from a poacher's trap the previous September whilst walking in the grounds of the Grange.

'You mean that rag-rug you make such a pet of instead of keeping him to a kennel outside where he belongs.'

She knew he was only teasing her, for he liked the spirited little animal which managed well enough with a crooked leg that had been badly broken in the trap and set in splints by Timothy after the rescue. Many a time when she had been exercising Toby on the beach Richard had thrown stones or a stick to be retrieved, expressing admiration at such stout-hearted enjoyment displayed, a tail almost wagging itself off after a hoppity delivery with a barking eagerness for the next throw.

'Toby cannot help his looks,' she chided with a chuckle. 'I wouldn't change him if I could choose from all the pedigree dogs in the world.' Briskly she collected the pages of her mother's letter together, slipping in the one she had been creasing, and handed it to him. 'You read this while I make out the list of dinner guests for your important evening.'

He received it from her, but even as he was about to settle himself in a comfortable chair to read it through a thought struck him. 'You had better include Josh Barton.'

Donna looked uncertain, pausing on her way to the bureau. 'Do you think we should? This is Father's house. We ought to consider that if he knew what was happening he would extend no welcome to Mr Barton these days.'

'That's nonsense.' Richard was good-humouredly patient with her. 'Any quarrel in the offing will be between Father and me. I accept full responsibility for my business arrangement with the company that Barton represents. Remember that it was old Hamilton Barton, Josh's great-grandfather, from whom Father purchased most of the land around here on which to build the resort.' Persuasively he flicked his hand at arm's length towards the bureau. 'Add the fellow's name to the list of guests. I'll find out where he's staying when I see him again. He should be back in Easthampton for a further business discussion any day now.'

'Very well.' Donna pulled out the chair at the bureau and sat down. Drawing out a piece of paper she dipped a pen in the inkwell and wrote first the name of the young widow who was to be Richard's guest of honour, underlining it with a single stroke. Under it she wrote Josiah Barton's name, and without quite knowing why, she gave it a similar flourish, making the nib splutter.

3

The parting between Lucy and her maid was not sentimental. Alina was anxious to get back to Italy and she accepted the brooch that Lucy gave her in the spirit in which it was given, not as a memento, but as an adequate reward for duties well done. In solitary splendour Alina departed in the carriage, and Lucy was left alone in her hotel room.

She had decided not to replace Alina with anyone else; instead she would make do for the time being with the assistance of one of the hotel maidservants to step in and act as lady's maid when needed, for until her future plans were settled and she knew where she was to live, it would be foolish to encumber herself with a servant. At all costs she must be free and feel free. The years of being dominated by others were well and truly behind her. As to her plans, her first move would be to find the Grange and get her bearings. After that she must consider where to live and how to supplement her meagre income. Her dearest hope was that somewhere and at some time she would meet someone who knew her father well and would engage in talk with her about him. She wondered if all orphaned children built up a god-like image of their father as she had done, and supposed it to be most likely. And what of her mother? Dearly as she had loved to hear the nuns' description of her mother's looks, she had never projected the aura of a saint about the woman who had left her in care of others. Was that the reason? Without being aware of it, had she always sensed rejection? It was certainly true that at the present time her thoughts were centred wholly on her father and all that concerned him.

Slowly she crossed to the window where she separated and held back the swathed velvet drapes that adorned it, and looked beyond the promenade to the sea, which lapped a clear, bottle-glass green on a morning bright and crisp after the previous day's gloom. Some boys came frolicking into sight along the promenade, playing tag until, tiring of the chase, one pulled a handful of marbles out of his pocket and the rest followed suit, settling down to play. Lucy craned her head a little, but the distance was too far for her to see who was winning. As it happened, she had never played the childhood game of marbles, but in the adult realms of sophisticated gaming she was an expert, which was due entirely to Stefano and no one else.

She smiled softly at her memories of him. He had loved all games of chance, and it would be impossible to reckon up the hundreds of hours they had spent playing together or with other company. He had taught her everything, for in the convent she had known nothing of gaming in any shape or form, and she had proved an apt pupil, her wits and skill matching his. For his amusement, when playing on their own, they had sometimes cheated wildly, she learning from him the tricks of dealing and cutting that would have deceived the keenest eye, and many a time their jollity must have resounded down the corridors. One of the compensations of that strange marriage had been the unexpected joy that his dry wit and sense of humour had given her, so that the two of them had been able to share a joke in the most pompous of gatherings, and when once more on their own, would laugh out loud together.

The boys had begun to quarrel over the game of marbles, resorting to punching each other, and when one bolted, making his escape, the rest followed him, leaving the promenade as peaceful as before. She knew how pleased Stefano would have been to know she was in her motherland at last. He had always wanted happiness for her and had promised that one day she should visit England, fully expecting to escort her himself, for in spite of his advanced

37

years, when he married her he had been in good health, his occasional lapses of memory attributed more to absent-mindedness than the forewarning of a sharp and sudden decline in all his faculties. They had been married less than two years when at last it became obvious what was to happen, and there was nothing to be done. Tragically, as his health had deteriorated, so had his pleasure in life. They would still play cards together, but he became more and more forgetful until one day he had dropped the hand he held and sobbed in frustration and utter despair. She had leapt up from the table, flung her arms around him and hugged him to her like a child, resolving to eliminate from his life everything that made him more aware of his own increasing helplessness. They had not played again, and she knew he was grateful for being spared that particular humiliation.

Then almost overnight all that remained of that grand, good-humoured and kindly old man was a dribbling hulk, shambling pathetically about in a state of bewilderment that tore at her heart-strings. She had taken one look at the hard-faced male nurses appointed by Domenico to look after his father, and had consigned their duties to a minimum. Through her intervention Stefano was not confined out of sight to one set of upper apartments as planned, but continued to occupy the main rooms that he had always liked best. Leaning on her arm he took shuffling walks in his beloved gardens, and under her watchful eye he was never bullied or treated roughly by impatient hands. She brought him peace at the end of his life, the girl who had been sixteen years old when the nuns had arranged the marriage without consulting her. With affection she remembered him; he had never husbanded her in a physical sense, such powers being no longer his, although his family had thought otherwise and it had flattered his ego to let them and others imagine it was so. Neither had he ever abused her. It had been for a peculiarly compassionate reason of his own that he had made her his third wife, which he once confided in her, a twinkle in his eye that had made him look almost young: 'It would have been sacrilege of a particular kind to have left you shut up forever within those dusty walls.'

38

Lucy let the drapes fall back into position again and turned away from the window. Dear Stefano. She had loved him as a friend. All he had asked of her from their marriage was that she should keep her wedding vow of faithfulness, warning that many would try to bed her. She understood that his pride could not have endured it, but she had made up her mind to be true to him, and nothing had swerved her from that path. Had Domenico been in his thoughts at the time? She never knew. Yet in the end it was Domenico who, when all else failed, had raped her most brutally.

She paled at the memory, thrusting it from her mind as she went to the bed where Alina had laid out her finest riding habit of bright blue wool as a final duty before departure. When she had changed into it, fastening the jacket by its buttons up to the folded white stock at her throat, she put on the matching top hat, arranged the veil over her face, and with the folds of her skirt looped over her arm she left her room to go downstairs where a hired hack, ordered from the hotel stables, awaited her. A groom assisted her up the mounting-block and into the saddle.

As she rode along the street level with the promenade, the full tide was splashing waves against the railings. A long chain-pier in the final stages of construction appeared to be floating on its struts, the arched towers spaced along it being supported by inverted crescents of intricate ironwork, which gave the whole structure a delicate, lacy look, and at the head of it was a circular pavilion on which some workmen were erecting a flagpole. Easthampton itself shone in clean, pastel colours, a blending of stucco and brick, enhanced by fan-lighted doorways, verandas and curved railings, with colonnaded entrances to larger buildings. Overhead the seagulls screeched as they careened on spread wings, and in the streets there was the constant jingle of harness and the swish of wheels.

She did not ride out of the resort through its centre and past the house on the hill, but going by directions given to her at the hotel she took a side lane which would in turn bring her onto a bridle path that she could follow all the way to the outskirts of Attwood Grange. She had made up her mind to find alternative accommodation to the hotel as soon as possible. Her expenses there would be paid for by the di Castelloni estate for as long as she wished it, but she was impatient to be wholly independent, and after she had seen the Grange, the prospect of which filled her with joyous excitement, she would start looking for somewhere to live. She liked what she had already seen of East-hampton, but more important would be her getting to know the district that had been home to her father. She could strike roots and let hers merge with those of her fore-bears, thus banishing forever that feeling of being adrift and not belonging anywhere that had haunted her from the time she had been able to understand what had happened to her.

The lane was narrow and ran parallel to the sea, only a thick-branched tamarisk hedge and a stretch of grass be-tween her and the sparkling waves, while on her right hand was woodland, with walks for those who wished to enjoy the countryside within sight and sound of the sea. A deal of careful thought and planning had gone into the laying out of the resort by the father of the young man she had met the previous day. In the hotel she had come across a leaflet printed specially for visitors, which gave the history of Easthampton, a brief account of its origins as a fishing ham-let followed by a summary of its development into a resort from the time the first stone was laid in 1827 to a list of distinguished personages who had stayed there, including the present Queen when she was still Princess Victoria, and other, minor members of the Royal family. A whole page was devoted to the resort's founder, Daniel Warwyck, the unbeaten Champion of England in the prize-ring, who had retired after one of the greatest fights ever to be recorded in the annals of British boxing. A gentleman's son, he had broken with class and tradition to enter the pugilistic world, and through a combination of fists, brains and courage he had risen to the top of his profession and at the same time established himself as squire over one of the most popular and select resorts of the British seaside. A portrait sketch showed him to be a still handsome man, even allowing for some flattery on the part of the artist.

Lucy reined in her horse, her attention caught by the name on a gate set back from the lane. *Honeybridge House.*

40

The charm of the name as well as the building that she could glimpse through the trees at the end of a path enticed her into bringing the horse nearer the gate in order to take a closer look. The house was thatched and much larger than it had appeared at first glance, its walls made up of such perfectly knapped flints that each shone bronze or amber or topaz as if centuries of stored-up sunshine lingered in their depths. The windows were shuttered on the inside and the whole place had a closed and sleeping look. Was it for rent or for sale? No board was displayed to enlighten her. Digging in her heel she rode on along the lane, determined to find out more about Honeybridge House when her visit to the Grange was over.

She had chosen to ride there by way of the countryside instead of going by road because she wanted to come upon it as her father must often have done when he returned home along the same bridle path in the days when he had been as young as she. How wonderful it was to be riding under branches of the same trees, to view the same placid expanse of Downs. She took a deep breath, filling her lungs with the clean, cold air in which the saltiness of the sea blended with the country aromas of wood and budding green, pale primroses and damp earth. All this her father had known.

Although she had been watching out for the Grange, the sight of it came upon her quite unexpectedly. She had covered almost two miles and had reached a sloping cart-track when suddenly the tall hedge parted and she found herself gazing down into a saucer-shaped dell in which was set a magnificent, grey stone house, looking almost toy-like in its distance from her. She could see that the approach to the house was by a driveway from the east, which passed through a deer park and by a lake of tranquil, willow-shaded water to reach the balustraded forecourt.

She looked at it and loved it and coveted it as she had never yearned for anything before in all her life. It was the most beautiful house she had ever seen, and had Fate not betrayed her there would not have been an inch of it that she would have failed to know and cherish. There was no question of her being the rightful owner, since it had been sold elsewhere by her mother's own hand, but she could not believe that her father had wanted her to grow up away from it or that he had imagined for one moment that it would never be her home.

Her chin set. This was her hour. This was the time to mend the past. Somehow or other she would get to know the house, and she would make a start by breaching its boundary walls.

Her horse, placidly cropping the grass, was jerked out of idleness. At a canter he bore her down the slope of the cart-track, bushes and woods immediately veiling the house from her sight, but soon afterwards she had reached the main gates, which stood open, and was riding through. It was an intensely moving experience for her. She wanted to embrace each of the great oaks that bordered the drive, to dip her hands into the clear water among the lily-pads of the lake glinting beneath distant willows, to throw herself down into the grass and press herself to the Attwood earth from which she had sprung.

When the house in all the splendour of its gables and carved parapets and vast areas of mullioned lights loomed up before her, she dismounted and walked the rest of the way into the forecourt. There she looped the reins to the balustrade and went to gaze upwards at her father's house, absorbing its beauty with her eyes, her mind and her whole being. Blinds shrouded the windows, the entrance door within the massive stone porch was tightly shut, and not a person was to be seen anywhere, but there was a special peace in being entirely alone at such a time. She had come home.

A sob of mingled anguish and happiness broke from her. With eyes suddenly a-swim with tears, she ran forward up the short flight of steps into the stony chill of the porch, let the folds of her habit fall behind her, and set both hands upon the ancient iron handle to pull on it with all her strength, letting the house know she was there by setting a wild ringing echoing somewhere throughout the depths of it, a heart-beat to reflect her own. With a silent cry of appeal she strained every sense to feel some response enter into her from the lives lived out there down through the centuries by so many of her forebears.

'There's no one at home,' said a man's voice, deep and articulate and faintly amused.

The spell she had been weaving was completely shattered. She gave a low moan at the insensitive intrusion, seeing in her mind's eye the contact she had been trying to establish slip away from her like silken ribbons borne off on the wind to vanish into infinity. In cruel realization she came back to herself, seeing the inviolability of the barred door, the house an alien place of bricks and stones and mortar, she still the outsider and the rejected. She continued to hang onto the bell-handle with all her weight to stop herself from slipping to her knees in the enervation of despair that swept over her. Was there to be nothing after all? Then simultaneously her strength and spirit returned. Abruptly she released her hold, jerking her hand back to her side, but still she did not turn to see who had addressed her. Instead she stiffened her shoulders as she fought for control, fiercely blinking away all traces of her very personal tears in an overwhelming rush of terrible anger at an invasion of privacy at such a time and with such dire results. With a quick swoop she gathered up her long riding skirt and only then did she spin about to face the intruder, her eyes glittering with hostility through the azure mist of her veil.

'So it appears,' she replied icily, feeling a stranger even to herself.

He stood some little distance from her in the forecourt, his long shadow stretching before him, his words having carried clearly in the quiet air; under one arm he had some sheaves of papers and in his right hand he carried a brass measuring instrument that glinted almost as brightly in the sun as the gold watch-chain looped across his trim-fitting waistcoat. About thirty years old and over six feet in height, lithe and lean-limbed, he had an erect carriage and wide shoulders, his head tilted back as he returned her stare with singularly dark brown eyes, intelligent and sure. The upper lip of the well-cut mouth was adorned with a full moustache as black as the clipped side-whiskers and the hair that curled vigorously under the brim of his tall hat; a man possessed not so much of handsome looks as of a forceful, lustful presence, a vibrant air about him even in repose.

43

Lucy found herself hating him utterly, with a virulence that was completely at variance with her nature and all the more racking for it.

His eyelids hooded slightly at her tone and he continued to regard her steadily. 'Perhaps I can be of some assistance to you, ma'am.'

'I think not.' She saw no cause to talk further with him and left the shade of the porch to descend the steps and cross the forecourt to where her horse waited, but with a casual saunter he managed to bar her way.

'Whom did you wish to see?'

'It is of no importance.' Her note was firm and dismissive. She could tell she had antagonized him, but that was nothing compared with the inner wound he had inadvertently inflicted upon her. She felt gouged and hurt and half-drowned in the tears she had dammed up.

'I suppose the open gates led you to believe that Mr Attwood was in residence,' he prompted silkily, munificently, giving her one more chance to amend her attitude.

'I had no such thoughts on the matter.' With her nerves so near the surface she was becoming increasingly frantic to get away from him, but she would not indulge in an undignified display of side-stepping. She set her riding crop against the side of his arm, indenting his sleeve under the touch of pressure she exerted. 'Now will you please move aside and allow me to pass.'

His expression hardened, an onyx darkness all that showed of his eyes. 'I'm not sure that I should, since I have a responsibility towards these grounds in the owner's absence.' Deliberately he threw off the crop with a thrust of his elbow. 'Do you usually trespass knowingly?'

Trespass! He had called her a trespasser on her own ancestral ground. A kind of horror overcame her, the present becoming inextricably associated with the hour of her rape as Domenico's dreadful threat seemed to ring again in her ears that she would be called an impostor should she make any claim to her father's name, the line between impostor and trespasser becoming indistinguishable to her. Had she received a physical blow from the stranger's fist it would have been easier to bear than his awful taunt. Her look of shock faded as her face became suddenly contorted with the violence of her feelings. 'How dare you! If you knew me you would be shamed to proffer such an insult!'

Again she made to pass him, but once more he blocked her path. 'But I do know who you are, ma'am. You are the mysterious widow who arrived in Easthampton yesterday. Afterwards, everywhere I went people were talking about the Italian carriage and the red-haired passenger. Am I not right, Mrs di Castelloni?'

She could scarcely find voice to answer him. Her natural pride in her origins and her whole self-respect had been almost mortally assailed and her eyes flashed her loathing of him. 'That is my name,' she said biting out the words, 'but we are not acquainted, sir!'

She swept past him to her horse and with dignified swiftness took the steps of the mounting block and settled herself in the saddle, but he had cast the objects he held onto the parapet of the balustrade and darted across to grab the bridle, the knuckles standing out at a gleam through the kid gloves.

'Let me remedy that, ma'am,' he said tight-lipped, glaring at her with an aggressiveness that showed no man or woman ever pushed him aside. 'Josh Barton is the name. I trust you will remember it.'

Then he released the bridle and gave the horse a whack across the rump that set it bounding forward, and at a gallop she went away down the drive, not looking back, her temper aflame. He had scarred for evermore the memory of her poignant homecoming that she had waited her full twenty-one years to achieve, and she was half-wild with pain and disappointment.

Not until she was back on the cart-track and out of sight of the house did she slow her mount, letting it have its head quietly while she breathed deeply, seeking to regain control of herself. She had learnt a hard lesson that morning. Never again would she risk such a tearing down of her very soul by any who might question her true right to call herself an Attwood born. Until she had found a way to remove all shadow of doubt none should call her impostor or trespasser or any other name that cast a slur upon her. When she came

45

to the gap in the hedge and looked down at the house again she saw that the forecourt was deserted, and of Josiah Barton there was no sign. What was he? Landscape gardener? Surveyor? An architect, perhaps? She neither knew nor cared, and thrust the ominous darkness of him from her mind.

She rode until eventually the peace of the countryside began to give balm to her injured spirit, and a considerable time passed before eventually she turned the horse towards Easthampton and approached the centre of the resort once more by way of the lane where she reined in again to look at the house that had caught her attention earlier. What a secluded, intriguing place it was. And what a perfect location it had, within sight and sound of the sea while being isolated from the resort and other habitations by unspoiled woods. How much better it would be to stay there than at the hotel or in any other rented accommodation for that matter. Moreover, such a place had endless possibilities. She could picture it as a music school or a home for convalescents; perhaps a gallery for the display and sale of paintings and other works of art to the summer visitors; these were only three business ventures that an enterprising young woman with wit and intelligence and the need to earn her own living could enter into with every hope of success. None of these ideas were new to her, for she had mulled them over often enough, particularly on the journey home from Italy. One haunting fear of the possible aftermath of Domenico's attack had formed a barrier to any plan, but fortunately Fate had been kind, and whilst in London the evidence had come that she could look to the future without the handicap of an unwanted pregnancy.

Her horse stirred restlessly, knowing that it was not far from its stable, and after one last, lingering look at Honeybridge House she rode on into town, where she was overtaken by a gig accelerated into a spanking pace by its driver as soon as he had sighted her.

'Good morning, ma'am.'

She turned her head and saw Richard Warwyck holding whip and reins, his horse and the equipage as smartly turned out as he was with his yellow gloves and beaver hat. She

46

returned his greeting, expecting him to drive on, but he kept abreast of her.

'What a splendid day, is it not? Have you been riding along the sands?'

'No,' she replied. 'Is it safe to do that?'

'Safe as anywhere could be. No sinking sands along this shore.'

'What about rocks?'

'Only those that you can see among the shingle.' He nodded towards the beach and then half-turned to gesture with his whip towards the wall of Ring Park, which they were passing. 'That was built from rocks blasted out when my father cleared a section of the beach for his bathing-machines. It's a fine example of Sussex flintwork.'

'Honeybridge House is another.'

He raised an eyebrow. 'You've spotted that, have you? It's a little masterpiece, built a couple of hundred years ago at least. Easthampton has several ancient corners that have been kept as an integral part of the resort, the newer buildings complementing the old.'

'I have observed that much thought went into the planning of this town. Not that I have seen it all yet.'

'A pleasure in store,' he commented. The Warwyck Hotel had come into sight and he was forced to draw away from her as she rode towards it. 'Good day to you, ma'am.'

'Good day, Mr Warwyck.'

She was relieved that at this second meeting the curious feeling of having known him before had gone completely. It must have been brought about through a first show of neighbourliness in new surroundings which would have been old and familiar to her had she not been born in an alien land. Then again there crashed in upon her the distress caused by Josh Barton at the steps of the Grange, and after that she thought no more about Richard, not knowing that his thoughts remained full of her.

The next morning with spirits full restored she set out from the hotel once more, but on foot, and she went straight to an estate agent where she made inquiries about Honeybridge House. The man shook his head regretfully.

'I'm sorry, ma'am, but that house is neither for rent

nor for sale. We can offer you other equally attractive properties.'

'But it is closed up,' she insisted, thinking he might be in ignorance of the fact. 'Nobody is living there.'

'So are many other houses closed up out of season. They are summer residences and are not used at any other time of year.'

She was disappointed, having hoped to get it at a rent she could afford. How she would have found the means to purchase it if it had been for sale she was not sure; it would have meant selling all her jewellery and securing a loan, for nothing that she owned was of any intrinsic value. She had worn the di Castelloni jewels in the days when Stefano had paraded her for all to see, but it was Domenico's wife who would be displaying them now upon the broad expanse of her ample bosom.

The agent in his turn knew disappointment when it became apparent that the new client, in spite of her stylish appearance, had no interest in purchasing any other property and dismissed everything he showed her except simple accommodation at a low rent. He supposed she wanted it for a retired servant or a poor relation, which did happen sometimes. She finally picked out several addresses from the list which simply provided apartments in a private house with attendance.

'I'll take a look at these,' she said, tapping them with a gloved fingertip, and he copied them out for her, slid them into an envelope and handed them over. Expressing the hope that he might interest her in other properties at a later date, he darted forward to open the door for her. She thanked him and departed.

Looking up the addresses gave her the chance to learn the names of the streets and lanes and to discover the layout of the resort, which had a number of small squares, a steine with gardens and a Norman church. Now and again she would come upon a corner of the original hamlet in a cluster of ancient fishermen's cottages or in the Tudor barn being used as a storehouse for the Warwyck tile and brick industry which operated on the outskirts, leaving the resort unsullied and free from any noise. In the commercial streets there were plenty of small, thriving businesses, and it was from an assistant taking down a saucepan outside an ironmonger's that she obtained directions how to find the fifth and last address on her list, none of the others having proved suitable.

She approached it by a lane bordered by fishermen's dwellings, some with the framework of old boats forming porches to the doors, which would give some protection from the sea-weather when it blew inshore. Sea Cottage proved to be larger and better built than those humbler dwellings, having an air of prim gentility in lace curtains drawn back with silk loops at the windows and in the brass knocker that had come from some grander residence to adorn the new-painted door. The garden was large, simply because a vegetable patch to the rear ran down to a stout wall that formed a barrier against the sea, ground that could be put to no other useful purpose. Some dried seaweed clinging to the top of the wall showed that there were times when waves, higher than the rest, managed to splash over it.

The door was opened by a buxom, middle-aged woman in a dark print dress, a cap pinned to yellowish hair, which contrasted oddly with a face as weathered as if she spent day and night in the open air, and although her eyes, small and alert, had a cunning slant, there was a geniality in her smile that plumped out her cheeks still further.

'Yes, madam,' she answered to Lucy's inquiry, 'I'm Mrs Linden – Mrs Emmie Linden to be precise. Come in, do. The agent sent you, did 'ee? You're in luck, right enough. I've nobody staying at the moment, and you can pick which of the two apartments you like best. They are being redecorated at the present time. I likes to keep the 'ouse spick and span.'

A strong smell of house-paint and paste wafted in the air about her and bore out her words. Lucy stepped straight into a large parlour with a flagged floor and an open hearth in which a cheerful fire burned brightly. Willow-patterned plates on the dresser reflected the firelight, and a horsehair sofa was set at a comfortable angle to the blaze, all the more inviting due to the fading of day outside.

'I live downstairs with my daughter, Meg,' Emmie

49

Linden informed her, leading the way through a door in what appeared to be a filled-in archway, and Lucy found that they were in a side-hall where a second entrance led into the house. 'My guests can come and go as they please,' the woman said, seeing Lucy glance towards it.

Upstairs she showed Lucy into each of the apartments, both of which opened out from the landing. Although all the furniture was partially hidden under paint-splashed cloths and the newly-hung wallpaper had yet to dry out on the walls, Lucy was sure that for the time being she had found what she had been looking for in the set of apartments that faced south. The rooms, which opened into each other, were small, but both the drawing-room and bedroom had windows that looked out beyond the garden to the sea where she would be able to watch it in all its moods; moreover, the décor was innocuous enough, the paintwork white and all colours muted with nothing to jar the sensibilities. The rent, which included the cooking and serving of the food that she herself would provide, was within her purse's range, but this did not mean that she would not have to find some employment to supplement the drain on her income as soon as possible. In any case it would not have suited her temperament to sit back in idleness.

'Would you mind my giving music lessons here?' she asked.

'Not so long as folks ain't disturbed when the other rooms is let.'

That was fair. The music lessons were only a stop-gap anyway. 'Then I'll take these apartments,' she said, taking a final look around at her choice. 'When will it be possible to move in?'

Emmie Linden, who had lifted up some of the cloths to show that the furniture underneath was of good quality and nothing was broken down, answered with an eagerness that showed she was well pleased to let the accommodation at such an unseasonable time of the year. 'Just as soon as the bedroom 'as 'ad its final coat of paint and I've got everything shipshape again. Should we say the last day of the month? And I'd like the rent in advance.'

'That would suit me very well.' Lucy opened the cords of

her reticule and took out the money to pay the woman, who was eyeing her astutely.

'Do you 'ave a maid, madam?' Emmie Linden had realized from first setting eyes on Lucy that she had under her roof the young widow who had arrived in the grand carriage. The fancy name, the red hair and the slightly foreign look to her, even though she spoke English smoothly as any of the local gentry, all added up to her being the new arrival to Easthampton.

'No, I don't.'

'In that case my Meg'll be glad to do for you at any time. She's real clever in curling 'air and stitching and all sorts. As a matter of fact, it's 'er and Bob who's been doing the decorating for me. There's nothing she can't turn 'er 'and to.'

'Perhaps I shall be glad of her assistance at times. Is Bob your son, Mrs Linden?'

'Dearie me, no.' Emmie's ample bulk shook jovially. 'But 'ee might be my son-in-law one of these days. 'Ee 'as a mind to marry Meg, but she's in no 'urry to wed. She'll cook for you when I'm busy in the summertime. I'm a "dipper", you see, madam. That is, I'm in attendance at the Warwyck ladies' bathing-machines. When the ladies 'ave undressed inside the machines and come out in their bathing-costumes, I dips them under the water quick like. They don't 'alf shriek, but it's for their own good. A sharp splash under is real invigorating. I tell you, I'm like a mother to my ladies. I 'elp them in and out of their stays, saves them from drowning, and dries their tears when they're scared out of their wits by the waves. Most of the summer I'm up to my waist in water looking after them. Some come back year after year, saying they'd be scared to bathe anywhere else without me to watch over them.'

'I can understand that,' Lucy said with a smile. 'Do you swim?'

'Do I swim?' Emmie threw up her hands and clapped them together expressively. 'Like a fish, madam. You've never seen anything like it. And I dive. Oh, you should see me dive. Like a pearl-fisher, that's me when I dive.' It was obvious she was never modest about her talents, but her

51

conceit, although thoroughly bumptious, was so utterly natural that somehow it was impossible to be offended by it.

'Would you teach me to swim when the summer comes?' Lucy had long wanted to swim and it would be frustrating not to be able to strike out in the blue salt water when the weather was right.

'I'd be 'onoured, madam. When I've finished giving you lessons you'll be able to cross the Channel and back before breakfast.'

Lucy was amused by the absurdity of the promise, although such were Emmie's powers of persuasion, her complete confidence in all she said, that it would not be difficult to believe that she really could do what she claimed. 'Then I shall hope for a warm summer, Mrs Linden, because I have no liking for chilly water.'

Together they went downstairs, still chatting. At the door Lucy asked how long it would take to walk back to the resort along the sands instead of by the lane. 'About ten minutes at a normal pace,' the woman replied, 'but there's always the track through the woods, which brings you to the bridle-path out of Hoe Lane. That's a short cut.'

'Hoe Lane?' Lucy repeated. 'Isn't that where Honey-bridge House stands? I rode that way only this morning.'

'Did you? Yes, it's the same.'

Lucy decided to go back by way of the shore and Emmie walked down the garden path with her to point out the stone steps that led down to the beach. The shingle crunched and slithered under Lucy's heels as she darted between the rocks and reached the tide-rippled sands. There she half-walked, half-ran by the withdrawing waves, filled with exhilaration at having the whole stretch of shore to herself and well pleased that her search for accommodation had met with reasonable success.

Once in her hotel room she took off her bonnet and tossed it aside, removed her sandy boots, and flung herself back onto the bed to rest and relax, her billowing skirts settling about her. She would abide at Sea Cottage while she observed the pattern of the summer season and could decide how best to invest what little money she had into some lasting enterprise. In the meantime she would make known her willingness to teach music and Italian to interested pupils, but more important than that would be the discovering of the exact date when Mr Timothy Attwood was likely to return, and then she would call again at the Grange. No one should bar her admittance when that day came. On that she was determined. Woe betide anyone who tried!

4

'When do you expect Mrs di Castelloni to return?' Donna
inquired at the hotel desk. She had Toby with her on a leash
and he sat down by the hem of her hooped skirt, a small
brown dog with a spaniel look about him, ears soft and long.

'I have no idea, Miss Warwyck,' the clerk replied. 'She
goes out twice and sometimes three times a day. She did say
yesterday that she had walked as far as the wreck beyond
the bay on the sands, and was it possible to walk as far in the
opposite direction. I had to warn her against being cut off
by the tide.'

'Perhaps that is where she has gone this afternoon, seeing
that the tide is out. I'll leave my card for you to give to her.'
Donna opened the draw-strings of her purse to take one
from the embossed visiting-card case she carried, but at the
same time the clerk leaned quickly across the desk to her.

'Here comes the lady now. I saw her go by the window.'

Donna was in time to see the glass doors flash as a figure
entered from the street and passed between the forest of
green plants in the vestibule, a shadow against the coloured
glass until she came into the lobby, her face glowing from
the cold sea-breeze outside. Cosily clad in a sealskin jacket
with a pillbox of the same fur secured to her blazing hair,
she was to Donna totally unlike any girl who had appealed
to Richard in the past, for like his father he had an eye for a
beautiful woman, and Mrs di Castelloni, although far from
plain, did not come into that category. Yet she had some-

thing more than beauty; her appearance was dramatic, almost feline, and Donna's original qualms that her brother might have become entangled with a scheming adventuress flared up again. Determinedly she drew in her breath and took a step forward.

'Good afternoon, Mrs di Castelloni. I'm Miss Warwyck, Richard's sister. You met my brother on the day of your arrival. It's not unusual for Easthampton to receive visitors from abroad, but since I believe you to be a fellow countrywoman, I wished to do my part in making you welcome.'

Instantly a look of answering pleasure showed spontaneously in the visitor's eyes. Donna saw no calculating hardness there, but a genuine response at friendship's level, and the unexpectedness of it left her somewhat at a loss. Not normally suspicious of others, she was only on the defensive for Richard's sake. Nobody should hurt him if it lay in her power to prevent it.

'I'm delighted to make your acquaintance, Miss Warwyck.' Lucy thought it exceedingly gracious that the young woman had come to the hotel specially to meet her. Then, her attention caught by Toby's sharp bark of greeting and wildly wagging tail, she slid her muff onto one arm and stooped down to pat him. 'What a dear little dog! What's his name?'

'Toby.'

'Toby, is it?' Lucy fondled the dog's face between both her hands. 'Hello, Toby. You look as if you're full of fun.' Her voice changed. 'Oh, his leg.' She looked up at Donna. 'How did that happen? Was it under a wheel?'

'No, he was caught in a trap. Mr Attwood, the owner of the Grange, rescued him and left him in my care.'

Lucy returned her attention to the dog, hiding the intentness of her reaction to hearing the Attwood name. 'The disability doesn't seem to bother him.'

'No, he manages very well. Mind his paws. There is mud on them. We went for a walk on our way here.'

Lucy straightened up. 'That's what I've been doing – walking. I'm getting to know every inch of Easthampton, and when the weather improves I intend to wander the surrounding countryside until I have explored it all.'

'You can soon do that. Tomorrow is the first day of spring.'

Lucy let her shoulders rise and fall in blissful contemplation of an English spring. 'You must know all the best paths to follow across the Downs,' she said on an unconscious note of envy, and her face suddenly lit up inquiringly. 'Would you be kind enough to take tea with me and tell me about them?'

The invitation was accepted. With Toby trotting after them they went into the drawing-room reserved for ladies and sat on a padded corner seat by the fire where tea was served to them. Donna talked at some length about the district before asking Lucy how long she had lived in Italy.

Instantly Lucy was on guard against any probings into her identity, but she answered evenly. 'I was born there, although my late parents were English.' She went on to speak conversationally of her convent life and, without details, of her marriage to Stefano. Her listener's face showed true compassion. Donna, although far from won over, was not hard-hearted.

'You are so young to be left a widow. Was he of similar age?'

'No, he was many years older than I, but a dear, kind man.' Lucy took a sip of tea. 'So with no ties to keep me in Italy, I have come home to settle in England, and I think there can be no better place than Easthampton in which to reside.'

'I agree with you about my home town,' Donna acknowledged. 'What made you decide to come here in the first place?'

There was a pause before Lucy answered, choosing her words. 'I knew of it, having first heard of it years ago, and it was a natural choice. Fortunately I have already found some furnished apartments to move into, because I'm not in the position to stay on indefinitely at this hotel, comfortable though it is.' She went on to tell Donna where the apartments were and of her plans to teach music and Italian.

It was easy for Donna to conclude that widowhood had brought about a drastic change in Lucy's circumstances, for the carriage that had brought her to Easthampton had not belonged to a poor man. Yet Lucy did not seem the least put out by having to take a practical turn, and no doubt the rigours of a convent childhood were standing her in good stead. With Richard's promptings in mind, Donna pressed on by an indirect route to follow up the reason for her call. 'I hope you will let me introduce you to local society. There are always plenty of agreeable events being held at this time of the year, and when the summer season comes the resort will have even more to offer.' She went on to explain that a certain rivalry had grown up between Easthampton and the nearby market town of Merrelton. 'But Easthampton will have a trump card to play soon. A company of players is to put on melodramas throughout the season in the new theatre at the head of the pier.'

'Is this another of your father's enterprises?'

'Not this time. The venture is entirely Richard's, but my parents plan to be home from visiting in the New World in time for the gala opening of both the pier and the theatre.'

The conversation turned to other social activities beside theatre-going, which interested them both, and Donna asked Lucy if she played cards.

'Yes, I do,' Lucy replied, smiling to herself. Her guest would hardly suspect just how well she played! She took up the teapot again, and let her smile come through. 'More tea?'

Donna had one more cup, spoke of returning Lucy's hospitality without delay, and after a short while made her departure. She was not entirely pleased with her call; although some of her misgivings about Lucy had ebbed, others had not been banished. It was not that she did not like her, because she did, but she could see all too clearly that Lucy would intrigue other men as much as Richard, who would not be long alone in his pursuit of her. It could lead to untold complications and endless heartache.

When Donna arrived home she found her brother already returned from work, and before she could remove her coat and bonnet or release Toby from his leash she had to relate all that had been said. He was aghast when he heard where Lucy had taken apartments.

'Good God! She can't live there. It's not fitting. An ordinary lodging house that still has a bad name clinging to it. Why didn't you persuade her to look elsewhere?'

Donna, because she was already worried enough, lost patience completely. 'Don't be absurd. It was not for me to tell her where she should or should not live, and Sea Cottage is as respectable a place as any these days.' Her voice took on an edge. 'She's not your betrothed yet, you know.' As soon as she had said the words she would have bitten them back, but it was done.

'I know,' he said quietly, with a depth of feeling.

To make amends she hastened to tell him about the dinner party. 'I paved the way and I'm certain she will accept. I shall write the invitation this evening and you can put it in the post tomorrow morning.'

'I'll deliver it myself.' His face was as determined as if he were going into battle, and Donna, recognizing that look, which was common to both father and son, knew that nothing would dissuade him. He could wait no longer to see his love again. Her impression was that Lucy would not be easily won by anybody, for it was as if she had already made up her mind as to what her future would be. Donna sighed to herself. Time would tell.

Richard was in luck next day. Failing to find Lucy at the hotel, he happened to sight her on the promenade. She was standing at the rails with a telescope to her eye, looking out to sea. He took a slope up to the promenade in a few swift strides.

'What can you see, Mrs di Castelloni?' he asked, coming to rest a hand on the rails beside her.

She lowered the telescope at hearing her name and turned her face, bright and animated, towards him. Through meeting his sister her acquaintanceship with him was somehow strengthened. 'Mr Warwyck, I declare. I'm watching a ship. It's a clipper. Would it be on its way to Portsmouth, do you think?'

'Most likely it's in the tea trade and bound for China.'

'That's a more romantic destination anyway.' Proudly she displayed the telescope. 'I bought this for a few pence in a second-hand shop in one of the little streets. It's brass, you know. It will look splendid when I've polished it up, and I'll be able to watch the ships go by from my window.'

His brows drew together in a frown. 'At Sea Cottage?'

'Yes.' She had put the telescope to her eye again. 'How white those sails are. It looks like a swan on the water.'

'Sea Cottage is not Warwyck property.'

She thought his remark odd and irrelevant, but she answered him, still studying the ship. 'I know. The agent told me. It belongs to a landowner named Radcliffe, and Mrs Linden is the tenant.'

'Radcliffe died last year and it is his widow who owns the property. It should have been pulled down years ago.' He sounded angry over it.

'Why? Is the site of some special value?'

'It's not that.' He cleared his throat. 'Had you not been married it would be even more difficult for me to speak out, but there is a very good reason why you should not move in there.'

He had captured her interest and she regarded him keenly. 'Whatever can it be?'

'Sea Cottage was once a house of ill-fame.'

'Indeed?' She was startled by the information. Those small upstairs rooms, now that she came to think about it, had not always had communicating doors, for in each there were blocked-up doorways to the landing, either painted or papered over, the outline still visible. She released a long breath. 'Well, well. How long ago was this?'

'When my father was building the resort.'

'Was Mrs Linden living there at the time?'

'No, she took over the house later, but because of the house's reputation she had never been able to let apartments to a lady before. In my opinion it is impertinence on her part to have done so, and a betrayal of trust on the agent's not to have forewarned you. I intend to deal with him this morning.'

'No, you must do no such thing.' She was adamant. 'I like the apartments and I intend to stay there.'

'But Easthampton has a wide choice of places in which to stay!' He flung out an arm to encompass the resort lying behind them in a sweeping gesture.

She saw he was genuinely concerned that she should be prepared to reside in a house tainted by the past, but although appreciative of his consideration, she was not having her plans changed by anyone and it was best to put an end to the matter quickly.

'Admittedly there are two places that I would have preferred, but since they are out of my reach, Sea Cottage is my choice.'

'Which are they?' He looked as if he were prepared to move mountains to secure either of them for her, and she was taken aback by his vehemence.

'The first place is Attwood Grange and the second is Honeybridge House.'

He showed disappointment at his inability to obtain one or the other for her. 'The unattainable indeed,' he said tautly.

She supposed he was irked that for once the Warwyck power, which she had heard spoken of with sarcasm by some business gentlemen in her hearing at the hotel, was unable to override such a simple situation. He was an unusual young man with his fine features and stern blue eyes, a trifle too handsome for his own good, because it was easy to see that he was more than used to getting his own way. She was under no illusion as to why he was so attentive towards her. In the past she had been on the defensive against advances through loyalty to Stefano, and in theory she was now free to please herself whom she enticed or rebuffed, except that Domenico's violence still haunted her, the details still vivid, and the thought of being embraced or kissed filled her with a dread she had never known before. She had begun to comprehend the reason why she had felt no response to Richard's burning gaze upon her in the Italian carriage. A platonic friendship was all she wanted with him or any other man, and only time would tell if that state of affairs could ever change. Meanwhile, Richard Warwyck must learn patience or give up the chase and find someone else.

'So you see,' she said, snapping the telescope shut, 'I am fortunate in securing accommodation that will suit me well enough for as long as I wish to reside there.'

'You have a particular interest in the Grange, have you not?'

She had been expecting the question. 'The Attwoods had Italian property once. I lived near it at the convent.' Then deftly she changed the subject, not wanting it followed up, and began to stroll, causing him automatically to fall into step beside her. 'How is your sister today? It was most courteous of her to call on me yesterday.'

'She was delighted to meet you. I left an invitation written by her at the hotel before I happened to see you.'

'To a teaparty?'

'No, to dine with us at Easthampton House.'

Had he invited her to dine with him alone it would have been an assignation with one purpose in mind, but by involving her with his sister and his family home it put the whole matter upon an entirely different footing. She had no hesitation in giving a reply. 'I shall accept with pleasure.' She gave him her hand. 'Now I must bid you farewell. I'm about to visit the library and expect to be an hour at least browsing among the books.'

He watched her leave the promenade and cross the street to enter the portals of the library. He hoped that she would look back before disappearing through the door to give him a wave or a nod and glance, but she did not turn her head.

During the next few days Lucy made the last of the purchases needed to add comfort to her apartments at Sea Cottage, which she had revisited twice since taking them, supervising on both occasions the installation of some furniture to supplement that already there. On the eve of her move she dressed for the dinner party at Easthampton House with a sense of excitement, which had its roots as much in the prospect of the morrow as in attending her first social function of importance for a long time. She chose a gown of hand-made Italian lace in deepest cream, with ribbons of the same colour entwined in the coils of her hair. Pearl ear-drops and a brooch provided her only adornment, and she put a fur-lined pelisse about her shoulders against the chill of the evening as she rode to Easthampton House in a hackney cab.

She never forgot her first impression of the interior of the Warwyck home. Outside it had impressed her with its dignity, but inside it had the iridescent quality of a sea-shell, the silk panelling echoing the delicate sea-blues and greens of the furnishings, the touches of gilt that were more like the glint of the sun on sand than mere ornamentation. It was a house completely in harmony with its setting by the English Channel, and her curiosity about the man who had built it stirred again within her.

Richard, entangled through a host's duties with some other guests, did not hear her arrive. But suddenly through the open doorway of the drawing-room he saw her being relieved of her pelisse by one of the maids. From overhead the gilded gasolier shone down to capture her in an aura of light, and such desire for her rose in him that for a few moments he could only stare at her, utterly possessed. She turned in a ripple of lace, saw him and smiled. His heart almost cracked at the joy of it.

With haste he crossed the wide hall to greet her as she came towards him, seeming to glide in her bell-shaped skirt. 'We have all been waiting for this moment,' he said with enthusiasm. 'You are our guest of honour. Everyone is eager to meet you. Have you moved into your new home yet?'

'I take up residence tomorrow.'

'Is there nothing I can do at this late hour to make you change your mind?'

'Nothing,' she answered amiably.

They had reached the threshold of the drawing-room and as Donna came forward to welcome Lucy Richard consoled himself with his own thoughts. She would not be long at Sea Cottage anyway. He must not rush his fences, but he had never failed to get what he wanted and, what was more, he was equally confident that by the time he eventually won her he would be able to take her to live in Honeybridge House.

To Lucy's delight all the company was young, and the formalities observed did nothing to quell the general light-heartedness, most of the guests being well known to each other. One of the couples, George and Ruth Holland, were particularly friendly, having visited Italy and being eager to talk about it. They even exchanged a few words of Italian, and when they heard that she planned to teach the language they immediately asked to have lessons. They drew her with them into another genial group of guests, and she could tell that any occasion where Richard was host guaranteed an evening of good humour and wit and lavish hospitality. The introductions were complete when the last guest arrived. Lucy, engaged in conversation, followed the glance of others, and with a sense of shock she saw Josiah Barton framed in the doorway, his black hair and well-cut evening clothes stark against the soft glow of the hall behind him. He was immediately greeted by his host and hostess and fortunately he did not see her, so she was able to appear absorbed in talk with those she was with when the moment for introductions came and Richard caught her attention.

'Allow me to present Mr Barton, our most welcome newcomer to Easthampton – Mrs di Castelloni.'

With a full swirl of her hooped skirt she turned about, to regard Josh Barton with a complete lack of recognition. It was in defiance of his instruction that she should not forget him, and she triumphed inwardly at this scoring over the detestable man.

'How do you do, Mr – er – what was the name again?' she asked. Richard supplied it, and she gave Josh a deliberately superficial smile. 'Oh, yes. Mr Barton.'

'Ma'am.' His voice was curt and crisp, his gaze upon her almost bored as if it wearied him to be brought into contact with her again. Dislike and mistrust vibrated between them, each aware of the other's suppressed antagonism before the view of others, and when he passed on with Richard to meet the rest of the company she was left feeling that somehow he had countered her barb, setting her afire with resentment. But she refused to let him spoil the evening for her, and out of her natural exuberance she found herself the centre of whichever group she was conversing with, causing Richard to glance time and again at her with pride, whether he was at her side or in another part of the room, thinking that there had never been such an intriguing, fascinating creature as Lucy anywhere. Had it not been for her arrival in that extraordinary carriage, months could have elapsed before their meeting or, a thought not to be contemplated, he might never have met her at all. Since she had been married he was relieved it had been to an old man, because he would open up paths of loving to her that she could never have known before, a prospect that consumed him with impatience, and he had yet to kiss her.

Donna noticed the constant direction of her brother's gaze and wondered how many others had observed it. She thought Mr Barton had taken note; nothing much seemed to escape those alert and scanning eyes, but it would be of no interest to him, since he was only a business acquaintance and the invitation to him for this evening had been extended out of courtesy and not through any closer relationship. She could not quite make up her mind about him. Josiah Barton did not fit into the conventional image of a gentleman. There was a Yorkshire bluntness about him, an air of not suffering fools gladly, and an inclination to speak out with a forthrightness that did not always go down well in the commercial circles in which he moved as one of the country's leading contractors. Almost as if he had caught the echo of her thoughts, he detached himself from a cluster of people near the fireplace and came over to her. His thin, flexible lips drew back in a smile that revealed perfect teeth.

'I can't tell you how honoured I am to be here this evening, Miss Warwyck.'

'We are delighted that you were able to come,' she replied. 'My brother feared that you might have left again before today.'

'I leave in the morning.'

'I hope that you have enjoyed your stay in Easthampton.'

Not for the first time Josh noticed the tendency of the Warwyck pair to talk in a certain tone about Easthampton as if they were a royal family ruling their own kingdom, and he was irritated by it. Admittedly Easthampton would probably still be no more than a poverty-stricken fishing hamlet if their father had not pulled it up with him out of the mud and sand by his bootlaces. Yet, in spite of their attitude, he liked both Richard and his sister, understanding that they were both totally unaware of possessing an air of condescension in all matters concerning the resort, which must have been instilled in them from birth, and he realized well enough that neither wished to cause him any offence. But he came from a part of the country where a spade was called a spade and at times he felt as alien among the people of this southern county as if he bore a surname as outlandish as that possessed by the red-headed widow with her provocative hostility and firebrand sexuality. He answered Donna easily.

'Yes, but it's not my first visit to Easthampton. I came here on holiday once with my parents. I was eight years old at the time.'

She was surprised. 'Did you really? Where did you stay?'

'We had a house near the sea. I remember that particular August as a month of cloudless skies and hot sun. But perhaps the holidays of one's childhood are always like that in retrospect.'

'I suppose so.' Her dimple came and went. She was losing her shyness of him. 'Have you seen Honeybridge House where your great-grandfather took the sea air when he was a sickly child many, many years ago?'

'I took a look at it the other day and I must admit to a feeling of regret that in the last year of his long life my great-grandfather ever sold the house to Daniel Warwyck. It would have suited me well to spend my time in Easthampton within its flint walls. I suppose there is no chance of my renting it when my affairs bring me back to the resort for a longer period?'

Donna shook her head. 'Without wishing to hurt your feelings, I must tell you that my mother would never allow a stranger to live there. It belongs to Father, but he has always let Mamma decide what is to be done with it. You see, it was their first home, and Richard was born there. I first saw the light of day in this house, and he and I grew up here.'

'But surely Honeybridge House should be lived in,' he protested. 'It can do it no good to remain shut up indefinitely.'

'Oh, Mamma has a sewing-room there, and a caretaker lights fires sometimes to keep the place aired.'

'Quite an extravagance. A whole house in which to sew a seam.'

'Oh, it's more than that. Mamma just loves the place. She told me once that she feels it is part of her.'

'I could argue that it is part of me, too. After all, it was my family who restored the house and made it into a seaside home long before your father ever set foot in Easthampton.'

'I realize that. Did you ever know your great-grandfather?'

He narrowed his eyes a fraction in reminiscence. 'I can just remember him, but I can't say that I knew him, more's the pity. He was quite a character, a self-made, self-willed man who was never ashamed of his humble origins and that he made his pile of brass out of trade, although his sons and my own father chose to ignore the fact.' His voice became extremely dry. 'It is said in the family that I'm old Hamilton Barton all over again and they don't mean it as a compliment.'

She looked at him uncertainly, not knowing quite how to take his remark, but escaped having to make any comment by the timely announcement that dinner was served.

'My pleasure, Miss Warwyck.' Josh offered his arm and she took it, while the other guests moved forward in pairs to follow her brother leading Lucy across the hall into the dining-room.

At the table Lucy sat at Richard's right hand. The flames of the candelabra and the gaslight in the opaque glass shades on the walls struck sparks from the crystal and the silver; the centrepiece was a carnation-studded epergne trailing maidenhair fern in a feathery cascade to the damask cloth. Stiff shirt-fronts gleamed, the throats and arms of the lady guests showed pale, while silk, satin and lace shone taut over their rounded bosoms. In the background the servants moved, silently attentive, with barely the chink of a dish or the rattle of a meat-cover to disturb the talk, which was lively and stimulating, the atmosphere relaxed, flirtatious and genial.

As it happened, Josh was seated on the same side of the

table as Lucy, but at the opposite end, so that she was spared any accidental catching of his eye, and she was able to enjoy both the dinner and the conversation without thought of him.

Later, in the drawing-room after coffee was served, George Holland sat down at the piano while everybody else gathered round to sing together to his accompaniment. Since Lucy was not familiar with many English songs, he made room for her on the long music stool beside him where she could read the words on the sheets and turn them for him. Everyone sang with gusto and with the same happy exuberance whether they were singing of love and broken hearts, ships going down in storms, or patriotically of flag and Empire.

Lucy did not hear who it was who suggested cards, but within minutes a large card table had been opened up and they all sat round it to play a game called Risk. She had never played it before, but it was similar enough to others she knew, and within seconds she had grasped it. Betting on cards painted on a centrepiece reminded her of Faro, but there was also dealing and playing involved, the players discarding cards they did not need, and points being scored at the end of each hand. She was not sure exactly when she realized that someone at the table was cheating, but suddenly it was as if the clock had turned back and she was pitting her wits against Stefano, whose aim had always been to see how quickly she could catch him out. The piles of coins on the cards in the centre of the table began to mount. Whoever finally won the game was going to gather in quite a sum.

She began to shake inside, angry that someone was abusing the hospitality of the Warwycks by stooping to such duplicity, and under her lashes she watched the shuffling and the dealing, trying to listen through the buzz of talk for the telltale click that told an experienced ear that there was dealing from the bottom, but she could discern nothing to give the culprit away. Yet someone at the table was thwarting the scores to cash in at the end of the game when it would be too late to do anything about it. Who was the cheat? She looked from face to face around the table, but there was no one she wanted to suspect unless it was Josh Barton. After all, with the exception of herself, he was the only outsider, most of the others being friends of long duration. She began to concentrate her full attention upon him, and she noticed that a small drop of wine lay shining on the table at his right hand, spilled perhaps from a glass drained before the game began. Spilled on purpose! It was an old gambler's trick, giving a minuscule reflection of dealt cards. At that moment he looked towards her and caught her eye. He must have seen her blazing look of accusation, because his own gaze became stony, and when she picked up the cards he had dealt her she saw a way to thwart him of the ill-gotten gains for which he was aiming.

She summoned up all the skill she had in her fingertips, which she had learned to amuse an old man in his dotage, never realizing that the time would come when she could use it for some purpose. When it was her turn to deal or cut she made sure that Josh's knowing would be thwarted, and all her play was concentrated upon releasing his hold on the game. With ease she manipulated the cards, holding back and concealing with a sleight of hand that no professional conjuror could have equalled. Immediately the play had tightened, and she knew her opponent was trying to counteract her moves with a talent that came close to, but could not master, her own. She failed to see the growing hostility of one of the husbands, a young man named James Whalley, who suddenly sprang to his feet, threw down his cards, and pointed an accusing finger at her across the table. 'You are cheating!'

There was a moment of stunned silence in which everyone stared at him in horrified disbelief. Instantly she knew she had fallen into a trap herself and Josh was not involved. The rage of the real card-sharp had got the better of him, and in fear of being exposed himself he was denouncing her. She could not deny what he had said or explain that it had been for the good of all that she had sought to snap the evil tentacles on the game and set it free. But even as she sat dumb, wide-eyed at her misfortune, Richard moved swiftly from his chair, causing it to fall back with a crash, and seized Whalley by the shoulder and spun him round.

'Your accusation is inexcusable! I demand an immediate apology!'

'It's the truth! Ask her! Go on! Ask her how she managed to play all those aces!'

Josh spoke almost lazily from where he sat. 'First explain why you were using a reflector.'

Panic registered in Whalley's face. 'I deny it! You're lying!'

Richard put his hand under the table in front of the place where Whalley had been sitting, and he felt the marks where the reflector had been clipped on. 'Turn out your pockets, James,' he ordered grimly.

'I won't, damn it!' Whalley was all defiance, and again he pointed at Lucy. 'There's the guilty one!'

Richard did not as much as glance in Lucy's direction. 'Mrs di Castelloni's score is such that she would not have won as much as a penny from the game, which everyone around the table knows. Let us see the contents of your pockets.'

In the background Whalley's wife began to sob, and Donna went to comfort her. Furiously and with ill grace he emptied his pockets. A gold watch, a pocket handkerchief, a comb and some loose change were all that came to light. Richard glanced at Josh.

'Look in his sleeve,' Josh advised quietly.

At once Whalley snatched up his belongings and drew back warily. 'I won't remain in this house another second. It's a conspiracy. I thought you and I were friends, Richard, but you are being duped. If you ask me, I'd say that your jumped-up business acquaintance is in league with that scheming little –'

Richard hit him, stopping the foul word he intended in his mouth. Whalley reeled back, blood spurting from a cut lip, and missed his footing. As he fell his elbow struck the floor first, and out of his cuff shot a small, circular object that looked like a snuff-box. It landed at Richard's feet. He bent swiftly and picked it up, holding it on the palm of his hand as he snapped it open. There shone the half-mirror that had enabled Whalley to control the game.

'Get out,' Richard said coldly to him as he scrambled to

his feet. 'I've had my suspicions before this evening, but because we have been old friends, as you say, I refused to believe that you were capable of such behaviour. I pity your poor wife. You have made it impossible for either of you to be received again in the homes of any of us here. For her sake I shall ask that word of what has happened does not extend beyond these four walls, and I advise you to mend your ways.' He hurled the reflector into the fire where it smashed among the red-hot coals.

Whalley, holding the bloodstained handkerchief to his mouth, straightened his shoulders defiantly, glared once around the room at the stricken faces, let his gaze rest briefly on Lucy with a look of malevolence, and then he stalked from the room in the wake of his sobbing wife, who was being assisted along by Donna. Richard closed the door after them and turned to face his remaining guests, his cheeks hollow with distress.

'I'm sorry that you had to witness the downfall of someone whom most of us have known for a long time. You heard what I said, and let charity be shown towards Adelaide Whalley, who is an innocent party, of that I am sure.'

There were murmurs of agreement. Lucy, who was still sitting in her place although the rest had risen to their feet and gathered into small groups, wondered if she should disclose her part in the man's downfall, but unexpectedly Josh slid into the vacated chair beside her and gripped her wrist under the table.

'No pretty confessions for the gullible,' he muttered fiercely under his breath. 'God knows what your aim is or even who or what you are, but I think you're far from the lady you appear to be. Only a gaming-hall could teach such skill.'

A gust of fury swept the colour over her cheekbones. 'You are the most insolent man I have ever met!' She sought to free herself, but he kept his vice-like clasp upon her and went on speaking in the same low tones, compelling her to listen.

'What was done tonight was all for the good, although I don't doubt it was for some scheming plot of your own, but it will only cause the Warwycks more embarrassment if you come out with having some part in it. The only reason I did not denounce you myself is that Miss Donna has had enough to put up with for one evening. For her sake I'm ordering you to hold your tongue, or else she will never dare ask people to play cards in this house again. Whalley's fall from grace lays no blame at her door, but the presence of a truly professional card-sharp would.' His voice took on a dangerous edge. 'If you don't keep silent I'll say that Whalley was right in his accusation and could tell that you were about to thwart him in getting the jackpot. I can present proof of my own there, because I have a memory for cards and they can be checked on the table where they still lie. Anything you may admit to will only look as if you are covering up. Nobody will believe you.'

It left her no choice for the present, although she was determined that Richard should learn the truth from her. Wrenching her wrist from Josh's grip, her glare equal to his, she tossed herself up from the chair and went to rejoin the rest of the company. Donna's return to the room had kept attention away from that brief and violent interchange, which Lucy found had left her shaking from head to foot. The evening was at an end, everybody deeply shocked by what had occurred, some of the men remembering ruefully the many times when Whalley's 'luck' at cards and dice had taken every penny from them.

Richard would have driven her back to the hotel, but earlier she had accepted an offer from George and Ruth Holland to ride with them since they would be going in that direction. She bade Donna good night, and Richard stepped into the forecourt with her. 'I regret that your first visit to Easthampton House should have ended so disastrously,' he said, taking her hand into his.

She looked up into his face, which was in shadow, her own illumined by the soft gaslight streaming out through the open door. 'It was no fault of yours,' she answered, determined he should know the facts eventually, 'and one day I would like to talk about it to you.'

'It gladdens me to talk to you at any time.' He put her hand, cupped in both his own, to his lips.

With good nights being spoken on all sides she got into the carriage and sat beside Ruth. She looked back to wave to the Warwycks as the wheels turned on the gravel, but she saw Josh come to Donna's side in the lighted doorway, and quickly she lowered her hand, turning her head away. She kept her gaze to the front as the carriage took the curving drive down the side of the hill.

5

Two men humped and heaved Lucy's trunks up the stairs at
Sea Cottage, hampered by the narrowness of the flight, and
set them down in her apartments, but after they were
unpacked it was Meg, Emmie's daughter, who slid them
down again unaided to store them in the cellar. Young and
strong, with a mass of dark brown curls that sprang from a
point on her high forehead, she was less hard-featured than
her mother, but with the same astute sharpness to eyes that
seemed to have taken their colour from the sea by which she
lived, being grey and flecked with blue.

Such was her obliging nature that she had offered to give
Lucy a hand with the unpacking and then had practically
taken over. Everything was dealt with in a manner that
matched Alina's competence, and Lucy's thoughts rested on
her former maid with gratitude. In her state of shock upon her
departure from Florence she had given no instructions as to
what the woman should pack, relying upon her judgement,
and Alina had used her own initiative and included an ormolu
clock among other items received from Stefano on natal days
and at Christmastime, as well as more practical requisites
such as bed-linen, a Persian rug and a lamp bought once in
Venice.

'Did you like living in a foreign land?' Meg asked seriously
when all the chores were done. Her expression showed a
distrust as if she could not imagine anything worse.

Lucy suppressed a smile as she set the key into the clock

and began to wind it up. 'Italy has some beautiful scenery and many great treasures from the past, but I never felt that I belonged there. My heart was always in England.'

Meg's face showed that she comprehended that state of affairs. 'I know I'd have felt the same. I've been across to France many a time in Bob's big boat, but it's always been grand to come home again.' She released an exasperated sigh. 'Bob won't take me no more. He always seems to end up in a fight with a Froggie if I'm there.'

'He sounds a jealous man.' Lucy slotted the key away behind the clock.

'He is. Thinks he owns me, and he don't.' The wide, full-lipped mouth set mulishly. 'He won't neither if he carries on picking quarrels with every fellow that sets an eye at me.'

'How long have you known him?'

'All my life.' Her shoulders shrugged. 'Like I know all the boys in Easthampton that I grew up with. Mind you, I'm better educated than most of 'em.' She tilted her head back proudly and wagged it. 'I went to Lady Edenfield's charity school for twenty poor girls of the parish, and that's where I learned to read and write and cypher as well as sew better than anyone else around here. There's nothing I can't read what's printed in the English language.' She was as boastful as her mother, but somehow it was disarming, expressed as it was with a complete naturalness that was almost childlike. Yet there was nothing childlike about her appearance, although she was slender and short in height, because there was a decisiveness about her movements, an air of knowing why she set one foot before the other, and there emanated from her a generosity of spirit and a full-blown exuberance in being alive.

'Why haven't you put that education to some purpose?' Lucy asked with interest.

'Go into service, you mean?' Meg's tone poured contempt in that direction. 'That's what they expected of us in that school. They didn't dangle no higher carrot.'

'You could have become a pupil teacher and then gone on to a more responsible position.'

Meg threw back her head and gave forth a gurgling, infectious laugh. 'Me a school-marm?' She dug a thumb against her chest. 'Me? Indoors all day? I'd die if I had to do that.' Her curls shook vigorously about her healthy face. 'That's why you'll not find me in a cap and apron in one of the hotels or in a private house. I don't mind what I do at home, 'cause I likes cooking and I'm clever at it, and what's more I'm quick at cleaning house and laying fires and so on, which means none of it interferes very much with the way of life that suits me best – just being out in my own boat and dealing with my wicker-pots, which I make myself out of withies, and then tar 'em, and weigh 'em down with large flints to catch lobsters, crabs and prawns. The best anywhere!'

A step on the stairs accompanied by the clink of china announced Emmie's coming, and Meg went to open the door for her, the floorboards creaking underfoot. Being an old house, the timbers eased like those of a ship whenever anybody moved about the house, and since it was a wet afternoon with rain pattering against the windows and the waves splashing near at hand, it would not have been difficult to imagine one was afloat. Emmie came into the drawing-room bearing a new tea-set on a tray, which Lucy had bought in Merrelton at the market. It had been unpacked and washed downstairs. When the tray had been set down Emmie folded her arms across her stomach, and she looked about observantly.

'It looks real nice, madam. I 'ope that girl of mine 'as behaved 'erself and done the unpacking to your liking.'

'Yes, she has worked hard.'

'I'm glad to 'ear it. Now light the lamps, Meg, and then 'op it.'

Meg did as she was told and left the room. Lucy noticed that Emmie was hovering deliberately. 'Did you wish to have a word with me, Mrs Linden?'

'Just a minute of your time.' Emmie seated her rotund form with alacrity as Lucy indicated a chair. 'I do like to get to know my lodgers if I can, but don't you go thinking I'll intrude again, because I won't. I've not let the other apartments yet, but when I do it'll be to a respectable person who'll cause you no disturbance. I like to keep a quiet house with quiet folk in it.'

Lucy realized at once that Emmie was wanting to cushion

anything she might be expected to hear from others in the resort about the house's past, unaware that the information had already reached Lucy's ears. No doubt the woman imagined that she would not have moved in if she had heard, and feared to lose her if she did.

'A bit of smuggling went on from this 'ouse in the old days,' Emmie said with tremendous casualness. 'Like it did all along the coast. That was long before I became the tenant 'ere, of course.'

Lucy hesitated no longer, having decided it was best to bring the matter into the open. 'I have been told that it was more than smuggling that went on under this roof in the past.'

Emmie narrowed her eyes, immediately on the defensive. 'What do you mean?'

'I understand that Sea Cottage was once a bordello.'

The reaction to Lucy's words was dramatic. With a fiery show of indignation Emmie sprang to her feet. 'That's not true. I know. I used to come 'ere myself when I was young. Folk gossiped then like they do now and mud sticks to a 'ouse like it does to people. Don't you take no notice of what nobody says.'

'I don't intend to,' Lucy answered calmly. 'When I move from Sea Cottage it will not be through anything that happened twenty years ago or more, but because of some presently unforeseeable change in my own circumstances.'

Slowly Emmie sat down again, uncharacteristically at a loss for words. She gulped as if to revive her voice. 'You're a true lady, Mrs di Castelloni. None but a real lady can trail her skirt-hems anywhere and know they don't get dirtied. I appreciate your getting me and this old 'ouse back on its feet. I'm respectable and I keep the 'ouse respectable, and I can 'onestly say I've beaten a sense of right and wrong into my Meg to keep 'er on the straight and narrow.' She began to relax. 'I admit the company kept in the old days was not for churchgoers and their like. There was boozing and dancing and a bit of carrying on, if you get my meaning. Two brothers, both fishermen, shared the cottage after their Pa died, and they'd always been on the wild side, so it weren't surprising that the rest of us young 'uns in the 'amlet should come along of an evening for a laugh and some sport. There weren't nowhere else to go for the likes of us.' The cheeriness normal to her countenance returned, and she set her hands on her ample waist. 'You may find this difficult to believe, madam, seeing the size of my figure today, but I was a right nifty dancer in my time and many's the jig I've pranced on that big table downstairs to the tune of a concertina and everybody clapping and singing.'

It was not so difficult to imagine, for in spite of her bulk Emmie walked a buoyant step. Lucy wondered if there had ever been a Mr Linden and where he was, but he appeared to have been relegated to the past by the very absence of his name on all occasions, and most probably he belonged to those dancing days.

As darkness fell that evening a rough wind blew up, buffeting the walls and increasing the sensation of being marooned at sea. In its howling down the chimney, which made the fire of driftwood roar in the grate, Lucy did not hear the knock that came at the side-door, and continued with the book she was reading, not lifting her head. Downstairs Meg stood listening, but when no board creaked upstairs to show that the summons had been heard, she went herself into the side-hall to answer it. The light of the lamp that she picked up on the way shone full upon Richard, who stood under the lintel with the rain running off the brim of his hat and racing in rivulets down his plaid cape. His lips parted in a smile.

'Hello, Meg,' he said without surprise. 'It's a long time since I've seen you.'

But she had seen him. In the distance. Riding by. Talking to workmen during the construction of the pier. Dozens of hoarded moments that he knew nothing about. 'Then you must be going around with blinkers on,' she replied pertly, ''cause I'm still living at Easthampton same as you, and I don't intend to move nowhere else.'

'Neither do I, Meg,' he said, removing his hat as he entered. It was good to see her again, and he knew he could engage her in flirtatious talk for as long as he wished, whether she was already betrothed to Bob Cooper or not, because they had known each other by sight since childhood and more intimately after adolescence. But the pleasing memories evoked were not strong enough to delay the reason for his visiting Sea Cottage. 'Is Mrs di Castelloni at home?'

'Yes, she is.' Meg had not supposed that he had come to the house for any other reason than to call on the new lodger, but nevertheless disappointment tugged at her, playing tricks with the corners of her mouth and making them quiver. To hide her feelings she turned away for a moment while she put the lamp down on the table. As he made to shrug off his cape she moved quickly around to the back of him, taking hold of it. 'Let me take your cape for you.'

As it slipped into her charge she longed to run her palms over the broadness of his shoulders, smooth in a coat of cloth woven so fine that there was a sheen to it. Her fingertips seemed to hold their own memory of the rippling muscles that lay beneath it and her hands shook as she hung the cape on a peg.

'Are the lady's apartments upstairs?' he inquired, flicking his cuffs into place.

She nodded. 'The first door to your right on the landing.'

She watched him go up the flight, not in haste but with the alertness of anticipation. In one hand he held a nosegay of flowers which he had been carrying under his cape to protect them from the wind and rain. He had given her a flower once. A buttercup picked from the grass in which they had lain together the summer night when he had come home from school for the last time, and he had tucked the stem between her breasts with kisses. His mood, one of excitement and liberation, had brought him down alone onto the beach where she had been about to set out with her lobster-pots. Mellow with wine imbibed earlier with friends at inns on the coach journey home, he had sought her out for a purpose of his own, and she had gone with him into the moon-shadowed orchard of deserted Honeybridge House where she had succumbed to his wild tenderness. She did not know what happened to the flower, but she would have kept it and pressed it if more of it had survived than the one yellow petal that she had found still clinging to her belly the next day.

Lucy did not put aside her book when a tap came on her door, but only looked up from where she sat. 'Come in,' she said, expecting either Meg or Emmie to make an appearance.

But when the tap came again she did put a marker in the book and closed it before going to see who was there.

'Mr Warwyck,' she exclaimed. He stood leisurely awaiting a more direct invitation to enter, although as a widow she was not bound by the conventions of chaperonage. 'What a surprise.'

'Forgive the late hour of this call,' he said, 'but I've only just returned from a business trip to Merrelton and I wanted to bring you these.' He handed her the nosegay. 'A token of my good wishes for happiness in your new abode.'

'How kind of you. Come in.' She inhaled the fragrance of the flowers, which seemed like a breath of spring itself.

He ducked his head automatically as he came through the low-jambed doorway, and as he straightened up his face registered his appreciation of what she had done to the humble room. 'My word! This is splendid. I was certain you would do everything in your power to make your quarters comfortable and charming, but I feared that in the end the Radcliffe property would defeat you. Nothing that particular family ever owned or built amounted to anything.' With observant interest he prowled about the room while she watched him.

'I have heard your voice harden against the Radcliffes before. What is the reason?'

He threw her a glance over his shoulder. 'The late Alexander Radcliffe engaged in double-dealings against my father on more than one occasion. Never trust a Radcliffe became a saying in our house.'

'How many of them live at the Hall?'

'Only the widow now since the daughter married and went away. I've nothing against Mrs Radcliffe, but she has taken the old feud upon her shoulders and has no time for a Warwyck.' Then he dismissed the subject and complimented her again on the room, seeing her personality imprinted upon it, and he missed nothing. Her books were on the shelves, most of them in Italian, and by the fine clock on the mantel as well as elsewhere in the room there were small *objets d'art* in crystal, gilt and porcelain. A silk shawl draped the back of the sofa, hiding its shabbiness, together with cushions embroidered delicately with designs of birds and flowers, and on

79

the walls were several Florentine landscapes in oils. The overall effect was as though some of that alien sunshine held within the gilded frames had escaped to bring warmth and colour in the meagre-sized room. One item held his attention in particular; it was too grand to have been included in the rented furnishings and she could not have brought it with her. It was the upright piano in the corner. He tapped the polished surface.

'This is yours?'

'I bought it in Easthampton. It's not new, but I'm very pleased with it.' She went through a communicating door into an anteroom to pour water from the ewer there into a vase for the flowers. 'I have advertised pianoforte lessons as well as instruction in Italian in the *Easthampton Chronicle*.'

He did not follow, but leaned a shoulder against the doorframe. 'You did not mention that you played the piano the evening when you were at Easthampton House.'

'None could have bettered George Holland, who knew all the songs,' she countered, returning with the flowers and closing the door after her. She put them down on a side-table and with her back towards him gave a final touch to the arrangement of the blooms. 'I have to tell you that I was entirely responsible for Mr Whalley's denouncement that night.'

'I suppose you were, in a manner of speaking, since it was you whom he accused.' His voice took on a growl of fury. 'The blackguard! I should have beaten him within an inch of his life.'

She swung about to face him, suddenly tense, not knowing how he would react to what she had to tell him. 'I knew someone was cheating in the game, and I manipulated the cards to counteract the sharp's play.'

He frowned incredulously, pushing back a fall of fair hair from his forehead with spread fingers. 'You! How could you know of such methods?'

'My late husband taught me.'

'What!'

'Stefano loved cards. There was nothing he did not know about them. He had a collection going back to a fourteenth century Tarot pack from Lombardy, and the packs must have numbered hundreds, some so beautifully decorated as to be works of art, and others comical or curious or lewd. Nothing enraged him more than dishonesty at cards or any other game of chance, and over the years he had developed, as they say, a nose for a sharp's presence, so he devised ways to thwart such rogues. Only the foolish and the frightened gave themselves away, as Mr Whalley did, knowing that someone was on to them and surrendering to panic instead of sitting tight and suffering financial loss whilst surviving to recoup another day.' She raised one hand eloquently and let it fall again. 'So I was Stefano's pupil, and at your house I put into practice all I had learned from him.'

'The devil you did!' He tilted his head, displaying his amazement. 'You are the most remarkable woman.'

'You're not angry?' Relief flooded through her veins.

'Angry with you? God, no!' He thumped a fist against his palm in emphasis. 'I'm only astonished at the calmness you maintained. Whalley had it coming to him, and there's no telling how long he would have gone on with his dishonourable conduct if you had not outwitted him.' His eyes held hers on a slow nod. 'I realize that it needed more courage to tell me about it than actually to bring down the fellow. Am I right?'

A serious smile touched the corners of her mouth. 'It did. You are very understanding. What do you think your sister will say?'

'I don't intend to tell her, and I suggest we keep the whole matter a secret between ourselves. There is no point in your having such a talent if the whole world knows about it, and in any case Donna does not want the catastrophe spoken of again.'

She compressed her lips briefly. 'Josh Barton knows.'

'Does he? Well, he can keep his own counsel, I know that.' He reached out and took her fingers into his, smoothing them with his thumbs as he looked down at them admiringly. 'Play something on the piano for me. I'm sure hands as lovely as yours must excel on the keys as they do with the cards.'

'What would you like to hear?' Her fingers slipped from his clasp.

'Whatever you feel like playing.' Eagerly he went to the

piano and pulled out the round-topped stool for her. Then he took a box of lucifers from his pocket and lit the candles in the piano's sconces for extra illumination. 'There. Everything is ready for you.'

She sat down on the stool, conscious of his rapt attention upon her, but within minutes she forgot all else but the music and was perfectly tranquil in her mind, swaying almost imperceptibly as she played as much for herself as for her listener. He had seated himself on the sofa, his elbow on the arm of it, and he watched as keenly as he listened. Never again was he to hear as much as a snatch of Mendelssohn without recalling her profile bathed in candlelight, the red-gold fire of her hair, and the pale flicker of her hands upon the keys. She was unlike any other woman he had ever known, surrounded by an air of mystery that he meant to delve into until there was nothing he did not know about her, spiritually or physically. It was a hunt for treasure beyond price and he would go on seeking and searching where she led until at last he had total possession of her. The music she was playing was like an echo to his thoughts.

When she came to the final notes they seemed to him to linger in the air, almost palpable, and as she withdrew her hands from the keys into her lap she turned her head and looked towards him. He could not speak. There was too much love in him. Abruptly he thrust himself away from the sofa, and before she could make any move he seized her in his arms and snatched her up from the stool, covering her mouth with his in a kiss of fiercest passion.

Instantly frantic to disengage herself, she tore her lips free from the loving onslaught, and he was aware that she had become rigid in his arms, her whole body trembling violently as if she might fall unless he continued to hold her.

'Let me go,' she appealed desperately, her face still averted from him, her head bent back on her long, white neck. 'I beg you.'

Out of the strength of his love for her he forced himself to take heed of her plea, for his blood was running so hot for her that he was scarcely his own master, but he eased his embrace until she was able to stand alone, her outstretched hand groping to catch the piano for support. Only then did she seem to recover, breathing deeply, but still kept her face averted, her eyes closed, a nimbus of candle-glow over the curve of her cheek.

'Now it is I who must ask if you are angry with me,' he said in anguish. His whole aim had been to take time in his courtship, wanting her to feel secure in the knowledge that he was not to be classed with those who considered attractive widows to be fair game, and now he had landed in that very trap. At all costs he must salvage what he could of their previous harmony in order not to lose her completely. 'Forgive me. The music quite carried me away. It was only a kiss. But a kiss between friends.'

He did not expect her to believe his excuse, but it was an olive branch that she could accept or reject, and he would know how the situation stood. She seemed to be making a tremendous effort to regain her equanimity, but so dilated were her pupils that her eyes retained a tormented look although she managed a faint smile as her words came breathlessly.

'I've never had my music approved with such ardour before.' She moved a few steps from the piano and tucked back into place a strand of hair that had slipped loose in the furore. 'I'm no more angry with you than you were with me over the cards, but since neither incident will occur again and the seal of friendship has been duly given and received, our acquaintanceship may continue without the danger of similar mishaps if –' she repeated the word to give emphasis '– *if* I have your word on it.'

She was warning him off severely, and he understood that, but having for a few awful moments expected to be banished completely, he merely took heart again, concluding simply that she was not ready yet in her widowhood for deeper involvement. His respect for her increased even beyond its present bounds, because in spite of some distress, she had made no foolish show of outrage, and had sought with dignity to hide the embarrassment he had inadvertently caused her. Was there to be no end to his reasons for loving her? He must be patient from now on and bide his time, and meanwhile he had the memory of her mouth and the feel of her softness in his arms both to succour and torment him.

He knew he must leave. To linger would not be appropriate. Taking a step backwards in the direction of the door, he surveyed her across the room, hands in his pockets to show she need not fear that he might reach for her again.

'I hope you'll play the piano for me again some time,' he said, giving her one of his rare grins, which took away his look of being older than his years. 'I promise to keep my show of appreciation to quite conventional applause.'

Without doubt the right words had been used, and she responded with a more relaxed smile as she took up the lamp to light him out on to the landing, lifting it higher to show him every tread of the flight down, as the hall below was in darkness. After he had put on his cape and taken his hat into his hand, he looked up at her as she bade him good night.

In answer he said her Christian name once, using it to her for the first time. 'Lucy.' He could not bring himself to utter any formal parting, however mundane. Nothing to snap a single golden thread of the love in which he held her. To bid good night upon the fiery longing in him was akin to goodbye.

No sooner had he gone from the house and Lucy withdrawn into her apartments again than a waiting figure moved in the inky blackness from the corner of the hall. Meg, holding her cloak about her, lifted the latch silently and slipped out into the slashing rain to run after Richard. He, hearing her footsteps, turned as he was about to get into his waiting brougham, and she caught hold of his arm.

'Give me a ride as far as Ring Park,' she begged, swaying against him as she blinked in the rain. 'I'm afraid for my boat in this rough wind that's blown up, and I must check that it's beached high enough.'

He looked down into the pale oval of her upturned face, her warm femininity emanating from her like an inviting bouquet in the harsh night, and a few seconds went by before he replied. 'I'll take you to where it lies. Get in.'

'You're a sport.' She flung her arms about his neck and planted a smacking kiss on his cheek before running round to the other side of the brougham to gather up her petticoats and clamber in beside him as he took his place at the reins.

She wriggled with pleasure as he fastened the leather cover over their knees. 'I'd have got soaked to the skin walking there in this downpour.'

He said nothing. When she snuggled against him for further protection he still kept his silence. With the raindrops thudding on the brougham roof, he drove her away with him into the night.

In her bedroom, Lucy tilted the swivel-glass on the toilet-table as she regarded her reflection with mingled regret and sadness. Her whole being had rejected with a kind of blind panic the loving in Richard's kiss. She liked him. She could say that she had developed a fondness for him and welcomed his pleasant company. Yet it had been as she had feared, and she had been as violently resistant to his touch as she had been to Domenico's. Was that dreadful occurrence in the Florentine villa ever to come between her and any man she might be drawn to? She shuddered, covering her face with her hands. Had Domenico's violation condemned her to endless loneliness?

With the despairing thought weighing her down, she swung away from the looking-glass, and it was then that she heard a hammering transfer from Emmie's front door to the one below. Once more she picked up the lamp, but this time it was to light the stairs for herself, although she was no more than halfway down when the caller, tired of waiting, burst open the door and clumped with heavy boots into the hall, raindrops showering off his fisherman's coat.

'Where's Meg?' he demanded fiercely of her.

She guessed at once that this was Bob Cooper. 'I have no idea. Is something wrong?'

'Aye, she ain't 'ere after telling me she weren't going out nowhere. The whole 'ouse apart from your windows is in darkness.'

Lucy's concern subsided. For all she knew, Meg might have gone out deliberately to escape his company. He was by the very nature of the calling he followed a heavily-muscled man, with huge, calloused hands that were balled into fists at his sides. Freckled and sandy-haired, his features had a pugnacious mould to them, even allowing for his present mood.

'Perhaps Meg has gone to meet her mother at the Crown Inn?' she suggested, knowing that it was Emmie's favourite haunt.

'I've come from there.'

She was not surprised. It was easy to see that he had had more than enough to drink. 'Then she could have gone on an errand somewhere.' Inspiration struck her. 'Since it is such a rough night, Meg could have gone to see that everything was safely secured at her hut –'

He cut her short. 'There ain't nobody beaches a boat safer than Meg. I 'elped 'er pull it up onto land myself only this afternoon, and I told 'er special that I'd be calling at eight o'clock sharp tonight.' His nostrils flared. 'I ain't going until I've seen 'er.'

So determined was his stance and so squarely were his booted feet set apart that it looked as though he were prepared to wait the night through in the dark and narrow hall. Lucy felt some pity for him. Since he had made an appointment, it was thoughtless of Meg to leave him high and dry. 'I'm sure Mrs Linden would not mind if you waited in her parlour,' she suggested. 'The door through to it is never locked.'

His temper eased somewhat at her calm tones. It had been almost more than he could endure to have given himself Dutch courage at the inn only to find Meg absent when he arrived at Sea Cottage. 'Yes, madam.' He could not begin to pronounce the lodger's foreign name, but pulled off his woollen cap as much in belated deference to her as in preparation for staying. 'I'll do that. My apologies for disturbing you, and you'll 'ear no more from me. I'll wait quiet till Meg comes 'ome.'

He went through into the parlour, the warmth setting his wet clothes a-steam, and he took off his coat and hung it out in the kitchen before returning to throw another log on the hearth and settle himself down in a chair to wait. He did not light a lamp, having some thought of taking Meg by surprise and challenging her when she did return, because he would have no lies or evasions from her: it would have to be a reason of utmost importance to make her break her appointment with him. He dived his hand into his pocket and brought out the purchase he had made last time he had taken his fish to Merrelton market. Holding the tiny, crimson box in the palm of his hand, he opened it, letting the garnet ring it contained catch the firelight. It had taken every penny he had received for that week's delivery and more, but he did not begrudge the cost. Meg was worth it. She would be proud to have a betrothal ring. It would be something to flaunt on her pretty finger at her friends, none of whom expected more than a wedding band on the marriage day.

Snapping the box shut he looked again at the moon-faced clock on the wall, its pendulum swinging to and fro. Where the devil was she? Impatiently he got up from the chair again and went to the window to peer out, but all he could see was the spray of the crashing waves rising ghost-like above the wall at the end of the garden.

He must have dozed in the firelight, the ale he had consumed and the warmth having a combined effect, because when the key turned in the lock he sat forward with a jerk, momentarily at a loss to know where he was. Then he saw her, but she failed to see him in the shadows, though she was illumined for him by the embers' rosy glow. She was dishevelled by the rough weather and as she slipped back her hood he saw her hair had fallen from its pins and was tumbled about her shoulders, her face holding a dewy look as if her thoughts had stayed in some far-off place and only the shell of her had returned home.

'Where the devil 'ave you been!' He sprang up and slammed a fist down on the long table between them, the chair overturned by the suddenness of his rising to hit the wall as it fell. Her eyes stretched wide and her whole face became a mask of fright, her mouth dropping open on an intake of breath as she jerked back, flattening herself against the door. His voice thundered at her. 'I said I'd be 'ere at eight o'clock and so I was. But where was you?'

She had been caught off guard, having forgotten completely that he was coming to see her, but she recovered instantly, seeming to crouch before she sprang forward against the table's edge, her arm shooting out as she hit him hard across the face. 'Don't you dare talk to me that way,

Bob Cooper! I'm my own mistress and none questions my coming and going.'

'Well, I do!' He grabbed her by the wrist and hauled her half across the table while she kicked and struggled, half-tangled in her cloak, shrieking at him to set her free. Every other man he knew would have struck her back for the blow she had dealt him, blacking her eyes for her, but even in his anger with her he was fearful of his own strength and wanted nothing more than to bring her to heel. Holding her pinioned in his arm he took her chin in his hand and jerked her face upwards in order that he might look full into it. 'Where was you?'

She gave up struggling and took to lying, able to tell by his breath he had been in one pub or another, and yet not knowing if she had been glimpsed in the Warwyck brougham. She managed to speak through lips twisted by his pressure. 'Miss Donna sent for me. She had heard I gave that dog of hers a kick when it came lifting its leg against my boat. I had a right old lecture on kindness to dumb animals.'

He did not disbelieve her. Meg was capable of giving anyone or anything the toe of her boot if her boat was involved, and he himself had seen the Warwyck girl concern herself over the treatment of animals other than her own dog, once scolding a man on the beach who was beating one of his donkeys which was declining to give someone a ride. It was just like the Warwycks to summon a visit to that house on the hill as if it were Buckingham Palace.

'It didn't do you no 'arm to 'ave a lecture,' he said, his face relaxing into a grin. 'I only wish I'd been there to see it. Give you a real ticking-off, did she?' He gave her a loving hug before easing his hold on her, his good humour restored. He had her to himself, her Ma was out and with any luck would not be back for another hour, and the widow upstairs would remain there. As Meg slid her feet to the floor and unclasped her cloak, he took it from her, and she shook her hair free, intending to put it to some rights as she plucked out the remaining pins, and heard the last one fall to the floor.

'Drat!' she exclaimed with a stamp of annoyance. 'Where did it go? Light the lamp. I can't see in this gloom.'

She crouched down at once, spreading her hands over the rag-rug, but instead of doing as she had told him, he went down on his knees beside her, not to seek for the lost pin, but to take her by the shoulders, causing her to look at him with impatience unwaned.

'Never mind the pin,' he urged. He had seen her with her hair loose many a time, but he thought he had never seen her looking quite as she did on this night, with her face in fire-glow and shadow, her curls a tumbled cloud of darkness. 'I've a present for you. Well, it's more than a present.' He dived his hand into his pocket and brought out the ring-box, which he held out to her. 'Open it and you'll see what I mean.'

She glanced at him twice uncertainly before she reached out slowly and took it, half-suspiciously, sitting back on her heels. He watched her face as she opened the box, and saw her eyes widen and her red lips part in astonishment. Then, closing the box again, she lowered it to her lap as she regarded him with a look of total misery that he was at a loss to understand.

'It's a betrothal ring,' he explained stumblingly. 'Like the gentry 'as. Don't you like it?'

'Of course I do, you fool,' she cried shrilly, raising clenched hands as her mouth fell agape in anguish, and for the second time she went for him like a tigress, beating his head and face with the flat of her hands, sobbing without tears and shouting abuse at him until he restrained her and held her down upon the floor, leaning over her.

'You shut your shouting or I'll do it for you!' He shook a threatening fist within an inch of her nose. She quietened, coming back to her senses and seeing she had spurred him beyond the point of restraint, and she rolled her despairing face away from him, looking towards the fire. The giving of the ring was the only romantic, tender thing he had ever done for her. Why had it had to happen on this of all evenings?

'I'm not marrying nobody who can't give me a home of my own,' she muttered stubbornly. It was her old excuse, thrown at him more times than she could remember, but she meant it. It was his ill luck that he could not afford to buy a place, and since he was independent, owning his own boat, he did not qualify for one of the cottages or small terraced houses built by the Warwycks for those they employed.

'That's it.' He gave her a little shake in his excitement. 'I've got a 'ome for us. I didn't want to tell you till I 'ad it licked into a bit of shape.'

She stared at him. 'Where is it?'

'Along the track at Denwin's Corner. I've rented the cottage by the woods there.'

Her scorn burst forth. 'That hovel! That ruin! What do you think I am? A gypsy wouldn't live in it!'

'Wait until you've seen it before you say that.' He spoke urgently, wanting to convince her. 'God knows 'ow long it's been empty, but there was nothing wrong with its walls and rafters. I've mended the roof where it 'ad fallen in, and cleared the whole garden patch. I've even dug ditches to drain it. You won't know the place when I've finished with it.' Swiftly he reached out and took up the ring-box, which had rolled from her lap in her attack. Seizing her hand he thrust the ring on to the third finger of her left hand, bruising the flesh of it in his haste. 'That's why I bought you this. I mean right by you, girl. I always 'ave done.'

Slowly she sat up and looked at the garnet glinting in the firelight. It was the prettiest thing she had ever seen. She had never owned a real piece of jewellery before.

'How did you get the tenancy?' she asked tonelessly, her eyes seemingly magnetized by the ring. 'Did you go to the Radcliffe steward?'

'I found out it weren't Radcliffe property. Neither does it belong to the Grange. It's a rogue piece of Warwyck land that juts out from the meadows to the south. I went to speak to Mr Richard on the matter, and 'ee said I could 'ave it at a low rent with an option to buy later.'

Without moving her head her gaze swivelled under her lids towards him. 'Mr Richard?' she said woodenly. 'How can he make such a promise? Daniel Warwyck has never sold an inch of Easthampton land that belonged to him that I know of, so why should he start now?'

'Mr Richard gave me 'is word that it'll be all right. 'Ee

won't go back on it. You forgets I know 'im from the spar-ring ring.' He reached out and smoothed her hair back from her forehead. 'Say you'll come and look at the cottage with me tomorrow.'

After a few moments of hesitation she nodded abruptly. 'But you better take the ring back until I've seen it, because I'm not promising nothing till I have, and even then I might not.'

It was hard to think of parting with the ring, but as she went to pull it off again with some reluctance, his hand folded over hers, checking the removal of it. 'Keep it on. I'm not afraid of you being disappointed. I've worked 'ard on the place. It'll be like a new pin for you before I've done with it. You'll see.' He sought her mouth with his own and out of habit she let him kiss her, her mind pondering the events of the evening, but when he began to make overtures she recognized, she broke his embrace about her, striking away his arms. 'No larking about. I'm in no mood for lark-ing about.' The coldness of her voice was at variance with the levity of the words she used, but he saw nothing odd in it, having heard them often enough before. With an inward sigh and a promise to himself that it would be different when they were wed, he got up from the floor and lighted the lamp as she had originally instructed him, with a taper from the fire.

After he had gone she took off the ring and tied it on a ribbon around her neck. She wanted no questions from her Ma or anybody else until she had fully decided what to do. Sooner or later she must marry, and since there was no chance of getting the man she truly loved, she supposed that Bob was as good as any and better than most. But not yet. She was not ready to have the banns called for a while yet.

Slowly she lifted her head and glanced at the raftered ceiling. How much had the widow heard of their quarrelling? A rumble of anger and some shrieking, but no more. It was a stout house with thick walls that knew how to keep secrets. Her gaze returned to the flames on the hearth by which she stood. She had a secret. This night she had stolen passion that intuition told her had been aroused and spurned by that same woman. In the blackness of her beach-hut, on a bed of dry nets, with the sea roaring and the rain hammering the tarred roof, she had welcomed and loved and given, receiving Richard's body, but not his heart. He might never come again to her, but that did not mean to say she would not continue to wait and hope.

When morning came she set off to meet Bob at the steps of the Assembly Rooms as arranged. Normally she wore a woollen cap or a sou'wester like the men when she was going to be busy with her boat, and on sunny days she would clamp a ravelled straw leghorn on her head, but seeing that this was an occasion of importance, destined perhaps to settle the course of her life, she put on her Sunday bonnet and her best dress. As soon as she was out of sight of Sea Cottage and her Ma's eye, she took out the ring and put it back on her finger.

Bob's glance went to it at once and he grinned, easing his wide shoulders and holding his head back on his neck with suppressed pride. She noticed that he had also smartened himself for the outing, a clean neckerchief about his throat, and he was wearing his one good coat that did not fit very well, but had a flare to its hem that was quite dashing. Assessing him with her sharp eyes, she thought again that he would do well enough. She could not have abided an ugly man, and he was far from that.

'Come on then,' she ordered. 'Let's get on with it.'

Once the place known as Denwin's Corner had been on the far outskirts of Easthampton, but with the growing of the resort, habitations had spread, the road had been improved, and Meg noted that she would not be far from neighbours or a small store that sold everything from flour to bootlaces. Neither would it be far to reach the beach, because on any other day she could take a short cut across the Warwyck meadows.

The cottage lay at the end of a short track and when they reached the gate, which was one Bob had made to replace the original, taken long since for a tramp's fire, she stood there and looked critically at the cottage while he waited with bated breath for her reaction. It was small, but stoutly-built, the passage of time having failed to disintegrate the thick walls, and he had re-thatched it with the aid of a fellow fisherman who had once been apprenticed to a thatcher before the sea had won him. The windows had been newly glazed, and the re-hung door, which was battered and much worn as if it had been kicked about after being wrenched off its hinges, was neatly mended and had a new lock that shone with brassy brightness against the old wood. All around the cottage the grass had been scythed, and the charred remains of a bonfire showed where dead bushes had been burnt and rubbish destroyed. She could have a good vegetable patch there, and plums would grow on the ancient wall that divided the garden from the woods. Without a word she opened the gate, and he went ahead to unlock the door for her.

It opened into the largest room, which had an ancient wall-bed in the corner. She went on a tour of inspection and came back to him. 'That'll have to go,' she said, nodding towards the wall-bed and giving him the first indication that the cottage met with her approval. 'I wouldn't want that taking up space. You could put it together again in the next room. No sense in wasting anything.' She took a step towards him and rested her hands against his broad chest, looking up into his face, her own expression softening. 'You've done well to get this place, Bob Cooper. I'd move into it with you tomorrow if I was ready to wed, but in the meantime you can take it that I'm promised to you definite.'

His face creased up in his jubilation. 'That's what I've been wanting to 'ear, girl. You won't keep me on the 'ook too long, will you? Seeing as I'm already paying rent on the place, I figured on moving my traps in as soon as possible, so it'll soon be shipshape.'

'That's a sensible thing to do.' She slid her arms up and about his neck, feeling that he deserved some reward for his initiative and thinking she might have come to love him if she had never set eyes on Richard Warwyck. 'I'll tell you as soon as I'm good and ready to go to the altar. Maybe when the summer is over and before the year is out, but I don't know yet. We'll see.'

Before the week was out she began to wonder if she had acted wisely in giving him her promise when she did. His possessiveness and jealousy, far from decreasing in the security of knowing she belonged to him, seemed instead to increase a thousandfold. He began to resent the cheerful *badinage* she exchanged with their fellow fishermen, showed a sullen face when she served her prawns and lobsters and fish to male customers with her usual quips and repartee, and became more demanding in his approaches to her. She renewed a vow made to herself that he must never ever suspect that she loved another, let alone what had happened between them, or else she could expect murder to be done.

It took all her strength of will not to follow Richard with her eyes whenever he drove by that part of the promenade where she and the other fishermen were allowed to sell their catch every day of the year. He did not as much as glance in her direction.

6

Lucy's hopes of financial reimbursement through the giving of music and Italian lessons failed to materialize. She wondered if the address of Sea Cottage had anything to do with it. If people had long memories, they would associate the house with its unsavoury past, but she was reluctant to change her accommodation, which suited her in all other respects, and tried to think what else she might do instead of teaching, because her need to earn money was becoming quite desperate.

The problem was much on her mind one soft spring morning when the nearby woods were full of bluebells and the mildness of the breeze carried promise of better weather to come. Instead of taking the path through the trees into town, she decided to go by way of the beach, and took the steps down from the garden to scramble over the shingle amid the rocks onto the crisp sands, realizing how convenient it must have been for smugglers in the old days to bring their boats into that quiet spot hidden from any curious eyes.

As always when going along the shore, Lucy made for the water's edge, and followed it as the wavelets broke and rippled on the incoming tide, swallowing up her footprints as she went. When she came level with the main buildings of the town she passed the length of beach where the fishermen kept their boats, Meg's among them, their tarred black huts draped with nets and set about with lobster pots, giving off a fishy aroma that mingled with that of salt and hemp and seaweed. Suddenly she noticed Donna ahead of her near the pier, and Toby with her. Increasing her pace, she was soon sighted in her turn, and when they were within earshot of each other they exchanged greetings, while Toby came bounding up to her with his hoppity gait.

'How are you today?' Donna inquired. She and Lucy had seen each other only the previous afternoon when Ruth Holland had been at home and they had taken tea with her. There had been other occasions since the dinner party at Easthampton House that had enabled them to talk together, because Donna had kept her promise to introduce Lucy to local society, and invitations had snowballed. Invariably Richard was present, but although Lucy could tell that his ardour had not waned, there had been no repeat of the embrace she had suffered at the piano, for whatever his hopes, he was keeping his word that their relationship should remain at friendship's level.

'I'm well, thank you. Isn't it a beautiful morning?'

Donna nodded in agreement. She wished she could dispel the doubts she had of whether Lucy was right for her brother. Although she kept her thoughts to herself, she still harboured unease, and the old fear that Lucy might not be all that she seemed. Since the incident at the card-table she had spoken to Adelaide Whalley, who had sought to denounce Lucy to her in defence of her husband, and although Donna had reminded herself that nothing could dispel the evidence of the reflector, the persistent accusation had done nothing to banish the original fear that Lucy was an adventuress out for her own ends. 'Have you walked along the shore from Sea Cottage, Mrs di Castelloni?' She could not bring herself to suggest that they should use each other's Christian names, although from some agreement made at a time unknown to her, Richard and Lucy now addressed each other in that manner. 'Down, Toby!' Her inquiring note switched to one of affectionate exasperation as Toby leapt about Lucy excitedly. 'You are covering the lady's coat with sand.'

Lucy was patting him, laughing at his barking exuberance. 'A little clean sand will do no harm.' She took the remaining few paces that brought her to where Donna stood. 'I always come by way of the shore when I can, but although you told me that you often exercise Toby on the sands, this is the first time I have seen you down here.'

'Toby has been in pain with his damaged leg for a little while, scarcely able to put it to the ground, but he has become so lively again I feared he would run riot if I did not let him work off his excess energy.'

Lucy gathered up a pebble and threw it for him, watching as he lolloped off to get it. 'He certainly seems all right today. What was the cause of the pain, do you think?'

'A twinge of rheumatism, I believe. Anyway, I'll be able to consult Mr Attwood very shortly now. He will know whether it is or not.'

Lucy, shading her eyes against the sun with her hand as she watched the dog retrieve the pebble, felt the skin tauten over her cheekbones. 'Is he coming home?' she asked in suspense, not seeing the look of contented anticipation that came over Donna's face as she made her reply.

'Next Monday. Richard had a letter from him yesterday.'

Briefly Lucy closed her eyes tightly at the import of the news that had been given her. The Grange was going to take on life again, with windows opened and doors unbarred. Soon she would enter there. Soon she would make herself known to it and feel herself enfolded by a past that was rightfully hers.

From a distance there came a hail. 'Hello-o-o-o!'

They turned simultaneously and saw the far figure of Richard waving to them from the rails of the pier, which shimmered in its cream and white paintwork. When he saw he had attracted their attention, he cupped his hands about his mouth again.

'Come and be the first patrons of the pier!'

Donna threw Lucy a sparkling glance. 'Shall we? I have not been on it yet.'

Lucy was eager. 'Oh, yes.'

Side by side they went up the slipway onto the promenade with Toby at their heels, and by the time they reached the entrance Richard was there waiting for them.

Like the circular pavilion at the head of the pier, the entrance was adorned with an onion-shaped dome painted the same aqua-blue, and its ironwork ornamentation was a glossy white. The price of admission was displayed at a penny, and since the pier was not yet officially opened and the paint on the gates still wet, he led them through a door in the ticket office onto it. The white-planked deck stretched far ahead under the ranked arches, making the distant pavilion appear quite diminutive. Donna ran forward and clapped her hands.

'How delightful! I have been looking forward to this. When the tide is in it will be just like strolling on a ship's deck without the inconvenience of the *mal de mer*.'

With a full show of enthusiasm, which was unusual for her reserved nature and an indication of her extreme excitement, she hurried on inquisitively, followed by Toby, and the two of them darted from the railings on one side to those on the other, she to exclaim over the view to the east and to the west, while the little dog wagged his shaggy tail in bewilderment at their zig-zag path. Richard, concerned that Toby might skid too far under the railings and fall to the sands far below, called to Donna that she should put him on his leash, which she did, seeing the danger, and the two of them continued on their way. Keeping a strolling pace after them, Richard explained to Lucy the purpose of having such a pier, which was unique in being the longest yet on the south coast.

'It is time Easthampton kept abreast of other resorts and surpassed wherever possible. It should offer a wider scope of entertainments for its visitors. Brighton has had a chain pier for over twenty years, but to mention that place to my father is like showing a red flag to a bull. Not that he has any personal aversion to Brighton; in fact, he and my mother met and married there, but he wants to keep Easthampton exclusive and quiet – too quiet.'

'And you don't agree with him?'

'No, I don't.' Forcefully he thrust his fists deep into his pockets. 'Times change and things must change too. Over the past few years Easthampton has been stagnating in many ways, and I will have progress.'

'Well, your father has come around to building a pier, so that is one step in the right direction, is it not?'

He smiled grimly. 'It was a result of many skirmishes over the office desk. When I finally won the battle he adopted the scheme as wholeheartedly as if it had been his idea in the first place, which is the reason why the grand opening is to wait upon his return.'

'Your sister told me that the theatre in the pavilion was entirely your venture, too.'

He looked pleased she had been told. 'I'm glad to say I had no opposition to that suggestion. When we are in agreement, my father and I get on well together, but it is when my ideas become too revolutionary for him that the trouble starts. A bone of contention between us before he went away was my wanting to see a railway branch line built direct to Easthampton from the nearest junction.'

Her own aversion to the railway flared up within her, but she was curious to know why Daniel Warwyck opposed it. 'What can he possibly have against that?'

'He argues that he created a sea-bathing resort that was different from all the rest in being a select retreat for gentlefolk, whatever their means, and will not have its character changed. His point is that therein lay its phenomenal success and its continued prosperity. You see, he believes in all sincerity that a railway line to Easthampton will open the floodgates to all and sundry, because cheap railway fares are enabling every Tom, Dick and Harry to reach the seaside these days. Those who come to Easthampton always arrive in their own carriages, as you did. He wants to keep it that way.'

She made no comment. He put his own interpretation upon her silence.

'I know what you're thinking, Lucy,' he continued with a nod. 'It may be difficult for you to believe, in the light of what I have told you, but my father does not despise those of his fellow human beings who occupy a lower station in life. His enthusiasm for the pugilistic world in which he still moves at every opportunity proves that, and he would begrudge nobody – whether roadsweeper, factory-hand or sewer-worker – a trip to Easthampton if they came singly with their families. But it is the hordes that he wishes to keep at bay, and the excursion trains with their cheap fares are starting to bring hundreds down to fill the beach at Brighton and other places. Over the years he has become fanatically obsessed with keeping Easthampton a place of peace and tranquillity, where there is still the original personal touch and he can greet every one of the visitors who come, keeping up traditions he started when he first put Easthampton on the map as a sea-bathing resort.'

'How strange that a man who experienced such violence in the prize-ring and all the wild life that goes with such a profession should hanker for perfect peace in his surroundings,' she mused, far more in sympathy with the retired pugilist than his son could possibly suspect.

'I often think that is the very reason,' he confided. 'A reaction to all he endured in the past.'

They caught up with Donna at the head of the pier where it widened out into a full circular shape, accommodating the large pavilion while leaving a broad walk around it for those who would want to face the sea in all weathers. Painters and carpenters were working inside the theatre, and when Richard opened the door for his two companions to enter, they were assailed by the smell of glue and paint and sawdust.

Lucy looked about her in amazement that such a place could exist out to sea. It was quite a small auditorium, but ornate, with gilded cherubs holding hands over the proscenium arch and cavorting along the front of the gallery, in which seats were being fitted. Yet there was no orchestra pit, and she questioned Richard about it.

'There is no room for a full orchestra, as you can see,' he said, 'and the acoustics are such that a pianist and a violinist will suffice.'

'Oh,' she said thoughtfully. Then again: 'Oh.' While he went on talking, she decided to apply for the post of pianist without delay. 'Have you appointed a pier manager?' she asked.

'Yes, he is usually around here. Sam Robertson. An excellent fellow I've promoted from assistant manager at the Assembly Rooms.'

Donna expressed a wish to see back-stage, and since the work there was completed, they were able to see into the two dressing-rooms, one for men and another for women, which were cramped and an odd, half-circular shape due to the construction of the pavilion in which they were housed. It seemed to Lucy like a tiny maze behind the scenes, and she did not envy those who would have to scurry about there, although gaslight had been installed and on the stage the footlights were the latest design.

When the three of them came out of the pavilion again they faced the panoramic spread of Easthampton and the Downs beyond, and once again Donna went ahead, exclaiming at the fine sight that was presented. Lucy congratulated Richard on the building of the pier.

'I'm sure it will prove a most successful venture.'

'As long as you like it, that is enough for me,' he answered her. He saw the quick look she gave him under her bronze lashes, which shaded to darkest brown at the tips, and in her eyes was the understanding he had intended. She knew he meant exactly what he had said.

She called twice at the Assembly Rooms before she found Sam Robertson there. He received her in his office, a thin man in his late twenties with alert, businesslike eyes and a narrow mouth. Without making any reference to Richard, for she wanted to get the post on her own merits, Lucy said she had heard that a pianist would be needed for the new theatre and she wished to apply for the post.

'I had better hear you play then,' he said.

He led her into the ballroom where there was a grand piano, and she played for twenty minutes. That was longer than was necessary for him to make his decision, but he found it pleasurable to listen to her, being an able pianist himself and recognizing a superior touch. He had had two other applications, both from men, and had half decided on one, but he thought it would be a far greater attraction to have a woman pianist, and with such magnificent hair and fascinating looks she would be an asset to the theatre. Her foreign name would look eyecatching on a bill-board too.

'You shall have the post,' he said to her, leaning an arm on the piano as he looked keenly as her.

She was intensely relieved. With no music pupils of her own, and only Ruth and George Holland learning Italian, her financial position was by no means secure. The salary she would receive as a pianist was modest, but it would certainly bridge the gap.

'Thank you, Mr Robertson,' she said. 'When shall I meet the violinist you mentioned earlier?'

'In my office tomorrow morning at eleven. You can start rehearsing together at the theatre as soon as it is finished.' He shook hands with her, saw her to the door and returned to his office, satisfied that he had made the right choice.

The violinist, Mr Bernard Bartley-Jones, proved to be a rubicund gentleman with a rich voice to match a great thirst, which he had attempted to quench at The Crown on his way to Robertson's office. He greeted Lucy with an old-fashioned gentility, the fumes on his breath rising as though from a tap-room.

'Your servant, ma'am.' His bow, in spite of his portliness, was elegant, and his clothes, although shabby, were of good material. 'I feel sure our partnership will delight the ears of our audiences as you will delight their eyes.'

'Mr Robertson has told me that you have played before the Queen.'

He rolled his eyes upwards in homage to the memory. 'I was first violinist with a London orchestra then, and enjoying better days.'

He was to refer often afterwards to his better days, which Lucy guessed to mean the time when he did not have to carry a bottle permanently in his tail-coat pocket more than to a higher financial status, although without doubt the two were linked. But whether he was gloriously inebriated or merely mildly intoxicated, he still played the violin well. One afternoon when they had finished rehearsing an overture suitable for the presentation of a heavy drama, she asked him why he did not consider returning to the orchestral world.

He gazed around at the newly-finished theatre where they were, and gave a long sigh. 'My health would not allow it.

Now, instead of playing for royalty in the light, I must stay in the shadows to play before a former pugilist.' With flamboyant disdain he pointed with his bow to the box opposite to the one under which her grand piano had been placed, where they could accompany the performances of the players without obstructing the view of the stage. A large W for Warwyck was entwined with moulded ribbons on the fascia of the box. When Daniel Warwyck or any of his family attended a play, they would have their own reserved seats waiting for them, as if they were the very royalty mentioned.

'A former pugilist who was once Champion of England,' she reminded him, folding away her music. 'That is a proud title.'

'Fisticuffs,' he exclaimed with contempt. 'What a use for God-given hands.'

She had risen from the piano stool and stood gazing towards the box. 'I'm looking forward to playing when Daniel Warwyck is present. Everything I have heard about him has whetted my curiosity.'

The violinist was not interested. He was waiting to leave, and she had been entrusted with a key for locking up. 'Shall we meet at the same time tomorrow?'

'Not tomorrow, Mr Bartley-Jones. I have another engagement. We'll say the day after instead.'

As she emerged from the theatre she saw a bill-poster at work putting up details of the opening production of the Asquith Theatre Company. The illustration was lurid, the colours crude, showing a half-naked man spread-eagled on the back of a horse, which was struggling out of a raging torrent onto a rocky bank while being pursued by swimming wolves and attacked by an eagle. Underneath, the title of the play was emblazoned in crimson letters:

MAZEPPA
or The Wild Horse
Lord Byron's Beautiful Dramatic Tale
Delineated by a Moving Panorama and Living Horse

There followed a list of additional treats in store for the audience during the performance, which ranged from scenes on the Steppes of Tartary to others on the precipitous slopes of the Carpathian mountains.

With a smile she turned away and her step was light as she trod the pier back to the promenade. She was looking forward to seeing all that was promised on the poster, but in the meantime she had something far more exciting ahead of her than anything that could be produced on a stage. Tomorrow she was going to call at the Grange. Mr Attwood had had four full days in residence and she could wait no longer to see inside her father's house. And that was the treat in store for her tomorrow. Tomorrow!

7

The great oaks of the Grange created a speckled pattern of sun and shade along the drive as Lucy held the reins of a hired gig, her hair enhanced by the brilliant green of the tilted pillbox and frilled gown that she wore. Ahead of her the house with its blinds drawn up and its windows open to the balmy air bore a far more welcoming look than it had done on her previous and disastrous visit.

As she drew up at the entrance a groom came running from the stables to take the horse and help her alight in a rustle of silk. This time, when she tugged the iron bell-pull, the door opened almost at once. She swept across the threshhold instantly and stood within the hall of the house that spiritually she had come to make her own.

'I wish to see Mr Attwood,' she said firmly.

The footman who had opened the door, dark-clothed and white-gloved, questioned her respectfully. 'Is the master expecting you, madam?'

'No, but Mr Warwyck may have prepared him for my visit.' She was taking a chance that Richard had dropped some word of her interest in the Grange to Timothy Attwood, for they must have met since his return.

'Your name, madam?'

She gave it, and the footman showed her into an anteroom to wait. She was pleased to have time to study at leisure a room in which her father must have received visitors many times, and she took an almost childish delight in seating herself in each one of the elegant chairs. But as time went on and nobody came she began to tap her foot impatiently and then indignantly. Finally, when a glance at the locket-watch she wore on a chain told her that half an hour had gone by, she sprang up and went back into the hall. It was deserted.

Standing alone in the middle of the floor she forgot that she was fuming, forgot everything as her gaze dwelt on every detail of that grand hall and she saw herself dwarfed by it in the reflection thrown back by the tall pier-glasses set against recessed panels. A stone staircase rose to meet an encircling gallery, and overhead mythical gods and goddesses graced a delicate sky on the domed ceiling. She could see that portraits of ancestral Attwoods adorned the walls of the gallery, but from where she stood it was impossible to see them in any detail. Suppose there was a portrait of her father among them!

Almost of their own volition, her feet began to mount the staircase, her gaze fixed upon the portraits. When she reached the head of the flight she had forgotten all else but the chance that within a few minutes she would be looking upon the face of Lionel Attwood. Absorbed, she studied each Attwood visage before passing it, wondering if she would see some resemblance to herself, but those ancestors of previous centuries, be-wigged, be-ruffed, or dressed simply in country clothes with gun and dog, gave back no likeness that she could recognize, and since she had inherited her flaming hair from her mother, there was no link with the one lady who flaunted an auburn love-lock upon a creamy shoulder.

She came to the end of the row, but branching off to left and right were long corridors hung with more paintings. It was as if she were in a trance, unable to halt her search now that she had started upon it, and she took the right-hand corridor, some vague idea in her mind that if she failed to find her father's portrait there she would turn back and explore the other. But these paintings were mostly landscapes. She bit her lip in frustration, increasing her pace until she had seen them all, and when the end of the corridor was blocked by double doors she swung about to retrace her steps with a desperate urgency, not noticing that her wide skirt flicked hard against a small, delicately-legged table on which stood a large, blue-patterned vase. Too late she saw the table tilt and the vase topple. She threw out her hands to try to save it, but with a tremendous crash it hit the floor and smashed into innumerable pieces about her feet. Overcome by dismay, she stooped automatically and picked up a piece. In the same instant the double doors were whipped open, and with the shining fragment in her cupped hands she faced Timothy Attwood.

'In the devil's name, what is going on here?' he exclaimed loudly, breath drawn in for further verbal abuse, but he checked himself when he saw it was no servant he was confronting, and he amended his tone if not his bewilderment. 'Who on earth are you, pray?'

In her immediate confusion he appeared quite wild and alarming, exuding vitality, his physique being of that type of bone-thinness which comes from compressed energy. Fashionably leonine locks and side-whiskers made a curly aureole of shining gold about his head, the brightness held in his brows and lashes. As she recovered herself she noted that he had a jaunty air about him and was quite debonair, his clothes cut in the latest style, the lapel of his frock-coat sporting a crimson rose, and the lively face with its narrow, green eyes, long nose and pointed chin looked as if its owner extracted a deal of enjoyment from life and would be a total stranger to boredom.

'I'm Mrs di Castelloni,' she said shakily.

Before he could make any reply a voice that she recognized instantly with a further sinking of the heart spoke drily from within the room. 'It is the visitor who has been waiting ever since we lost ourselves in a last-minute discussion of those new plans.'

Timothy Attwood smote his forehead with the heel of his hand in self-reproach, and looking beyond him into the room she saw Josh Barton sitting at a table spread with papers and maps. 'What a couple of boors we are, Barton!' Timothy exclaimed before giving her a wide smile that creased up his eyes to make them no more than twinkling slits. 'Forgive me, ma'am. It is no reflection on you that I did not see you earlier.

As you heard, time flew by unheeded.' Setting his fists on his hips with elbows jutting, he eyed the broken pieces of the vase under a raised eyebrow. 'Did your impatience with being kept waiting reach smashing point?'

His humorous note did nothing to dispel her mortification. 'I knocked against the table.'

'So I can see!' He was getting some good-natured amusement out of her confusion. 'What are you going to do about it?'

'I'll replace it, of course. There must be other vases of that design.'

'I'm afraid not. It happened to be unique.' His tongue was in his cheek.

Already pale, she went even whiter. 'Then you must let me know its value in order that I may recompense you for its loss.'

He was enjoying himself hugely. 'I never take money from a lady. It's an old-fashioned principle of mine.' Not unkind, he took compassion on her distress. 'Come, ma'am, forget the matter. I'm only gaming you. In truth, I can't remember that I ever looked at the wretched vase and could not describe it now if a thousand guineas should be wagered on it.'

A gush of relief released the mainspring of her own sense of humour at the harmless little joke he had played on her, and she uttered a spontaneous, lively laugh to which he immediately responded, throwing his head back on a shout of mirth that showed every white tooth in his head. Their mutual merriment broke down in seconds the social barriers that could have taken weeks to overcome. Her youth seemed to join with his, and for Lucy it was as if he had thrown shutters wide to sunshine. Never before had she met anyone who obviously found it possible to look on the bright side of things, and it brought home to her how starved she had been throughout her life of joyful laughter with someone of her own age.

'Nevertheless I must make amends for that wretched vase,' she insisted, and somehow her repeating of his words on it made them laugh again.

'I'll try to think of something.' It did not appear impertinent to either of them that he should reach out and link his hand with hers to draw her away from the fragments lying about the floor. 'Come along, and don't cut through the sole of your shoe on any of those pieces. I had said I would go down to you, so I fail to understand why you were allowed to make your own way – and unescorted. I'll have the servant responsible by his ear for it, I promise you.'

Josh spoke from the table where he had risen at her entry, a spread of papers before him. 'Perhaps Mrs di Castelloni came to find you on her own initiative, Attwood,' he said in that deceptively easy voice of his. 'She has a way of making conventions go by the board.' He made a little bow. 'Have you not, ma'am?'

Out of the happiness of her mood she refused to be goaded, although the hard glint in his eye left her in no doubt that he had not forgotten she was waiting downstairs, but had chosen not to remind Timothy of the passing of time. It was as if he were engaged in some sharp game with her in which there were no rules, but which only they knew how to play. Timothy had turned from closing the doors, unaware that anything was amiss.

'You have met each other before, Mr Barton tells me.'

'Yes, we have.' Then she addressed Josh as she accepted the chair he had pulled forward for her. 'You are correct in assuming that no servant is to blame.' Sitting back, she returned her attention to Timothy, who had perched his weight on the table's edge. 'I have to admit to inviting myself into the grounds the first time I made Mr Barton's acquaintance, and I have taken an advantage again today.'

'How?' Timothy chuckled in anticipation.

'I came to look at the house in your absence, and on this second visit my curiosity quite overcame me and I started viewing all the paintings I could see in the hope of finding a portrait of Lionel Attwood. I grew up in a convent on the Adriatic coast not far from the churchyard where he lies. For as long as I can remember I have wanted to visit the place where he lived and, if possible, to see a likeness of him.'

Timothy showed surprise and thumped the table top with his fist. 'That's right, by Jove! He did die in Italy. What on earth made you so deucedly interested in that distant cousin of mine?'

'A natural curiosity.' She was getting adept at cloaking her past. 'I was an orphaned child of English parents, and his tomb was a link with England.'

'Well, well.' Timothy folded his arms. 'From what I've heard, Lionel Attwood was never much of a ladies' man. Quite the reverse, in fact.' He was confident that she saw no significance in his words, and he had not intended that she should. 'But I'm sure he would have been flattered by your interest in him. Take a look at his portrait, by all means.' He gave a casual nod across the room. 'There he is.'

She turned her head towards the Adam fireplace, and within an ornate frame above it was the painted likeness of the man who had died almost at the moment of her birth. For a few minutes she sat completely motionless, staring at the finely-featured face with the meditative expression, a poet's mouth, and shining golden hair dressed in the fronded style of the Regency.

Slowly she unfolded herself from the chair and advanced towards the portrait, her hands clasped together against her chest, her gaze fixed unwaveringly on those grey-blue eyes that seemed to look into her own. Coming to a standstill below it she took in every detail of the painting. He was dressed soberly in a snuff-coloured coat, his cravat plain and folded in fan pleats across the high collar, his only jewellery a gold fob-watch and an opal ring. In the background lay Attwood Grange and the green swell of the Downs, conveying his affection for his house and the local countryside. Across the years her heart spoke its filial love to him and she half-closed her eyes, trying to imagine that his life-like hand might move and touch her cheek in benediction.

In the room neither of the men spoke. Josh, engaged in stacking the papers together, paused in his task to watch her sharply and observantly. Timothy, waiting for her to finish looking her fill of the portrait, eyed her differently. Richard Warwyck had told him of the widow who had moved into Sea Cottage, but it had been at a local committee meeting that they had both attended the day after his return to Easthampton, and he had not paid much attention, merely gathering that for some obscure reason she was interested in the Grange. Warwyck, whom he listed as a business acquaintance although they did meet socially, had not prepared him either for Lucy's youth or her unusualness. She made other women he knew, whatever their age, pale by comparison. Had he not been drawn to Donna Warwyck, for whom his feelings were very close to love, he might have lost no time in pursuing this young widow who had come so unexpectedly into his life.

Lucy broke the silence. 'Exactly when was this portrait painted, do you think?'

He shifted from the table and went across to her side, looking up at the painting with her. 'I can't tell you the date without searching through the Grange records, but I would say about 1818, before the consumption laid a full hold on him.'

'From the date on his tombstone, that would make him twenty-two years of age,' she said promptly.

'He had already made the Grand Tour then, and many of the treasures in this house are those he brought back from his travels. It was through him that the gardens were laid out as they are now, and it was he who redecorated and refurbished the house, using the best craftsmen of the day.' He tilted his head at the painting. 'It must have been a year or two after he sat for this portrait that he had to return to Italy for his health's sake. It was on a subsequent return home that he married, and he and his wife lived at the Grange for a short time before he left it with her, never to return.'

'Is there a portrait in this house of his wife?' In suspense she waited for his reply.

'No, there isn't. That is quite surprising, because Claudine Attwood was said to be a fascinating creature. But then, as far as I can remember from the family history, they had not been wed much more than a year when he died. If a portrait of her was painted during that time, it is most likely that she kept it with her, because after his death she never returned to the Grange.'

'Why not? Do you know?'

He shrugged. 'From the manner in which she dissipated the rest of her short life, I should imagine she found it a dull place. My uncle bought it from her to keep it in the family, but he never lived in it, having no wish to uproot himself from his own home in Hertfordshire, so it had been closed up for a long time when I became the owner of the Grange.'

It was difficult to suppress her anguish. The ache for what might have been was useless torment, but for the moment she could not check it. This dear house in all its quiet beauty had stood unloved and unwanted throughout all those years when she had been growing up homeless in an alien land. She drew in her breath, conscious of being in a highly emotional state, and the strain was telling on her. What was more, she had begun to realize how closely Josh was observing her. She would ask no more questions at the present time.

'We must be boring Mr Barton with all this talk of the past,' she said with forced lightness, compelling herself to move away from the painting.

'On the contrary,' Josh remarked, slipping the papers into a leather folder. 'I'm a man who looks to the future in all matters, but that does not mean I don't appreciate what the past has bequeathed us.'

Timothy was busying himself with a decanter and glasses. 'I'm sure you did not know that Mr Barton is a railway man, did you ma'am? That's where his great talents lie. He'll have the whole of southern England veined with tracks before he's finished with it.'

She knew a sense of horror. So that was what he did. For a moment he seemed superimposed upon a backcloth of the misery and despair that the railway had brought to the local peasants in the faraway Italian district that she had known, the demolishing of the humble homes, the gouging of the pitiful acres, the smoke of fires. As if a bell of warning were clanging a deafening knell against her ears, shutting out all else, she recalled that morning in the grounds of the Grange when he stood with an air of having interrupted some task he was engaged in to address her.

'No, I did not know,' she said confusedly. She had heard someone refer to him as a man with commercial interests at the Warwycks' dinner party, but that was all.

'Well, that's not surprising.' Timothy came with a glass of Madeira for her. 'It was considered expedient to keep Mr Barton's business in the area *sub rosa* until he and I had fully discussed matters between us, but he is one of the best contractors in the country. Only Richard Warwyck and one or two others were in the know, being similarly involved in affairs of compensation and so forth.' He handed another glass to Josh and picked up his own. 'I bid you welcome to the Grange, ma'am, and you too, sir. I think a toast would be in order. To the London and South Coast Railway Company. May good luck favour it, and may its Easthampton branch line cross Attwood land for the benefit of all concerned.'

Both men drank the toast, but Lucy continued to hold her glass with its contents untasted, scarcely able to believe what she had heard. 'Is the railway to violate this estate?' she demanded hoarsely.

'I suppose it is a violation in a manner of speaking,' Timothy admitted cheerfully, 'but I deem it an honourable sacrifice in the cause of engineering advancement.'

'I think the whole idea is monstrous!' she exclaimed, setting down her glass so abruptly that the wine almost slopped over.

Timothy was somewhat startled by her fierceness, but Josh appeared unconcerned, taking another mouthful of wine and then deliberately draining the glass in a manner that somehow seemed like an insolence directed specially towards her. With his dark Cossack looks she would not have been surprised if he had hurled the glass into the fireplace, but he merely held it for a second or two before putting it on the table. 'The days of coaching are over,' he pointed out to her. 'We have moved into a new age of steam and electricity and industrial power. The railways are part and parcel of that system.'

'But not here!' she protested heatedly. 'The railway would not be linking up with factories or mines or shipping docks – only to the seaside.'

Timothy approved her concern for the estate, some part of which was farmed by tenants, and the rest consisting of a fine stretch of parkland, a fit setting for the old house, but a choice had had to be made and he had made it, subject to certain conditions regarding the site of the branch line's terminal. On his lawyer's advice he was withholding his signature to any deed until that part of it was settled and the Company had been compelled to go along with him in the matter. 'One cannot stand in the path of progress,' he pointed out to her a trifle pontifically.

She was incredulous. 'Progress! Is it progress to let

vandalism loose? Are you to give preference to a railway company over the responsibility of keeping intact land that has been handed down for you to hold in trust for generations of Attwoods who will come after you?'

He was intrigued by her passion. It radiated excitingly from her whole person, and he could not take his eyes from her. 'I have given serious thought to my responsibilities, you can be sure of that, but I also welcome the spread of the railways. As for the Grange, I shall dispose of it later. It was never my intention to make it a permanent residence.'

He was in ignorance of the fact that he was hacking away at the very roots she had aimed to thrust down, threatening to leave her as much adrift as she had ever been. With the Grange in the possession of strangers she would suffer a complete and final loss of identity, cut off for ever from the Attwoods who had lived in it. 'Is everything signed and sealed?' she asked in as level a tone as she could manage.

'Far from it.' Timothy cast a wry glance in Josh's direction as if it amused him to have the Company dependent upon his whim. 'A deal of difficulties have to be ironed out first. Is that not so, Barton?'

Josh had finished fastening the buckle on his leather folder and he nodded. 'Local opposition from certain quarters is inevitable, but I am confident it will not prevail. There will be nothing that we have not dealt with successfully in other parts of the country. However, until matters are settled to everybody's satisfaction, no date for the first pickaxe to go into the ground can be set. In the meantime, I'm extremely busy with a number of other arrangements that have to be made in this area.'

Lucy released a pent-up breath. So nothing yet was irrevocable. It was like a reprieve, a precious breathing-space in which she could do something to change the course of events.

'It could be said that the branch line stands or falls by my decision in the end,' Timothy declared to her with continued amusement. Josh looked less pleased. Lucy ignored him and concentrated on Timothy.

'What power you hold, Mr Attwood,' she said softly, eyes brimming with admiration. She saw him preen, well pleased, and knew a sense of power all her own. Only then did she shift her gaze in the direction of Josh Barton and it glittered with challenge through the dip and sweep of her curiously shaded lashes, and the stare he gave her back was intent, aware and penetrating. It was as if for a few crystal seconds they were able to read each other's thoughts, and both knew that they were launching into a conflict greater than any of the minor skirmishes that had gone before, with no holds barred and a tremendous future at stake. He must fight with every weapon at his disposal for his aim, and she would pitch against him all her feminine wiles to save the Grange and its land from dissolution.

Deliberately she gave a pretty shrug of her shoulders, as if for the moment the lull before battle continued. Picking up her glass, she smiled at Timothy over the rim of it. 'Whatever happens, Mr Attwood, I'm sure you will see that everything turns out for the best, and I drink my toast to that.'

She saw how he was looking at her, his admiration transparent, and she felt a surge of exhilaration, as if the fate of the Grange had already passed into her hands.

'I'll be going,' Josh put the leather folder under his arm, 'and I'll see myself out.' He shook hands with Timothy and nodded to her, bidding her goodbye. Then he went from the room, the renewed murmur of their voices following him until he had gone some distance along the corridor.

'Damnation,' he muttered under his breath. Then he added a few more expletives to himself as he went out into the sunshine and flung himself into the seat of his cabriolet, which had been brought to the entrance. The whip cracked through the air over the horse's head and he was bowled away at a spanking pace. At the gates he looked back over his shoulder, but the length of the drive combined with the angle of the house to prevent his seeing again the window of the room where the woman he wanted more than he had wanted any woman before in all his thirty years was dallying with young Attwood. With a jerk, he jammed the brim of his tall hat more securely over his glowering brow and on skidding wheels went out into the lane.

It was late afternoon when Timothy handed Lucy into his

curricle, having dispatched a servant much earlier to return the gig to the hiring stable for her. He had asked her to stay to luncheon with him, and afterwards they had strolled together in the grounds, resting for a while on a white wrought-iron seat under the trees, which gave them a fine view of the house across the lawns. Deliberately she kept away from the subject of the railway and concentrated on questions about the history of the Grange and the Attwood family, which he answered freely, painting images of their joint ancestors, unaware how he was filling in parts of a great void in her life. She realized as he talked that their kinship to each other was extremely distant, that of cousins many times removed, but since it was her father who had done so much for the Grange, she felt she had the greater right to decide its future and was not troubled by conscience in her determination to manipulate Timothy and events towards that end.

As he drove her back to Sea Cottage they talked of horses and riding, he telling her that he sometimes rode with friends along the sands, and expressing the hope that she would join them in the near future. She accepted, and was told that an extra horse should be brought for her from the Grange stables, which she remarked was both thoughtful and courteous of him.

'I have enjoyed my visit to the Grange,' she said as they were about to part.

'I hope you will honour me with your company often,' he replied. Briefly their eyes held. He had intended no more than a conventional politeness, but somehow a warmth had come involuntarily into his voice that went beyond the bounds of it.

'Good day, Mr Attwood,' she said, as if nothing untoward had occurred, turning in at the gate of Sea Cottage and closing it. He waited until she had entered the house and then departed.

He went straight to Easthampton House. Only later was he to wonder if by turning at once to Donna it had been to seek confirmation as to the direction of his feelings. Any doubts he might have harboured at the time vanished at the sight of her. She was in the garden picking flowers, and did not see him as he approached noiselessly across the lawn. One by one she was placing the blooms in an open trug, a

Paisley shawl about her shoulders, a rose-coloured ribbon set flat across the middle parting of her shining hair. It was to be their second meeting since his return, for he had called to see her the day after getting back to the Grange, but then she had had some other young women with her and the chance to converse had been limited. He was delighted to find her alone.

'Miss Donna.'

She swung about on a start of pleasure that suffused her face before she collected herself behind that wall of reserve that he wanted so much to breach permanently. 'Mr Attwood! How agreeable of you to call.'

'Isn't it time you called me by my Christian name? I asked you to in my letters.'

She caught her breath and her eyes shone. 'Very well – Timothy.'

'You must know I'm Tim to my closest friends.'

The colour deepened in her cheeks. 'Tim.'

'That's better.' He gave her a grin, wide and approving, and took the trug from her to place it on a garden seat. Then he took both her hands into his. 'It's splendid to see you again. The months of winter have been long and dreary.'

His meaning was unmistakable. He had missed her! She was overwhelmed, quite dizzy with happiness. 'I found them wearisome myself,' she admitted, letting caution slip. None suspected that beneath her cool veneer there churned a passionate nature equal to any of her Warwyck ancestors. She was a deep and secret person, and not even with her closest friend had she ever exchanged the giggling confidences common to the rest of the love-struck girls she knew; only Richard had plumbed the depths of her feelings for Timothy, simply because, knowing her as he did, he had seen more in her expression than she had realized whenever he had handed her unexpectedly a letter from the morning's post bearing the dear, familiar writing.

The pressure of Timothy's fingers upon hers increased a fraction as he looked penetratingly at her. 'May I hope that my absence contributed to the dreariness of those months from October until this first day of May?'

Her lashes were lowered, not through coquetry, but as a defence against revealing her inner self, a trick she had played all her life to disguise her emotions, having learned early on that a show of feelings inflamed even further any conflict with her father.

'It could have been a factor involved,' she conceded, with enough play in her voice for him to have made no mistake about it.

He gathered both her hands into his clasp, causing her arms to fold against him as he took a step towards her. 'May I kiss you, Donna – my dearest?'

The question was superfluous since nothing would have stopped him, but not knowing how she would react to anything other than the mildest caress of the lips, he constrained himself, keeping to the chastest of kisses, and because he did not expect to meet it, he mistook the amorous shudder that passed through her for one of shyness and affronted modesty, a misapprehension that appeared to his eyes to be confirmed by the hasty withdrawal of her hands from his and her quick move away from him. He put her at her ease.

'We had little chance to talk together the other day when I called, but I trust we can amend matters throughout the summer.'

'Yes, Tim.' She was composed again and smiling, nothing to show that she had not dared any response to his lips with her own, fearful that love might carry her away to an excess of kisses. 'You will remember that I asked you to take a look at Toby next time you came.'

'And where is that wicked mongrel we rescued from perdition?' There was a teasing note of laughter in his query.

She answered him in mock reproof. 'You're as merciless as Richard. Toby is the sweetest creature. Let us find him.'

The little dog came obediently at the sound of her voice calling him, lolloping across the lawn from the direction of the stable, long ears flying. He greeted her and the newcomer with a wriggling exuberance.

'You're getting fat, old chap,' Timothy said when he had calmed down some of the dog's excitement, and set him on a stable bench, holding him with firm and sensitive hands. 'Too many tit-bits at table, I'll be bound.'

Donna could not deny it. 'He was scarcely more than a poor little skeleton when we found him,' she pointed out.

'You had to build up his strength again, but it is as wrong to overfeed as it is to underfeed, and the extra weight has not been helping his disability.' Carefully he handled the misshapen limb. 'I know of a liniment that should help his rheumaticky pains, because that is what is afflicting him at times. I'll get a bottle made up for you.' He put the dog back on the ground and they left the stables, Toby following them until he spotted the groom's cat and went off after it in a fruitless chase.

'Do stay to tea,' she invited. He accepted, and she had it served on the bamboo table in the veranda, amid the foliage of ferns and a vine that made a leafy ceiling of the glass overhead. They sat in basket chairs, and over the white and gold cups, the raisin scones and the buttery seed cake, they exchanged full news of whom they had seen whilst he had been absent from the Grange and what they had done, filling in gaps left by their correspondence and their wholly inadequate reunion in other company. As they talked, his mention of the Grange itself brought Lucy's name to the tip of Donna's tongue, her intention being to inform him of the widow's Italian link with his home, but he forestalled her.

'I made the acquaintance of Mrs di Castelloni when she called at the house today. She spoke most highly of the kindness shown to her by you and your brother.'

'Did she?' Donna always knew unease when caught unawares by Lucy's name.

'I intend to include her in riding parties when people come to stay at the Grange, but why should we wait until then? Let you and I ride with her along the sands one day, dine afterwards at an inn, and come back by road if the tide is already on the turn. Another day we could take a gallop across the Downs. What do you say to that?'

Her immediate thought was to refuse. Although she loved horses as she loved all animals, Donna did not care to ride if she could avoid it. She had never conquered her nervousness in the saddle, a fault with which her father always showed his impatience, being a superb horseman himself, and it was one more bone of contention between them. She had shed more tears in childhood than she cared to remember through his scorn of her horsemanship. But not to go with Timothy at his invitation would be to deny herself his company, and she believed he had inveigled the situation in order that they might ride together with Lucy as chaperone. She summoned up her courage.

'Yes,' she decided firmly. 'Let such an outing be arranged as soon as possible.'

'That's capital!' he endorsed, well pleased.

They were to meet the following evening at Anna Edenfield's house, and when Donna arrived Tim was waiting to come forward as soon as her hostess had welcomed her. Anna had inherited the house from her late grand-parents and lived in it with a maiden aunt as chaperone, a strait-laced lady who put a severe restraint on all social proceedings there. Her expression was consistently disapproving, although this was a decorous card-party with little chance of intimate conversation, the couples making up fours at rosewood card-tables adorned with silver dishes of sweet-meats and nuts for refreshment during play. Donna often wondered how Miss Roberta, who rarely smiled, could be so sour in nature when in looks she so much resembled her kind and dignified late brother, Sir Geoffrey, who had not only been Daniel Warwyck's patron, but had backed him financially in the great gamble of establishing Easthampton as a resort. Donna concluded that it must be spinsterhood that had turned Anna's aunt into such an old dragon, and in spite of the warmth of the room a shiver passed through her as if someone had stepped on her grave.

8

———◆———

Timothy lost no time in making arrangements for the first of their riding expeditions. Before the end of the week Donna found herself mounted on her mother's mare, which was called Bonnie after a favourite horse once owned by Kate Warwyck, and she rode stiffly beside Lucy as Timothy led the way on a dappled grey down a slipway to the shore. Fishermen with their boats drawn up on the beach paused in whatever task they had in hand to stare after them, only Meg having no time to spare a glance, being busy with the cording of snapping claws while getting a catch of crabs ready for the cooking pot.

As his horse reached the sands, Timothy waited for Donna and Lucy to come one on either side of him, and then the three of them kept abreast for some distance. He and Lucy, immediately engaged in lively conversation, failed to notice that Donna did not join in, her concentration fixed, the high white stock about her throat hiding the nervous pulse that resulted from being in the saddle once again. She could give no thought to the sunny brightness of the afternoon and the glory of a setting of tide-swept sands, crisp as toast, with the luxuriance of the thick tamarisk hedge rising above the shingle and a bastion of rocks that followed the curve of the bay. She had thought that love would give her courage, and somehow she had managed to convince herself that she would forget all the old qualms while with Timothy, but a welcome lapse in riding, seized since her father had finally thrown up his hands in despair at her incompetence shortly before his departure to America, had done nothing to restore her confidence, and as soon as she had stepped onto the mounting block an attack of shivering nerves had possessed her and would not be banished. Often she had tried to analyse her fear, trying to discover whence it stemmed, but she could recall nothing that remotely justified her misery in the saddle.

From the pier, Richard saw the three of them put their horses into a trot, leaving three separate trails of hoof-prints in their wake, each indentation taking on the appearance of a silvery horse-shoe as the sea-water from the outgoing tide seeped back into the hollows. He was more than surprised to see Donna in the saddle and erroneously credited Lucy with giving her the necessary encouragement to ride. He considered Lucy to be an ideal companion for his sister, who was inclined to gather about her friends of the same disposition as herself, and Lucy with her bright spirits and enthusiasm for life could do much to draw her out of herself. For the same reason of temperament he approved Donna's affection for Timothy Attwood and hoped a match would come of it; she needed someone to break through the shell she had built around herself as a protection against their father's constant criticism, which had subdued and conditioned her over the years. Privately he believed it was bitterness over the death through measles of two younger and more favoured daughters that had finally hardened their father's heart against the least loved of his children, who had survived the dreaded attack. He himself had been away at school and escaped the illness, but the memory haunted him still of his father coming to break the news and take him home to one funeral that had followed close upon another, when the hearse, a-flurry with black feathers and purple drapery, drawn by six ebony-hued horses, had seemed incongruously large to carry those small, white coffins to a last resting-place.

Along the sands the sun flashed suddenly on the bridle of Lucy's chestnut as it tossed its head in eagerness for a swifter pace, and Richard forgot the past in contemplation of the present. He was seeing Lucy often. He made a point of calling in at the Pier Theatre when he knew she would be there, included her with others in a party when he had tickets to a concert or some other function at the Assembly Rooms, and it had become expected that he should join the Hollands for supper after their Italian conversational sessions with Lucy, in order to drive her home afterwards. So far he had not attempted to kiss her again, determined to lay a foundation of such strength to their relationship that when he did reach for her again, she would come of her own free will into his arms.

The three riders were drawing steadily away. For once his duties irked him, and he would have liked to be with them, hearing the quiet scrunch of sand and the cry of sea-birds overhead. He did not notice Josh, with whom he had made an appointment, approaching him from the entrance gate that he had left open.

'Good day to you, Warwyck. What have you sighted at sea?'

'Nothing at sea, but Attwood escorting my sister and Mrs di Castelloni on an outing.'

Josh went to the telescope set up on a stand bolted to the deck for the use of future patrons who wished to enjoy a view of the resort and the shore in some detail, and he put it to his eye. Immediately the lens held Lucy within its circumference, and even from that distance he could see that she and Timothy were engaged in animated talk together while Donna trotted her mare in silence a few paces behind. Richard, glancing at his pocket watch, did not notice how Josh's lips tightened ominously or the manner in which he struck the telescope away as he moved from it, a resolve made to deal effectively with Lucy di Castelloni before her womanly meddling complicated still further an already difficult situation. Only that morning he had met Attwood again in the Warwyck office, and enough had been said for him to gather that Lucy's argument had had the effect of putting a goad to the young man's conscience over keeping the estate intact, and although there appeared to be no real threat of a change of mind, the risk was always there. He could not imagine anything more galling than to lose a contract worth many thousands of pounds through her interference. Not only the contract, but his reputation for being able to overcome all obstacles in the way of his railway tracks was very much at stake.

With the pier lying far behind them, Timothy twisted in the saddle to look back at Donna, reining in for her to draw level with him again, something he had already done several times, which made the ride somewhat erratic. Why she did not keep up he did not know, but he supposed her to be trying to set the pace, and resolved not to pull ahead of her again.

'Did you hear, Miss Donna?' he inquired, lapsing back into a more formal mode of address in the presence of a third person. 'I have just said that I think it's time the old ballroom at the Grange was put to good use again. It must be many years since music and dancing were known within its walls – not since Lionel Attwood's time, I'll be bound – and I've a fancy to let the house have a last merry fling.'

'I thought you told me that you were keeping that wing of the Grange closed up,' she answered, hoping that he would not notice the strain she felt across her eyes or how awkwardly she rode in comparison to Lucy's ease and grace.

'So I have, and I had intended to keep it padlocked, but I think it would be only right to carry on the festivities of the opening of the pier and theatre upon your parents' return with a ball at the Grange. Do you think your parents would like that? I'm most anxious to get your father into a good mood.'

Inwardly she was thrown into blissful confusion by his remark. Did he mean that he wanted to soften her father's attitude towards the railway, for she knew Timothy to be Richard's help and ally there, or was it more personal than that? She was certain the second reason was the one, and she gripped the reins still tighter and was thankful that she had her mother's gift of retaining a look of composure no matter how great the turmoil of her thoughts.

'I cannot think of anything better suited to humour Father than a ball practically in his honour,' she said with perfect truth. Her father had known the adulation of the prize-ring crowds in his youth and still enjoyed being fêted in the public eye, much like an actor who must play to an audience on any occasion, even when he has long since left the boards.

'Then it is settled. A grand ball it shall be.' He smiled from one to the other of his riding companions. 'I trust you two ladies will honour me with your presence and allow me more than one dance with each of you.' When they had promised him, he added to Lucy: 'I'll make a point of including Mrs Olivia Radcliffe of Radcliffe Hall on the guest list. After we talked that day at the Grange I remembered suddenly that she was related to Lionel's wife, Claudine. They were sisters, in fact, and there were just the two of them, no others in the family. Since you are interested in him, I thought you might like to meet his sister-in-law. She could probably tell you quite a lot about his life and his travels and so on.'

Such startling information uttered in such matter of fact tones caused Lucy almost to doubt that she was hearing aright. Her mother's sister was living locally! Her own aunt! Someone with whom she had the closest of blood ties. Olivia Radcliffe of all people! Her thoughts raced. She had never known that she had anyone on her mother's side. Claudine had told the nuns that she had been orphaned some years previously and had no one to stand by her in her grief. Why had she lied? Had she not been on speaking terms with her only sister? But then, hard as it was to accept, it seemed that her mother had been an inveterate liar who told tales to suit herself and her own ends.

'That should be extremely interesting,' she managed to say, choking back a thousand questions.

Timothy gave a nod, moving his horse closer to hers as he skirted a rock sticking out of the sand, but disturbing a pool in which it was centred, ripples passing away from the passage of hooves. 'In the past the Radcliffes and the Attwoods were always friends and neighbours, but my uncle never lived at the Grange and I'm still virtually a newcomer; thus I have only the slightest acquaintance with Mrs Radcliffe and her daughter, an only child who is married and lives elsewhere. I met them for the first time when I attended the funeral of Alexander Radcliffe, the late master of the Hall, last year shortly after inheriting the Grange.'

Lucy fought down an almost uncontrollable urge to put her whip to the chestnut she was riding and gallop at once to the Hall to declare herself and demand recognition, but cool common sense prevailed. It was highly likely that Olivia Radcliffe was as much in ignorance of her existence as everybody else, and it would only be folly to burst in upon the unsuspecting woman. Better by far to bide her time wisely and meet her aunt at the Grange as Timothy had planned. Such an appropriate setting would be conducive to an amiable meeting, and if good fortune was with her, the striking likeness she bore to her mother should be enough for Olivia to speak out the truth of her own accord, finally putting an end to those years in limbo and making a whole person at last of Claudine's only daughter.

She turned her face full of appeal towards Timothy. 'Would you grant me a favour?'

'Anything,' he replied cheerily.

'Would you arrange for me to talk with Mrs Radcliffe in the room where Lionel's portrait hangs?'

'That can be done.' He smiled, shaking his head. 'My word! You are deucedly taken with the fellow, are you not? But there, I suppose I can understand it, seeing that you regarded him as a link with this old country of ours throughout those impressionable years when you were growing up in a foreign land.'

Neither noticed that their companion had dropped behind again. Bonnie, following through the rock-pool, had slithered sharply on a submerged ledge, causing Donna such a heart-pounding start of fright as she had thought herself about to be tossed from the saddle, that she was paying little attention to the conversation of the others. Timothy wheeled his horse about to come to her side, Lucy following suit.

'Are you game, Miss Donna?' Timothy inquired, smiling.

She supposed he was making some reference to the ball again, and she answered him with a kind of desperate brightness, afraid he might suspect her terrible cowardice of which she was ashamed. 'Yes, yes,' she exclaimed vaguely.

'Right! One! Two! Three! We're off!'

Merciful heaven! It was to be a race! He and Lucy were

away from her in a thud of hooves and a shower of sand. She had no choice but to follow, and she gritted her teeth as she urged the surprised mare on. Whether Bonnie, who was used to Kate Warwyck's complete control, seized the chance to show a quirk of ill-temper at her rider's ineffectual handling, or whether the sight of the other two horses pounding ahead aroused some long dormant competitive spirit could never be known, but whatever the reason, Bonnie hurled herself into the race, succeeded in getting the bit between her teeth, and promptly strained every muscle to overtake and out-length. Donna was seized by panic. The sound of the waves blended with the thunder of hooves and the rush of sea-wind to create a roaring in her ears. She shut her eyes, gripping hard with her knee about the pommel, seeming to hear again her father's exasperated shout that she could not possibly fall riding side-saddle if she was sitting properly, but the remembered gusts of his wrath only served to enervate still further her feelings to a state of utter helplessness, her only thought being that she must not disgrace herself by crying out or she would die to see the same contempt upon Timothy's face as she had seen upon that of her parent so many times.

The race was to a distant wing of water not yet drained back by the sea, and Lucy arrived at the edge of it a few seconds after Timothy, who had hauled his horse spectacularly back on its haunches. But before they exchanged one word, a riderless Bonnie shot past them to plunge into the water, throwing up huge spumes to half-drench them in spray. Both wheeled about in dreadful concern, to gallop back to where Donna lay motionless on the sands.

Timothy was the first to get there, hurling himself from the saddle to kneel beside her, and he was relieved to find her shaken by the fall she had taken, but unhurt. Lucy, who had caught Bonnie's reins, came riding up, leading the water-subdued runaway with her.

'I'll help you back into the saddle,' Timothy said when Donna had recovered herself, resting against his arm until he assisted her to her feet, but she turned her ashen face towards him, her eyes frightened.

'No! I can't! I don't want to!'

'But you really should ride back,' he encouraged patiently, recognizing a loss of nerve that could be in danger of never being regained. 'It's the only way after a tumble.'

'No!'

Lucy added her persuasion. 'Your mare is quiet enough now. We'll ride one on either side of you.'

'Leave me alone!' Donna's voice trembled on the brink of hysteria, and she swung away, stumbled to one knee and scrambled up again to run from them blindly. Timothy caught her up and seized her by the arm to check her flight, bringing her to a reluctant halt. She could not look at him, so great was her sense of folly and shame.

'Just be calm,' he said quietly. 'The choice is yours. But I'm asking you to try. For me.'

It was a measure of her love for him that after some hesitation she did take a step towards Bonnie, who had been led by Lucy to stand by a rock that could be used as a mounting-block, but as soon as she smelt the sweat of excitement and exertion that hung about the mare, the last threads of her courage went completely. It was as if she were paralysed.

'No,' she said tonelessly. 'I'll walk back.'

Although she did not see Timothy and Lucy look at each other, she somehow sensed the exchange of compassionate glances. It seemed to her to be the crowning humiliation. It had been as her father had always predicted: she had made a complete fool of herself, and had she been stripped naked she could not have felt more vulnerable and exposed to scorn. Setting her gaze ahead, she began to retrace the way they had come, Timothy walking beside her, leading his own horse, while Lucy continued in the saddle, Bonnie's reins still in her hands.

He attempted conversation, keeping it light-hearted as if nothing had happened, and Lucy supported him, but Donna only spoke when she had to, and then in monosyllables. Irrationally, she found herself furious with them for trying to put her at her ease. All her smouldering distrust of Lucy flared up, and she could no longer distinguish between love and hatred in her certainty that Timothy was despising her in her cowardice.

It was the longest walk she had ever known back along the shore and up through the town to 'her home. Sympathetically, Lucy offered to stay with her, but she refused with some bluntness, wanting to be alone in her wretchedness.

'I'll call and see how you are tomorrow,' Timothy said, swinging quickly back into the saddle and inadvertently giving away his eagerness to depart, being utterly thankful that the whole disastrous expedition was at an end. It had been quite an eye-opener to see the mulish set of Donna's mouth, and she had revealed a defiant, ill-tempered side to her character that he had not suspected. Good God! Anybody could take a fall, and there was no need to radiate hostility over it. He could not understand her, he really could not.

Neither he nor Lucy mentioned what had taken place as he returned with her to Sea Cottage, but when she had dismounted he spoke the thought that he believed to be in both their minds.

'It looks to me as if Donna has finished with riding for the time being, but there's no reason why you and I should not continue to take outings together sometimes.' A pause. 'Is there?'

Since everything possible to coax Donna back into the saddle had failed, Lucy had no compunction in accepting, her smile merry, quite dazzling him. 'I think it would be extremely agreeable. You see, I'm set on winning the race next time.'

He saw she was laughing as she went up the path into the house with her quick, light step. Indoors she immediately became aware of cigar smoke. The piquant aroma hung about her as she ascended the stairs. She had never seen Emmie Linden with anything other than her clay pipe, but if the woman had decided to indulge in a more noble smoke, it made a pleasant change.

Humming to herself, Lucy did not more than remove her hat and gloves upon reaching her rooms, before going to a drawer and taking out a map of the district, which she had purchased in a second-hand shop at the same time as the brass telescope. During the strained talk while escorting

Donna back to Easthampton House, there had been mention of the extent of Warwyck land, and she was eager to settle a point in her mind. Drawing out a chair, she sat down at the table and unfolded the map, spreading it out to study it even more closely than before. It showed the Grange and Radcliffe Hall, but it was too old a map to show Easthampton as anything but the fishing hamlet it had been in the past. With her fingertips she traced the boundaries of the two great houses, and it was easy to see that if all the rest of the land to the south of them belonged to Daniel Warwyck, as she believed it did, there was no chance of the railway branch line coming though by any other way than by the Company's purchasing some part of any one of the three estates.

She lifted her head, hearing Meg moving about in the neighbouring apartments, which were cleaned thoroughly every week to keep them in readiness, and decided the girl would most surely be able to advise her on what she wanted to know. Going out onto the landing she smelt the cigar smoke again, only stronger this time, and as she went through the open door into the other apartments she half expected to find Emmie there with her daughter. But Meg was alone, making up the bed with clean linen.

'Have these rooms been let?' she asked with some surprise. She had been told that there was little chance of that happening before the influx of summer visitors began towards the middle of the month.

'What? Mm? Oh, it's you, madam.' Meg did not pause in her work, unfolding a crisp sheet with a jerk that sent it snapping out across the bed, and reciting the old bed-making jingle in song-song notes as she tucked it in. '*If a handsome man you wish to wed, then settle the foot before the head.* Yes, they have been let. To a business gentleman who has moved his traps in from the Royal Hotel where he's stayed before, 'cos he'll be coming and going regular in the months to come and wants a more settled abode. His name is –'

Josh Barton's voice spoke laconically from the doorway. 'That's all right, Meg. I am acquainted with the lady.'

Lucy knew a dreadful spasm of fear. Why fear should

predominate over anger at his invasion of her domain at that moment she did not know, but she was caught off-guard by the thought of his sharing a roof with her, and she was slow to turn and face him where he stood. He was leaning a broad shoulder against the door-jamb through which she had come, a cigar in the corner of his mouth, his thumbs hooked casually in his waistcoat pockets. By rights he should not have continued smoking in her presence, but since she had arrived uninvited in his rooms, he obviously saw no reason in his arrogance to stub the cigar out. In any case, conventional pleasantries were superfluous between them, because she understood, as he did, that they had become enemies for whom pretence of any kind was unnecessary. She had been mistaken in thinking of their conflict as a deadly game. By coming to Sea Cottage he had brought war itself onto her own ground.

'I had not expected that we should find ourselves living in the same house,' she said icily. 'After all,' she added, unconsciously repeating what Richard had once said to her, 'Easthampton has a wide choice of places in which to stay.'

'Sea Cottage was recommended to me.' He was speaking the truth. It had been recommended, but only after he had learnt the forwarding address she had left at the Warwyck Hotel when the clerk had said that at the height of the season overnight travellers unable to be accommodated by the hotel were sent to Mrs Linden's house.

From the bedside, Meg was watching them anxiously. The widow looked as if she might pack her bags and depart then and there, and if that was the risk involved, then Mr Barton must go, since business gentlemen were two-a-penny, while ladies of distinction were not. Her mother had pinned great hopes on Mrs di Castelloni giving high tone to their home, because the legend of the Italian carriage lived on, as did the widow's aura of mystery. The best supposition that Meg had heard yet was that Signor di Castelloni had been killed fighting a duel with his wife's lover, and she was half inclined to believe it, for such happenings were commonplace in the novelettes that she read. She gave a start as the widow suddenly spoke to her.

'Come to my drawing-room after you have finished here. I would like some information.' Lucy's finger tapped the map she held and then she made to leave the apartments, addressing Josh once more. 'Rest assured that we shall see little of each other. Normally I keep to my own quarters whenever I'm at home.'

He stood aside to let her pass him, her wide skirts brushing both sides of the door as she went through, but he stepped out onto the landing after her, letting his voice follow her departing back. 'Nevertheless I would like a short discussion with you soon. We could always round it off with a harmless little game of cards – provided we keep to the rules.'

She could have been deaf for all the notice she took of his sardonic jibe, but he had the satisfaction of noting the involuntary tilt of her head before she vanished into her rooms, out of his sight.

Meg recounted the whole occurrence to Bob that evening at the Denwin cottage, while she sat on the window bench swinging her legs idly, watching him take down the old wall-bed in the living-room. Being in an agreeable mood, she had allowed him to take advantage of its broad spread before the dismantling, responding to his rough lustiness with a hot-blooded appetite of her own and managing to keep at bay the gentler yearnings of her heart.

'I thought she was going to stalk out of the house then and there,' she said on the salacious note that accommodates gossip. 'You should have seen how she glared at him with daggers drawn, and he no more amiable towards her.'

'Hmm.' Bob was not interested, concentrating on his work and wanting to keep as much of the wall-bed intact as possible to save extra carpentry. The side had been removed, wooden supports taken out, and not a nail to be found in it, so there was no telling how old it might be. With all his strength, making the biceps stand out through the sleeves of his shirt, he wrenched at the base and with a crumbling of plaster and a cloud of dust brought it out from the wall. Something went clattering down to the floor. So there were nails in it after all. But a moment later his conclusion was proved wrong.

'Hey! What's this?' Meg sprang up as a coin came rolling across the floor. She bent and scooped it up. 'It's a sovereign! A golden sovereign! Let's see if there's any more!' She went scrabbling about in the dust behind the bed and he pulled it farther out to give her more space, wondering if they had stumbled on some long-dead cottager's treasure trove, but there was no aperture in the wall and it looked as though the coin had been lodged by chance down the side of the bed. Her excitement grew as she discovered another sovereign, and being as eager as she to see how many more might be there, Bob crouched down by her to join in the raking of the dust and dirt with his fingers. In all, five more sovereigns came to light, together with several shillings and two small, round buttons which Meg thought were silver, although they were too blackened by time to be sure about it, and the design on them impossible to decipher. She sat down on the bench, and as Bob sat with her, she spread the spoils between them.

'It looks like a flower on it,' she said, turning one of the buttons this way and that. 'If it *is* silver, they're gentry buttons and no mistake.' She raised her head from her scrutiny and her eyes reflected her puzzlement. 'How do you think they got there? And the money, too? Stolen?'

He scratched his neck meditatively. 'No, shouldn't think so. Nobody in 'is right mind would stuff shillings down the back there even if it was deemed a safe place for the sovereigns, which it wasn't, seeing they've been stuck there for years and was lost as far as anyone getting 'ands on 'em again. I reckons the coins got there by theirselves.'

'How?'

'Tossed out of a pocket or a purse.'

She looked scornful. 'Who would sit on that old bed and throw money about? People who lived in this place would have been poor as church mice – like what we are.'

'I don't say it was done deliberate. Remember the first time I brought you 'ere and we tried out the old bed?' A bold grin crinkled his eyes and he reached out to fondle her breast. 'A sixpence flew out of my pocket when I was snatching my coat off. I reckon a gentleman took 'is plea-sure with the daughter or wife of a cottager 'ere and lost 'is sovereigns in a similar fashion. That would explain the buttons, too. Burst 'em off 'is weskit in 'is 'urry.'

She threw back her head and laughed. 'You're a bad lad, Bob Cooper, but I'm not denying it's a fair explanation. I'll ask Ma who used to live here in the old days. Of course, it could have been before her time, but I'll find out what I can.'

When they left the cottage, she kept charge of the coins, saying that it would be a nice little nest-egg when they were married, and he made no demur. At home, after he had left her, she put them with some other carefully hoarded money in a drawer and was about to toss the buttons into the same box when she decided that they should be examined carefully first to assess their worth. She could always sell them.

Fetching the silver powder she mixed it in a saucer and began to clean the buttons. Emmie came in while she was still at work in the circle of lamplight.

'What 'ave you got there?' she asked her daughter.

'Two buttons. Bob and I found them up at Denwin Cottage.'

Emmie hung up her bonnet and shawl before coming to sit down at the table and pick up one of them. ''Ere! These are silver, ain't they!'

'Yes, and quite fine. Who used to live at that cottage in the old days?'

'It's been empty well over twenty years, but I can tell you that the buttons wouldn't 'ave belonged to the family what did live there last. The parish paid for 'em to go off to Australia as settlers and I remember seeing them go. They 'ad everything they possessed in three bundles, and their only piece of furniture was an old chest of drawers with rope around it, which held their toasted bread and the rest of their victuals for the long voyage.'

'And before them?'

'The man's parents after 'is grandparents, I suppose. That was the way of things in the old days.' She squinted again at the button. 'I can't see without my spectacles, but there's some kind of pattern. A rose, is it?'

'I don't know yet.'

'Well, I'm off to bed. Are *they* in?' She made an inquiring jerk of her head towards the ceiling.

'The widow has retired, but Mr Barton is dining out.'

Meg finished polishing the buttons and was studying them thoughtfully when Josh returned. She heard him enter the house by the side entrance, and although she knew he would not come into their part of the house, she closed her hands instinctively over the buttons to hide them. Only when his tread had gone up the stairs did she open her palms again to look once more at the pattern she had released from the tarnish of twenty-odd years, a period she had been able to estimate by the sovereigns that had been unearthed with the buttons, none of which had béen minted before 1817. It was not a rose, but a pair of clenched fists finely chased upon the silver buttons. She would not dare to sell them. It was not that they were surely unique and could be easily recognized by anyone who had ever seen them before, but because she had an uneasy suspicion as to whom they might belong, and if Bob's theory of how they came to be lodged between bed and wall were correct, would the rightful owner want them returned? On the table the two buttons shone as brightly as moonlight on the sea. In a way she wished they had never been found. The initials on them, *D.W.*, most surely stood for *Daniel Warwyck*.

At Easthampton House, Donna was going across the stable-yard in the moonlight. After Timothy had ridden away with Lucy she had wept a quantity of tears, lying face downwards on her bed with her arms clasped about her head. Toby had whined outside the door for a long time before she had finally stirred and opened it for him. Gathering him up, she had hugged him close, continuing to weep, but beginning to understand that it was the shock of the fall that was magnifying the disgrace she felt in her own mind over her stupidity. Later she would go and saddle up and make herself ride down to the beach and back. She might even take a canter along the sands. Indeed, she would go now!

At the stable-door she stopped, aware of a return of that sharp terror. The sweat started on her palms and upper lip.

Desperately she struggled for control, reminding herself that unless she overcame the sick dread lying heavy in her stomach she would never ride with Timothy again, and if she were left out of invitations to ride, who knew what else she might miss. Richard had not won Lucy yet, and Timothy was no different from other men in letting his gaze be drawn, as if by a magnet, towards the young widow whenever she was near.

Woodenly, reminding herself of an automaton wound up to jerk out its arm, she reached for the ring of the stable-door, but even as she pulled it open she knew she could not go through with it. She could no more saddle up Bonnie and take a ride than she could have flown through the air. With a sob she released the handle, which fell back into place with a clang, echoing after her as she ran back into the house.

At noon next day, when Timothy called on her, she received him in the garden room, nothing in her outward appearance to show the emotional storm that had swept through her the previous day, or the restless, anguished pacing of waiting for him to come. He had recovered from his disappointment in her and even his hurt that she should have rounded on him for no reason, a wealth of affectionate feeling spilling through him at the prettiness of her, but he had ridden again with Lucy only that morning and the excitement and pleasure of it were fresh in his mind, making him more aware than he might otherwise have been of a certain loss of communication with Donna. Totally against her will she had withdrawn tightly into herself, something she could not control in times of trouble, although with all her heart she wanted everything to be as it was before between them. As a result, an unusual seriousness was set upon him and he felt constrained, his talk lacking its usual lilt and banter. Tactfully he avoided all reference to the scene on the sands, apart from expressing the hope that she had fully recovered from the previous day, and a lack of discussion served to intensify the awkwardness that was there.

'I took a look at the ballroom earlier today,' he said, keeping to a neutral plane. 'It has been swathed in dust-sheets for years, but I've already set preparations in motion for the dancing there.'

She looked pleased. 'By coincidence a letter came from my parents this morning, giving the date of their return towards the end of this month.'

'Excellent. Has your brother set the date of the Grand Opening of the pier?'

She nodded. 'It is to be the twenty-ninth of May – just a week after their return.'

'Then we shall have a Glorious First of June ball at the Grange. What could be better?'

He left soon afterwards, but not before he had kissed her hand and her lips at the moment of departure. She was elated, all sorrow banished, seeing the kiss as being tantamount to a proposal. She had no doubt at all that he would speak to her father as soon as the ball was over.

Timothy, driving away, bitterly regretted his impulsive action. He had thought to bridge the gap he had felt widening between them, but instead, at the contact of her soft lips, he had found himself wishing that it was Lucy's mouth upon which he could set his own.

9

Lucy arrived at the pier to find a scene of great activity. The theatre company had arrived, and from the wagons, drawn up at the entrance, were being unloaded basket hampers, crates and rolls of canvas scenery, to be carried along the length of the pier into the theatre. Dodging past two men arguing how best to get a piece of scenery through the gates, she made her own way along the deck and entered the theatre to find it a bustle of noise and colour. Suddenly the whole place had come alive; the house gaslights were being tested and the footlights were aglow. The odd echoes that had made a hollow sound of voices had gone, and there was even a different aroma prevailing, a mixture of greasepaint and perfume, new clothes and old, and that of a special blend of magic that was impossible to define.

Richard and the pier manager were engaged in talk with a beetle-browed man, and all three turned as she drew near. 'Allow me to present Mr Asquith,' Richard said to her, 'who has just arrived with his company.'

She acknowledged the man's bow, undaunted by the fierceness of his eye as he addressed her. 'I had not expected a female pianist,' he declared forcefully. 'I'll remind you that we are presenting melodrama, ma'am. Not a drawing-room tea-party. I look for plenty of thunder and lightning in the music.'

Robertson scowled at him, resenting any reflection on his judgement in appointing the young woman. 'You'll not be able to fault Mrs di Castelloni's playing, or that of my violinist,' he retorted tetchily.

Asquith made no sign as to whether the statement had had any effect, simply snapping his fingers to draw the attention of someone crossing the stage. 'Fetch me one of those folios on the chair.' When it was handed to him across the footlights, he checked the contents and then gave it to Lucy. 'Here is the musical score of *Mazeppa*. Be ready with it tomorrow at two o'clock when rehearsals begin.' With that parting shot he swung away, drawing Robertson with him with some complaint about the lighting, and leaving Richard and Lucy on their own.

She released a smiling sigh. 'Well, well. I'll have to work hard between now and tomorrow.'

Richard shook his head dubiously as they turned to leave the theatre. 'Are you sure you·want to carry on as a pianist?' he inquired. 'Asquith looks a bully to me.'

'No, he's not,' she replied confidently. 'He only wants the best accompaniment that he can get for his productions, and without conceit I feel I can match his requirements.'

'I've no doubt of that,' Richard assured her, pride in her accomplishments showing in his smile. They had come out of the theatre into the sunshine, and he was reminded of what he wanted her to see that day. 'Come over to the rails,' he said, taking her by the elbow. 'You're about to see a sight that has become traditional, not only at Easthampton, but in all bathing resorts of importance.'

At the rails he stood gazing towards the resort, his eyes screwed up against the sun. She tried to follow his gaze, but could see nothing different about the view except that since her first visit to the pier the trees had reached full foliage and awnings made bright spots of striped colour, supplementing those of permanent attachment to the houses, which were fashioned of painted metal and trimmed with filigree ironwork. High on its hillock, Easthampton House gleamed like an opal in the sun. But Richard had been watching for something.

'There!' He pointed in the direction of the road that came into town by the hillock to encircle Ring Park. 'Over there. Under the trees.'

Then she saw it. A long caravan of huge-wheeled bathing-machines drawn by plodding carthorses was moving along at a steady pace, making for the seafront. Each horse was being led by a man, and as they drew nearer she saw there were no shafts to the machines, but only chains, which glinted and rattled.

'That is the true sign that summer has come,' Richard said with a grin. 'More sure than a skyful of swallows. The season has opened. Bathing days have come once more.'

She tried to count the machines, estimating that there must be fifty or more, and saw that they were striped pale blue and white with the name *Warwyck* in black letters on the sides. Some had hoods folded back against them, and these turned to the right when they came level with the promenade, while the rest turned to the left, all peeling off from the line as neatly as if it were a rehearsed production from the theatre itself.

'Those with modesty hoods are going to take up their position on the ladies' bathing beach,' Richard explained. 'When lowered, the hoods allow ladies to emerge from the front door of the machine and go down steps straight into the water, without being seen in their bathing costumes. A dipper waits to plunge them under and makes sure that nobody gets drowned.' He nodded in the direction of the rest. 'Those are making for the male section of the beach. Swimming for gentlemen in the buff is allowed before eight o'clock in the morning, but after that a full-piece costume must be worn. A rowing-boat patrols to make sure the ladies' privacy is not invaded by some strong and lecherous swimmer from that particular quarter. Shall we go down to the beach? I want to check that all is in order with the machines.'

They found Emmie Linden down there, giving orders on the placing of the machines on the high shingle as if she were a general in charge of troops. As each machine was lined up beside its neighbour, the chains were unhooked from the horse's harness and they were led away, all except three which were retained to pull the vehicles up and down to the water.

'Let me present Beauty, Major and Lion,' Richard said,

clapping the necks of each of the three great horses in turn, causing the amber nostrils to flare questioningly and a head to toss with a jingle of bridle. Lucy resolved to bring them some sugar-lumps on the day of her first swim.

A shout took Richard from her side away to the slipway where a horse had taken fright and made one of the wheels slide sideways, causing the machine to tilt perilously. Lucy saw ropes and strength put to the rescue before wandering off by herself along the shingle to inspect those already in place. She noticed that short flights of wooden steps were tucked away fore and aft under the machines, ready to be let down when needed. Wanting to see inside, she pulled out the steps in the rear of one machine and went up them to push open the door and enter. She found herself in a good-sized space, with the other door in front of her that would open to the sea when the machine had been drawn hub-deep into the water. A slatted seat ran on either side of her, and there were hooks for clothes, a round mirror advertising Jenkins's Sausages and Meat Pies in red lettering, and tiny shutters covering square peep-holes in each corner for peering out to see if the coast was clear. Standing on tip-toe, she slid back a shutter and looked out at the long stretch of beach.

'Looking for me?'

She spun about and saw Josh in the doorway, check-suited with a wide-brimmed hat, which he doffed as he entered. 'I'm exploring,' she said, drawing back from him. 'I've never seen or been inside one of these machines before.'

He closed the door behind him and they were enclosed together within planked walls that shone with a new coat of white paint in the warm light that came in through the open shutter. 'I've never had any use for one myself, being a dawn swimmer by choice.' Leisurely he seated himself. 'I saw you down here from the promenade. It's quite a good place to talk. At Sea Cottage you have been avoiding me.'

It was true. During the short time since he had moved in, she listened and watched in order not to meet him on the landing or the stairs, ignored his knock on her door on two occasions whilst holding her breath and hoping he would think her out, and had torn into shreds a note left with the request that she should suggest a time when he could see her.

'I can't think that we have anything to say to each other.'

'Why? Because it seems as if it has already been said?'

She sat down in the furthest corner from him. 'Since you wish to bring it out into the open between us, I endorse what I said at the Grange that day. I'm totally opposed to the railway going across Attwood land. Let it go by some other route.'

'There is no other route available. It would mean cutting through the Warwyck brickfields or over Radcliffe land, and Mrs Radcliffe has given a negative answer and will not be persuaded. Don't think I haven't tried. The London and South Coast Railway Company has no wish to pay Attwood's price, although of the three routes it is the best one.'

Her aunt! He had spoken to her aunt, who was as concerned for the land of the Radcliffe estate as she was for that of Attwood. It showed they had much in common. 'You met Mrs Radcliffe then?' She had turned her face from him, not sure how well she could hide her feelings.

'Yes, I did. She was adamant.'

'What did you think of her as a person? Kind? Dignified? What sort of impression did she make?'

The questions puzzled him and he stroked his chin once before he answered her, wishing she would look directly at him. 'It struck me that Olivia Radcliffe was one of those docile-looking women with backbones of iron. Once her mind was made up about something, nothing on this earth could change it.' Stubborn as a mule was the description he had used to himself, but it was no way to speak about a lady. 'The only other alternative would be to lay the tracks across Warwyck land, but that is also out of the question.'

She looked at him then. 'Why? Richard is in favour of the railway.'

'But his father isn't. What's more, the route would have to be along the richest seam of clay in the whole area, and to destroy it would cut down the Warwyck brick-making industry. Neither father nor son would agree to that. As it is, we need a Warwyck site for the railway terminal building.

That is the final hurdle when Daniel Warwyck returns from his travels, and he and his wife are sailing by steamship from New York today, I understand.'

'And if you don't get the site?'

'It will simply be built at the end of the Attwood run. Not so convenient for passengers, but the Company will come to terms with hired transport to convey people to and fro over the short distance into town, and there is nothing Daniel Warwyck or anybody else can do to prevent that. In other towns and resorts the railway station is similarly situated and presents no great inconvenience to anyone.'

He is bluffing, she thought. He would not like to be thwarted on that last hurdle, even though an Attwood site could be substituted. Without doubt he wanted to concentrate on completing final arrangements upon Mr Warwyck's return without her complicating those already reached with Tim Attwood.

'Do you know,' she stated calmly, 'I don't think you're going to get the Attwood run. What do you say to that?'

He studied her for a moment. Then he moved from where he was sitting onto the seat on her side, sliding himself along to thrust his face towards her.

'I say that I'm willing to consider a truce if you tell me what you aim to make out of your sojourn in Easthampton and give me a chance to help you achieve it in some other place. I'm not without influence and can pull strings for you in the right direction. What is it, eh? An advantageous marriage? Wealth, power, and politics? You can do better than young Attwood, you know.' His glance ran assessingly over her. 'You could aim for a title with every chance of success. Surely you must have thought of that.'

She pressed her back hard against the wall behind her, keeping her temper under tight control. 'No, I had not thought of that,' she answered in dangerously dulcet tones. 'How very remiss of me.' Then she jerked away as he came closer still, finding his nearness overpowering.

'What is your real name?' he questioned keenly, unrebuffed. 'Di Castelloni was imaginative, I grant you, but it has a fairground ring to it. Did a circus supply you with that extraordinary carriage you hired to make an impression

143

when you arrived in town? Quite a stroke of genius.' He gave a short laugh. 'God knows how you found out enough about Attwood's late third cousin or whatever the kinship was to make your Italian story credible, but you're a clever woman and I would rather have you on my side than against me. What's more, I should hate to see such talents wasted, which is why I'm prepared to make you a business proposition.'

His arrogance and patronizing audacity left her almost speechless, but she found breath to answer him, a-shudder at what that proposition might be. 'I don't want to hear it and I cannot endure your objectionable company another second!' She sprang up to dart from the machine by the way she had come, but he was on his feet instantly and blocked her flight, driving her back against the other, still-bolted foredoor.

'Not so fast, Lucy. At least hear me out.'

Lucy! He had dared to address her in so familiar a manner in preparation for more familiarities to come. The confines of the bathing machine seemed to hold her like a trap, the old nightmare of Domenico's violence descending upon her again and bringing her close to terror of the man she faced alone there. 'I owe you no explanation or confirmation of my past,' she gasped, 'but I was married to Stefano di Castelloni and I did live in Italy as I have told all whom I have met.'

'But there's more, isn't there?' he probed perceptively, his dark eyes hard on her. 'Details that you do not care to disclose for reasons of your own, and I want to ensure they do not cross my plans. In exchange for your departing from Easthampton, I can practically guarantee a brilliant remarriage for you within a matter of weeks or months according to your eagerness to get to the altar.'

She stared at him wordlessly. He took her lack of verbal response to mean that at least she was prepared to listen to what he had to say, and he sat down again, quite relaxed, and straddled his polished boots on the opposite slatted seat, creating a barrier of his long legs between her and the door through which she had tried to leave.

'My sister Charlotte is married to Sir Roger Macdonald,

who is an up-and-coming politician as well as being of a most noble family and probably one of the richest men in the country. I have been in touch with Charlotte who, wishing to oblige me, her elder brother of whom she is extremely fond, will extend to you the hospitality of their London home and their other grand residences, which include a castle in Scotland, and you'll have a splendid time.' He grinned benignly, showing the spread of his white teeth, and slapped a hand upon his knee in emphasis. 'There! You could not have a better offer than that, I warrant you. Once wed, you can come to Easthampton as often as you like for all I care, but keeping away until you are is one of my conditions, and I don't have to elaborate the reason why. Now, what do you say?' One of his slashing black eyebrows lifted expectantly, showing he had every confidence in an affirmative answer.

She drew in her breath. 'I say you may go to damnation, Josh Barton!'

Hurling herself around, she shot back the bolt of the foredoor by which she was standing, but he threw himself to his feet and before she could get it open to jump out, he had caught her hard against him. She knew blind panic. It was as if the clock had turned back and she was struggling again with Domenico. She uttered such a piercing shriek that instinctively he clapped his palm across her mouth, cutting the sound short, and above his hand her eyes stared at him, huge with fright. He could actually feel the tumult of her heart against his chest, and yet to him her terror, which he could tell was genuine enough, seemed to war with the sensuality that emanated from her, her mind at odds with her body which he held moulded to his. She was a total contradiction; the more he thought he knew her, the less was the discovery. His manhood was savage for her. Had she been willing, he would have taken her then and there upon the sand-gritted floor, but the time was not yet.

He breathed deeply, and slowly removed his hand, all the time his eyes holding hers, and the moisture of her soft lips was left upon his palm, striking cool against the air. She did not shriek again, but the frenzied beating of her heart had not eased. It seemed to take her a few moments to realize he had released his arm about her, at the same time of removing the pressure upon her mouth, and nothing was holding her captive but the contact of their two bodies. Her panic appeared to return a thousandfold and she gave him a thrust away from her, hauled open the door she had unbolted and leaped out. She did not lose her footing on the shingle, the drop being no more than a couple of feet, and the yards of her skirt-hem created a great swathe of tiny pebbles in front of the machine as she turned in the direction of the slipway, where the hold-up had been cleared and the machines were rolling down with much creaking of their wheels as before. He followed her with his sun-narrowed gaze as he lounged there in the open doorway, saw her speak to Richard and then take the wooden steps up to the promenade, her green bonnet ribbons flickering over her shoulder as she disappeared from his sight. He made to take the same exit from the machine as she had done, but his foot knocked against something and, looking down, he saw the music folio lying where she had dropped it. He picked it up, put it under his arm and swung out of the machine.

Absorbed in her thoughts, the violence of her nerves subsiding, but not her anger at the insult of Josh's proposition, Lucy turned for Sea Cottage by way of Hoe Lane. It added to the heat of her resentment that instead of keeping calm she had reacted like a soul out of Bedlam when he had held her to him; at least with Richard she had kept her poise and her dignity. Was it that he had shown a loving passion, alarming enough with the memory of Domenico's assault still raw, whilst intending no harm to her, whereas with Josh it had been a different matter? He, with that hard and quiet embrace, that silencing of her cry, had conveyed either by intention or otherwise, a resolute and unwavering determination to fulfil ultimately a selfish need of her akin to Domenico's own. She hated him as she had hated her stepson, but with Josh there was the ever-present needle of fear, which she had not known towards Domenico until those last dreadful minutes. She would not rest until she had turned Timothy's decision totally away from letting Josh Barton and his railway ruin Attwood land. Her whole future as a person in her own right depended upon it.

'Morning, madam. Nice day, ain't it? Just right for a bit o' weeding.'

She lifted her head sharply and saw Bob leaning on a spade in the garden of Honeybridge House. 'Why, Bob,' she exclaimed, welcoming with some relief a diversion of her unhappy meditation. 'I didn't know you were a gardener.' She had spoken to him several times since the evening he had come to see Meg at Sea Cottage, and had bought fish from him on a number of occasions.

'When not in my boat I does all kinds of work to bring in a bit extra, seeing as 'ow I'm doing my own cottage up at Denwin Corner.' His voice held a note of pride at that achievement, and he jerked his head in the direction of the flower-beds. 'I'm clearing up 'ere in readiness for Mr and Mrs Warwyck's return. They'll be 'ome very shortly from the New World now, I 'ear, and Mr Warwyck won't tolerate a weed in any garden or park what is 'is responsibility.'

'Most admirable,' she endorsed. So Daniel Warwyck owned the house as he owned almost everything else in Easthampton. No wonder Richard had classed it as being as unobtainable as the Grange when she had mentioned the place to him after first seeing it. If the house had been hers, she would not have parted with it either, but she did not think she would have let it remain unoccupied, and expressed her thought. 'I find it sad that such a pleasing house should stay empty and shuttered.'

'It ain't empty, far from it,' Bob said in contradiction. 'It's full-furnished like it was when old Jem Pierce moved in to end 'is days after a prize-ring life. Don't ask me why it ain't been let since. Mrs Warwyck comes now and again to make sure all is in order, just like what she did in Jem's day, bringing 'im food she'd cooked special up at the big 'ouse, and nursing 'im in 'is last days. Maybe it's being kept for when Mr Richard weds, because it's a family 'ouse and too large for a bachelor on 'is own. Old Jem kept 'alf the rooms locked up when 'ee 'ad it. If you're interested, madam, why not take a look around the garden and the orchard. Mrs Warwyck wouldn't mind. She's real Christian; a more kindly soul you'd not meet anywhere.'

Lucy was tempted, but she shook her head, stepping away from the gate. She had no right to intrude on private property there. It had been different at the Grange, where she belonged. 'I'll wait until I'm lucky enough to see Mrs Warwyck here one day.'

''Ere. Wait a mo! Take this.' He held out a rosebud over the gate. 'It's an early flowerer. It gets all the sun on the south wall, and it snapped off when a thorn caught in my shirt.'

She took it, thinking it should have been Meg who was receiving it, but she saw it meant no more to him than the weeds he had been digging out. It was a tender bud, its petals barely showing, but she could tell it was of a type that was quite honey-coloured, which was well suited to the south wall of a house that bore such a delightful name. She was about to turn away when she remembered what she had heard at the theatre.

'If you want some other work, Bob, I know that local people are needed to walk on and off the stage in the opening production of *Mazeppa*. You could apply to Mr Robertson.'

Bob gave a bellowing guffaw. 'Me? On the stage! I'd be that nervous I'd fall over my own feet. Wait till I tell Meg. That'll give 'er a good laugh, too.'

Lucy smiled at his enjoyment of what he had taken as a joke, and continued on her way. In her drawing-room she put the bud into a slender vase and placed it in the window. As she adjusted the silken ties of the lace curtains, she saw Josh coming through the gate, the forgotten folio under his arm.

At his knock she opened her door to his hostile visage. Instead of handing over the folio, he held it half behind his back and leaned a hand against the jamb. 'I'm not in the habit of taking no for an answer,' he said grimly, his eyes steely. 'Think over my proposition with less haste, and thank your good fortune for the second chance I'm giving you to accept it.'

Under her shaded lashes, her gaze burned her fury. 'Are you not afraid of my cheating your sister's grand acquaintances at the card-tables?'

He snorted. 'No, I'm not. Had you wished it you could have wiped the board at Easthampton House that evening, but that's not your current policy. You'll take no risk against the bigger jack-pot that you're aiming for.' He brought the folio forward and thrust it into her hands.

She breathed deeply. 'You are right, of course. Only a fool would risk her future, which is the reason why I'm keeping to the path I have chosen. It is you who should remove to London, or wherever else a railway is needed, because I can assure you that you are wasting your time at Easthampton.'

He looked at her as he had done when he had grabbed the reins of her horse, his lids brought so close together that only the black glitter of his eyes showed. 'We'll see,' he mocked. 'Oh, yes, Lucy. We shall see.'

As he threw himself off to his own quarters, she closed the door and leaned tensely against it, her arms clasped about the folio. Never in her life before had she made such an enemy, but she would counter with her wits every move that he made.

To her relief he left Sea Cottage early next morning, giving her door a thump as he passed it, as if in rebuke for disturbing his rest with the late hours she had kept in playing through *Mazeppa* and her recommencement of the procedure shortly after dawn. She continued playing to show her indifference, but when the side door banged after him, she reached the window in time to see that he was departing in his cabriolet with a hand-valise suitable to a short absence.

That afternoon she arrived at the theatre on the dot of two o'clock. She had become thoroughly familiar with the score of *Mazeppa* and acquitted herself well enough for Asquith to give her a nod, lips compressed, but no comment. She knew all would be well.

But as the days went past, and Lucy relaxed in Josh's absence from Sea Cottage, nothing seemed to banish the aroma of expensive cigars that he had left in his wake. She kept her windows open wide to get rid of it, but whenever she thought it had gone, a whiff of it stirred from the curtains or met her on the stairs when she returned from rehearsal, until eventually she assumed she must be imagining it, so strong was his haunting of her, and so great her dread of his return.

IO

Josh's return to Easthampton was completely overshadowed by another arrival, far more important to the resort, which took place the same day: Daniel and Kate Warwyck came home from their far-away travels in the New World.

Kate let herself into Easthampton House and was glad that she would have a minute or two to herself before it became known that she was there. Daniel was not with her, having insisted upon alighting at the office, where Richard had rushed out to hug his father and leapt into the carriage to embrace her. She had wept with joy to see him again, her handsome son with his good heart and kindly ways, holding his face between her hands as she kissed him on one cheek and then the other. It was odd to remember sometimes that although conceived in love, he had been born at a time when she and Daniel had been bitterly estranged, and it had taken a major crisis to bring them together again.

Perhaps that was why, even after all these years, she did not feel totally at home in Easthampton House. It had not been built for her, but for another woman in Daniel's life, and she had always felt that the house had never forgiven her for usurping the other's place. Yet Daniel had made his own choice between them and had cleaved to her, his lawful wife, to whom he was still the most ardent of lovers. But that did not mean his devotion to her had kept him faithful throughout the years of their married life. While at his sister

Jassy's home in New York, his eye had roved in the direction of a senator's wife, a flamboyant beauty with that particular shade of red-gold hair that was always his weakness, and whether anything came of it she did not know, but there were a number of evenings when prize-ring dinners and reunions left her alone with her sister-in-law and husband whilst the clock ticked the hours by with agonizing slowness. She had learned to live with his infidelities, to understand that against his own will a craving hunger for the woman he had rejected would be with him until the day he died, but comprehension and compassion did not lighten the burden of knowledge that she had to bear, for she loved him not a whit less than on the day she had first set eyes on him from the dusty auction-ring of a Brighton marketplace. Although many men had admired her, she had remained totally his from that day forth, and had never wished it otherwise.

How quiet it was in the house. She stood quite still at the foot of the central staircase, a tall, graceful woman in her early forties, with a classic mould to her features and spun gold hair in which no grey was discernible. The gaze of her blue eyes travelled slowly over the ivory walls and pastel furnishings in their sea-colours, all bathed in the diffused sunlight pouring down through the glass lantern in the domed roof. From a gilded frame Daniel's long-dead father looked down at her, a reckless gaming man who had left his penniless widow and three children dependent upon the charity of his miserly brother, which had resulted in Daniel losing his inheritance of the family home and making his own way in the world with empty pockets and only a pair of fighting fists to his credit. Yet the face in the painting had the dashing Warwyck charm still to be found in Daniel's younger brother, Harry, who came to see them from time to time, always in a new carriage flashier and more designed for speed than the one before, ever the best of matched thoroughbreds straining at the laces.

Through the open doors of the Green Drawing-room she could see her own portrait hanging in the place of honour above the marble fireplace. It had been painted shortly after Daniel had become Champion of England in the prize-ring, and she held the victor's colours in her hand, the blue and green silken squares drifting lightly against her skirt as she sat there with the sea shimmering in the background. There had been a new serenity in her face when that portrait had been painted, a knowledge in her eyes that Daniel loved her above all other women, and yet, such were the tricks of light and shade in this glorious, opal-tinted mansion, that to her it seemed that life was quite drained from the likeness, leaving it no more than a skilful application of oil-paint upon canvas, her true self hidden even from the most discerning.

The softest of sighs escaped her. Easthampton House had always rejected her. Even after all these years there was no welcome for her in it. It tolerated her, but did not acknowledge her as its mistress. But why should it, since she had always loved her first home with Daniel best of all, the unpretentious and simple Honeybridge House, which was still her refuge and her haven.

'Mamma!' Donna had appeared at the head of the stairs.

'My dear child!' Kate flung out her arms. The girl came down the flight at a run, hooped skirt swaying, one part of her mind registering that her mother had taken on a new, almost ethereal look, with a brittle thinness instead of the slenderness that had always become her. Blaming Daniel for having dragged Kate halfway round the world, determined to see that she had rest and care to restore her from her travels, Donna swept into her mother's arms and there were tears and laughter as they embraced joyfully, each full of questions with answers getting confused. Finally Kate held Donna back from her at arms' length, her head on one side. 'You are looking well. How good it is to be back with you again.'

Around them the whole house had begun to stir, the servants realizing that their mistress had returned, and they came from all quarters either to bob a curtsey of welcome or, after bows, to lend a hand in unloading the travellers' baggage. Only then did Donna look for her father. 'Where is he?' she asked.

'Surely you can guess,' Kate answered with indulgence towards him as the two of them slipped arms about each other's waists and went into the drawing-room. 'He must needs stop off at once to delve into matters at the office and see how everything has been run in his absence.'

'Oh.' Donna looked disturbed. It was no use pretending to herself that she did not care that business affairs were more important to her father than seeing his only surviving daughter again after six months, because she did, but there was more than that causing the worried contraction of her brow.

Kate lost her smile. 'What is it?' she asked anxiously. 'What is wrong?'

'Nothing with the business, Mamma. There have been no difficulties there that Richard has not been able to settle, or with the pier and the theatre where the Grand Opening has been arranged for next Saturday. It is just that Richard has gone ahead on his own initiative and given his support to Josh Barton, who is the contractor concerned for the branch line that the London and South Coast Railway Company wants to run through to Easthampton. He has more or less guaranteed a site for the terminus on Warwyck land.'

Kate put a fluttering hand to her face and sank down in the nearest chair. 'Merciful Heaven! He *knows* that his father will not hear the railway mentioned, let alone have anything to do with it. Has Richard gone out of his head?'

'Far from it. He is looking to the future and I'm with him. Easthampton can only lose through Father's stubbornness and be left behind all the other resorts.'

'Your father does not care what happens elsewhere and never has done. He built Easthampton to be different from all the others in the first place, a select resort offering the best of entertainment, where the sea and the salubrious air could be enjoyed by a select number of visitors, without crowding or vulgarity.'

'I know that, and such an aim was admirable when it originated, because only persons of quality and equal social status were involved, but times are changing fast. Many more people can afford to visit the seaside than in the old days, and can you in all conscience, Mamma, say that it should be denied them?'

Kate shook her head and rose from the chair to wander across to the window where she gazed out at the distant, sparkling waves. 'Everyone should have the chance to see the sea. I had never seen it until your father took me down onto the sands at Brighton the day we met. I remember kicking off my shoes and paddling in my stockinged feet, laughing with exhilaration at the glory of the sensation and the freedom that was mine that day.'

'You, Mamma! Paddling! Showing your ankles! I can scarce believe it. You are such a modest person.'

The corners of Kate's mouth became indented on a secret smile. Modest? She? Always with others, but never with Daniel, not even on that first, loving, abandoned night they had spent together in the room of a tavern with a name she could not remember. How little it was that offspring knew or guessed about those who parented them.

'What are you going to do about the branch line?' Donna prompted her. 'Are you going to side with Father or follow your conscience and back Richard? It's best that you decide before they come home, because there is bound to be terrible trouble over it.'

Kate passed her fingers across her tired eyes. In her yearning to be back at Easthampton with journeying done, she had not expected to find herself on the edge of a volcano. Loyalty to Daniel, which flowed like her own blood through her body, prevented her from giving her daughter a direct answer. 'I shall talk to them both. A compromise can surely be reached somehow.'

'Yes, let us hope so.' Donna dropped her defensive attitude which she had assumed in support of her brother, and patted a cushion on the sofa invitingly. 'Come and sit down. I'll ring for some tea. Let me take your coat and bonnet.' Her voice took on a lightly teasing note. 'You have come home to stay, you know.'

Pray God I have, Kate echoed silently, untying her bonnet ribbons. Who would have thought the day Daniel bid as high as twenty-one guineas for her in the Brighton marketplace, after her first husband, an uncouth country fellow, had put her up for auction, that he would fill her whole life with love and those to love. She counted her blessings daily and would do so until her last breath.

The afternoon passed and dusk fell. Still Daniel and

Richard did not appear, but Kate knew better than to go to the office. Daniel had never welcomed her presence there, believing as men did that a wife should never concern herself with anything beyond the sphere of the domestic circle, and Richard was enough like his father to be of the same mind. In the past she had dared Daniel's wrath many times to champion the rights of his workmen in a variety of ways, from seeing that they received adequate compensation for injuries to making sure that children employed worked only short hours and were kept away from the danger area of the kilns. Daniel had never refused a petition of hers yet, and in his own way did far more good than most people suspected, but he never liked it to be known.

She and Donna took supper together. 'Why don't you go to bed afterwards?' Donna suggested. 'You look exhausted.'

'I am tired,' Kate admitted, 'but I'll wait up until they come in.' She knew how to deal with Warwyck men on home ground. She had had plenty of experience handling Daniel and Harry as well as Richard. They roared and shouted and raised the roof, but as long as she stood firm they eventually calmed down and could be persuaded to reason. Yet it always drained her emotionally and physically, and with the effect of the long voyage and the carriage journey home dragging at her, she would have to summon up all her reserves of strength for the confrontation.

When her menfolk returned she saw that it was worse than she had feared between them. Daniel, whose towering height matched that of his son, came storming into the hall to hurl aside his hat and cane, not even the angry congestion of his features able to pale the fact that in spite of his forty-odd years he was still a powerfully handsome man. If anything, with the nostrils of his strong nose flaring wildly, his fury only served to heighten the drama of his flashing eyes beneath the thick, black brows, and accentuate the thrust of a ruthless chin, while the thinning of the sensual lips by temper did nothing to detract from the fine cut of them.

'*Your* son!' he roared at her, rendered almost speechless by rage as he pointed a violently shaking finger at Richard, who had slammed into the house close on his heels. 'I hope you're proud of *your* son!'

Kate made no answer, her gaze following him as he stamped into the drawing-room with Richard in his wake. Richard had always been *her* son in the face of any youthful misdemeanour and, in latter years, during any quarrel between the two men, but whenever Richard excelled or won praise, Daniel was always quick to make the prior claim. Taking a deep breath she drove tiredness from her, set physical weakness aside, and quietly entered the drawing-room after them, closing the door to save disturbing the rest of the house.

Upstairs, Donna, who had retired early, put down the book she was reading. What was happening down there? She watched the clock on her chest-of-drawers. One hour passed and still no further sound was heard. Unable to control her curiosity any longer, she turned back the bedclothes and reached for a wrapper, thrusting her arms into it. On slippered feet she left her room and went along the passage to the landing. But she had barely reached it when the drawing-room door was opened by Richard, and her mother came out into the hall.

'Good night, Richard,' Kate said to him. 'Chat about America with your father now and let matters rest as they are for a few days.'

'Nothing has been solved,' he answered stubbornly. 'We have reached an impasse.'

'But you are talking to each other, and that would not have happened if you had carried out your intention to pack your things upon your return this evening and flown out of this house in that dreadful rage. At least the rest of your business together can be conducted daily in a civilized manner without the railway making a battleground of everything. Naturally you will want to remove to your own bachelor quarters again as soon as possible, and I'm grateful that you gave up your total independence to look after Donna whilst we were away.'

Donna spoke from where she was leaning her arms on the balustrade, making her presence known. 'We in this house looked after *him*,' she joked. 'He was not hard done by, Mamma. Cook insisted on preparing every single meal to suit his taste, remembering all the puddings he liked best.

That's why he has put on all that disgusting weight.' She laughed as he gave her a brotherly retort, and came lightly down the stairs. 'I'll greet Papa before you rejoin him.'

From the drawing-room Daniel's voice boomed out. 'Don't keep your mother talking in the hall, Richard. I have poured your glass.'

Mother and son exchanged smiles, and Donna went past them into the drawing-room. Daniel turned with a glass of Madeira in each hand, expecting to see Richard, but instead it was his daughter who came towards him. As always, against his will, warring with his deep paternal protectiveness and his natural love for her, he knew again that flicker of revulsion that she should have the look of William Warwyck about her. It had been with her from babyhood, that particular colouring and the shape of the deep-set eyes, and although by nature she had nothing of his uncle's meanness, he attributed all her faults and failings to a regrettable link with a branch of the family that he had always wanted to forget.

The moment passed as quickly as it had come, and he put down the glasses to embrace her fondly as she reached him, kissing her on the cheek. She kissed him back, but with disappointment that after such a long absence his eyes had held no spontaneous spark of pleasure at the sight of her, but had been glazed over for those few telling instants with that bleak look she knew all too well. It was always the same.

'I'm glad you're safely home again, Papa,' she said awkwardly, but sincerely.

'Thank you, my child. Did we wake you from your bed? Would you like a glass of wine?'

She declined, but they talked for a few minutes until she felt her duty was done and left him again to go up to bed, exchanging a final good night with her mother and brother on the way. Upstairs her bedroom door closed after her.

'I'll leave you to have that drink with your father now,' Kate said to Richard, and she gave him a little pat on the arm to send him back into the drawing-room. As the door closed behind him, the last ounce of her sustained strength seemed to ebb away, and she looked towards the stairs with despair, wondering how she was going to get to the top. But she did it. One step taken slowly at a time with the support of the banister rail, and then the blissful expanse of the waiting bed.

She was stretched across it, lying where she had collapsed and sound asleep, when Daniel came to bed. He removed her shoes, and with fingers long experienced with frills and stays and hoops and ribbons he undressed her, and she stirred only when he pulled the bedclothes over her nakedness to reach out her arms to him, still in sleep. When he had climbed in beside her, he gathered her to him and kissed her closed eyes and her brow.

'Kate, Kate,' he murmured. 'To think that I had actually turned away from that auction ring so long ago, and almost lost you.'

She awakened late, rested and refreshed, to prop herself up against lace-edged pillows and take breakfast in bed, her daughter sitting on the chaise-longue to talk to her while she ate. Toby, specially privileged on this home-coming, lay stretched out at Donna's feet, his head on his paws, seemingly aware that he was in unfamiliar territory and doing nothing to risk banishment. Kate learned that Daniel had been up and out of the house by eight o'clock, going off to inspect the brickyard and the work going on there. As for Richard, before leaving for the office, he had given instructions for his clothes and other belongings to be packed up in readiness for collection by a servant sent by the housekeeper in his own bachelor quarters, for he would be moving back there after dinner that evening. Kate thought it was as well. In present circumstances, father and son seeing each other at various times of the day was enough, without extending business into leisure hours under one roof, with possible fireworks resulting. Donna was wearing a gold locket-watch that Daniel had given her that morning and it swung prettily on its chain. Kate nodded towards it.

'Did your father tell you he chose your gift himself in New York?'

Donna looked surprised, cupping the watch gently in her hand. 'No, he didn't.' She followed her action instantly with a sharp shrug of her shoulders as if the lapse was of no importance to her. 'You must remember that in my company his mind is usually elsewhere.'

Kate leaned back against the pillows. 'He cares for you more than you realize, and I know you're fond of him, but there is a clash of personalities. Somehow you always antagonize each other, and I want things to be better between you.'

'How?' Donna's eyes were full of the old pain and bitterness. 'And why? He won't be satisfied until I'm married and out of this house. He would give his permission if a tinker should ask for my hand, just to be rid of me.'

Kate's eyes did not leave her daughter's face. 'In that case, you should have no anxiety if a truly presentable young man should ask instead. I could not help noticing from all you have said of Mr Attwood since yesterday that you have become on more familiar terms with him. He is called Tim now in every mention of him, and you have mentioned him a great deal.'

'Have I?' The dimple in Donna's cheek deepened and her gaze took on a sparkle. 'He is becoming most attentive, and an invitation arrived this morning, which Father opened, for us all to attend a June ball at the Grange, which he confessed to me is primarily in honour of the new pier and to put Father in the best of humours.'

'Then we shall all be there and ensure that Mr Attwood's good intentions come to pass.'

Later in the morning, Kate went into the garden and picked the sweetest-scented flowers she could find, taking only tiny blooms. Donna came out onto the veranda where she sat tying them into three separate bunches with double-edged white satin ribbon. 'Do you want me to go with you, Mamma?'

Kate shook her head. 'No, thank you. Don't be hurt, but I would like to go alone.'

'I understand.'

It took Kate a quarter of an hour to reach the churchyard on foot. She pushed open the lych-gate and followed the path until she came to the shade of the yew tree under which three small graves lay side by side, each with its own marble headstone. Victoria, Hannah and Edward, their ages ten, seven and four respectively when the dreadful fever resulting from measles had taken them from her. She and Daniel had returned heartbroken from the funeral of the two little girls to find that Edward had died in their absence. How she had survived such bereavement she did not know, and tragically grief and shock had brought about a miscarriage shortly afterwards, the fourth she had suffered throughout the years. Afterwards she had been advised against any further pregnancy and that advice, reluctantly accepted on her part, had been taken.

In a rustle of striped beige silk she knelt down between two of the graves, tenderly removing leaves and pieces of dried grass that the sea-wind had blown across them, and then moved to the third. Absorbed in her loving task, she failed to see the pedestrian in the church lane, who paused on his way at the sight of her, and leaned his arms on the gate. When all was cleared of debris and she had fetched fresh water for the flowers from a tub in the corner of the churchyard, she took up the posies she had brought and gently implanted a kiss in each before arranging them in the marble urns carved with angels that adorned her children's resting-places. She was unaware that the spectator, waiting to speak to her, at this stage had moved on, not wanting to pry into these private moments that came from her own memories. Not until she came out of the gate into the church lane did she come face to face with him, both held within the shade of her tilted brown lace parasol.

'Why, Mr Barton!' she exclaimed, genuinely pleased to see him. 'I heard you had taken up temporary residence in Easthampton. How are you?'

'I am in the best of health, I thank you, ma'am. And you?'

He was, she thought, looking at her with an extremely alert appreciation in his eyes, and she found it flattering, glad that she was wearing one of her prettiest bonnets. Continuing on with courtesies, she fell into leisurely step at his side, inquiring after his father and mother, and trying to work out how long it was since she and Daniel had last visited them in London.

'Ten years exactly,' he volunteered.

'Is it really all that time?'

'I recall coming home to spend a few days with my parents before going north, and finding you there.'

'That is clever of you to remember so precisely.'

How could he not remember? He had been twenty at the time and she the first older woman to whom he had ever been attracted. Not the last, but very much the first. They talked on generally, keeping away from the reason for his presence in the resort, until they reached the end of the lane and paused on the pavement of a main thoroughfare, prior to going their separate ways. 'How soon may we have the pleasure of your calling on us at Easthampton House?' she asked.

He gave her a wry glance under his brows, compressing his lips briefly. 'Ah! Much as it would delight me to accept your invitation, I fear your husband would not uphold you or wish for my company at the moment. I have not seen him yet since his return, but your son has prepared me for violent opposition to the business that brings me to and fro at this time. You are most kind, but until matters have settled themselves, I must be content with seeing you and your family at the homes of mutual acquaintances and anywhere else we might happen to meet.'

'You speak frankly,' she commented with faintly raised eyebrows, but not displeased in any way.

'Is it not best, ma'am?'

'It is, of course. But you must not suppose that my husband will hold a personal grudge against you simply because you are on opposite sides over the railway. It will be the same with Mr Attwood, who can be said to be instrumental in the whole matter. Socially Daniel will remain on good terms with him as he will with you.' She inclined her head. 'Remember that my husband was a pugilist, and no matter how fierce and hard the mill, he never bore malice or fought vindictively, which is the reason why he won such honour in the ring. He is a fair man.'

'I know that, ma'am. But since I mean to win the railway bout with – to quote a phrase from your husband's sporting days – no holds barred, I cannot in all conscience inflict my presence on him without his own expressed wish.'

'You must do as you think best. I only hope that everything will be solved amicably and without delay. I should not like your gracious and hospitable parents to consider that we had shunned you.'

'They shall not gather that impression, my word upon it.'

'Please convey my kindest regards to them next time you are in contact.'

He promised that he would, and she parted from him, thinking no more of the encounter.

In another part of town, Daniel, leaving the brickyard, snapped open his gold hunter and noted the time. There should be some activity going on at the pier theatre by now. It had been deserted the previous afternoon when Richard had shown him around it, and he wanted to judge the acoustics in the auditorium from every part of it, for nothing irritated him more than not being able to hear properly in a theatre. A punch in one of his many prize-fights had left him with partial deafness in one ear, although his conceit would never admit to it.

He entered the theatre and crossed the foyer to look about him. The pay-box was shuttered. From the auditorium there came the sound of a woman singing Zemila's song, which burst forth in volume as one of the doors swung open and a young man emerged in full Tartar costume, complete with face-covering helmet and spear.

''Day, sir,' the apparition greeted him. 'I 'eard you was back, Mr Warwyck.'

'Good Lord! Who are you?' Daniel replied in astonishment.

'Bob Cooper of the craft *Mary Anne*.'

'What the devil are you doing in that garb?'

'I'm walking on in this 'ere play. That's what they call it – walking on, but it's more than that. Bashing spears and marching and 'ollering.' Bob did not sound over-pleased with his situation. 'I finish with it after this production, but I 'ears Mr Asquith was asked to open with something real spectacular, and lots of local folk 'ave been taken on for it.'

'Why aren't you on the stage now?'

'I was sent to see if there was any sign of the 'orse being used in the production.' He went to the door and looked out. 'Yes, there it is!' He banged his spear against his shield. ' 'Urry up!' he bawled to the stable-lad leading a docile white horse up the pier. 'You're late!' He came back. 'I'll 'ave to leave you, sir. I'm in the next scene.'

Daniel, thinking that surely no horse had ever been more greatly miscast as Mazeppa's wild mount, watched it go past the entrance in the direction of the stage door at the rear of the building, and then decided to take a look at the auditorium from his own box, not having been in it the previous day. He went down a scarlet-papered corridor until he came to a white door which he opened, blinking a little in the dazzling brilliance of the footlights after the subdued red gloom he left behind him. Voices rang out stentoriously from the stage where the players strutted and gesticulated in their colourful robes against a back scene of a Tartar tent. He had seen *Mazeppa* twice before in other parts of the country and recognized that he had arrived towards the end of the second act.

He leaned forward to look towards the gallery and down into the pit as the curtains swished together on Act II to the accompaniment of rumbling chords supplied by the piano and violin. In the third row a heavily built man, whom he guessed to be Asquith, rose to his feet to shout some comment, which was duly acknowledged by those at the side of the stage before he reseated himself.

Deciding it would be only courteous to go down and make himself known to the man, Daniel was on the point of rising from his chair when his glance happened to fall on the pianist, who was changing her sheets of music around in preparation for the next scene. He stared, almost in disbelief, experiencing the uncanny sensation that momentarily the clock had turned back. Such red-gold hair shining, such an oddly familiar tilt of the head. How like someone he had known a long time ago. A very long time ago.

Lucy, her music ready, leaned forward to catch a word from Mr Bartley-Jones, who was adjusting a violin string and wanted her to give him a note. She obliged, her finger still on the ivory key, and idly glanced about her. Her attention was caught by a movement in the Warwyck box. She raised her face and looked straight at the man seated there.

Claudine! For Daniel the world seemed to stop, his heart contracting sharply. Yet even as the name echoed through his mind, he knew it to be an illusion, a trick of sight and light. Claudine had been dead for more years than he cared to remember, though the aching for her had never left him.

Lucy had no doubt who he was. None but Daniel Warwyck would sit in that box with the air of being master of all he surveyed. The lights of the auditorium enabled her to see that he was an extremely dashing man, his black hair winged with grey, his heavy shoulders in the dark frockcoat giving strength to his immensely attractive presence. This, then, was Richard's father. She smiled at him.

Daniel swallowed hard. The likeness to Claudine tore at him, all the torment he had suffered crashing over him, but then curiously it passed, leaving a calmness in its wake. It was as if a search was over.

He waited in a frenzy of impatience for the rehearsal to come to an end. When Asquith delayed proceedings in the final battle scene, to arrange extra space for some local members of the cast in their unaccustomed Tartar and Polish uniforms, Daniel drummed his fingers on the arm of the chair, and again when the flickering red lights simulating the conflagration of the forest behind Mazeppa and his bride failed to flare brightly enough. Finally he flung himself out of the box, sought her name at the bottom of the poster in the foyer, and went to the stage-door to await her appearance.

When Lucy emerged from the theatre out onto the broad walk that encircled the building, she saw him standing there, a tall man made taller by the black stovepipe hat he wore, his grey silk waistcoat adorned with a gold watch-chain, an ornate sovereign fob dangling from it. His height towered over hers as he doffed his hat and took a step forward.

'I'm Daniel Warwyck,' he said, his penetrating gaze devouring her.

She thought him even more dramatic at close quarters

than in the shadows of the box. Her lips parted in a smile again, not knowing how it stabbed at him. 'This is an honour, sir. I'm acquainted with your daughter and with Richard. We are close friends. No doubt he has spoken of me.'

Daniel's face seemed to freeze at his son's name. A close friendship, he pondered. How close? 'No, he hasn't,' he remarked evenly. 'Throughout the time spent in his company since I arrived home yesterday I fear business affairs have been the sole topic of our conversations. He was remiss. Your name in print is all I know. You are Italian?'

She gave her usual explanation of birth and marriage. He nodded.

'There is in Easthampton an Italian chef who pretends to be French in order to serve the best English food on the south coast to diners at the Royal Hotel. I feel sure a word from me will produce any Neapolitan dish you may fancy. I should be honoured, Signora di Castelloni, if you would take luncheon with me and amend my son's omission.'

She appreciated his dry note and her eyes danced. 'That would be delightful. I confess I have been looking forward to meeting you, Mr Warwyck. No doubt you will be able to answer a thousand questions I have stored up about the beginnings of Easthampton as a resort and the families who lived in the district at that time.'

His lids lowered a fraction as if inadvertently she had put him on guard, but he answered her with such graciousness that she thought herself mistaken. 'My time is yours, ma'am.' He offered her his arm and she took it.

In the Royal Hotel they sat at a damask-spread table in a bow window with a sunny view of the promenade and the sea, waiters hovering around Daniel. She had difficulty in not staring at him, considering him to be one of the most alive and vital men she had ever met, but because she had been used in the past to the company of older men she was completely at her ease. She waived the chance to have an Italian dish, not at all sure that he had not fabricated the whole tale, and let him order for her, gripped by a sense of adventure. She had noted that in spite of his height and hard-muscled bulk, he was lithe, almost panther-like in his movements, and he had such a noble carriage that had it not been for a scar running down one cheek and another splitting one dark brow in twain, it would have been difficult to believe that he had ever put up his knuckles in the notorious prize-ring.

'I should like to hear how you won the Championship of England,' she said with no intention of flattery, but hitting upon an opening subject that suited Daniel best. Once George IV had royally commanded the same information, one of many honours bestowed upon him at the time.

'It took place near the ancient city of Chichester, not so many miles from here. I was fighting the reigning champion, one of the best fellows it has ever been my good fortune to meet in the ring or out of it. He fought a clean mill with no tricks and no crooked punches.' He related the event, abbreviating it and editing it for a lady's ears. Not for her the spurting blood and the crunch of bones, the sweat and smell and controlled brutality, the awful roar of a crowd thirty thousand strong, and the vile swearing of the whips seeking to keep back those spectators who, in their oblivion to all else but the mill fought to reach the ropes of the ring where two antagonists were beating themselves to a pulp for the highest honour that could be awarded anywhere in the science of self-defence. No sight for ladies, and yet, breaking all convention, two had been present: Claudine and his wife. Fickle, selfish, utterly self-centred, Claudine in her widow's weeds had finally committed herself to him by coming to the field that day, but he had turned from her to hand his victor's colours to Kate. Claudine had swept away immediately with her chin high, her black veil flowing, and he had never seen her again. But his rejection had broken her. He knew that from the way she had dissipated the rest of her life. Revenge, incidental at the time, had turned sour on him. Physically he had sought her ever since in the arms of any red-headed woman who remotely resembled her, but never before had he found anywhere the very essence of Claudine's magnetism that was captured in the oval face of the young woman seated opposite him, her attention hanging upon his every well-chosen word.

'It was a marvellous victory,' she declared when he had

concluded his account, and she patted the fingers of one hand against the palm of the other in silent applause. They had finished the dish of Emsworth oysters as well as the asparagus soup that had been ladled from a large, willow-patterned tureen to follow; both had portions of game on their plates with a coating of wine sauce rich with mushrooms and sprinkled with parsley.

'I retired from the prize-ring the same day, but you must realize that it all happened twenty-one years ago this coming summer.' His voice flowed smoothly. 'That was before you were born.'

'No, it wasn't,' she replied without thinking, not seeing the trap that had been set. 'That was my age only a few days ago. I was born in May.' Abruptly she bit off the words, flushing sharply. No matron revealed her age, not even one as young as she, but somehow in her enthusiasm for what had been related to her she had let her tongue run away with her.

He observed her keenly. So she was only two months younger than his son. A widow with a vibrant sexual allure, who still retained a girlish, vulnerable look across the eyes as if she had never known fulfilment. It was not possible, or at least the most highly unlikely state of affairs that he could think of. His own wish was making him place a condition upon her that did not exist. How charming he found her confusion over the slip she had made in revealing her age as he had intended. He leaned across to her, lowering his voice to a mock-conspiratorial whisper.

'Your secret is safe with me.'

She could not resist his deep chuckle, her own laughter gurgling from her. Richard was fortunate to have such a father. How she longed to question him outright about her own, but until she had met Olivia Radcliffe she must tread carefully. As she was trying to decide how best to make an opening that would link the resort's beginnings with the Attwoods at the Grange, he forestalled her.

'Tell me about Italy. I have never been there. Whereabouts did you live?'

She told him no more and no less than she had told anybody else, but without warning he came out with the question she had dreaded being put to her and which so far nobody had thought to ask.

'What was your maiden name?'

She played for time, needing to quieten her nerves. 'Why do you ask?'

'Not mere inquisitiveness, I do assure you. It is just possible I might know your father's family, since I have wide connections that stretch from Sussex right through to Yorkshire and even further north, both socially and through my business connections. It's quite a small world, as the saying goes.'

He had no idea how small, she thought, not wanting to lie and yet not able to reveal the truth. 'My mother told the nuns that there was no family on either side.'

'She died whilst you were still in their care?'

'That is right.' She had not specified the intervening length of time to anyone, and without any deliberate intention on her part everyone had assumed that her mother had also died in Italy. She did not expect Daniel Warwyck to be an exception, and his next question brought confirmation.

'Your parents were laid to rest together, I suppose?'

'No, they do not lie in the same tomb.' Deftly she switched the direction of their talk. 'Richard told me that both his Warwyck grandparents died young. You must have known grief similar to mine in your childhood.'

'I did,' he admitted, drawn onto the path she had opened. 'I was eight and my brother only three when my widowed mother died a few months after giving birth to our sister, Jasmine, whom my wife and I have recently visited in America.'

She listened and could tell that he had known a bitter discipline from his bachelor uncle, William Warwyck, who had taken in the three orphans. At least her own childhood had been a gentle one without unfairness and cruelty, although his had had the family comfort of a brother and a sister. He went on to tell her of his fistic training from Jem Pierce, a retired pugilist, and by the time their luncheon was coming to an end she had learned much about his founding of Easthampton as a sea-bathing resort. She dared to broach the subject of the railway branch line, and instantly he was afire.

'It shall not go through, I promise you,' he declared, enforcing what she had hoped to hear. 'Companies who own transport boats on the Merrelton Canal are united in this fight, simply because they can see their trade being cut down. It would only be a question of time, once the railway was established at Easthampton, for Merrelton to be linked with it, and after that there would be no more commerce upon the waterways. There is proof enough of that further north, where boatmen everywhere have been thrown out of work, and their families made destitute and left to starve.'

'It seems impossible to build a railway anywhere without causing misery and destruction.' She told him what she had witnessed in Italy.

'The same has happened here with others than the boatmen. Whole streets demolished and hundreds of homes destroyed, quite apart from the rape of the countryside and the suffering left in its wake.' He gave her a penetrating look. 'How did you hear about the branch line going across Attwood land in the first place?'

She told him of her visit to the Grange when Josh Barton was there. 'I clashed with him then, and at every meeting with him since. The objectionable fellow has taken rooms in Sea Cottage where I am living, and I find his presence a constant annoyance. I have not admitted it to him, but in truth I would have no objection to the railway generally, and should favour such a quick and easy mode of travel and transportation if innocent people were not left to suffer, and were re-housed and re-employed by the speculators who made such enormous profits.'

He was already shaking his head and spreading his hands expressively, letting them hover over the table in front of him. 'We don't live in a perfect world, and greed and great fortunes go hand in hand. I myself have been guilty in the past of ruthlessness at times, but it is to my shame and I'm not proud of it. My battle this time will be to defend my resort, for as surely as I sit here, the railway would reduce Easthampton's prosperity and in turn create poverty and unemployment for the people who live in it. The nobility still come to Easthampton because it is a place of social consequence and has been since its foundation, and with them come their wealth and their patronage, enabling the town to thrive. It only needs a whisper of beaches crowded with trippers coming on day-excursions for those of importance to cancel their bookings and take themselves off abroad or to country estates instead, never to return. There are plenty of other seaside resorts connected with the railway for those working folk to disport themselves in, bringing no money with them and scaring away polite society. Every man to his rights and to his choice. I deny it to no one, but I'm conscience-bound to preserve Easthampton as a bastion for those who want its special amenities and those whose livelihoods depend upon their patronage.' He took a mouthful of wine quickly as if his throat had dried with the vehemence of his convictions. 'Well?' He set down the glass again. 'I have told you my reasons for keeping Josh Barton and his damned railway out of Easthampton, and you have told me that it offends you that an ancient estate is threatened with bisection. That makes us allies.' His powerful hand came across to her and she placed her own in it.

'Allies,' she repeated. 'In a common cause.'

He did not release her fingers immediately, but continued to hold them for a few moments longer, his gaze dwelling on her face. 'How shall we celebrate our victory?'

'Let the winning be done first.'

Once, long ago, Claudine had said much the same to him when he had spoken of gaining the championship of the prize-ring. Lucy, her fingers released, slipped the strings of her reticule over her arm and pulled on her gloves, fastening the tiny buttons as she rose from the table to leave the hotel with him.

Being on foot himself, he would have ordered a hackney carriage to take her home to Sea Cottage, but she would have none of it, saying she would walk. He remained on the pavement outside the hotel and watched her go. She was Claudine's daughter. He was convinced of it. The likeness was uncanny, to say nothing of her whole background, innocently described, which, when added to her fervent interest in the Attwood estate, reinforced that conviction. In the past there had been a tale of a stillborn child, but now he knew it to be a lie. It had been a live birth, but Claudine in her deviousness had chosen to hide the fact, even as Lucy had sought to conceal her true identity from him. Why the girl should take refuge behind her married name he did not know, unless it did not suit her purpose to reveal that she was an Attwood through some painful sense of shame about her father, although how on earth she would have heard of the shadows in his character was impossible to guess. Lionel Attwood had needed an heir and out of a sense of duty had married Claudine, who had come to hate the husband driven to her bed by that need alone, in a reluctance that had frequently defeated him. Yet he had not been a vindictive man; indeed, he had been gentle and generous by nature, well respected and well liked by those who did not suspect or were prepared to overlook the side of his life that was personal and private. Only rumour and the noticeable number of fine-looking young men included in his staff gave away the fact that the brilliant marriage was not all that it should be.

Lucy vanished from sight beyond a row of terraced houses. Daniel stood a few moments longer. Only to him had Claudine confided the misery of that marriage. He had no doubt at all why, in her release through widowhood, she had abandoned her unfortunate infant with accommodating nuns: it had been to allow her to return alone to England and to him, unhampered and unreminded by appendages from the past. Claudine had wanted a new beginning. It had come, but not in the way she had visualized; instead, it had been a despairing path into the oblivion of debauchery and death. Lucy should never know his rejection. There was nothing in all the world that he would not do for her. Fate had given him a second chance.

Even as he made to turn in the opposite direction to that which she had taken, he changed his mind and went through an archway into the stables at the rear of the hotel. It was his habit to take a hack from either The Royal or The Warwyck when it suited him, and the ostler saddled up the best available. Without haste Daniel rode away from the centre of the resort, making for the outskirts, his mind so full of Claudine and the coming of Lucy into his life that he knew he could give no more thought to business that day and needed to be alone. He knew where he could find that solitude, a derelict cottage at Denwin Corner that he had ridden by a number of times over the years, but never entered since a night long ago when he and Claudine had had a clandestine meeting there.

He left the road and followed the track that led to the cottage, but when a copse of trees drew back to reveal the deserted hovel that he remembered, he reined in, his whole face registering disbelief. The cottage had been re-thatched and repainted, the garden cleared and the gate mended. Who had *dared* to take advantage of his absence abroad to exercise a squatter's ancient rights on his land! He'd have whoever it was out with a boot in his arse!

He dismounted swiftly, threw the reins over the fence-post, and sent the gate swinging back on its hinges. He did not deign to knock on the door of his own property, but took the latch, and had it not opened immediately he would have put his shoulder to it without a second's hesitation. The sunshine followed him into the cottage, and dust motes, disturbed by his stamping entrance, rose and rotated gently in the rays. He glared about him, and was immediately so assailed from the shadows by the past that he placed a shaking hand across his mouth as if he feared he might shout out against the curse that still afflicted him.

Claudine was everywhere. The bed was gone, the wall white-washed and a bench set against it, but he could see her still, naked in the soft hay that had been their mattress, their clothes lying about the floor where they had been hurled aside, and in his ears rang her cries of ecstasy and pain, for he had used her ardently and brutally out of lust and hatred. He had been infatuated with her, a terrible infatuation that had had nothing to do with love. Love was what he felt for Kate, a cherishing and depth of heart that he would feel for her until the day he died, but what he and Claudine had felt for each other had been passion of another kind, a total craving for each other that only being together could assuage. He had betrayed Kate that night as Claudine had played false to her lawful partner, and with the coming of dawn each had returned home, she to a husband fallen sick unto death, and he to an estranged Kate who – unbeknown to him at the time – had been carrying their son in her womb. Their son. Who was two months older than Claudine's daughter.

'I didn't hear you knock, Mr Warwyck,' Meg said pointedly from the doorway into the bedroom from which she had been watching him. Alarm at his noisy bursting into the cottage had made her move cautiously from folding away some clean linen she had brought there, and what she had seen of his stricken expression had caused her to stay quiet and unobserved.

'Meg Linden?' he exclaimed hoarsely, his anger vanquished by far more disturbing thoughts than the occupation of a cottage. 'What are you doing here?'

'I'm your new tenant, sir. At least, I will be when Bob Cooper and I are wed. Your son, Mr Richard, let him do the place up and has rented it to us with an option to buy later on.'

Daniel breathed deeply. 'The devil he has!' He slammed out of the cottage as forcefully as he had entered it, the door springing open again against the fallen latch. Meg took it and slowly pushed it closed, thoughtfully watching him depart through the diminishing aperture. He had looked quite distraught when he saw that the bed had gone. Did he suspect he had once lost two silver buttons with a give-away identification wrought upon them, and had he come back to seek them out upon hearing or seeing that the cottage was re-occupied?

That evening at home she took the buttons out of the drawer and showed them to Emmie, who put on her spectacles and studied them cunningly, but not before she had heard about Daniel's visit to the cottage that day.

'These buttons are 'is, right enough,' she said, sitting back in her chair at the table where they sat and unhooking her spectacles from her ears. 'Those initials are living proof, apart from nobody but 'im ever 'aving anything so fancy in that line around 'ere. Are you thinking of using them against 'im if 'ee should turn nasty over your getting the cottage to rent?'

'Did I say I had that in mind?' Meg retaliated sharply.

'No, you didn't, but if it's scandal you want, I can tell you a thing or two about the Warwyck family.'

Her daughter's face tightened warningly. 'I won't hear nothing against Mr Richard.'

Emmie chuckled and slapped her palm on the table. 'Not about 'im or 'is sister, but about their Uncle 'Arry and 'ow 'ee followed our Mr Daniel Warwyck to that cottage one night a long time ago when 'er up at the Grange, a real flighty piece of goods, came sneaking out for a bit of what she fancied.'

Meg stared at her mother. 'Go on,' she urged breathlessly.

Emmie leaned her head forward and spoke in low, confidential tones. 'There was a boating party for the gentry what was staying at the resort and from the big 'ouses around. Me and some of my pals were down on the beach with other ordinary folk to watch the jollifications in the light of flares stuck in the sand. Well, it 'appened afterwards, and 'ere's the way of it.' She lowered her voice still further and Meg almost had to strain her ears to hear what was said, although there was no chance of their being overheard. What she learned put a new interpretation to the drawn expression she had seen on Daniel Warwyck's face that day.

At Easthampton House he sat alone in the library, a decanter of brandy at his elbow, a glass in his hand. His reinforced anger over Meg's claim to the tenancy of the cottage had evaporated again before he was halfway home. He had battle enough on his hands over the railway without adding to the score against his son, who had only acted with common sense and in his own best interests in taking the chance to get the cottage restored with two reliable tenants in it. Daniel certainly had never thought of it remaining as a kind of hidden shrine to the past. Far from it. Indeed, he had left it to crumble away, taking its secret with it. Dammit, he still had a key to it somewhere.

Putting down the glass, he rose from his chair and went to hunt through the drawers of the desk, coming across the key at last where it had lain forgotten for many years. He weighed it thoughtfully on the palm of his hand. It was a link with the past and the present. A link with Lucy.

II

Sunlight flashed on the brass instruments of the military band that had come from Merrelton barracks specially to honour the pier's opening, and it made a stirring accompaniment to the cheerful noise of the crowd. People had travelled from far around, and the roads and lanes into Easthampton had held a steady flow of equipages of every kind that had brought families and parties to witness the event. Throughout the resort flags were flying, and windows were festooned with red, white and blue drapery, which had been saved in some cases from the Coronation. New bunting in the brightest of colours fluttered from archway to archway along the full length of the pier. Guests of honour and local dignitaries from the council conducting Easthampton's affairs were given special positions of vantage on either side of the entrance, across which a white ribbon had been stretched. Lucy, standing on the outskirts of the crowd, was just able to see Richard moving among them, and now and again she caught a glimpse of Donna's rose-trimmed bonnet.

The opening had been timed to coincide with the high tide, and by good fortune the balmy day had brought the sea to a vivid emerald, such a sun-glitter riding upon it that the show of parasols on the promenade resembled a pastel-hued mushroom patch. The fishermen, their own craft decorated, had boat-loads of passengers bobbing offshore, some people having decided to alight on the pier after the ceremony was over by the iron steps at the head of it.

Timothy, arriving among latecomers, spotted Lucy and promptly threaded his way through the crowd until he reached her side.

'Good morning! What a day for the celebrations.'

She was delighted to see him. 'It is indeed. A good omen for the pier's success, wouldn't you say?'

'I agree.' He was thinking how lovely she was and that there would be the devil to pay if his family ever suspected he had serious intentions towards a young woman who played the piano at a theatre. Donna had been the one he had marked out as a possible choice for a wife, but his amorous feelings there had waned, and try as he would, he could not recapture the first sweet flush that had kept him corresponding with her throughout the winter. He regretted having kissed her, a declaration of serious intention in the first instance, but on both occasions it had been to banish Lucy from his mind, although he had not quite realized it at the time.

He noticed now she was standing on tip-toe to catch glimpses of what was happening through the crowd. 'You won't see anything of the ceremony from here,' he commented, and then promptly raised his voice on an authoritative note to address those standing in front of them. 'Make way for this lady, if you please.'

Such was the note of command in a voice unmistakably that of a gentleman that people moved automatically, enabling him, stifling his amusement, to propel her forward to a much better viewing site. She made a laughing protest.

'That was quite unnecessary.' Then her laughter faded. She saw that she had come side by side with Josh Barton. Timothy expressed pleased surprise, shaking Josh's hand vigorously, but she barely acknowledged his greeting. He eyed her with a glint that seemed close to amusement of his own. They had not conversed at all since his return to Sea Cottage.

'This great day for Easthampton should be a lesson to you, Lucy. There was opposition to the pier from certain quarters when the idea was first put forward, but I have heard from Richard Warwyck that those who were most fiercely set against it are now the most enthusiastic.'

She was saved from any comment on this parallel drawn with his railway aims by the ripple and rise of a cheer gathering momentum at the approach of Mr and Mrs Warwyck in their open landau along the road from Easthampton House.

Kate would gladly have surrendered the honour of opening the pier to any one of the many local personages she felt were better qualified to do it, but neither Daniel nor Richard would hear of it. Her son himself came forward when the landau stopped to hand her from it, and that surge of pride in him rose up in her, making her determined to do justice to the occasion since all the credit for the pier was his. Applause resounded as she and Daniel moved towards the decorated entrance, through the passage kept clear by the crowd across the breadth of the promenade. Every woman, she knew, would be noting her fashionable straw bonnet with its gossamer veil and the delicate tones of her silk dress, which changed from pink to grey as the light caught it. She smiled and nodded to all around her, and had a special word with Anna Edenfield, who was among the guests of honour, since it was her grandmother, the late Lady Margaret, who had cut the ribbon many years before at the resort's foundation ceremony.

Lucy was observing Daniel, who was doing his own share of greeting the dignitaries, and it seemed to her that in spite of his apparently undivided attention directed towards whoever happened to be speaking to him, he was looking out for someone in the crowd. Beneath the brim of her leghorn hat her shaded eyes had the advantage of his unshielded from the sun, and she tried to follow the direction of his glances in open curiosity to see who was important enough to be singled out for acknowledgement by him. But he appeared to draw blank each time. Suddenly the breeze, which was playing tricks on all sides with ruffles and ribbons and dancing fringes, caught her leghorn's brim and flicked it upwards. Instantly he caught the fiery swoop of her hair, and she was no longer left in doubt for whom his eyes were searching, though the burning look he gave her held no sexual challenge in its depths. It was more as if he had been seeking confirmation of her presence in the crowd out of a quiet reason of his own, almost as though it were enough for him to look upon her face again, for already he had turned away to draw his wife to the place of honour for the ceremony to begin.

Richard addressed the guests and the crowd, welcoming them in a short speech that was crisp and to the point, before introducing his mother with praise and compliments. As the applause died down, Kate commenced the carefully rehearsed few words that she had to say.

'Ladies and gentlemen, this happy occasion is another milestone in the history of Easthampton. All of us, young and old, residents and visitors alike, will be able to enjoy a walk far out to sea on this splendid pier –'

A coarse voice interrupted her from the crowd, causing a stir. 'Not everybody, lady! Only those what gets to the coast in the first place! When's the railway comin'? That's what we wants to know!'

Kate went pale, but she continued with dignity. '– and in addition, there is the new theatre that is to present melodramas of distinction throughout the summer –'

She was shouted down again from another part of the crowd as Daniel became the focus of abuse. 'Stop acting the almighty, Warwyck! We wants the railway even if you don't!'

'That's right! Let's beat Merrelton to it!' bawled a third man, choosing an appeal guaranteed to inflame the sense of rivalry that existed between the resort and the market town, which won calls of assent from the rougher local element in the crowd, while those who had come from Merrelton booed their derision. Others, outraged at the disruption of the ceremony, voiced their disapproval of the interrupters, and scuffles began to break out between some of the men, even those in favour of the railway deeming it in poor taste to use such an occasion for demonstration.

Daniel clenched his fists at his sides, his face darkened with angry colour. 'Paid agitators!' he grated, wanting to deal personally with each one of them. 'I can smell 'em a mile off.'

Kate remained unflinching beside him, although some ladies among the invited guests had begun to draw back nervously, fearful that missiles might be thrown, a not uncommon occurrence at times of unruliness. Anna Edenfield clutched at Donna, asking apprehensively if there was not a policeman present to restore order.

Easthampton's sole representative of the law was in the thick of the throng, his tall hat visible amid the stovepipes, parasols and toppers as he tried to reach the troublemakers, but his way was being blocked deliberately by supporters. People began to scatter, gathering their children, some of whom had begun to cry. Richard's appeal for everyone to remain calm went unheard. Suddenly Josh shouldered his way through to stand in front of the Warwycks, and he threw out his arms wide, his shout ringing out.

'I'm your railway man!' He caught everyone's attention, the agitators giving him a cheer, and the scuffling ceased. 'Give your backing to me at the right time and the right place, but not today! We are here to rejoice that Easthampton has the longest and most handsome pier on the south coast, and we owe that to the initiative and in-genuity of Mr Richard Warwyck who – like his father – has only the good of this resort at heart. Now let us give ear to Mrs Warwyck who is going to open the pier for us!'

He had won the crowd over, and knew it. Good humour returned, and with it the holiday spirit, a rousing cheer going up. Kate, giving him a grateful glance, took the gilded scissors from Donna, and her simple declaration that the pier was open brought more approbation and applause as the snapped ribbon fluttered away to either side, leaving the entrance unbarred. As she and Daniel went through with the invited guests, everybody else began to move forward. Admittance was free that day, and the flow through the gate was smooth.

'Well done, sir,' Timothy said in praise as Josh rejoined him at Lucy's side, but she had no such compliment to pay, fuming with indignation.

'Your duplicity astounds me! That was all planned, wasn't it? A neat little trick to gain popularity and support while appearing as the benevolent peacemaker.'

'Here, steady on,' Timothy interposed in mild reproof, but Josh held up a hand.

'Let Lucy have her say. I always find her statements interesting.' There was a glint in his eye that showed he was laughing at her inwardly. 'I admit that the occurrence has done my cause no end of good. Some of the most influential people in the area are here today.'

'There! You see!' She had turned to Timothy. 'He doesn't deny what he has done. Are you to be party to these underhand schemes by supporting such a man?'

Timothy looked serious. 'I think Mr Barton and I must discuss this matter between us.'

'At your convenience,' Josh offered blandly. Then, as she moved away: 'Aren't you coming on the pier with us?'

'I've seen all I wish to see,' she replied with cool emphasis. 'Moreover, it's no rarity for me to traverse the pier.'

'We shall meet later, after this evening's performance,' Timothy reminded her. The Warwycks were giving a champagne supper party at Easthampton House, and Richard had invited them both.

'I'm looking forward to that,' she said with a soft-lashed look at him that she knew was not lost on Josh Barton.

Among those drifting towards the entrance was Emmie Linden, neat in bonnet and shawl, a silver brooch pinned to her ample bosom. She was looking seawards, able to see Meg and Bob with their boats filled with passengers, both of them expecting to do a roaring trade plying round the pier until the tide turned, and she did not notice the broad, stocky man sauntering nonchalantly through the milling throng towards her.

''Ello, Emmie! 'Ow's life been using you?'

For a moment she stared at his ruddy-complexioned face, the blue button-eyes sharp and crafty in their thickish lids, his side-whiskers sandy-hued and abundant, and then at once recognition dawned. 'Ben Thompson! You rogue, you! After all these years!' She took him by the shoulders and shook him exuberantly before standing back a step to look him up and down, for he sported a bright waistcoat with his check coat and trousers, a high-crowned bowler at an angle on his balding head. 'You look a proper swell. Times must be a bit different since you 'ad a boat bringing in a cask or two from over the water.'

' 'Ere! Keep your voice down.' His good humour ebbed slightly, his gaze shifting about to make sure she had not been overheard. 'I don't want all and sundry 'earing about the old days. I finished with that trade when I left 'ere.'

She gave him a dig with her elbow. 'Don't tell me you've ever followed the straight and narrow.'

'I 'ave, I 'ave.' He rocked on his heels importantly. 'Made many an honest penny working the race tracks and the prize-rings. That's where the blunt is to be made, I'm telling you.'

'I bet it is.' She chortled admiringly. 'But you'll never convince me you earned those togs you're wearing without bending the rules to suit yourself. You always were one step ahead of everybody else.'

His preening at her compliment expanded his thick gold watch-chain. 'You weren't so slow yourself, Emm,' he conceded magnanimously.

Her eyes narrowed inquisitively. 'What's brought you back 'ere?'

'A need for a breath of sea air. What else?'

She was unconvinced, showing jovial suspicion. 'You never did do nothing for no good reason. I bet there's more be'ind you coming 'ere than meets the eye.' She caught her breath on an explanation dawning. 'Was you one of those in the crowd –?'

He silenced her with a tap of his finger against the side of his nose, his fleshy lips parting in a grin of yellow teeth. 'We won't talk just 'ere no more. Let's find a quiet corner. Is The Crown still doing business?'

'Not 'alf!' Her chuckling voice mocked him. 'But don't you want to see over this fine pier?'

'I'll 'ave plenty of time for that.' He took hold of her arm and guided her about to stroll away from it with him. 'I've thought of staying around these parts for a while. 'Ow about your place, Emm? Where are you living now? Would you 'ave a room to rent?'

'There's Meg's room. She could turn out and share with me.'

'Meg?'

'My daughter.'

He snapped his fingers, emphasizing recollection. 'Yes, yes. I remember. You was in the family way last time I saw you. Did you and Joe make a go of it?'

'Fat chance I 'ad. He skedaddled off to sea and that was the last I ever 'eard of 'im.'

He had noticed her left hand. 'You're wearing a wedding ring.'

She set her shoulders and drew herself up, regarding him warningly. 'And why shouldn't it be there? Nobody never questions it, and I'll not 'ave you starting now. I'm respectable. I keep a proper genteel 'ome with well-to-do lodgers and no funny business. I'll ask *you* to keep a quiet tongue in your 'ead about the past, Benjamin Thompson, seeing as 'ow you're expecting the same from me.'

'Agreed, Emm. Agreed.'

When Meg came home between tides to rest and refresh herself she was less than pleased to find an unknown man, smelling strongly of ale, snoring on her bed, and all her possessions moved into her mother's room.

'Who is he? What's he doing here?' she stormed.

Emmie, inebriated from the time spent in The Crown, sat down weightily on the edge of the sofa and flapped her plump hands placatingly. ''S awright. 'Ee's an ole friend. Knew your Pa in the ole days. Can't turn 'way an ole friend.'

Meg scowled, setting her fists on her waist. 'Well, I don't like the looks of him. A crooked tyke if ever I saw one. I bet you did the paying in The Crown.'

Emmie wobbled her head. 'No, I di'n't. Not the firs' round anyway. Don' you fret, 'cos 'ee won' be at Sea Cottage all the time. 'Ee's in a way of business, comin' and goin' like Mr Barton, y'might say.'

'With the railway company, you mean?'

Her question had a sobering effect upon her mother, who staggered to her feet, looking alarmed, and grabbed her for support. 'Don't mention it! Jus' don' mention it to no one. Ben don' want it spread around. There was a bit o' trouble at the pier today –'.

'I know. I heard about it.'

'– and although 'ee di'n't say outright, I think 'ee 'ad a finger in it.'

'Nothing would surprise me about *him*.' Pithily.

Emmie pulled at her. 'We've gotta stay on the right side of 'im. Promise me you'll stay on the right side of 'im.'

'Why?'

' 'Cos 'ee knows a bit more about my younger days than I care to 'ave spread around, and that's the truth of it. It ain't fair to 'ave the good name I've built up for us dragged about in the mud.' She began to weep maudlin tears. 'I've been a good mother to you, brought you up proper, never done wrong to no one, and saved no end of dam' silly females from drownin', so why should I 'ave to suffer in the twilight of my years?'

Meg rolled up her eyes wearily. 'You're not going to suffer, so shut up, for God's sake. I won't say nothing about him and I'll keep the peace. Is that all right?'

'Take an oath on't. A proper oath.' Emmie reeled up and went to the dresser, snatched the heavy Bible from the shelf and swayed as she thrust it towards her daughter. 'Swear it!'

Meg sighed again and put her palm on the Bible. 'I swear.'

Emmie nodded, satisfied, and collapsed down again onto the sofa, still holding the Holy Book to her. 'You're a good daughter. None could 'ave 'ad better.'

'You rest there and sleep it off,' Meg advised, lifting her mother's feet by the ankles and setting them upon the sofa. Then, taking her own shawl from about her shoulders she spread it across the woman's legs and saw that she already slept.

Removing the Bible carefully, Meg replaced it on the shelf and went into the bedroom she was to share with her mother. She despaired at the untidy manner in which armfuls of belongings had been gathered up out of her room and deposited on the bed, but she set to and cleared some space in a chest of drawers where she folded her clothes away with her customary neatness. In her annoyance at the turn things had taken in her home, and her own physical tiredness from sailing around the pier with sightseers, she failed to notice that the little box containing her hoarded sovereigns and the two buttons was missing, overlooked by Emmie in the clearing of her room.

Long before the gala performance was due to start, people arrived in carriages and began to wander along the pier towards the theatre. Every ticket had been sold in advance, and against the darkness of sky and sea the gaslights made a golden chain to light the way, which was reflected in the water where boats were plying again, coloured lanterns at their bows. The foyer, a-buzz with excited voices, was already filled with guests, all in evening dress, and even those taking a side entrance to the humbler seats in the gallery had in the main donned their best clothes. An air of thrilled anticipation lay over the whole theatre as the auditorium filled up, programmes with silken cords rustling, jewels glittering, white gloves glowing, and a rising aroma of macassar oil, fragrant scents and powdered shoulders. Backstage, pandemonium reigned as it was discovered there was a jamming of the mechanism of one of the rollers around which the strip of scenery passed from another on the opposite side of the stage to give the illusion of the wild horse's gallop across the countryside. In the end Asquith himself took a spanner to it and made the correct adjustment, swearing all the time.

Lucy, who was allowed to share the actresses' dressing-room in order to change into her evening gown, gave a final touch to her hair before a looking-glass, a little dismayed to find that she was nervous. She stood back from her reflection, pleased that she had decided to wear her dark emerald silk, which would glow when the lights of the auditorium were up, but would blend into the shadows when the curtains parted.

Outside the dressing-room she found Richard waiting for her. He took both her hands into his. 'I've come to wish you luck,' he said proudly. 'Not that you need it. You're such a talented pianist. Father told me he heard you play at rehearsal and that he took you out to luncheon afterwards.'

'He was very kind.'

'But you haven't met my mother yet.'

'I shall do this evening at your home.'

'But there'll be such a crowd there. May I ask you to come to our box when the melodrama is over? I would like her to have a few words with you before she leaves the theatre.'

'I'll come to the box,' she agreed willingly.

'Thank you. Now I must get out to the foyer to meet my parents and Donna, who are coming with Timothy Attwood and two of our other guests.'

He departed. It was too early to go out to her piano, but as soon as the green curtain had been raised she would go through to the auditorium with Mr Bartley-Jones, who was presently seated on a hamper, returning a bottle to his tail-pocket and wiping his mouth with the back of his hand. It was suffocatingly warm backstage, and crowded in the cramped spaces as stage-hands and cast avoided bumping into each other. A stable-odour came strongly from the place where the horse was tethered, for he was nervous, affected by the pervading excitement, and he tossed his head and blew down his nostrils, promising a better performance as an untamed Tartar horse than on his previous, docile appearance at rehearsals. Bob Cooper in his costume as sentinel was moving forward to take his place in the castle setting on stage, and when the actor playing Mazeppa emerged from the men's dressing-room, fussing over the folds of his cloak, Lucy welcomed the diversion of helping him to adjust them. He gave her no thanks, totally absorbed in himself, and smoothed the artificial moustache that drooped down thinly from his upper lip in true Tartar style.

Then it was time for her to go out into the auditorium. She took a deep breath. Mr Bartley-Jones opened the door that was concealed on the other side by the panelling, and she went through it ahead of him, to be assailed by the buzz of voices and the rustle of programmes. He took her hand to lead her to the piano, and as she seated herself she saw that a bunch of violets lay on the lid. Tucked in them was a card. *D.W.* Nothing more. She was touched by his kind thought and placed them by her music. Two Warwycks had wished her well. Out of the corner of her eye she saw that the Warwyck box was not yet occupied, but she had no chance to look towards it again, because the signal that all was ready had been given. She and Mr Bartley-Jones struck up the thunderous overture.

Daniel, with his unerring sense of timing learned during his prize-ring days, had brought Kate and his party into the box at the moment when the music was inspiring a pitch of exhilarated absorption. Kate, always a credit to him, shone in iris-blue taffeta, an antique Chinese shawl about her shoulders, and since Donna had chosen to wear sapphire striped muslin and Anna Edenfield azure silk, Timothy had declared they were like a bevy of forget-me-nots, paying a compliment with a play on words that had charmed all three of them. When the ladies were seated at the front of the box, the menfolk, who included Anna's betrothed, a gentleman named Alfred Swain, took the rest of the chairs. The curtains parted. The eagerly awaited performance began.

There had been no time for Kate to observe the pianist who was to be their guest after the performance, and throughout the first act she was wholly caught up in the play. Enthusiastic applause came with the closing of the curtains on the bolting of the wild horse with Mazeppa bound to its back in a terrible punishment, and immediately Donna and Timothy engaged her in conversation, so that the piano stool had been vacated for the interval when she looked towards it.

'Doesn't Mrs di Castelloni play well, Mother?' Richard said, leaning over her chair a moment later.

'Er – yes, she does. Indeed she does,' Kate agreed sincerely.

'Here she comes again now.'

Kate glimpsed the young widow as the lights lowered again, caught the burnished glow of a smoothly dressed head and the pearly gleam of shoulders, and then turned her attention towards the stage, feeling strangely uneasy. She no longer found it possible to concentrate on what was taking place among the Tartars, the conviction laying hold on her that she had seen Lucy di Castelloni somewhere before. But how was that possible? According to Richard, and to Daniel who had made her acquaintance, the widow had come straight to Easthampton from Italy where she had lived all her life. Again and again Kate put the ivory opera glasses to her eyes, not to study the players on the boards, but to observe the face of the young woman of whom her son was enamoured. He thought it was his own secret, but those who love can never resist the pleasure of talking about the loved one, however casually the name drops into the conversation, and where Donna had given herself away transparently, it had only needed a word or two here and there for Kate to grasp that it was no ordinary attunement developing between the lovely young widow and her son.

And Lucy di Castelloni was lovely. The opera glasses showed that with perfect clarity. Her hands on the keys travelled gracefully, completing a chord and then alighting in her lap until it was time to play again. It was as she sat there, poised and still, the lights from the stage capturing her face as if in a cameo, that it came to Kate why it seemed she had seen Lucy di Castelloni before. It was as if a figure had stepped out of the past. Kate stiffened. Her heart began to beat uncomfortably. It could have been a softer, gentler Claudine seated there.

Kate was never to remember anything of the rest of the play. Her mind was totally occupied with trying to piece together everything she had heard her son and daughter as well as Daniel say about the newcomer in their midst. Daniel. Had he noticed the likeness too? He was sitting behind her and there was no way in which she could see if he was observing the pianist as she had done.

The melodrama came to an end at last. The cast took many bows, for they had done well and it had been an ambitious production for a small stage. It was not long before Lucy arrived at the door of the box where Richard swept her in, and she and Kate faced each other for the first time.

'How do you do, Mrs Warwyck,' Lucy said, thinking how fortunate Daniel's wife was to have the classic facial bones that held a beauty no passing of time could dim, her complexion flawless, her eyes sparkling and somehow enhanced by the fine corner lines that denoted the passing of the forty years' milestone.

Kate heard herself make some reply, offering congratulations on the rendering of the musical score, but all the time she was registering every detail of lash and skin and eye and voice of the young woman facing her, seeing with a kind of awful clarity another, fainter likeness as if a phantom had shifted almost imperceptibly to reveal one other behind it. A suspicion, more dreadful than anything she had ever known, drummed into her, making it difficult for her to keep the smile upon her lips.

'Are you ready to accompany us?' she inquired. 'Good. We will leave, then, or else all the rest of the guests will have gathered at Easthampton House before us.'

Not quite knowing why, Kate glanced from her husband to her son to encourage the general departure from the box, but both were looking at Lucy, and what she saw in their faces made her want to scream out. Daniel's expression bordered on doting, and Richard's was rapt with love.

12

In his office Richard looked up from a ledger in surprise when his visitor proved to be Meg Linden. He rose to his feet at once and came round the desk to greet her, caught again by that tug at the heart that he had known repeatedly since he had first become aware that the dipper's daughter with her sun-browned face and sea-faded clothes was growing up, as he was. The days of her saucing him with face-pulling behind his nursemaid's back were gone, to be replaced by a taking on of curves, a hiding of her ankles in careful modesty and a new lustre to her wind-swept hair.

'This is an unexpected pleasure,' he said, pulling a chair forward for her. 'What brings you to the offices of Warwyck and Son?'

She hesitated before taking the crimson leather seat, ill at ease in the formal setting of oak panelling and carpeted floor, but when she did sit down she settled herself firmly, as if determined not to leave until the cause of her visit had been resolved to her liking. He guessed her cotton dress was new, and although it held the crude green of a cheap dye and was over-ornamented with braid, it somehow suited her, and as he perched his weight on the edge of the desk facing her he could see that her faded straw bonnet was a shade darker where fresh trimming had not fully covered it.

'It's your Pa,' she began. 'I chuffed him off the other day for coming into Denwin Cottage without as much as a knock, and although I was polite about it, I've worried about it ever since.' She leaned forward anxiously. 'He'll not turn Bob out of there, will he? I could tell he didn't know you'd rented the place to anybody.'

Richard folded his arms and spoke in reassuring tones. 'Don't you worry yourself about it, Meg. He did mention he had been to the cottage, but he said nothing to me about wanting Bob or you out of the place.'

'That's a relief.' She tilted her head sideways at him with sudden impishness. 'You'd have had to find me somewhere else if he had, wouldn't you? Seeing as you gave your word to Bob on the tenancy.'

He threw back his head on a laugh. 'Yes, I suppose I would. What about Buckingham Palace? Would that have suited you?'

She wrinkled her nose. 'No. Too grand. But I'd have settled for Easthampton House. Or that nice villa where you've got the upper floor.'

'Would you indeed?' He was still amused.

She caught her breath, not quite looking at him. 'But without Bob, of course.'

A quietness took over the office. To both of them the ticking of the longcase clock in the corner seemed to have become magnified. Beyond the windows, the sounds from the outside yard, hooves, shouts and rumbling wheels, came faint and subdued.

'Don't you love him?' His voice was flat, cautious, and he did not really want to know the answer.

'He'll do.' Her crisp, phlegmatic utterance was belied by the tell-tale folding and unfolding of her hands.

He moved from the desk, feeling burdened by her unspoken misery, and went to stand looking out of the window, his hands clasped behind him. 'When is the wedding to be?'

'I'd told Bob not until the autumn, but now it's to be sooner. Ma's taken in an extra lodger and I don't like him. I'll be glad to get away from home. That's why I was worried about losing Denwin Cottage.'

He recalled Lucy mentioning that there was someone else staying at Emmie Linden's place, and anything remotely concerned with her was of interest to him. 'Why don't you like the fellow? Is he abusive? A drunkard, perhaps?'

'He drinks a bit, but no more nor less than Ma does. No, it's just that he's a creepy sort of man. One who looks as if he'd steal from a blind man's cup.'

He made a mental note to find out more from Josh Barton about the stranger there, and as he turned back to Meg he saw she was on her feet, ready to leave. Regret swept over him that she was approaching marriage without the joy with which he would meet his to Lucy when the time came, and he was filled with pity and pain.

'You know it's unwise to let a temporary unhappiness at home drive you into this union before you're ready for it.'

She shrugged resignedly. 'What difference will three or four months make? None. Better it's Bob than anyone else, since he does care for me and he'll not beat me like some men would, or use me ill. Jealousy is his only real fault, quite like a sickness with him, but I'll cure that sooner or later.'

'That may not prove as easy as you think. A man's character is moulded young, and if there's jealousy in his nature it can rarely be banished.'

She tilted her face to his. 'But he'll have no cause for it. No cause – unless you should ever need the comfort of my arms again.'

His rebel body stirred in opposition to his heart, for she had caught him off guard, sending those flickering images of her through his brain, and he gave a soft sigh of embarrassment, shaking his head, and taking hold of her by the wrists.

'I'm to be wed myself before long if all goes well.'

She went quite white, but nodded dumbly. Then, taking him unawares a second time, she twisted like a corkscrew out of his clasp to thrust her ripe mouth hard against his, her arms limpet-like about his neck, and as abruptly broke from him.

'I'll love you all my life, Richard Warwyck. If ever you need me, I'll be there.'

She darted from the office, leaving the door open behind her in her haste, and when he went to close it she had already gone from sight.

*   *   *

He saw her again the same evening when he went to the pier theatre to meet Lucy and take her to the ball at the Grange. Meg had her boat and Bob's ready on the beach, and even as Richard reached the stage door, Bob came out in a rush to make his way at a run down the pier, anxious to catch the tide for a fishing trip, the other vessels having already sailed. Neither of them noticed him.

Lucy came out of the theatre soon afterwards and he could tell at once she was at a high pitch of excitement which had little to do with the performance she had just accompanied for she could talk of nothing else all the way to the waiting carriage but that she was to meet Mrs Radcliffe at the Grange and hear all about Lionel and Claudine Attwood.

'Olivia Radcliffe is not a very friendly person,' he warned as the carriage moved off, wondering if she was aware how happily she had tucked her hand into the crook of his arm, but she refused to be daunted.

'She will be to me,' she declared joyously. 'I'm sure of it. You must remember that I'm no part of that old feud that your father shared with her late husband.'

'I meant with people generally,' he said, but she was not listening, chattering on about her feeling that the evening was going to prove a turning-point in her life, and what a lot there was going to be to talk about when it was all over. The glow of the passing street-lamps made the interior of the carriage light and dark by turns, and he smiled at the excited animation of her lively face, and was puzzled, but not perturbed.

Supper was over when they arrived, and the dancing had commenced.

Timothy, who had known that they would not arrive until after the theatre performance was over, came to meet them in the entrance hall as Lucy's cape was taken from her, the silk lining slithering away from the heavy frills of her ivory satin gown.

'Is Mrs Radcliffe here?' she asked at once.

'Yes, she is, and willing to see you alone,' Timothy reassured her, looking pleased that he was able to indulge her wish, and he offered her his arm. 'Let me take you into the supper-room. There's half a banquet left, and I'm sure I can tempt both of you to some champagne.'

'A capital suggestion,' Richard laughed, rubbing his hands together in agreeable anticipation, but Lucy held back.

'I don't want Mrs Radcliffe to see me until the moment of our meeting,' she insisted.

'Neither shall she.' Timothy offered his arm again. 'We'll go into the supper-room from this direction, and then you can see her first, if you like, through the doors that open out from it into the ballroom.'

But Olivia could not be seen from that point after all, for she had seated herself some distance away in a gilded alcove with some other matrons of her acquaintance. Lucy merely sipped her champagne once and toyed with a little food, having no appetite, but Richard ate heartily, Timothy replenishing his glass, the three of them alone in the room. Through one of the half-open doors she saw people she knew rotating past on the shining floor, among them Donna with one partner and then another, Kate in Daniel's arms and then again with someone else, Josh Barton dancing two consecutive dances with the same dark-haired girl, both of them appearing to be enjoying each other's company immensely, all as one waltz succeeded another before the music changed to a gavotte. At any other time Lucy's foot would have tapped impatiently to be among the dancers, but on this night she had a far more serious matter on her mind.

Richard and Timothy began a discussion about the disturbance at the pier's opening, and Lucy immediately paid attention. 'I questioned Josh Barton after your accusation,' Timothy said to her, 'and he said he had nothing to do with it, although he admitted giving his sanction to demonstrations in other places that have been designed to stimulate public opinion in the railway's favour.'

'In other words, rabble-rousing,' she remarked critically.

Timothy sighed a trifle ruefully and rested a hand on Richard's shoulder. 'I suppose you're aware that Lucy is as set against a branch line across my estate as your father is against any rail link with Easthampton.'

'We have talked about it, have we not?' Richard gave her a benevolent glance, not seriously troubled by her opposition since he considered it to be a whim, linked to her childhood idolizing of an Englishman unknown to her in a foreign grave. Once the branch line was built and the deed done, she would think no more about it.

'Surely I should be meeting Mrs Radcliffe now,' Lucy said, unable to wait any longer.

'Certainly. I'll tell her you're here.' Timothy moved to the door.

'Just give me a few moments to get up to the room of the portrait ahead of her,' she begged. He agreed, and Richard went to open the door back into the hall for her, which she sped through, her satin skirt whispering, and then on up the stairs and along the corridor to the upper drawing-room lighted for her coming. She halted in dismay. Josh was standing with his back to her, looking up at the portrait of Lionel Attwood.

'What are you doing away from the ballroom?' she demanded, flustered and wanting him gone with all speed.

He faced her, white shirt-front with pearl studs gleaming, his boutonnière a dark red carnation, and lazily he indicated the cigar he held and the open glass doors onto the balcony and the warm, dark night. 'Attwood uses this as a smoking-room. I came to take advantage of that facility.' He had discarded his white gloves, which lay on a side table, and a gold signet ring on his finger shone as he took a puff on his cigar again to illustrate his point, regarding her through the curling smoke. 'I might ask you the same question.' One corner of his mouth tilted in a smile, his eyes cynical. 'Come now, confess. You smoke yourself, but are afraid the rest of the company would think you fast if you should show yourself with a cigarette between your lips. You need harbour no such fears with me. I'm a broad-minded man where you are concerned.'

She had closed the door behind her and now advanced further into the room. 'I have an appointment to meet someone –'

'A tryst?' he interrupted. 'Who is it this time? Young Attwood or the Warwyck lad?'

'Neither. Oh, please go.' She almost wrung her hands in her agitation. 'I have arranged to meet Mrs Radcliffe in this room to discuss a private matter.'

He gave a half-bow in deference to her request. 'In that case I'll absent myself without delay.'

She released a sigh of relief, already overwhelmed by nervousness, and then swept across to the open balcony doors, to breathe in the cool air. Her cheeks were burning, her heart palpitating, and she pressed her hands to her sides in the frills of her skirt as she took one deep breath and then another, looking out at the dark landscape. He opened the double doors to the corridor, but paused in the doorway.

'If your aim is to try to persuade Mrs Radcliffe that she should sell a strip of her land to the railway and thus save the Attwood estate, you know that we would not be enemies on that point, although I can hold out no hope for you in your pleas. As I told you before, I found the lady quite adamant.'

She did not as much as glance at him, remaining in profile as she continued to gaze ahead. 'Good *evening*, Mr Barton,' she articulated pointedly in dismissal.

'It's too early to say that to me, because I hope to see you again before the night is over. In fact, I plan to dance with you later, but don't expect me to commiserate with you over failing with Mrs Radcliffe. I have warned you.'

Exasperated beyond all control with her nerves so near the surface, she turned with a stamp of her foot. 'Oh, go to the devil!'

Then she froze, her face paling. Behind him in the doorway stood Olivia Radcliffe. How long she had been standing there unnoticed by either of them was impossible to tell, but her composed stance with feet together and folded hands suggested it could have been throughout the exchange of remarks. The element of surprise that Lucy had planned to capture had been lost, and the look of instant recognition which she had hoped to see in Olivia's eyes had come and gone if indeed it had ever been present.

'I beg your pardon, ma'am,' Josh said smoothly to the woman, drawing aside. 'I did not see you there.'

'Of that I am aware, Mr Barton,' Olivia replied drily. She

entered the room and he went out, closing the doors and leaving her alone with Lucy.

Immediately Lucy dipped into the deepest curtsey. It came spontaneously from her respect, her longing and the conviction that she had met one of her own kith and kin at long last. 'Ma'am, I am honoured,' she said shakily.

'So you are Signora di Castelloni. I hear you are an accomplished pianist. I am not a theatre-goer myself, but I have friends who are, and they have praised you in my hearing.' She moved across to a striped upholstered chair and sat down in it, a blue sheen rippling across her black silk gown, and indicated that Lucy should take the one opposite her. 'Now, what did you wish to see me about? If it is about the railway, this meeting of ours can end here and now, because when I make a decision I know to be right, I never go back on it.'

That was easy to believe. There was nothing imposing about Olivia Radcliffe, who was short in stature, small-boned and thin, her hair grey and half-covered by a black lace cap. But her face, which looked as if it had been moulded in a gentleness that had become embittered by the years, held a stubbornness of expression even in repose, the lines strong from an aristocratic nose to the corners of the pursed lips, the eyes behind the silver-rimmed spectacles sharp and direct, missing nothing. She watched as Lucy did not take the chair, but went to stand under the portrait of Lionel Attwood, her hand resting on the marble mantel.

'I wish to talk of kinship,' Lucy began, feeling uneasily at a disadvantage, since she had lost those first few precious seconds that could have provided some guidance as to what ground she had to go on. 'A topic that must be as dear to your heart as it is to mine. I will tell you now what I have disclosed to none other since my arrival in England a short time ago.' A pause, not for any dramatic effect, but because it was a traumatic moment for her. 'My maiden name was Lucy Attwood.'

'Well?' Olivia unclasped her net-mittened hands and put them together again inquiringly.

'Do you not see any likeness in me to someone once known to you?' Lucy held her breath for what she would hear, but Olivia's expression did not change, although she sat back as she let her gaze travel from Lucy's face to that of the man in the portrait and back again.

'If you mean to my brother-in-law, dead these many years, I cannot detect the slightest resemblance. Our host informed me that you particularly wanted to talk to me in this room where Lionel's portrait hangs, and I suppose this was your reason. Surely you should ask him about it. My name was Clayton before I married, and the Claytons were never related to any branch of the Attwoods until the marriage of my sister took place.'

Lucy took a step towards her. 'That is where the kinship lies.' A footstool was located near Olivia's chair and she sat down on it, the frills of her skirt rippling out around her. 'Let me tell you my story. You are the first to hear all the details I kept from others, because I needed to find the right source to confirm my identity, of which I have no proof.' Out the story came. Lucy did not take her eyes from Olivia's immobile face all the time she talked, relating all that had happened and leaving nothing out, even to her youthful despair when Sister Alice had taken her into the room at the convent where Stefano awaited her, to see for the first time the man purchasing her for his own, no matter that the settled price went in the guise of a generous donation to the coffers of the convent for the benefit of the poor and needy. She had wept, unable to control her tears, but Stefano had spoken kindly to her, silencing with a wave of his hand the accompanying nun's sharp reprimand. Unfolding his handkerchief of finest linen from his topcoat pocket, he had dried her tears as they flowed and promised her she could have anything she desired to bring a smile back to her lips.

'Will you take me to England?' she had asked with still brimming eyes, unconsciously testing him.

He had looked at her thoughtfully under his grizzled brows. 'Is that what you want more than anything else?'

She had nodded. 'To see my father's home. To know where I belong.'

'Then you shall go. I will take you there.'

From that moment she had loved him, innocently and

asexually, and never had any cause to retract that depth of feeling, for it had been no fault of his that his health had begun to fail even as plans for a visit to England were being made and his doctors had forbidden travel.

Her tale continued, and although she could not bring herself to speak of Domenico's rape she did tell of his threats and how at last she came to England and the Grange. 'I am your sister's child,' she said in conclusion, and she held out her hands to Olivia in a spurt of appeal. 'Let me hear you say that without doubt you know me to be Claudine and Lionel Attwood's daughter!'

Olivia's mouth twisted and her eyes were cynical. 'Mercy! You are an actress beyond compare, Signora. Had I not been in possession of all the facts surrounding the last days of my brother-in-law's life in Italy, I might have been taken in by your grand display.'

Lucy blinked in stunned disbelief at what she had heard. 'Aunt Olivia – I know you to be my aunt – you cannot in all conscience deny that it is the truth I've put before you.'

'Conscience?' Olivia reared in her chair, her eyes flashing. 'Do not dare to question my conscience. It is clear on all points. My sister's child was stillborn and that I heard from her own lips.'

'She lied! God alone knows why she lied, but she did! Look at me! Look into my face! See the colour of my hair! Can you still deny me?'

Fractionally Olivia's gaze shifted, swift enough to have been no more than a glaze of light across her small-framed spectacles, but even when Lucy would have cried out that Olivia knew it was true and must speak it, there blazed such a look of hatred at her that instinctively she sprang up from the footstool and drew away. Olivia was also on her feet, quivering with the outrage that possessed her.

'You are no Attwood! No child of my sister and her husband! You are a cheat! A trickster! Go back to wherever you have come from! Never let me set eyes on you again!'

She stalked from the room, the lappets of her cap fluttering, the ramrod stiffness of her back daring any attempt to call her back. She left the doors open behind her.

Lucy did not move. She seemed to have been numbed

completely by the blow that had been dealt her. Later the pain would come, but not yet. Later there would be tears, but at the present time her eyes were as dilated and dry as if they would never cry again. A circular looking-glass on the wall reflected her where she stood, with the open way to the balcony behind her, and as though observing a stranger, she saw that her visage was waxen. But the creature who had called herself Lucy Attwood was a stranger, a false myth upon whom Stefano had placed a name of real value, giving some surface substance to one who had been nothing. And was still nothing. One without an identity.

A faintness overcame her. She passed her fingers across her eyes, but the dizziness did not leave her, and she felt suffocated. Blindly she turned into the soft draught of the night air, going out into the darkness, and was vaguely aware that somewhere to the left of her some light streamed out from another room. She stumbled against the stone parapet of the balcony and clutched at it, knowing she was going to faint and there was no stopping it. She swayed and saw the black lawns and starlit lake swing up at her, making her realize that she was leaning across the parapet in danger of tipping over it, but there was no strength in her limbs to save her.

Suddenly she was grabbed and jerked away by powerful hands. 'No need to end it all yet,' said Josh's voice.

Instantly she knew resentment, not because she sought death, but because the oblivion that was on the brink of overcoming her promised a welcome respite from the tearing anguish that consumed her.

He shook her, making him hear her out of the abyss into which she was sinking. 'I'm reluctant to admit it, but I would miss you if you weren't here.'

It was as if he stabbed life back into her with his taunting. She gasped, struggled, and the exertion swept her into total blackness.

He carried her back into the room and laid her carefully on the silk-upholstered sofa, arranging cushions behind her head. Briefly but thoughtfully he looked at the portrait of Lionel and then back at her. Then he delayed no longer in summoning assistance.

She recovered consciousness to the acrid aroma of a vinaigrette which was being wafted under her nose by Donna, with Anna Edenfield hovering by the sofa on which she was lying. There was no one else present.

'No, don't sit up,' Donna advised, adjusting the cushions behind her. 'You've been in a swoon for quite a little while.'

'We were considering whether we should send for a physician,' Anna said, her face still showing her concern, and she offered a glass of water. 'Take a sip.'

Lucy obliged and then rested her head back on the cushions again, closing her eyes. And it all came back to her: the whole dreadful scene with Olivia Radcliffe and then Josh's voice coming out of the darkness at her. Where had he come from? What was it he had said? Unable to sort out the confusion of her thoughts, she put her hands to her face and began to moan.

She could not stop. The girls fussed over her, but she only rocked to and fro, and her moaning would not cease. Donna went to fetch Kate, who came from the ballroom floor, appearing ethereal in her cream and gold gown, as Lucy glimpsed her through the visor of her lashes, before covering her eyes again. She heard the soft, low-timbred voice of Daniel's wife giving instructions, and the pop and slip of long evening gloves being unbuttoned and removed.

'Send a servant for a light blanket and another for a pot of Indian tea. Then both of you go back to the dancing and leave Mrs di Castelloni to me.'

'What's the matter with her?'

The matter, Kate thought, was that the young woman on the sofa seemed to be suffering from extreme shock, which was not the usual result of a faint caused by tight stays and too much exertion. 'She has been in a deep faint. You should have called me before.'

'I'm sure that dreadful Mrs Radcliffe upset her. I was dancing a *Schottische* with Tim when Mr Barton came hurrying for assistance, saying he had found her in a faint. Tim said that she and Mrs Radcliffe were going to talk about the portrait and some of the family history up here, so whatever could have happened?'

'Where is Mrs Radcliffe now?'

'She went straight home.'

Kate refrained from saying it was the best place for her, and shooed the girls off to do her bidding. She shook some lavender water from a phial in her pearl-embroidered reticule onto a clean handkerchief and applied it to Lucy's brow. She appeared calmer than she felt. There was a question that had to be put to young matrons at such times in order to know if professional care was needed, and she did not know how to voice the query in dread of what she might be told. But it had to be done.

'Are you in the family way, Mrs di Castelloni?'

Lucy raised her face with a look of such astonishment that the answer was given before it was put into words. 'No. Indeed not. Quite, quite the reverse. I quarrelled with Mrs Radcliffe.' She rolled her head away and moaned again.

Kate went to answer a tap on the door, trembling herself at the release of tension, after the denial of what she had feared. She knew Richard to be a young man of honour, but with a widow certain barriers were already down, and the Warwyck men were hot-headed and extremely sensual by nature. She took the blanket from the servant on the threshold, and no sooner had she spread it over Lucy than the tea was brought. She poured the tea hot and weak and well sugared, which she managed to persuade Lucy to drink. It had the desired effect, and after giving her a second cup, Kate sat on the edge of the sofa, facing her.

'It's not difficult to quarrel with Olivia Radcliffe,' she said. 'Since she has no time for the Warwycks I never come in contact with her, but I know those who do, and with the passing of years she has become quite bitter and sharp-tongued. Even Daniel felt some pity for her husband, because when his health began to fail she gained the upper hand and never ceased to upbraid him. Yet she took up cudgels on his behalf long after he – poor man – had laid them down, and continues the feud with Daniel whenever an opportunity presents itself.'

Lucy could tell that Kate was talking simply to bring her out of her distress and onto a more even keel, but there was nothing she or anyone else could do to lighten the blow that Olivia had dealt her.

'It was very kind of you to come and look after me,' she said with a sigh, 'but I should not keep you from the ball downstairs any longer. I'll rest for a little while and then go home.'

'I think you should stay the night. There must be thirty bedrooms at least in this rambling house. I'll tell Mr Attwood and make arrangements with his housekeeper. She will see to everything.'

Lucy raised herself on one elbow. 'I don't want to impose.'

'You would not do, I know.' Kate smoothed a fold in the blanket back into place. 'Mr Attwood would be the last one to want you to leave his house while still feeling unwell.' She moved to the door. 'I'll ask him to come and reassure you. Good night.'

As Kate went back along the corridor in the direction of the ballroom, she pressed her hand against the pain in her side, which was something that had troubled her periodically for years, ever since she had had a bad fall during a free-for-all when Daniel and his workmen had fought a bathing-machine proprietor and a gang of thugs for right of access to the beach. During latter months it had bothered her with increasing frequency, but she had kept it to herself as she had ever done, and she closed her eyes tightly and briefly in a vain effort to banish it again through strength of will, thinking that it always seemed worse when she was upset or strained, as she was now.

Although Kate had no proof that there was a blood-tie between Richard and Lucy di Castelloni, intuition told her that he must never become involved with the young widow. She could not tell her son what she suspected, and to try to argue or cajole the young out of an unsuitable love affair only cemented still further the bonds that should be broken, and Richard would be more stubborn than most. But she hoped with all her strength that somehow his present course of action could be deflected. Since the evening at the theatre she had listened and observed and totted up every tiny fact that had come her way, and although she knew what it would mean to Donna, she had not failed to pin her hopes on her observation that Timothy Attwood, for all his gentle attention to her daughter, was sexually drawn to Lucy as to a magnet. At the champagne supper party after the gala opening performance of *Mazeppa*, she had noticed in the tautness of her nerves, which had given a crystal sharpness to everything that happened, that Timothy's glance was forever settling upon the young widow, and although Richard gave him little opportunity, monopolizing her company, he had seized whatever chance there was of talking to her or handing her a glass or into a chair and out of it, even when Donna was at his side. Had she not had enough such glances herself in her time to know the unspoken thoughts behind them?

It was no surprise to her to find Richard pacing the floor at the foot of the stairs. He dashed forward as soon as he saw her. 'How is she? May I go up?'

His hand was already on the newel-post, but she restrained him, wanting to cry out that he must turn his heart from the young woman she believed Daniel to have fathered. 'No, you must let her rest. She'll be quite recovered by morning.'

To her relief he accepted that he must do what was best for the patient, and after she had informed Timothy of the arrangements made, and looked for Josh Barton, of whom there was no sign, she went to rejoin the friends she had been sitting with. Some little distance from her, Daniel was in fine form, thoroughly enjoying the company of those gathered around him. She looked across at Donna, radiant as she danced with Timothy, and almost wept that she should wish that he would jilt her beloved daughter and wed another.

Lucy lay looking at the portrait of Lionel on the wall, and when the door opened she did not turn her head at once, thinking it was the housekeeper returning to tell her that a room had been made ready. As the sofa faced the fireplace, she did not see it was Daniel until he came round and stood looking down at her.

'We're just leaving,' he said, smiling, 'and I haven't had a chance to speak to my ally yet this evening. How do you feel now?'

She sighed. 'Foolish for having caused a fuss.'

'Think no more about it.' He took hold of a chair by its back and swung it forward to sit by her, looking thoroughly pleased with himself. 'I've something to disclose to you that will make your eyes sparkle and bring the colour back into your cheeks.' To give emphasis to what he had to tell, he lapsed into prize-ring phrases. 'Tomorrow the first round of the bout will be ours. Josh Barton will be dealt a facer in the morning that will stretch him the length of the ring.' He made a pugilist's fist with his powerful hand and grinned widely as he struck a blow through the air in illustration. 'I've not been idle since my return, and my lawyers inform me that I can baulk the entrance of a railway line into Easthampton on all sides, right out as far as Denwin Corner, and a terminus two miles away from a passenger's destination is not much of a facility, is it? To show the Railway Company finally what I think of 'em, I'm having foundations dug on the site that Richard has been angling for on their behalf, thinking to win me over. Work starts in the morning on a new theatre to replace the one that was burnt down a few years ago. It will be bigger and better than the one on the pier, which will continue to have a summer season. As there is no other site suitable for a terminus in Easthampton, that will put an end to the matter, and if that isn't a serious deterrent to Josh Barton's plans, I don't know what is.'

He gave a bellow of laughter as he slapped his thigh triumphantly, and she sat up, congratulating him. Neither heard Timothy come into the room, and he looked taken aback at such jollity when Lucy had been left to rest and recover. 'I don't want to hasten your departure from my home, sir,' he said, 'but Mrs Warwyck is in your carriage and has been waiting there for several minutes.'

'Yes, I'm afraid I stayed longer than I should have done with the invalid. Good night, my dear.'

Timothy looked over his shoulder at her as he turned to follow Daniel out. 'I'll return shortly.'

She twisted from the waist to rest her arm on the back of the sofa, gazing seriously at him over it within the lamplit aura of her hair. His dazzled glance returned again to her before he disappeared. Olivia had failed her, but that did not mean that her roots were not buried deep in Attwood soil, and she would not let that claim be cut from her. Daniel had acted decisively in turning down the Railway Company once and for all. It was her turn now to act as positively.

When Timothy had seen his last departing guests into their carriages he looked at the clock in the entrance hall and with disappointment realized that Lucy would have been asleep for an hour or more in the room that had been made ready for her. Thrusting his hands into his pockets, he took a last look into the ballroom where the musicians were packing up their instruments, and then he ambled tiredly towards the staircase.

'Was it a successful ball?'

He lifted his head sharply and a smile broke across his face. 'Lucy!' He had forgotten in his pleasure at seeing her sitting on the top stair that he had never before addressed her by her Christian name, but he always thought of her as Lucy and it seemed perfectly natural to use it now. 'Yes, I suppose it was for those who came,' he said, putting his hand on the banister rail and beginning to ascend the stairs towards her, 'but not for me.'

Her eyebrows lifted. 'Why?'

'I did not have one dance with you.'

'But from what I could see from the supper room, it seemed as if the prettiest girls in the county were here to partner you.'

He dared to put what he was feeling into words. 'I would have exchanged them all to have held you once in my arms.'

She accepted what he had said with not so much as a blink of her lashes, knowing she had him in the palm of her hand, and at the same time experiencing such a deepening of her original liking for him that she felt singularly calm and at peace. He swung himself down onto the stair beside her.

'Have you quite recovered from your faint?' he asked.

She nodded. 'I should go home.'

'No!' Then more quietly: 'It's pointless at this late hour when the housekeeper has made all the arrangements for you.'

'Perhaps it is. In any case, I want to talk to you. To ask you something.'

'Anything.'

She turned her face to his. 'Don't sell that land to the Railway Company.'

Somehow he had half expected that was what she was going to say, and he was not totally unprepared. He looked at her, pressed his lips together while he considered how to answer her, and looked at her again with some sadness.

'You think I'm a monster, I know; quite lacking in aesthetic values, and a boor beyond par for slicing up the estate, but it's a question of money. I simply cannot afford to run the place. It was left to me without the necessary for its upkeep, and therefore it has to go.' He shrugged unhappily. 'It's as simple as that.'

All her bones whitened in her face and her lips felt dry. Not once had she suspected that a very real financial burden lay upon him. 'I thought you had no such problems. I have heard talk of a town house, an estate in Norfolk and a country seat in Bedfordshire.'

'That's all true, but only Beacon Manor, the Bedfordshire place, is mine. My father died years ago, and my mother owns both the London house and the Norfolk home where she resides permanently. Until such time as I inherit from her, I must manage with one country residence and the use of a London *pied-à-terre*, which will become mine eventually.'

She dipped her head, fighting against despair. Railway or not, the Grange would have to be disposed of anyway. Unless ... 'Why not sell your Bedfordshire property instead?' she questioned eagerly, alight with hope again. 'I cannot believe it can compete with the Grange for country views and it lacks the benefit of the salubrious sea breezes!'

He looked shocked and was thoroughly disconcerted. 'I can't do that. Beacon Manor was bequeathed to me by my mother's parents and has belonged to that side of the family for two hundred years.'

'Is that longer than the Grange has been owned by an Attwood? I think not! I've been told that an Attwood laid the foundation stone in the year following the Armada! Is it not true that Queen Elizabeth granted land and bounty in recognition of service rendered by him as captain of one of her ships?'

He sprang up, feeling trapped, and took a step or two along the landing, hammering a fist down upon the balustrade. 'Yes, but nobody I know personally ever lived in this house. My uncle never did, and in any case he belonged to a distant branch of the Attwoods and only left me the place because I happened to be the last male in line.' He moved restlessly, much troubled, his face averted from where she had drifted with a rustle of her skirt to stand a few feet from him. 'The Grange is still strange to me, not a home. Not like Beacon Manor. I know every inch of it. I practically grew up there. I learned to shoot and ride and hunt from there. It means far more to me than the Grange or anything else.'

Silently she came within touching distance. 'More than me?' she asked, scarcely above a whisper.

His head was slow in turning, but when it did his eyes were full of love, as if he could no longer hold back all that had been dawning in him. 'No, nothing more than you,' he said in the same soft tones.

She had the sensation of being reborn and reawakened, all shadows banished from her life by that loving murmur. He put an arm about her and no shadow of Domenico came between them as he cupped his hand against the side of her face with trembling tenderness and lowered his mouth to hers. Sensitively, almost as if somehow, with the special perception of lovers, he understood how brittle the moment was for her, how fragile the barrier between response and panic, he let his lips caress and soothe, reassure and love, and when he knew he had won her and there would be no bucking away, he gave vent to his passion, felt her lips part and her arms clasp themselves rapturously about his neck.

When the pressure of their embrace lessened they stayed within the loop of each other's arms, he as full of wonder as she that such should have happened to them without warning and as neither had imagined it could. Both were beyond further talk, smiling at each other, breathless and more than a little dazed. She had come far in those jewelled seconds, but she could risk no more yet.

'Good night,' she whispered, drawing away from him.

In the room where she was to sleep, she went to the window and looked out at the grounds. The estate was saved. She had no doubt at all about the decision that Timothy would make, but the miracle was that her struggle to save her father's home had brought her love. Never had she known such joy.

By the time she returned to Sea Cottage the following afternoon, Josh had already departed to confer with the Railway Company over Daniel's new move. His absence added to her happiness.

13

Meg stitched the final blue glass button on her wedding dress, bit the thread between her strong teeth and smoothed the muslin bodice flat. She had never seen prettier buttons. They were Venetian and given to her by the widow. Mrs di Castelloni had pointed out one of the small paintings in her sitting-room, which depicted a scene of the Grand Canal with strange-shaped boats on the water. Meg thought Venice a fine place for her bridal buttons to have come from, and whenever she dusted upstairs she stole another look at the painting. Her dress was the same dark blue as the Canal, trimmed with some hand-made white lace that she had bought once from a Romany, and with a new bonnet wreathed in roses from the garden, she thought she would knock everybody's eyes out when she went to the altar in nearby St Mary's Church the day after tomorrow.

A sigh escaped her as she put the needle back in its flannel case. It was a poor state of affairs when making friends envious of one's wedding rig-out was the highlight of the day, not that some of them wouldn't have given their eye-teeth to have got hold of Bob. She should think herself lucky, but it was hard when the heart yearned for another, a cloud ever at the back of the mind to dim the brightest of sunny mornings. Love was a curse and a nuisance, and how much wiser were those who partnered up without giving much thought to it.

Carefully she gathered up the surplus glass buttons,

thinking she would keep them with the silver buttons in her sovereign box, and with the wedding dress over her arm to be hung away she went into the bedroom that she still shared with Emmie. She pulled open a drawer, lifted the lid of the box and made a space among the small treasures it contained for the buttons. Then she frowned and began to scrabble about in the box with her fingers, craning her neck over it. The five sovereigns were there, and she had checked them when Ben had returned the box to her several days after he had taken possession of her room, but in snatching it from him she had forgotten, in her anxiety, two of the other items it had contained. The silver buttons weren't there!

Furiously she slammed the door shut and stalked out of her room to his bedroom, knowing she would have no compunction in turning everything he owned out of drawers and cupboards until she found the buttons he had annexed. But his door was locked. She fumed, setting her arms akimbo, knowing he would not be back until late from the Brighton races, one of several racecourses that he frequented within a fairly wide radius. Perhaps she could get in the window.

Outside the house, she cupped her hands against the glass and peered into his room. The window was fastened, but she knew how to get it open, having climbed back into the house that way more than once. Getting her fingertips on the edge of the frame she began to shake it, and in a matter of minutes the fastening slipped and she was able to pull the window open.

She wrinkled her nose in distaste as she dropped into the room. It reeked of violet-scented macassar oil and stale tobacco and male sweat. She was glad she was getting away. It would have taken a bucket of disinfectant to rid the room of that man's odour. Opening the cupboard door, she began the task of searching through his clothes. She failed to find the buttons, and the last place left to her was a locked drawer in the top of the chest, but that was no barrier, because she knew the key of the commode had the same lock, and within seconds she had the drawer open. She was surprised at the contents. No silver buttons or valuables of any kind, but neat stacks of letters and papers, with a cord around some, segregating them from the rest; among these was a packet of letters addressed to the same lady at an address in London, all in the same masculine hand. Among a few lying loose, a line on one of them leapt out at her: *I implore you to keep silent and allow me more time to pay.* Her gaze fell upon another note which was also from a debtor in dire distress. Unable to stop herself, she flicked through a wad of papers and saw they were memoranda of debt from various people, addressed to Ben and signed in each case by the borrower.

Suddenly she felt nervous, realizing she had stumbled on a side of his business that he certainly would not want her or anyone else to know about. With a care she had not shown before, she darted her hands in and out of the drawers, trying to ensure that everything was as it had been before, and hung up again the clothes she had let fall in the cupboard. But once outside the house again, with the window pushed back into place, she lost her nervousness, and indignation over her missing property surged back again. She set off in the direction of the beach, determined to present her grievance to her mother without delay.

Everywhere the resort was busy. The sun had been out earlier, encouraging a display of soft muslins, flounced lawn and thin silks among the visitors, who had taken up all available accommodation in the town since mid-May, some for the whole season. There was extra traffic in the streets — elegant barouches, landaus and broughams, and everywhere there were wagonettes and pony-carts that conveyed well-dressed children on outings of their own in the charge of governess or nurse. Meg had to wait at the kerb to cross over to the promenade, held up by a stream of dog-carts on the way to some sporting expedition, and she looked askance at the weather, thinking that those setting off in such high spirits would have a storm to face before they returned again. She had an eye, nose and ear for weather. It was more than mere practice from residing close to the sea and making a living by her boat. She could literally hear when a breeze was on the point of gathering new strength unto itself, and she could read every shade and variation in the sky. By the time the tide was full those rising waves, filling her nostrils with salt, would have spray whipping across white-tops, but for the moment the shawls and wraps that had appeared were enough to keep their wearers protected from the seemingly innocent breeze that was increasing with every passing minute. As she went down the slipway to reach the bathing-machines, those in use drawn up in an irregular line, most hub-deep in the rolling water, she saw another warning sign in the flapping canvas of the Punch and Judy show, which had a laughing crowd around it, some of the ladies holding onto the brims of their leghorns, the ribbons on the children's hats fluttering and dancing.

In the water, Lucy was having her sixth swimming lesson, which Emmie had declared should be her last, seeing that she had mastered the strokes, could progress some distance without going under, and was able to float on her back indefinitely.

'Good. That's the way,' Emmie intoned monotonously as she had done with so many pupils in her time, while her eyes darted in all directions, keeping a watch on the foolish and the frivolous females bobbing in the waves around her; any one of them was likely to get out of depth and give way to hysteria before one could say Jack Robinson. She frowned, seeing Meg come down to the water's edge, her straight expression showing that something was amiss. Leaving Lucy to her swimming, the woman waded shore-wards, water pouring from the long skirt of the dark blue serge dress she wore – the traditional outfit of the 'dipper' together with her straw boater, much yellowed by salt and sun, which bore her name in bold letters on a ribbon around the crown.

'Well? What is it?' she asked as soon as she and her daughter were within earshot.

'My silver buttons!' Meg expostulated. 'They're missing! Gone! There's only one person who'd have taken them –'

'Ben did.' Emmie calmly set her water-shrivelled hands on her hips. 'But I give 'em to 'im to sell. 'Ee got five bob each for 'em. I put the money in the caddy on the dresser and clean forgot to tell you.'

Meg was aghast, not knowing whether to be outraged more by the audacity of her mother conniving with Ben to

214

sell her property or by the meagre amount he had obtained for them. 'Ten bob! The cheat! They were worth far more than that! Ten quid more likely, and I bet that's what he got!' Her voice cracked. 'How could you have let him have them without asking me?'

Emmie was undisturbed. 'I did it for the best.'

Meg thrust her face forward. ''Ee's a real cur, that fellow! I know! You must get rid of 'im. 'Ee's got to go!'

'Well, 'ee ain't going.' Emmie jerked her chin stubbornly. 'I've told you that before. As far as I'm concerned, 'ee can stay as long as 'ee wants.' A flicker of satisfaction showed in her eyes. 'As a matter of fact, I quite likes 'aving a man of my choosing about the 'ouse again.'

Meg groaned and flounced back to the promenade, throwing up her hands in frustration. Emmie's mouth compressed into a little smile before she returned to see if Lucy was ready to be helped back up the steps into the bathing-machine.

When Lucy had dried and dressed herself, pulling in her stays on her own as she always did – although this was a service by Emmie included when payment was made at the Warwyck ticket office situated nearby – she put a comb to her hair in front of the circular mirror on the wall and tamed some damp tendrils into place. It had been difficult to keep her balance, for the horse had been hitched up to draw the machine back out of the water onto the dry sands, but now it had come to a standstill and the rattle of chains told her the horse had been unhitched and led away. She took her tapestry bag from the peg where it had been swinging to and fro with the movement of the creaking wheels, and slipped it onto her arm, popping her comb in beside the musical score of the new melodrama that was to follow *Mazeppa* in the Asquith Company's repertoire. Shooting back the bolt of the door, she paused uncertainly, seeing that in the few minutes that she had delayed, the tide had already crept under the steps, making it difficult to get down onto the sands without getting her shoes wet.

From the direction of the promenade, a voice hailed her. 'Don't move! I'll help you.' It was Timothy bounding down the distant slipway, the flare of his sack coat swinging out to reveal its silken lining, his hair shining bright as a golden sovereign. He did not slow his pace until he came to a halt at the steps, grinning at her breathlessly.

'Ready? Here we go, then!' He set a foot against the lowest step to balance himself, set his strong young hands on her waist and half-lifted, half-swung her onto the dry sands. Instinctively she caught at him to keep·her balance as she landed, and instantly his arms were about her. 'My dearest, dearest Lucy. I have something wonderful to tell you.'

'What is it?' She was tip-toe with anticipation.

'Not here.' He had looked about and seen they were being observed. 'Let's get away from all these people somewhere along the sands.'

They began to walk eastwards, he hurrying her along by the hand so that she was almost running, half-pressed against him, both of them laughing as she implored to be told and he shook his head again and again, enjoying the postponement of the joy he knew would be hers. Not until they had come under the overhanging cliffs, past the barnacled wreck of a ship, and with several clusters of rocks to form layered screens and hide the distant resort in the curve of the bay, did he stop at last and face her, taking her other hand into his, capturing all her fingers.

'Now you shall hear what I have to say.' He was still smiling, but seriousness had taken over his expression, awing her a little as she waited. 'I have turned down the Railway Company. I've written to Josh Barton that he can have neither the land nor the extra site for a terminus, which was to stand against Mr Warwyck's ultimate refusal.' He took a deep breath. 'I'm selling Beacon Manor. Attwood Grange and its estate shall remain inviolate.'

Her lips parted, but her voice seemed to have deserted her, although her whole face reflected her emotions. Her throat revived huskily. 'I do love you.'

It was what he had hoped to hear her say, but had expected to speak first. He was deeply moved. 'And I love you, Lucy. With all my heart. I beg you to marry me. The Grange could never become a home for me without you. Tell me that you'll be my wife.'

By marrying a theatre pianist and selling his Bedfordshire

home, he knew he had put himself beyond par with his mother and his family, but he did not care a toss. Somehow he knew he would have lost Lucy with the going of the Grange and its land, and he gloried in the sacrifice that he had made for her, knowing he could have offered no greater proof of his devotion. But she was hesitating, not giving him the simple affirmative answer he had thought to hear, and a terrible anxiety overcame him.

'I'll make you happy, I swear it. There's nothing that I would not do for you.'

She was shaking her head at his fears, and she answered him carefully. 'There is something I must tell you first of my origins, something of great importance, which I disclosed to Olivia Radcliffe on the evening of the ball. I have to warn you that she rejected my story as being totally untrue.'

'So that is why you were overcome. It only confirms my certainty that what you will tell me is the truth in its entirety.' He nodded towards the banked shingle in a hollow under the cliff. 'Let's sit down over there. I want to hear all you have to say. We have all the time in the world.'

She sat down where she could lean her back against the cliff, and he seated himself beside her on the shingle, but slightly lower so that he could look into her face. He supposed he was about to hear some tale of illegitimacy, but not even that social stigma could set up a barrier against his love for her.

'My father,' she began, with her head lifted in pride, 'was Lionel Attwood.' It did not occur to her as she talked that in no way had her belief in herself as an Attwood been shaken after the initial shock of Olivia's rejection. Vaguely she associated some resurge of spirit with Josh Barton in the darkness, but she had not seen him since, for he had not yet returned to Sea Cottage since bearing Daniel's letter of final dismissal of the offer for the terminus site to the board of the Railway Company.

In their sheltered cove they were out of the rising wind and too absorbed in the telling and the listening, the gentle questions and the answers, to notice that clouds had gathered low, turning the encroaching waves to a sombre olive green. Neither did they realize that the tide was coming in fast.

'Now your name shall be Attwood again,' he said, moving up on the shingle to enfold her in his arms. She clung to him, kissing him back, loving him for himself, for his banishment of the darkness of Domenico, which he had achieved almost without her realizing it, and most of all for his faith and belief in her that was to make her one with the past, a whole person in her own right.

The first heavy spots of rain disturbed them, and they scrambled to their feet, scattering the pebbles, and kissed and laughed and hugged each other again, amused that the weather should turn against them, but jubilant in the knowledge that nothing could affect their happiness.

'We had better make a run for it,' he said, catching her about the waist to hurry her along with him. The drops were pitting the sand, and the spume flew from breaking waves thundering in, spreading out with a suddenly alarming swiftness. Perhaps she sensed the danger before he did, that the strip of sand had become perilously narrow and they must use all haste to escape getting cut off by the tide. Too late she remembered the warning given to her at the hotel when she had first arrived at Easthampton, that to go beyond the wreck when the tide was coming in was to risk getting trapped.

'My God!' He jerked her to a halt. They had come round the first great wall of rock, and ahead of them the sea had washed in to the base of the cliffs. Swiftly he looked upwards, but such was the overhang that although the cliffs were no more than fifteen feet high, and considerably less in places where the land began its descent to the bay, an obstacle was presented that would be impossible to climb without ropes slung down from above. They could neither go back to the hollow where no one could see them, nor get as far as Easthampton without being swept up in waves that would defeat the strongest swimmer. He gave her a grin that hid his true misgivings. 'I'm afraid you'll have to get your feet wet after all. My aid at the bathing-machine steps was all in vain. We must reach the wreck and attract rescue from there.'

She grinned back at him, trying not to show she was desperately afraid. 'Let's go then.'

At first the water was comparatively shallow, but as they progressed, she hampered considerably by her full skirts, it soon became thigh-deep. Twice she almost fell, caught by the force of a rolling wave, but he held on to her with all his strength, his face contorted against the wind and rain and spray. Both of them were as drenched as if they had swum the short distance they had traversed, his hair glued to his head and fronded about his face, hers protected to some extent by her bonnet, though the straw flopped limply now and the ribbons had turned to soggy strips that whipped against her throat. She made to throw her tapestry bag away, not wanting to be burdened with it, but when she told him it only contained a copy of the musical score for the new play that could easily be replaced, he reached out and grabbed it before it sank.

'We'll keep it. It could help to get us rescued.'

How it could help she did not know, and it was too much effort to ask, for she needed all her breath and energy to plunge on, step by step. She had lost both shoes, and had to dig her toes into the sand to propel herself forward, always helped by his arm about her.

'Not much further now,' he encouraged, thinking to himself that the dark shape of the wreck through the rain looked hardly any nearer than it did when they had first begun to wade towards it. They ploughed on, becoming buoyant at times when a wave carried them on its swell, and he struggled to regain lost ground, fearful they might find themselves dashed by a breaking wave against the cliff-face where the water was churning back on itself.

She shut her eyes, partly to protect them from the stinging spume, but also because she could not bear to observe the slow progress they were making. She seemed adrift in an endless nightmare of roaring sea and howling wind, chilled through as though the seawater had entered her veins, and all that was real to her was the closeness and unfailing courage of the man holding her to him. To her shame her physical strength was ebbing, every step being a buffeting against the force of the tide, and had she been alone she could not have withstood its onslaught. His voice came to her through the crash of waves meeting the cliffs.

'We're there, my love. We've reached the wreck.'

She opened her eyes, blinking against the sting of salt, and saw the barnacled hulk soaring above them. It lay jammed into the rocks onto which it had been driven during the storm that had wrecked it, and it was these that offered a foothold to get aboard. Afraid that she would be torn from him if he climbed up first to pull her out of the water, he showed her where to get a grip and then heaved her up on to a rock, helped for the first time by the depth of water. The surface was slippery with seaweed rising and falling like green hair as the tops of the waves ran over it, but she managed to crawl onto the neighbouring rock, which was higher, only aware that she was weeping by the strange warmth brimming from her eyes, that chilled before it reached her cheeks. Behind her Timothy had climbed out of the water, tearing the knee of one trouser leg in the process, his feet bare, shoes and socks lost long since, and had it not been for his pallor and the strain across his eyes, his triumphant expression might have led her to believe that he was convinced that all danger was as good as past. But she knew, as he most surely did, that at full tide the wreck was always covered.

'We'll get aboard, and then I'll see what can be done to attract attention,' he said, going ahead of her to find the best way to clamber onto the wreck. The bow had smashed into the rocks, but was several feet higher than the stern, as if it had risen up in its death throes, and he could see that somehow he must get Lucy for'ard to ensure the longest time before the sea swallowed the hulk as it did twice daily, gradually pounding it to pieces. Gaping holes in the deck bore witness to timbers torn away for driftwood, but a place by a splintered stump, which was all that remained of a mast, would give her some safety and something to grip when the waves grew higher.

'Don't be afraid,' he said, coming back to fetch her. 'I'll be able to see Easthampton from the remains of the bow, and that means people there will be able to see me. A boat will put out and take us to safety in no time at all.'

'How will you attract attention?' she asked, holding onto his coat as she followed him, the wet rock surface cutting into her bare feet.

'With the aid of your music,' he replied confidently, giving the tapestry bag a swing. 'You'll see.'

She was mystified, but did not doubt him, touched to the heart by this show of optimism designed to give her hope and encouragement. When they reached the point where they were to climb over the bulwarks onto the slanting deck, she pressed her face into his shoulder. He thought fear had overcome her.

'You'll not fall into the sea, I promise you that.'

She shook her head, lifting her face to his, heedless of lashing rain and spray. 'It's just that I don't know how to tell you how much I love you this day.'

His chilled knuckles stroked her cheek in the tenderest of caresses, and he rested his brow against hers. 'We'll have the rest of our lives in which to talk about it. Years and years and years.'

It was not easy getting on board, owing to the angle of the deck, but she managed it with his help and took her place by the mast-stump, sitting crouched by it. She found being on the wreck no less alarming than wading through the sea, for it shuddered continuously, and through the gaping holes in the deck she could see the trapped water churning furiously. She caught her breath in terror for Timothy's safety as he began to clamber up to the bow, and she cried out when a piece of plank he used for a foothold loosened and almost cast him down, but he grabbed at a rail and saved himself.

She watched him settle himself against a jammed timber, and then he took the musical score from the tapestry bag which he jettisoned, and it slid soddenly down the slope to vanish through a hole in the deck. With his gaze set in the direction of Easthampton, knowing that it was a slim chance that they would ever be seen in the greyness of the rain, he began the painstaking task of taking the score apart, peeling off the damp sheets and throwing each one separately as high into the wind as he could manage. Some rose on the current of air, dipping and whirling like seagulls on the wing, but others fell flatly to stick to the deck or toss into the water to be swamped by the rising waves, which had begun to boom against the sides of the wreck and crash over the stern. When all the sheets were gone, he took off his coat and held it above his head at arm's length where it flew and whipped like a banner, their last hope of being seen. All around them the white-capped sea was mounting for full tide. Once he thought he saw a boat in the distance, but when he rubbed a hand across his salt-swollen eyes, there was nothing to be seen except the endless waves rising and falling. When his arm was aching as if all the muscles had become fixed, he shifted the coat to his other hand, glancing towards Lucy to shout an endearment, to take some of the wide-eyed tenseness from her face that was turned constantly towards him.

She could not catch what he said in the noise of the sea, but she saw his expression change to one of dismayed disbelief as he looked beyond her. Throwing a glance over her shoulder, she saw a wave riding higher than the rest and advancing with the speed of a charger.

'Lucy!' His full-throated warning thundered at her, and he was starting to slide down to reach her and try to pull her clear. She scrambled towards him, heard the deafening roar of the breaking wave, felt the wreck heave and shudder under the onslaught, and then cold, white foam enveloped her. Through it she saw him go. Whether his heel slid on a sheet of music she was never to know, but as she was hurled aside by the force of the water, she saw him in a tangle of arms and legs borne past her over the side of the hulk. When the water drained, she was alone, clinging to the bulwarks, with no sign of him in the seething backwash.

When Bob Cooper and two other fishermen came rowing out of the rain to bring their tossing boat alongside, she did not see them, and when she did, her rescue only confirmed her loss.

14

She wore no black for Timothy. A resolution once made was not broken. At the memorial service in Easthampton's parish church of St Mary, others looked askance at her dress, which to her was the blue of the sky above the Grange when she had first met him. After the service she went alone down to a deserted part of the shore and threw a bunch of wild flowers onto the water.

They had found him when the tide ebbed, a few hours after her rescue, lying on the shingle not far from where they had sat together. Nobody had seen his signalling, but it was there that Meg had sent Bob and his fellow fishermen to search for them after Emmie, returning home to take a rest until full tide was over and wanting to keep any further argument about the silver buttons at bay, had told with her usual salacious appetite for gossip of the lady lodger making off towards the wreck with the young nob from the Grange. Meg had run all the way to the pier, and when she was told that Lucy had not yet appeared for rehearsal, she had sought out Bob and sent him off with his companions in the boat.

Timothy had not been laid to rest locally, but had been taken far away to Norfolk, to be placed in a family tomb, the last male Attwood in line. Donna, who had gone into deepest mourning, had travelled the long distance with Richard to be there.

'We were to be married,' Donna said. Her face was

pinched and pale behind her black veil when she came to call on Lucy as she lay in bed recovering from the ordeal suffered the previous day. 'Tim was going to speak to my father at the first opportunity after the ball, which was given for the sole purpose of ensuring goodwill. He is the only man I've ever loved or shall ever love. I lost him because he took it into his head to walk with you along the sands.' She held up a black-gloved hand quickly as if she expected Lucy to make some excuse. 'I'm not blaming you. I'll never blame you. I ask only that you make amends by ensuring that my brother never suffers by losing the love of his life through denial as I'm suffering this day through the snatching away by death.'

Lucy stared at her, a silent scream running through her head that such a demand should be made of her at such a time. It overlaid all else that had been said. She rolled over with a despairing cry and buried her face in the pillow, and it was then that the tears she had not yet shed overcame her. When her terrible sobbing finally eased through exhaustion, Donna had long since gone from her bedside.

Later, when some few days had elapsed and she was calmer, she saw how Donna must have seen more in Timothy's courteous attentions than had been there, recalling mention of correspondence over their rescue of Toby, and how such an interpretation could have been put upon what he had said in her own hearing about the ball. Perhaps he had indulged flirtatiously, but to a serious-minded girl like Donna it would amount to a declaration. It seemed that she must again hold her tongue on the truth, for she had no right to destroy the dreams which were all that Donna had left of the man she had believed to have been hers.

She herself had her work at the theatre to occupy her mind and her time, for which she was exceedingly grateful, not knowing how she would have coped with her sorrow without it. At Easthampton House, Donna was refusing all invitations, was not at home to visitors, and was withdrawing more into herself as the days went by, wanting Toby as her only company. Daniel came to tell Lucy news of the Grange when its future became known to him.

'You had best sit down,' he advised with compassion,

understanding more of what it meant to her than she supposed. They were in her drawing-room at Sea Cottage. 'You're not going to like what I have to tell you any more than I did when I heard it.'

She obeyed, and sat quite straight and still, her hands in her pale muslin lap, while he strode about the room. Her likeness to Claudine was at times more than he could bear, and on this day the feline mould of her face seemed more marked in the sadness that lay behind it.

'The Grange is going up for sale,' he announced heavily. 'The late Mr Attwood's will, which would have been altered should he have married, leaves everything to his mother. She wants to dispose of the Sussex property as soon as possible. I hear that the Railway Company are aiming to get the whole estate for little more than they would have had to pay that poor, lamented young man for the land they wanted.'

She put a hand across her eyes and a red-gold gleam passed over the shining smoothness of her hair, making it a physical effort for him not to reach out and rest his palm upon it. 'All is lost, then,' she said chokingly. Timothy's last-minute change of mind had been to no avail when the new owner had no mind to anything except disposing as quickly as possible of the one place that was associated with her son's demise.

'It appears so.' He clasped his hands behind him, looking down at her, wanting to tell her of the stratagem he had in mind, but knowing it would be unfair and make the blow worse if he allowed her to cherish false hopes. He had already spoken to his lawyers and his bankers, but no loan was secured yet. 'I can't bring myself to visualize the district swarming with navvies while sitings are dug and the viaduct near Merrelton goes up.' He balled his fists. 'Or Josh Barton crowing over the two of us.'

Josh! She lifted her head sharply at the import of this additional bad news. He had still not been back to Easthampton since his departure upon receiving Daniel's dismissal of all hopes of the terminus site, although he had continued to pay Emmie by post for the retention of his apartments. She had become used to the quietness of the house with his prolonged absence and Meg married and gone from home. In her present state she did not know that she could face his taunts and triumph over her.

'What's the matter?' Daniel asked.

She sprang to her feet. 'I can't stay here if Josh Barton returns. I could not endure his presence as a neighbour again. It was bad enough before, but it would be a thousand times worse now.' She had taken a frantic pace or two towards Daniel and then she stopped, gesturing despairingly. 'But where could I find anywhere else at the height of the season? It was difficult to find somewhere suitable when I arrived in March, and it would be virtually impossible to find a single room untenanted now.'

A pause. 'I know a place.'

'You do?'

He gave a slow nod, seeming to have come to a momentous decision. 'You can rent some property of mine in Hoe Lane that has been standing unoccupied for want of the right tenant for a number of years. It's furnished throughout and high time it was lived in again. We'll not quarrel over the rent, which could be whatever you are charged for these apartments in this house, and would be paid quarterly.' By introducing a business note he was seeking to show that he had no ulterior motive and – perhaps for the first time in his life – he had none, wanting only to help her in any way that lay open to him.

She could not believe her good fortune. 'You don't mean – you can't mean Honeybridge House?'

'You know it, do you?'

'I've admired it every time I've passed it. I was once given a rose from the garden and kept it until it dropped its petals.'

'Well, then, in a day or two you may pick as many roses there as you wish. Honeybridge is yours to live in for as long as it suits you. I'll see that you get a key without delay.'

'I can't thank you enough.'

'No need to thank me at all. The pleasure is mine.'

She tilted her head as she regarded him seriously. 'You're a kind man, Mr Warwyck.'

He uttered a wry laugh, shaking his head. 'There's many

who wouldn't say that. I've made as many enemies as friends in my time. As I once mentioned, I've been a hard taskmaster, sparing no one even as I never spared myself.'

'Maybe I've come to know you better than most people.' She meant it. There was goodness in him, no matter what else.

Something close to pain showed in his eyes and he spoke gruffly. 'Pray God you have, my dear.' Again he began to prowl about the room. 'May I ask you a question? A very personal question?' He cut the air with the edge of his hand in reassurance. 'I intend you no offence.'

'What is your question?'

He came to a standstill, his nostrils flaring as he breathed deeply. 'My wife tells me that my son is in love with you. I'm not divulging a secret, because every woman seems to know when a man is in love with her. Am I not right?' He did not wait for confirmation. 'You once spoke of a close friendship with Richard. May I ask how close it has become? In other words, do you reciprocate his feelings?'

'No. This he is aware of, so I'm not divulging a secret either.' A catch took hold of her throat. 'I have loved someone else. Nobody could take his place.'

He was both relieved by what she had said and contrite that he had caused her distress. 'Forgive me. I've upset you. My concern is as much for you as it is for my son. He is young yet for knowing his own mind in matters of the heart, and might have led you to believe that he is more settled in his aims than his years allow.' It was the only excuse he felt would be acceptable to her, and he was treading carefully. It came to him that he had given similar advice years before to his own Kate when he had warned her against his brother, but then it had been because he, without being aware of it, had wanted her wholly for himself. In another way, all reasons set aside, was he being equally possessive this time? He hoped not, and his gaze searched her face. 'I would not have you hurt. Better my own life should go first.'

Her colour came and went. She could not interpret his attitude towards her. It was neither that of seducer nor amorato, although at their first meeting he had reacted to her as so many men did. 'I appreciate your concern.'

The corners of his well-cut mouth lifted in a serious smile, and she reflected it, suddenly feeling that they were in complete accord. He decided a hint of his plans would not go amiss. 'Josh Barton and the Railway Company haven't beaten us yet,' he said. 'We'll go down fighting.'

'You hearten me,' she declared warmly.

After seeing him out she went immediately to give notice to Emmie and found her drinking ale at the table with Ben, who immediately rose to his feet with an obsequious show of good manners that she would not have expected of him. 'Will you join us in a glass, madam?' he asked. He and Emmie had been reminiscing about the past, he probing more into her tale of the night she believed Daniel Warwyck had lost two silver buttons at Denwin Cottage. At the time Emmie fancied young Harry Warwyck, and had followed him after a gentry's boating party, only to discover that he was dogging the footsteps of his elder brother. She had sensed something was up and with that insatiable curiosity that was hers then as it was now had waited in the darkness to see what would happen. Like Harry, she had remained under the cover of trees and seen Claudine Attwood go into the cottage where Daniel, all unaware of being spied upon, had waited. Outside, Harry kept a steady vigil for an hour or more, and she, frightened by the terrible sternness of his face, had not dared to approach him or let him know she was there. How long Daniel and his light-o'-love had stayed that night in the cottage she did not know, for she had run home herself after Harry had departed.

It was a tale Emmie had kept to herself, not risking involvement in any trouble at the time, and her tongue had only loosened over the silver buttons, first to Meg, and then to Ben when he had offered to sell them. His present jovial mood had much to do with a hunch that rarely played him wrong, that somehow or other his crafty ability to cash in on the misfortunes of others might get a line onto the Warwycks one of these days. With the habit he had of repeating his words sometimes, he said again to Lucy: 'A glass? Just to wet the whistle?'

She declined, but Emmie insisted on plumping up cushions on the sofa for her to take a seat. When she had said that she would pay her rent until the end of the month although she expected to leave within a couple of days, Emmie was somewhat mollified, but she was less disappointed than she might have been at losing the widow's tenancy, because since she had become a theatre pianist it was no longer possible to boast that there was a real lady living at Sea Cottage. After she had left them, Emmie released her breath in a long, low whistle.

''Oneybridge, eh! Bet that'll put the cat among the pigeons.'

''Ow d'you mean?' Ben set down his tankard and wiped the foam from his upper lip with the back of his hand.

'Well, it ain't been rented since old Jem Pierce died. You remember 'im. It's going to cause talk with Daniel Warwyck setting up a woman piano-player in it.'

Ben gave a guffaw. 'You've a wicked tongue in your 'ead, Emm.' The reluctant admiration in his tone was somehow underlined by the thoughtful glint in his eye. 'I'd like to 'ave a gander at 'Oneybridge for old times sake. I remember going there once to a lively booze-up that weren't at Dan Warwyck's invitation.'

'I bet you do.' Her face looked morose. 'You and Charlie Brent 'ad to get out of town real quick afterwards, and my Joe did a bunk the next day.'

He paid her no attention, talking more to himself. 'Charlie and me 'ad a right profitable sideline going in the running in of French brandy by night, and Warwyck put an end to that with 'is nosing into matters that 'ee 'ad never concerned 'imself with before.' He drained his tankard and set it down on the table with a vicious whack. 'Yes, I ain't never settled that score with 'im.'

Daniel arrived home at Easthampton House with just enough time to change for dinner without haste. He liked routine, his meals at a set hour, and everything well-run and organized, which came from his years of pugilistic training and its regular time-table. Kate had it all down to a fine art, making sure he was never disturbed by petty domestic problems or harassed at times when he needed quietness in which to relax after a busy day. Above all, she was always

pleasing to his eye, his visual satisfaction as unchanged as
was the pleasure of the physical relationship, that still surpassed the occasional amours that meant nothing to him.
Their love was like a good wine maturing over the years,
and the young who imagined there was no reward in middle
age had much to learn. Kate had so much in her favour and,
what was more, now she was older she was much less
strong-willed and obstinate than she had been in the past.
Or was it that he had mellowed with the passing of time and
never dismissed out of hand any petition she made to him as
he had done in the early years of their marriage?

But he was not looking forward to telling her of the renting of Honeybridge. In his dressing-room, as he slipped his
waistcoat over his stiff-fronted shirt, he felt tense and ill-
tempered as a result of it, none of the customary balm of the
pre-dinner hour descending upon him; he even found that
he was arguing with himself over the right to let his own
property. Damnation! He was master in his own house,
wasn't he? Kate must accept his decision, and she would, he
was sure. But not without trouble. He sighed heavily,
reached for his evening coat and put it on, automatically stepping back to view his appearance in the cheval-glass. His
own reflection glowered back at him, but by the time he was
descending the curved staircase he had managed to compose
his expression to one of geniality.

Kate saw as soon as he entered the drawing-room that
something was wrong. In nearly a quarter century of marriage she had learned to read him like the proverbial book,
but she made no sign, for it had never been her way to fuss
and question, and in any case such a wife would have driven
Daniel out of his mind. She went instead to pour him the
glass of sherry-wine that he liked as an aperitif each evening, a habit developed since he had taken her on a first trip
to Paris many years ago.

'Where's Donna?' he asked, taking the glass from her.

'She is having a light supper on a tray in her room.'

His frown threatened. 'Why? Is she ill?'

'No, but she does not feel like coming down.'

His voice took on edge. 'I recall that it was the same
yesterday evening and the evening before. Last week she

dined with us only once out of seven and then after toying with her food retreated from the table before dinner was half over. She has spent every day since her return from the funeral in her room, refusing to see all callers, even Anna. It's time she began to pull herself together.'

Kate spread her graceful hands in sympathy for her daughter. 'It's early days yet, and she is deeply grieved by Timothy Attwood's death.'

'Weren't we all? But life must go on.'

'She was in love with him. I will remind you that they were to be married.' Kate's voice was suddenly choked. She had clung faintly to the hope, albeit to her dear daughter's cost, that Timothy would decide it was Lucy he would prefer to wed, which would have solved the terrible problem that hung like a dark cloud over her. Now, as far as she could see, there was no one to come between Richard and the young widow.

Daniel gave a derisive snort. 'Donna had hopes, I don't doubt, but he never once showed any inclination to speak to me.'

'He was going to after the ball.'

'Ha!' He was malevolently triumphant, easing his own uncomfortable sense of guilt over what he had to tell his wife later by venting his irritation against a familiar target. 'Donna was mistaken there. I gave him ample opportunity when I met him by chance the next day at the club.'

She was on the defensive. 'Naturally he would have expected to call formally here at your own home.'

His eyes narrowed. 'I invited him back to the house to view my new hunter. We had a drink together in this very room afterwards. You had gone with Donna to the dressmaker's or milliner's or some such establishment.' He flicked his fingers impatiently in his inability to recall their exact whereabouts. 'He could have asked me a dozen times over for her hand, but I noticed he avoided mentioning her, even when I thought to aid him by bringing her name into the conversation.'

She looked sad. 'He probably lost his nerve, the poor young man. You're not an easy person from whom to ask favours, you know.'

His glower returned. 'I never noticed it holding you back,' he snapped heatedly.

She remained silent, refraining from the retaliation that he would have welcomed, knowing that he was inviting a quarrel, and when he stalked to the bell-pull and jerked it she was sure it foreboded some ill-tempered whim. The butler appeared almost at once. Daniel lifted that stubborn Warwyck chin.

'Tell my daughter that her father expects her to join him for dinner in precisely two minutes.'

Kate bit her lip, but said nothing. The reply came as she had expected. His daughter regretted that she was indisposed. He did not dismiss the butler. 'Inform Miss Donna that she has exactly one minute left in which to make an appearance.'

As the butler went again, Kate made her appeal. 'Daniel! Leave her alone. Within a few days she will be herself again.'

'Within a few days she will have sunk into an apathy that will make an old woman of her before her time. There's all the difference in the world between grief bravely borne and wallowing in morbid sentimentality. She has seized upon young Attwood's drowning as an excuse to escape from God knows what. Ever since early childhood she has accepted setbacks without struggle, failure without battle. I will not have a recluse in my house!'

The butler returned. 'Miss Donna gave me no reply, sir. Dinner is served.'

The clock in the hall had begun to strike. As always, dinner was on time. Without a word Daniel went out into the hall, not to cross to the dining-room, but to take the stairs two at a time, not pausing until he reached his daughter's door.

'Donna! Come out this instant.'

The key turned against him in the lock. It was like a slap in the face, a flaunting defiance that made him long to smash the lock with his heel and drag her out bodily, but she was not a child, and for all her faults he would not expose her to such embarrassment before the servants. Inexplicably he was deeply hurt, as he was always hurt when she disappointed him, seeing it each time as an unnatural lack of filial affection. Abruptly he turned away and descended the stairs. As he reached the last tread a maidservant came from the direction of the kitchen with a tray of supper covered by a cloth. It came to him how he could bring Donna out of her seclusion.

'Take that back again,' he ordered. 'In future no food or drink is to be taken upstairs without my permission.'

The girl looked startled. 'Not at all, sir? Very good, sir.' She went scuttling through the green baize door to proclaim the strange development to the rest of those below stairs.

Daniel ate his dinner doggedly. Instead of the usual contented conversation shared with Kate, a silence reigned. He had no appetite, but would not show it, drinking more wine than was his custom, pretending not to notice that she had no interest in what was set before her. In a show of nonchalance he ate his way through each course, and when the cloth was drawn, the port placed at his right hand and the servants had left them alone, for Kate always sat on with him when there were no guests, he rose to fetch a second glass which he put before her, filling it with the ruby wine. He ignored her protest.

'Drink it. It will do you good.'

She thought he was setting the scene for a more amiable discussion about Donna, and was prepared to meet him halfway, taking a sip of the port to prove it. He took his chair again, reclining back in it as if completely at ease, while steeling his very stomach for what he had to say.

'I've rented Honeybridge House to Mrs di Castelloni.'

She went deathly pale. The glass slipped from her fingers, smashing on the table and sending a ribbon of port pouring over the edge onto her skirt. He jumped up and dabbed with a napkin to stop the flow, but she brushed his aid aside, making him leave the cloth sodden on the table between them.

'Honeybridge is mine,' she said in a whisper.

He answered with a careless smile. 'I know you've kept a sewing-room there, but that was only to ensure that fires were lit and the place kept aired. In any case, how often do you sew these days? The times when you made your own dresses have long since gone.'

'You gave Honeybridge to me,' she persisted in the same stunned whisper.

He was genuinely astonished. 'How can you imagine that? It's not true.'

'You told me once that I should never have to leave Honeybridge ever again unless I wanted to.'

'But you did leave it. Over twenty years ago. You came of your own free will to Easthampton House and called it home. Here we became husband and wife again, here we renewed our love, and here the rest of our children were conceived.'

'But Honeybridge has remained my haven.'

Her dreadful, white-faced calm was almost more than he could bear. He had expected anger that she had not been consulted, a flare of her temper that could match his own and with which he could deal, but not her restrained quietness that was making him feel as guilty as if he had robbed her of life itself. He took refuge in anger of his own.

'How can you say that?' he demanded hotly. 'Jem lived in it throughout his retirement, and you never objected to his being a tenant.'

Her lips were so pale and dry that she seemed scarcely able to move them. 'Jem understood.'

'Understood? Understood what?' He was blustering fiercely, and he threw himself up out of the chair, dismayed that he should feel jealousy of an old friend long gone because Jem had known some part of Kate's heart that apparently had never been disclosed to him.

'Jem knew that I must be free to come and go there if I was never to be overpowered and defeated by the woman for whom this house was originally built!'

He made no pretence of not knowing whom she meant. 'Claudine is dead!' he ground out.

'Not for you. Never for you. To my knowledge, not once did she ever enter this house, but her mark was put upon it no matter how you tried to convert it to my taste and hold me in settings that would not have been of her choosing.'

Her perception infuriated him. She had not spoken above

234

a whisper, but she had countered him on all sides and his temper erupted. 'So that's how you have despised my efforts all these years to make you happy here! Nothing I did meant anything to you!' He wanted her to storm at him, to give him a chance to ease his conscience and glory in a quarrel with her, and to end it as their quarrels had always ended – with reconciliation in each other's arms, the subject of their differences forgotten or at least shelved temporarily and never seeming so grim when discussed afterwards. But this restrained, mask-like Kate was beyond his handling.

She did not seem to hear what he had said, or else dismissed it out of hand as being groundless abuse, knowing as they both did that there was no truth in his accusations. She continued to speak in that same, strange, muted tone.

'That stranger must not take my place at Honeybridge. Tell her the house is mine.'

A wave of crimson suffused his face, his anger more at himself than at Kate, but he laid the blame with her. 'I'll do no such thing. I've told her she can have Honeybridge and have it she shall. I never go back on my word.'

He hurled himself out of the room. Her voice suddenly took on strength and her cry echoed after him. 'But you have to me!'

The front door slammed behind him, making the house shake. It was a retreat and a defeat, but no amends would be made. She remained in the high-backed chair at the table, immobile as a statue. It came to her that when she had first viewed Easthampton House she had had an awful vision of herself alone in it, with Daniel gone to Claudine, and at last the reality had come upon her. Donna was shut away, Richard had left home and her other children were dead. As for Daniel, it was the second time in his life that he had made a choice, but this time she had lost, and Claudine's image had won. The red-headed girl with the looks, walk and allure of Claudine was to inhabit peaceful Honeybridge, trailing turbulence and trouble in her wake.

She did not know whether she sat there at the table for ten minutes or half an hour, but suddenly she rose with a sensation of suffocation and rushed from the dining-room to fetch a key, and then went out of the house. The warm summer night met her, full of stars, and below the hill the lights of the resort lay in golden brilliance. She gave no thought to a carriage, but hastened down the drive to the gates, the gravel cutting through the thin soles of her evening shoes. Avoiding the main streets, she darted through a long, dark twitten, came out on a little-used path bathed in moonlight, and disappeared again along a track through the woods to arrive in Hoe Lane. Had she met anyone *en route* to greet or accost her, the remnants of her self-control would have snapped for all to see. As if she had arrived at sanctuary, she thrust the key into the door of Honeybridge and rushed into the house, feeling its peaceful atmosphere fall over her like a cloak. But somehow that only increased her sense of loss, and she uttered out of the fathomless depths of her despair an impassioned, rending cry.

'Jem! Jem! Dan's taking this house from me!'

Her own voice echoed back at her, and the last threads of control snapped. She ran as though demented into one room and then another, almost as if in some way she could gather the house unto her for safekeeping, and when she came upstairs to the bedroom where Jem had spent many hours in the last year of his life, she flung herself down by the large leather chair from which he had watched for the coming of his beloved Warwycks through the gate, and she threw her arms across the cushions as if she might yet embrace the old man who had been her special champion. Sobs were racking her. It seemed as if her head and heart must split in her torment, and unable to contain her anguish she reeled to her feet again and was not aware that she was beating her fists against the panelled wall. Neither did she know that in her distraught state she had failed to close behind her the door into the house.

In the lane Josh sauntered along, taking the evening air after the journey that had brought him back to Easthampton. After depositing his baggage in his rooms, he had come straight out to exercise his limbs, thinking the journey from London would be very different once his local branch line linked up in turn with Merrelton and thence to the metropolis. He had half a mind to look in at the pier theatre and catch the last act of the latest melodrama being performed, for he had caught glimpses of the posters as he drove through the resort, but on second thoughts maybe he would wait until tomorrow evening and see the whole performance of *The Highwayman's Revenge*. However, that would not stop him being at the stage door when Lucy came out. He wondered how she had recovered from the shock of Timothy Attwood's drowning. It had been shock enough for him to read about it in the newspaper, for he had liked and respected the man, and his sorrow at such a tragic waste of life was deep and genuine.

As Josh came abreast of Honeybridge House he glanced towards it and saw that the door stood ajar, but no lights showed within. It was the first time he had ever seen his great-grandfather's old home open. Had carelessness left the door unlocked, or was there an intruder?

He went swiftly through the gate, and on the threshold he pushed the door wider to listen. A thudding somewhere sounded like a distorted heartbeat, almost as if a box or drawer was being hammered to get it open. He no longer had doubts that an illegal entry had been made, and he closed the door fast behind him to prevent any dash for escape. Silently he began to ascend the stairs, balling his fists ready for attack and defence. When he reached the landing, he ran lightly to the open door of the room from which the thudding came.

'Mrs Warwyck!' he exclaimed in astonishment, able to see her clearly in the moon-washed room.

At the sight of his broad-shouldered frame in the doorway, Kate mistook him in her hysteria for Jem, forgetting that it could not be, or that towards the end age and sickness had crippled the old man, and she flung herself towards him.

'Dan's letting his daughter have Honeybridge!' she cried in anguish. 'You must stop him, Jem! He won't listen to me!'

Instinctively he held her as she fell against him, and when he saw that in addition to all else an irrational disappointment had been added to her misery as she comprehended her mistake, he continued to keep her fast to him, seeing that she scarcely knew where she was or what she was saying in a state bordering on dementia.

'Kate, Kate, nothing can be worth this distress. Kate,

listen to me.' It was no time for formality. He had a woman on his hands who seemed ready to put an end to herself, not like Lucy who had merely lapsed into a faint at the edge of the parapet. Her head had fallen back on her neck and she threw herself about helplessly, her sobbing pitiable. He tried to soothe and quieten by enfolding his arms about her, seeking to give her comfort through a simple human contact that would make her realize that she was no longer alone in her troubles and he was there to do whatever he could in the circumstances. But she fought him off, wrenching herself away from him, and in staggering free she half-fell across the end of the bed where she clutched at a carved post at the foot, setting her forehead against it and continuing to give way to total despair.

He seized the opportunity to find a lamp and put a light to it. As he adjusted the wick, it occurred to him that it would be as well if nobody else's attention was drawn to signs of occupation at a late hour, and quickly he closed the inside shutters over the windows before turning to look at her in the lamp-glow. Her head was bowed and he could not see her face, for her hair had slipped from its pins and lay across her heaving shoulders like a silken shawl. Down the layered skirt of her gown a wine-stain showed dark against the grey moiré, and the toe of her shoe showing beneath her hem was soiled by grass and earth. Had she walked some distance? Not unusual by day, but never after dark.

He went to sit on the end of an ottoman at the foot of the bed where he was opposite her, and where, by lowering his head, he could see into her face.

'Kate,' he said again with compassion. 'You know me; not well, but you know me. Talk to me. Tell me the nature of your distress. It will remain within these four walls. It's doing you harm to torture yourself in this manner.'

She could have been deaf for all the notice she took. He reached into the pocket of his coat-tails and took out the hip-flask still there from the day's journey. Pouring a measure for her into the silver top of it, he begged her to take a sip, as he held it towards her, but it was dashed from his hand, and she rolled away from his insistence, throwing her arms over her head and renewing her distracted weeping.

Fearing she would sob herself out of her senses completely, he moved to the bed beside her and pulled her into his arms, forcing her to listen to him. 'Why shouldn't Donna have Honeybridge? Is it the end of the world that a daughter wants to leave home?'

'Donna?' Her head jerked up and her eyes were staring. Suddenly she burst into wild, hysterical laughter. 'Not Donna! It's his daughter by his paramour who's taking Honeybridge from me! His daughter by Claudine!'

He struck the laughter from her on one side of the face and then the other. She went rigid, the red marks showing up on the pale skin, and then as suddenly she drooped towards him. He put the flask to her mouth and tilted it, making her swallow the brandy until she coughed and gasped and thrust it away, causing it to splash and add further stains to her gown. He put aside the flask and his arm went about her as her head came to rest against his neck. He stroked her face gently, stunned by what she had revealed to him.

'I've told you a terrible secret,' she said, low-voiced.

In silence he agreed with her. It had been surprise enough at the Grange when from the balcony where he stood smoking in the darkness he had heard Lucy's raised voice declare herself to be the late Attwood's child and Olivia's merciless denial of her closing the interview. It had explained Lucy's obsession with the Grange and her desperate concern for its future, and the strange, adoring look he had seen on her face when she had first gazed at the portrait of Lionel Attwood. But this! That she had been born the wrong side of the blanket and was no more Attwood by right or lineage than he himself, was information that could have the gravest consequences.

'Who else knows of this matter, Kate?'

'No one except Daniel himself. I have read his knowledge in his face whenever he has looked at her. He thinks I have lived in ignorance of a night he spent with Claudine.'

'Perhaps you are mistaken. Why should Lucy not be Lionel Attwood's child?'

'Because there is in her a facial resemblance not only to her mother but to the Warwyck family too. Not to Daniel's

uncle, of whom Donna reminds him – to her constant misfortune – but to his own sister, Jassy, and even to a daughter
of my own whom I lost when she was only ten. Whether he
has seen that special likeness in his love-child I would not
know.'

'Love-child? That is a generous word to use. Not many
wives would be so magnanimous.'

'Perhaps, but what else can one call a spell that had lain
across him since their first meeting? Surely you as a man
should be the first to admit that it is possible for any one of
your sex to feel passion for two women at the same time,
albeit in different ways.' She raised her face to look up at
him, causing a strand of her loosened hair to fall across her
eyes, which he brushed back for her.

'Naturally I admit to it,' he answered, his gaze dwelling
on her. He was thinking that it would have been no great
difficulty to stir up his own affections for her, even though
Lucy ran through his heart and his veins, giving him no
more peace now that he had come to love her than she had
done when everything she had done or said had made him
impatient with her almost beyond endurance. Originally
Lucy had offended his pride with her high-handed indifference and show of contempt, which was something he had
never been used to from women, never known before.
Maybe it was that alone which had made him set his sights
upon her with an unerring aim, and he knew it to have been
jealousy as much as the certainty he had recognized from
the start that she had the power to twist young Attwood
about her finger against the railway when it so suited
her.

Finally the unfortunate fellow had used his retained right
to withdraw from the proffered contract, but it had been to
no avail. Lucy had lost even as she had won, and his own
conviction that she was destined for him was unshaken. The
thought gave rise to another.

'You say that nobody else knows?' he checked. 'What of
your son and daughter?'

She sat up within the circle of his arm. 'Neither of them
has the least idea, and for all our sakes as a family it must
remain so, because I would not have them turn against their

father. That was why I was thankful that Timothy Attwood displayed an interest in the widow –'

He interrupted her. 'Say her name. Say Lucy.'

Her face dragged in her misery and the tears re-shone as she shook her head.

His arm tightened about her. 'You must. If you are to accept and overcome the circumstances that brought you to this pass tonight, you must use her name.'

Her mouth quivered, but she obeyed him bravely. 'Lucy.' She drew breath, but with no lightening of spirits. 'There. I've said it.' A dreadful sadness lay in her meditative gaze. 'How odd that I've been able to speak her mother's name always while that of the innocent party in it all has threatened to choke me.'

'Is it so strange?' he consoled. 'She is living proof of what inwardly you hoped had never happened.'

'I suppose so.' She covered her eyes with her fingertips, exerted pressure on the lids as if to banish weariness, and then opened them again, but her voice revealed that she was almost at the finish of her strength. 'It's not every day I see my son, but whenever I do I wait and hope and listen for some indication that his love for Mrs di – for Lucy has waned, but if anything it seems to strengthen. Only yesterday he talked of her needing him more than ever in their mutual loss of a friend and the aftermath of suffering it has caused her. He never suspected as I did that Timothy was set on taking her away from him.'

'I find that hard to believe. I found it obvious enough myself.'

'Did you? But then you're not besotted with Lucy as he is. The Warwyck men are all alike. When they set their hearts and their minds, there is no turning them aside, and the thought of failure does not occur to them.'

He mulled over for a few moments how he should re-assure her. 'What would you say if I told you that I too am in love with Lucy, and mean to have her?'

She stared at him. 'Is that true?'

He nodded. 'I'm not besotted, because I see her faults even as she sees mine, and I welcome that. A docile, doting partner would suffocate me with boredom.' A corner of his mouth twisted upwards in amusement. 'There'll be no fear of that with Lucy. She can take me as lover or husband, whichever suits her best, and I see no reason why Richard should ever learn of his blood-tie with her.'

She regarded him thoughtfully. 'You're an unconventional man.'

'Does that displease you?'

'No. I think you might win Lucy dishonourably where my dear Richard is prepared to lay the world and himself at her feet. Women are contrary creatures, and I'll pin my faith on that.'

He was unable to keep back a grin at the comment, his white teeth showing beneath the trimmed black hedge of his moustache. 'I'd say you had backed a winner then, Kate.'

She was deep in her own thoughts and took his face between her hands. 'I wish you luck. The whole structure of my family life and perhaps even that of my marriage itself depends on your success.'

She kissed him. He had not been expecting such a demonstration of gratitude, and she caught him unawares with her lovely mouth, soft as it was from her suffering and still with the salt of tears upon it. His embrace tightened and he kissed her back, leaving her in no doubt that the way he had looked at her in his father's house and more recently in the church lane was evidence of an admiration that bore no heed of the years that divided her age from his.

She left him then to go into her sewing-room where she kept a comb and spare hairpins. He went downstairs to the hall to wait for her, and stood looking about him until she reappeared, having re-dressed her hair, while about her shoulders she had draped a length of lace from the sewing-cupboard to make a shawl, long points of it arranged to cover the wine and brandy stains upon her skirt.

He walked her home along the same deserted route by which she had come. At the steps of Easthampton House they bade each other good night, parting with the warm touch of her fingers in his, her eyes briefly eloquent. As he turned away he happened to glance up at the house, sensing someone's gaze, and at an upper window he saw Donna looking down at him. She looked like a harbinger of death with her peaked face and black clothes. The curtains swirled as she swung back into the room and the light was extinguished.

Josh walked back through the gas-lit streets to the pier, which had been his original destination, and found the last of the theatre crowd was dispersing. He waited by the pier entrance, and before long various members of the cast came away from the theatre in twos and threes. When Lucy appeared, he saw he had been forestalled by Richard, whose arm she was holding.

He drew away, and neither of them noticed him as they came through the gate, talking seriously together, and directing their steps towards The Warwyck, where Richard was obviously taking her to a late supper. Without doubt no more time must be wasted, or else, on the rebound of her languishing over Timothy Attwood, Lucy would be imagining herself in love with her own half-brother. For Kate's sake, to say nothing of his own, he must make good his boast soon that he would eradicate all competition.

For the second time that evening he went through the gate of Honeybridge. Whether Lucy would take it into her head to visit the house before retiring at Sea Cottage he had no idea, but he had a feeling that curiosity about her new abode would get the better of her. He found a garden seat, swung up his legs and crossed his ankles on one end of it, and set his hands behind his head to wait for an hour or two.

It took less time than he had expected before the gate clicked, and a glance at his pocket-watch in the moonlight showed that it was barely midnight. Lucy was alone. As she put the key in the door he was already drawing close to her, and as she crossed the threshold he was hard on her heels. She gave a frightened cry even as he spoke her name and she recognized him.

'Where on earth did you come from?' She had let Richard leave her at Sea Cottage, and had gone indoors only to borrow a lantern from Emmie to light the path back through the woods to Hoe Lane, wanting to explore Honeybridge on her own, and now Josh of all people appeared. She had had enough of difficult men for one evening: Richard had shown he was less than pleased that she had become the tenant at Honeybridge, when she had greeted him excitedly with the news that his father had had the key sent to her during the second interval of the performance. Although he had not stated the reason for his lack of enthusiasm, she felt certain it was because he had not had the authority to let her rent it when she had first spoken of the house to him. But whatever it was, she had been made acutely conscious that tension and disappointment were high in him, and her attempts to soothe matters had met with no success.

'I heard you were moving from Sea Cottage,' Josh said.

She sighed, misjudging the source of his information. 'Why couldn't Emmie hold her tongue for five minutes about my leaving there?'

'Are you taking up quarters tonight?'

'Of course not. I'm just going to take a look at Honeybridge.'

'Let me look around with you.'

She leaned her head back wearily against the half-open door. 'I'm in no mood to do battle with you at the moment. I came here to be quiet and alone for a little while. It's best you go.'

He set his hand on the flint wall under the lintel, resting his weight against it. 'Let's create a temporary truce. We'll make it of an hour's duration if you like, with not a word mentioned on either side about the Grange or the railway or anything else over which we fail to see eye to eye. But let me accompany you into Honeybridge. It belonged to the Barton family years ago.'

'Haven't you ever been in it before?'

He gave a quick grin that was faintly wolfish in the moonlight. 'Once. Quite recently, in fact. But I was only in the hall and one other room. I really would like to be allowed into the house with you. My great-grandfather spent the summers of his childhood in it.'

She hesitated. At least it seemed they had an interest in common. No other appeal would have moved her. 'Very well. You may light a lamp if you're able to find one. This lantern has a poor wick to it.'

In the hall he moved with alacrity to take a lamp from the

niche that he had noticed earlier, and when it was lit he held it high for her to look about the hall, which was square with a central staircase and doors leading off on all sides. She turned to the one nearest to her, which opened into a dining-room, her shadow racing before her over the dark panelled walls and the long table flanked by high-backed chairs, the old wood shining with the polish that comes from years of care and plenty of elbow grease. Set into one wall was a great open hearth, ancient dog-irons supporting logs made ready for the chill of still distant autumnal days. Her whole face showed her pleasure in all she saw, and she pirouetted with a bell-swing of her skirt to look about her at every detail.

'This is a beautiful room,' she declared softly, running fingertips along the surface of the table and letting them alight with a butterfly touch on the back of the chairs. 'So plain and simple, but enriched by old welcomes to this board.'

He was as charmed as she by it, but it gave him greater pleasure to observe her delighted reaction as their tour took in one room and then another downstairs, everything mellow and faded, occasionally worn to the point of shabbiness, the colours muted and misty. Overhead the ancient beams hung low, making him dodge his head at times, especially in the kitchen, where the copper hood of the big, black range winked reddish lights in the lamplight that were reflected back by the rows of pans on the walls.

Upstairs it was the same, the ceilings sloping with dormer windows making interesting angles, some of the beds four-posters, others with flower-painted headboards in a style of the previous century long out of fashion, and over all the scent of lavender strewn in cupboards and drawers to keep the rooms fresh and sweet-smelling. Except one, that had a more piquant aroma to it.

'How odd,' she exclaimed. 'This bedroom smells of brandy.'

He would have shepherded her out again, but perversely she was set on discovering the origins of it, saying that perhaps the old man who had last lived in the house had stored a keg somewhere in the room and it was leaking. She began to open cupboards, only to find them bare. Kate had smoothed the patchwork quilt back into place and reopened the shutters, so that there was nothing to show that anyone had been in the room that same evening. Josh set down the lamp, rested his hands resignedly on his hips, and thought that it seemed his destiny to kiss a lovely woman for the second time in these same surroundings. With Kate it had been pleasurable, combined as the kiss had been with affection for her that had lingered over the years, but with Lucy it would be much, much more. He watched her in her search, bright and fleeting and light as the moonlight vying with the lamp's glow, until she came at last to the chest by which he was standing. Apart from the sprigs of lavender encased in muslin bags, each drawer was empty. She shut the bottom one and straightened up.

'Isn't that strange?' she remarked, her mind occupied with the mystery. Then she saw how he was looking at her.

He read her thoughts. 'There's a truce between us. Remember? Nothing stands between us. For whatever remains of the brief hour agreed upon, we are simply a man and a woman who have been attracted to each other for longer than either of us has been willing to admit, least of all to ourselves.'

She could not deny that he had made an impression on her as no man had done before. His very maleness had had a searing effect at their first meeting, but he had come like a sword between her and the Grange and he had continued to divide her from it. That made the barrier between them unassailable. She shook her head, drawing back from him, and came against the foot-post, but then jerked away from that too and the association that it presented. He made no move, merely watching her and waiting, tall against the dark tones of old wood and the muted crimsons, russets and ambers of the furnishings held free from the shadows by the lamplight. Had she chosen to take half a dozen steps she could have been through the door, for he was not barring it, and by his relaxed stance he showed he had no intention of stopping her forcibly if she should decide to make an exit. Perhaps he knew before she did that she would not leave.

His eyes held hers. All else deserted her but an awareness of being alone with him without animosity for the first time, the stillness of Honeybridge's age-warmed atmosphere working some extraordinary effect upon her, making the outside world unreal and far away. It was as if the house had taken up their truce and given it some special benediction.

She saw him come towards her and felt a seething, uncontrollable excitement rise darkly in her. Almost incredulously she observed her own arms rise as he put out his own towards her, and as his embrace slid about her she clung to him, her lips parting as he sank his mouth upon hers. They kissed as if to assuage a terrifying hunger, wildly and passionately, such a fire ignited in each of them that when he lifted his mouth from hers it was only to take it captive again, she as eager as he for the blending of lips and the amorous pressure of limbs. When his caressing hand came upon the smooth firmness of her breast, silk and cambric thrust aside, she strained against him, and when he began to slide her gown from her shoulders, it was as if she were being peeled from a calyx to feel the sun at last. Then, without warning, the spell was broken.

It was no more than the creak of a floorboard somewhere in the house that had disturbed the quietness. It was almost as if Honeybridge, tiring of holding time at bay for them, had given way to the night-time settling of ancient timbers and floors and furniture, with no more thought for the man and woman who had been on the brink of further discoveries of each other. Reality swept back over Lucy, bringing with it the realization that she had almost succumbed to the one enemy who was set to cut away her last tenacious links with the past.

Abruptly she tore herself from him, jerking the shoulder of her gown back into place, trembling in every limb. 'The truce is at an end!'

He caught her by the wrists. 'You can't say that now.'

She flung up her arms to break his hold, whirling away from him. Out of the door she went and down the stairs, her heels pattering, and he was after her, skidding across the hall floor to get between her and escape, slamming the flat of his hands against the wall on either side of her to keep her trapped.

'Lucy, Lucy, Lucy,' he breathed dangerously, lowering his head to bring his eyes on a level with hers. 'Don't set us back where we started.'

She avoided looking at him, turning her face one way and then the other as if she feared he would fasten his mouth upon hers again if she remained motionless. 'We have never progressed beyond that point, not even in that room above. It was a moment of illusion, because you'll not give up until you've destroyed a great house and its lands that have come to mean as much to me as life itself.'

'Forget the house! It's not going to be demolished. Others may come to care for it more than you.'

'That's impossible. It could never mean as much to strangers as it does to me. Timothy meant it to be a home for me.'

He gave an impatient nod. 'As he meant to make you an Attwood again, no doubt?'

She was aghast, her mouth open and quivering as she pressed herself back against the wall. 'You listened that night at the Grange! You eavesdropped on a private conversation.'

His forehead contracted, showing his displeasure at the accusation. 'Through no fault of mine, mark you. I was on the balcony three rooms away and had you and Olivia Radcliffe not raised your voices I would never have heard what passed between you.' He moved in close to her, speaking in softer tones. 'Forget the Grange. You need nothing that has ever belonged to an Attwood to give you the identity you seek. I'll make you the woman you want to be. With me you can look to the future and forget all about the past.'

'I don't want to forget the past!' she burst out frantically. 'I loved Timothy –'

'You only loved what he represented. You set your cap at him for that very purpose and that purpose only.'

She made no denial, for he spoke the truth of her original intention, but in avoiding his hovering mouth, which was only awaiting a pause in their heated talk to descend, she had strained her neck away, her cheek against the wall, and beneath her lashes noticed what had been there all the time for her unseeing gaze: the dining-room door was ajar. Her attention became riveted on it with a new alarm. Josh had closed it after them on their tour of exploration, and she recalled the creaking of boards that had come so abruptly when they had been on the point of making love. It was more than the midnight contractions of old timbers that she had heard.

'There's an intruder in the dining-room,' she whispered.

He jerked his head back from her slightly and followed her glance. Before going upstairs with the lamp he had lit one of the wall sconces in the hall, and if he threw the door wide he would have full illumination into the dining-room combined with an element of surprise in overpowering the intruder.

He moved quickly and silently. The door flew back on its hinges with a crash, and he recognized instantly the figure sitting in one of the dining-room chairs, which had been turned away from the table, one elbow resting on the polished surface. It was Ben Thompson.

'What in hell's name are you doing skulking about in this house?' Furiously Josh seized him by his coat and yanked him to his feet, ready to hurl him across the room. Hastily Ben sought to placate him.

'I'm not skulking, sir! Far from it! I was waiting to see you most urgent.'

Josh shook him violently. 'In the dark? Trespassing on other people's property? You're a damned liar, Thompson. What did you come to steal?'

'Nothing!' Ben was thoroughly agitated, for Josh had made a fist under his nose that could smash it to a pulp. 'I saw you enter the 'ouse from the end of the lane, and by the time I reached the door to give it a knock the lamplight was upstairs, and –' he cleared his throat uncomfortably, '– I guess I wasn't 'eard. I swear I didn't see the lady and thought you was on your own, or else I give you my oath I'd never 'ave tried the door and come in to give you a shout.'

Josh spoke through his teeth. 'I don't believe a word you're saying.'

Ben flapped his arms, half choked by the grip on his coat, which was pulling his cravat hard across his throat. Had he wished, he could have put up some defence, but it was never his policy to risk physical violence to his person, which was the reason why he had chosen to sit in apparent innocence by the dining-room table instead of making a run for it. He should have left before by the small window through which he had forced an entry, but he had never knowingly let slip a chance to investigate other people's troubles and affairs for possible gain. Had his presence not been discovered he might have learned much more, but he must count himself lucky that it had not taken place earlier, for as an insurance against the risk of being nabbed he had had time to put back the few small items of value that he had pocketed.

'You gotta believe me, Mr Barton, 'cos it's the gospel truth. As sure as 'eaven is my witness –'

'Don't blaspheme!'

''Ow was I to know you was meeting Mrs di Castelloni 'ere? I understand the ways of the world, and as soon as I 'ears a lady's voice upstairs I wouldn't embarrass 'er by letting 'er know that I knew she was there.' He attempted a man-to-man smirk, which was difficult with the pressure on his throat, and then immediately regretted it as he was shaken violently again. The cravat was given another twist, and he clawed at it, falling into a fit of coughing, his face turning purple. Lucy, who had been watching from the open doorway, hurried forward and pulled at Josh's arm in an attempt to loosen the iron hold.

'You'll strangle him!'

'Gladly!' Josh retorted with relish, although he slackened his grip. 'I know his kind.'

She addressed Ben sternly. 'I don't believe you either, but I'll not have you throttled for it. Had your entry into this house been as you said it was, you would have left immediately you realized Mr Barton was not alone.'

'It's that danged front door.' Ben rubbed his throat painfully. 'It won't open without waking 'alf the neighbour'ood and you'd 'ave thought I was sneaking out like a common thief and it would 'ave given the game away in any case.'

She looked at Josh. 'It's right that the hinges squeal most dreadfully.' She saw by his inexorable expression that he took it as no excuse. She spoke to Ben again. 'I think you had better let us hear what the special reason was for your sneaking into this house in the first place. A matter of some urgency, I believe.'

Ben looked from one to the other of them, thankful that the ripe piece of information gathered from one of his sources that evening could be put to good use. 'It was for Mr Barton's ears alone.'

Josh flung him back in the chair and wiped one palm off against another, with his mouth twisted in disgust. 'There can be nothing you have to tell that Mrs di Castelloni can't hear.'

'Awright then. Maybe she should 'ear it, seeing as the matter was referred to between the two of you in the 'all just now.' He got to his feet and took a few paces out of range, making a half-bow to her. ''Ere it is then. Daniel Warwyck 'as put in an 'igh bid for the Attwood estate. 'Ee's prepared to top whatever the Railway Company offers. There won't be no place for your rail-tracks there.'

He thought he had never seen two people react so differently to the same piece of news. Josh Barton's whole face tightened as if it had turned to stone and the widow's expression became one of incredulous joy. She clasped her hands together and closed her eyes as if it were the most wonderful thing she had ever heard.

'Get out!' Josh growled. 'Get out before I throw you out.'

Ben grabbed his hat from the floor where it had fallen and ran. It had been an expedition from which he had gleaned much, and with time and thought he had no doubt that he could put it all to good use when an opportunity presented itself. He might even be able to kill two birds with one stone, so to speak. He had actually been putting a small gold clock into his capacious pocket when Warwyck's half-crazed wife had come bursting into Honeybridge. It had been a nasty moment, but he had hidden himself successfully, as he had done again later when the widow had begun her prowling tour. In between he should have got away unnoticed with his spoils, but the information he had learned from Kate Warwyck had made him stop and think, delaying his departure until Josh Barton had returned to occupy the garden seat, cutting off all escape.

Ben grinned to himself as he slowed his pace to a saunter, tipping his hat forward complacently. In all, it had been a good night's work. Once indoors at Sea Cottage he went to a secret hiding place in his room and checked to make sure the silver buttons were still there.

At Easthampton House, in the small hours, Daniel reached to draw Kate to him, not with any apology for his loss of temper over Honeybridge House or with any reference to their quarrel, only wanting desperately to heal the breach between them before it widened beyond all reason. Kate, being Kate, did not hold herself from him, but enfolded him to her in loving arms. He had never known it otherwise, not since she had once rebelled in the early years of their marriage against his autocracy and chosen to live apart from him, leaving him to a loneliness that he never wanted to experience again.

'Dear, darling Kate,' he murmured in his kissing. 'How I love you. Oh, how I love you.'

She held him to her passionately, her eyes closed. The question of the tenancy of Honeybridge House was unresolved, but for the time being she gave no thought to it. With all his faults, he loved her as he had never loved anyone else. It was all she had ever wanted.

15

———◆◆◆———

Donna's door was not opened for four days. Her own marble bathroom, which had been installed with others only the previous year, when Daniel had modernized the facilities of the house upstairs and down, enabled her to maintain her customary fastidious routine until physical weakness began to take over. As for food, she felt no need of it, finding sips from a glass of water sufficient for her sustenance. Toby had not been in her room when she had made herself a prisoner, and she wept sometimes to hear him whine and scratch the door for admittance, but for his own sake she could not let him in. Other requests for admission she ignored. Lying on the chaise-longue, she listened without reply to her mother's pleas, her brother's coaxing and quite often her father's ranting. He had never liked to be crossed, but innocently and helplessly she had displeased him all her life, and had she not been numbed of all feeling, it might have given her intense satisfaction to provide him at last with real cause for displeasure. She genuinely wanted to cut herself off from the outside world and stay in solitary seclusion. It was safe and peaceful and she could devote her thoughts to her lost love. Everything Timothy had ever said to her now became magnified with meaning; she saw declarations of love in all that had passed between them. So vivid had her imagination become that at times it seemed she saw a gold band upon her finger and believed herself to be a true widow mourning a husband. On the evening of the fourth day she began to hallucinate. It was hearing her talking to herself that made Kate fly down the stairs for help to get the door forced open when Richard came bursting into the house, white about the mouth with anger.

'Where's Father?' he demanded.

'He's not here. I want you to –'

He broke in across her words, pacing the hall and shaking both fists in exasperation. 'What do you think he's done? He's mad! Mad! In spite of all I've said to dissuade him, he's bought the Grange!'

She did not care about business deals at that moment. 'Donna's ill! I know it! You must come upstairs and get her door open.'

He saw then how frantic she was. 'Good God! Hasn't she come out of that room yet?'

'No, and your father said she must unlock it herself.'

He pounded up the stairs to his sister's room, feeling as exasperated with her as he was with his father. He set his hands aggressively on his hips and shouted through the door to her. 'Donna! This is your last chance. Unlock the door or I'll bash it down!'

He did not notice that Kate had not followed him all the way. Halfway up the stairs she had been caught by such a stab of pain in her side that for a few moments she could not get her breath, leaning against the banister rail, and when the pain ebbed again her brow was beaded with moisture. Hastily dabbing at her temples with a lace handkerchief, she forced herself on again and arrived as Richard, all patience gone, put his weight to the door.

She rushed after him to the figure lying on the chaise-longue. The room smelt musty and was in some disorder; a hairbrush lay where it had fallen, Donna having lacked the strength to bend and pick it up again; an overturned glass of water had spread a white mark on a polished table by her side, and bed, cushions and her clothes were all rumpled and untidy. Richard had stepped across to sweep back a curtain and open a window, letting in the sea air.

'I'll send for the doctor,' he said, 'and fetch some food up myself.'

Kate nodded, her arms about Donna. 'Cook has some

beef-tea and calves-foot jelly waiting for this moment. Send maids to change the bed-linen, and then you can lift her into the bed for me.'

At the theatre, Daniel was backstage talking to Lucy. She had hugged him in her jubilation at hearing that the sale of the Grange to him had been confirmed, and he now confided his plan that was to make it a profitable investment.

'Easthampton has long needed another hotel, and the new Grange Hotel will accommodate those who wish to combine the quietness of the countryside with a seaside vacation.'

There was no more time to talk. Mr Bartley-Jones was signalling that it was time for them to go through to the auditorium, and with a quick word of farewell to Daniel, she hastened away, reflecting on his whole attitude when he had patted the newly-delivered deeds in his pocket. It was almost as if in the end he had purchased the Grange as much for her as to keep the railway at bay.

A few days later, Josh drove his cabriolet through the gates of Radcliffe Hall. From an upper window Olivia's daughter sighted him. Sophia, a tall, dark-haired young woman, was on a brief visit to her birthplace from Edinburgh, which had become her home upon her marriage to a Scot, James Stuart, just six months before her father died. Already she was looking forward to her return, not only because she loved her husband dearly and missed him, but because she was heartily tired of her mother's tirades against the Warwycks. She liked them no more than her mother did, having been brought up to a knowledge of their brutal ways and ruthless scheming – indeed some of her earliest memories were of her father's brooding outbursts against Daniel Warwyck – but hatred was an uncomfortable emotion with which to rub shoulders, even when not directed against oneself, and it seemed to her that since her father's death her mother had become more obsessed than ever before with a loathing of the Warwyck family. Personally, she thought it was due to her mother not having enough to occupy her mind since her only child had married and gone away, and to Sophia's great joy she believed herself to be *enceinte* at last, which would provide a new interest for Olivia Radcliffe. When her first-born as well as the other children she hoped to have were old enough, she would dispatch them to Radcliffe Hall for summer holidays, where they could benefit from the sea and country air away from the dampness of Scotland, and give comfort and pleasure to their grandmother in her old age.

'Mr Barton has arrived,' she said. 'Do you want me to leave you alone with him?'

Olivia looked up from where she sat at her embroidery frame and leaned back in her chair, removing her thimble. 'Yes, my dear. We have business matters to discuss that would be quite beyond you. Return when he has departed and we'll take tea together.'

When Sophia had left the room, Olivia moved across to check her appearance in a gilt-framed looking-glass where she patted the smooth wings of hair on which perched a lace cap with the daintiest of lappets. When her visitor entered, he found her waiting, poised and composed, with her back to the summer-screened fireplace above which hung a large Canaletto. Its golden colours blended with the August sunshine that superimposed its own pattern through the mullioned panes upon the multi-hued Persian carpet.

She greeted him simply by name as if to remind him he was associated in her eyes solely with the sordid world of trade. 'Mr Barton.'

He bowed. 'Good day to you, ma'am.'

She saw the guarded glitter in his eyes, knowing he was aware that she would not have sent for him unless she had reconsidered some aspect of his plea for the railway which she had dismissed out of hand at the time. 'Please sit down,' she invited, taking a seat opposite him and spreading her purple-shaded skirt. Leisurely she picked up a folded copy of the *Easthampton Chronicle* from the table by her chair and indicated a news item on the front page. 'It appears that Mr Warwyck managed to be one step ahead of you again. He has bought the Attwood estate and plans to turn the Grange into an hotel.'

'That is correct.' It was no easy thing for him to admit he had been routed. 'I hear that so determined was he to outbid the Railway Company that he secured the property before he had actually raised the loan. Had his bankers failed him, it could have caused him considerable financial embarrassment.'

'He has always taken chances,' she observed drily, 'but this time it will give him no advantage.'

Josh leaned forward in sharpened interest, liking her no more than he had done at their other meetings, but if one did business solely with those whom one liked, little would ever be achieved. 'What exactly do you mean?'

'I have not changed my mind about letting you have one inch of the Radcliffe estate that surrounds the Hall, but there is another strip that is of no use to me and about which I have kept silent, waiting to see how Daniel Warwyck fared in tilting at the Railway Company.'

'Where is that strip?'

She smiled a thin smile. 'Before Daniel Warwyck came to Easthampton, buying up land from your great-grandfather for a song, the Radcliffes still owned a plot or two which had somehow been left from the days when the Bartons had been the purchasers, and although those have been sold in every case since to various individuals, this one strip does remain, simply because it is the rout of a lane, once a cart-track, that leads from the Radcliffe boundary to Sea Cottage. Should you wish to purchase this strip, you could run your railway into the heart of Easthampton and build its terminus within sight of the sea.'

He displayed no reaction to her dramatic offer, too wary and too experienced to take anything at its face value. 'Warwyck must know about this land,' he pointed out emphatically.

She gave a slow nod, her expression complacent. 'He does indeed, and has never worried himself about it, since it is a right of way used by all. But it is not a turnpike – it is still a private road.'

He knew more about such matters than she did. 'Nevertheless, when such a right of way has been exercised for many years, it would need an Act of Parliament to close it, and I can assure you, ma'am, that such intervention would not be forthcoming.'

She retained an attitude of supreme confidence, her demeanour unchanged. 'It would not be necessary in this case, Mr Barton. My lawyers have delved into records going back to the fifteenth century. Since the route would still be used by the public, albeit on railway wheels instead of those on a cart or wagon, there is nothing to prevent you putting down your iron rails and setting your terminus on the site of Sea Cottage and some neighbouring dwellings which I am prepared to sell to you.'

He released a long breath. 'I think we had best look at a map of Easthampton and its district before we proceed any further,' he said, taking one from his pocket and rising to his feet to spread it out on a circular table. 'I think you have omitted one important factor.'

She came to stand beside him in a crisp rustle of petticoats. 'What is that, Mr Barton?'

He found the route she had offered and followed it with his fingertip from Sea Cottage up through the outskirts until it came to Denwin's Corner. 'This is Warwyck land. As you can see and must surely know, it makes a triangle with the boundaries of the Attwood estate – now the new Warwyck property – on one side, while the Radcliffe estate lies on the other. How –' Here he jumped his fingertip forward across the broad spread of the two estates riding side by side to the open land several miles to the north, and back again. 'How am I going to get the railway to and fro across this stretch? Put wings to the locomotives?'

She laughed delightedly as if he had made some extremely amusing joke. 'Not at all. The right of way, made by deed of gift three hundred years ago as a settlement of debt and set down in black and white, albeit in Latin, from an Attwood to a Radcliffe, crosses the Attwood estate from north to south. I have the document in a strongbox in this very house.' Her whole face became a mask of malevolence. '*That* is something that Daniel Warwyck does not know! It has probably been forgotten by the Attwoods over these many years, simply because the Radcliffes have not exercised their rights since they rode that way with hawks and falcons on their wrists.' She jabbed her finger at the map and then at herself. 'But it is mine to sell. No law in the land can alter that. I am offering you a more direct and far better route for your railway than the one that was originally lost to you!'

So he had won. It was not in his nature to gloat in victory, and not a thought of it entered his head. He merely felt satisfaction at reaching his goal at last while acknowledging that he had had a worthy opponent in Daniel. As for Lucy, she would see the Grange and much of the estate left intact, but the connection was no good to her, and the sooner she was severed from it the better.

'Well, then, ma'am, it seems we're in business after all.'

'Indeed it does.' Olivia had opened a drawer from which she took out a map that had been specially drawn up to show the route in detail and to scale, and with it she had the papers prepared by her lawyers to cover the sale. 'No doubt you will wish to study the map and consult your lawyers, Mr Barton. I suggest you take these copies with you, and return at the same time the day after tomorrow, when my legal representatives will be here expecting to meet those of your Company. You and I can then put our names to the papers.' She smiled at him sweetly and extended her hand to him with every show of graciousness.

But there was nothing sweet about her thoughts. She was savagely triumphant in her striking of a blow of vengeance against Daniel Warwyck on her late husband's behalf as well as that of her seduced and ravished sister. And yet towards the end of their lives she had hated them both, though not as much as she hated Daniel for inadvertently destroying her happiness and theirs. If he had not pursued her sister relentlessly, commanding her to him with a deadly attraction, Olivia was sure Claudine would have married early away from Sussex and Radcliffe Hall, which would have put an end to Alexander's passion for his sister-in-law and left their own marriage unscathed.

After Josh had gone she resumed her seat at the embroidery frame and took up her needle again to stitch automatically, her thoughts elsewhere, the stabbing rhythm an indication of her vindictive reverie. Years ago she had been the gentle one of the Clayton sisters, but a streak of hardness must have been dormant in her in her youth, and it had certainly come to fruition after the birth of her only child. She had suffered a nervous breakdown, and had remained tetchy and difficult ever since, unable to banish any grievance, which in turn fed upon slights and hurts from the past. She had shed no tears when Claudine died. Whether her sister had ever betrayed her with Alexander she could never be sure, but she had never let him forget that she had caught them in each other's arms in this very room. Her heart had been like steel when she had brought Alexander to tears as he ailed towards a premature end of life, managing to goad him into admitting one day that he had loved Claudine although she had never loved him in return. What a weapon it had placed in her hands to use against him, for heaven alone knew how their flirting, touching, snatched kisses, and all else had tormented her in the days when Claudine had been under their joint protection at the Hall, though she had hidden it under a cloak of pride. Now it was her turn to revenge herself, taunting him with her special knowledge of how men had always pursued Claudine like dogs after a bitch on heat, and nothing had sorrowed him more than her jibe that of them all, the girl had loved his old enemy, Daniel Warwyck, and that he, Alexander, the proud and boastful, had never managed to get the better of a common pugilist. Sometimes since she had wondered whether Alexander knew that Claudine was carrying Daniel's child when he went to see her off to Italy with Lionel. It was highly probable. Claudine was full of cruel tricks and would have enjoyed mocking him for his failure to win her.

Olivia rested her needle against the taut tapestry held within the frame, bringing her thoughts to a more recent occurrence. She had had the same steeliness in her heart again when Claudine's daughter had begged for recognition. It had given her a considerable start to see such a likeness in the young woman, but fortunately she had had time to recover from the initial shock before her presence on the threshold of the room had been noticed. Why should she acknowledge Daniel's by-blow as her niece? Claudine's confession on her deathbed of a child by him left in an Italian convent had failed to penetrate the hardness that the years had scaled upon Olivia. Let the brat remain. Those born the wrong side of the blanket had no place in respectable society. Well, now that daughter had come home, thinking herself to be Lionel's child, which added to the exquisite irony of the situation. Not from her lips should the truth of Lucy's parentage ever be learned.

Sophia, re-entering the room, paused involuntarily at the look of malice completely contorting her mother's absorbed face. But her footstep had been heard and Olivia's expression cleared and melted into a little smile as if the vindictiveness of her thoughts had never been. At such times a veneer of the mildness that had once been hers lay upon her features. Only she knew how the cruelty of others had mangled her very soul.

16

On the first day of September the surveying was completed, and within a few days Josh's navvies began to move in, additional labour being recruited locally all the way along the staked-out route. Emmie had not been given notice to quit Sea Cottage, for the terminus was not to be sited quite şo far south in the lane, but at a more convenient level for easy access through to Ring Park and the centre of the resort. Those who were being compelled to leave cottages that stood on the Radcliffe strip of land went in turn to the Warwyck offices, seeking help there, for it was known that no compensation would be forthcoming to tenants, and Mrs Radcliffe had made it clear to those who had approached her that they must shift for themselves. Richard made what arrangements he could for them against the actual day of vacating premises, but it was not easy to find homes for over thirty families, even though many were in Warwyck employ. Only Meg and Bob had not been to see him, and he supposed they were arranging their own alternative accommodation.

'We did talk of building some small terrace houses out by the brickyard,' he said one day to Daniel in the office. 'I think we should delay no longer. I wouldn't want to lose some of those workers through their being forced to move away to Merrelton or further afield. They're good men, and at least three of them are talking of emigrating.'

Daniel was looking out of the window. 'We can't do it. We must rein in all expenditure.'

Richard looked up from his desk. 'I don't understand you.'

Daniel swung around to face him, his expression grim. 'With the news of the railway branch line being established, my shares in the Merrelton Canal Company plummeted. I need hardly remind you that I lost heavily on other canal boat shares in the north for the same reason a few years ago.'

Richard sat back incredulously and threw down the pen he was holding. 'Didn't you get rid of those Merrelton shares when I first advised it? I knew they would slump at the first whisper of the railway's interest in this area, and I gave you fair warning. All along I've invested every penny of my own money in the railways, but it's nothing compared to what you could have made.'

'It went against my principles to invest in an industry of which I want no part.'

Richard sighed as he lowered his head, rubbing a finger and thumb across his forehead. That was typical of his father, whose scruples over certain matters could not be assailed. 'What else?' he asked uncompromisingly.

'The building of the new theatre is costing a great deal, as you know. Then there's the Grange.'

'Ah. The Grange.' Richard could not hold back a faintly wearied note. The Grange had become a bone of contention between them, and as a rule they tacitly agreed not to discuss it since it was Daniel's independent venture. Unfortunately the intonation was not lost to his father's ears. Daniel thumped a fist on the desk.

'Yes! What should have presented prosperous returns threatens to become a white elephant. And you know why. My God, yes, you know why. Your cursed railway is the cause. Already the majority of our most distinguished visitors to the resort, who have been coming year after year, have made it known that they will not be returning next summer. We face the prospect of villas unoccupied and hotels half empty. Did you know that three privately-owned summer residences have been put up for sale this week alone?'

'The railway had to come,' Richard answered doggedly. 'It was inevitable sooner or later. Other visitors will come instead.'

'Of course they will,' Daniel retorted bitterly, 'but they'll come for a day's excursion or a week in a cheap lodging-house at the most. The nobility and the gentry have brought prosperity to this town. Where is the trade to come from that they provided? Who will feed those who have relied on summer employment?'

'I admit I see a decline for a year or two, but after that I'm convinced a new prosperity will be provided by those who come to spend money earned by the sweat of their brow in the factories, shops and offices. You must remember people are better paid than they used to be.'

'In Easthampton they are!' Daniel retorted. 'I raise the men's wages whenever loyalty and effort are due for reward, and I've instituted those bonus schemes of yours. But workers in other parts of the country are not so fortunate. How are they to patronize the seaside?'

'Other resorts flourish on the patronage of the middle class and the less fortunate. Easthampton will do the same.' Richard rose from his chair at the desk and went to clap a hand companionably on his father's shoulder. 'Perhaps things aren't as bleak as you fear where the Grange Hotel is concerned. Lucy and I have talked over changes to the resort that are inevitable through the coming of the railway, and she has some ideas of how we might make an all the year round success of the hotel, which could bring Easthampton winter visitors on a scale that we've never known before. She's at home today, because there are no more rehearsals at the Pier Theatre now that the season is closing. Let's go along to Honeybridge and take her with us out to the Grange now.'

Lucy welcomed them. She and Daniel had already gone together to view the railway marker stakes that sliced through the Attwood estate, standing in silent commiseration at their shared defeat. Josh had broken the news to her himself and she had thrust him away in her distress when he would have taken her into his arms.

'Put on your bonnet,' Richard said cheerily. 'I want you

to present your ideas for the Grange to my father on the spot.'

At the Grange, cleaning-women were applying a last polish to the floors after the trampling of feet through the house for the auction, for almost everything except family portraits had been put up for sale. The portrait of Lionel Attwood had already been taken down when Lucy went to view it for the last time, leaving only a darker rectangle of azure silk panelling to show where it had hung. It was perhaps the saddest moment of all for her that she had made it no goodbye.

Daniel had bought much of the furniture as well as many other items, so the house was by no means empty as the three of them went through to the ballroom. She darted away from the two men to take up the centre of the floor beneath the crystal chandelier, which even without lights sparkled like a waterfall, and she flung out her arms as if to encompass the whole area.

'Here,' she declared in a ringing voice, 'will be staged before invited spectators prize-fights between reputable opponents through the courtesy of Mr Daniel Warwyck, undefeated Champion of England!' The echoes seemed to tinkle amid the crystal droplets. She let her arms go slowly to her sides, watching Daniel anxiously for his reaction.

Suddenly he threw back his head and gave forth a tremendous bellow of laughter. She began to laugh, too, joining in with Richard, who caught her hand as she ran back again, both of them jubilant to see such a spontaneous show of approval. Daniel threw an arm about their shoulders.

'We'll do it! By God, we'll do it! With the law getting so mealy-minded that it's almost impossible to stage a good mill without interference by the beaks, we'll have our choice of fighters, and I'll bring over from the United States that young negro I told you about, Richard, who has a punch like the kick of a horse.' He could scarcely contain his enthusiasm, and he released his clasp around them to pace about the ballroom, deciding exactly where a ring should be roped out, the stench of sawdust, blood and sweat already in his nostrils, the air vibrant with that special excitement of a prize-fight, and he ached to be young again, when the crowd had roared for him and the spoils of victory were his alone.

Yet he had much to be grateful for in the present. All thanks to Lucy. Would that his legitimate daughter had a quarter of her spirit, but Donna, although the key to her door had been removed to prevent further self-imprisonment, still kept to her room, ate almost nothing, and although she would speak a little to Kate and Richard, she refused all communication with him as if the filial tie had been completely severed, never suspecting the terrible distress it caused him. Added to the whole awful matter was the physician's diagnosis of Donna's strange behaviour as the early symptoms of the dreaded decline, and Daniel longed to see her make some effort to free herself from it.

How different was Lucy in temperament. She was a fighter. Should any man need proof that she was his own flesh and blood, it was marked enough in her. He longed to tell her she was a Warwyck, but he had to think of Kate. Although Kate probably was not always aware of it, he had put her first from the day he had first realized how much he loved her, and he had hurt her enough over the matter of renting Honeybridge. Never had he thought she would take it so hard, but ever since it seemed to him she had lost much of her bloom, almost as if she were ailing, though when he had questioned her about it she had denied emphatically that she was in ill health. He was not convinced. He thought he would have a word with Dr Houston next time the physician called on Donna. Perhaps Kate was simply coming prematurely towards that difficult time in a woman's life, but whatever it was, he'd not cause her endless anguish through revealing the sordid facts of his greatest infidelity after so many years.

His glance fell upon Richard, who was arguing happily with Lucy over some point she had raised. Quite apart from Kate, he would lose a son if he ever let it be known that Lucy was his daughter. Pray God he never had to speak the truth to prevent a union between them, but so far she had made it plain enough that friendship was all she looked for from the lad. Lad? No, a man with a man's will and a man's desires. Maybe he should confide his certain belief in their relationship to Lucy, but how would she react? It was obvious she cherished the Grange secretly as her ancestral home, but would she welcome the knowledge that she had no place in it, and be shattered to discover she was his byblow, even though she would never know that he had fathered her during one black night of savage lust that had made him a stranger to tenderness? His expression was wry. Those fancy melodramas which she played for at the Pier Theatre could not hold a candle to the events of his life.

He returned his steps to the two young people. 'A regular programme of fights would fill not only this hotel, but all available accommodation in Easthampton as well.' Jovially he chucked Lucy's chin, almost as if they were acknowledged father and daughter, she smiling back at him. 'You're a clever lass. Do you have anything else up your sleeve?'

'A gaming-room upstairs. Faro, roulette, hazard and the rest.'

Daniel sucked in his cheeks in an expression of doubt, but his eyes were dancing. 'My dear young woman, the laws of this country are such that officially it is permissible to play games of chance, but not to play them for financial gain.'

'That doesn't mean to say it isn't done,' she argued. 'After all, we're not thinking of setting up a common gaming-house, but a private club.'

He laughed again, delighted with her. 'Quite true! By becoming a club and being strict in our rules, admitting members only, we'd have the law on our side. We could always enrol any guests staying at the hotel who desired an evening at the tables. It's a great pity that certain sanctimonious people in influential circles have put an end to the great gambling days of my youth. Their pernickety curbs have taken the zest out of high play and turned most gaming-men worth their salt from the tables to the race-course.'

Richard chuckled. 'Take care, Father, or else Lucy will be proposing we include horse-racing in the grounds too.'

'Why not indeed?' she voiced impishly.

At Richard's suggestion they went upstairs to locate a suite of rooms best suited for gaming-tables. There they chose one that consisted of four rooms opening into each other, with a concealed door in the wall that led to a rear staircase.

'That could be handy,' Daniel observed drily, 'should there be a need for patrons to vacate the premises in a hurry.'

The suite happened to include the drawing-room where Lionel's portrait had hung, and Lucy kept her eyes averted from the bare place. 'You will need a head croupier to supervise the rest and make sure that nothing underhanded goes on.' She made a dip of curtsey to Daniel. 'I'm applying for the post, since the Pier Theatre is closing for the winter and I'll be in need of employment. Richard will vouch for the fact that no card-sharp or dishonest croupier could evade my eye.'

Richard spoke up for her, seeing that his father was uncertain whether to take her seriously or not. Briefly he explained what had happened at the party at Easthampton House, and while Daniel was still asking her about how she had learned such skill, she took out of her reticule the pack of cards she had brought specially to give weight to her request, and shuffled and cut and flicked them in and out of fans and running falls with such lightning speed that both he and Richard watched in astonishment.

'Not only did Stefano collect packs of cards,' she said, still deftly manipulating those she held, 'but all his life he had collected gadgets used by gamblers to cheat at gaming tables, and had I not chosen to suspect Josh Barton through personal animosity at Easthampton House, I would have realized that it was a reflector and not spilt wine that was being used as an aid. I like to think that is the only mistake I've made since Stefano was first teaching me the signs to look for when a sharp is handling the cards.' With a final flourish that made the whole pack twist like a typhoon and fall back neatly into her palm, she set her head on one side and regarded Daniel with impudent amusement. 'Well, Mr Warwyck? Is the position of head croupier mine?'

Such an enchanting request would have been difficult to refuse in any case, but unbeknown to Lucy there were two other aspects in her favour: firstly, her vivid presence presiding in a gaming-room would be an immense attraction, and secondly, the all-important issue, she would of necessity have to reside at the Grange, which would free Honeybridge and enable Daniel to return it to Kate, and to make amends; this time Kate should have the deeds to it and be really able to call it her own.

'Yes, Lucy,' he replied, well pleased, 'you shall be head croupier here. I have no hesitation in appointing such a charming applicant.'

Just before they left the Grange a while later, Lucy had a few moments alone in the hall, and she swivelled round slowly to look up and about her, trying to establish some deep contact with her surroundings. But it evaded her, even as it had shut her out on the day of her first visit. What was the reason? What was wrong? Why couldn't she feel an integral part of the building's past even as she was moulding its future? Was the cause her failure to keep the estate intact? Yet surely it was better than nothing that an Attwood-born had the right to come and go within the house again. Why should the house continue to bar itself to her?

She knew the answer. It was staring her in the face, no different on this day than it had been when she had tried to make the house acknowledge her with a wild ringing of its bell. Josh had sliced his way between the house and her then, and he had continued to do so ever since. No wonder fear of him had persisted, irrational though it had appeared at times, always the intuitive knowledge that he was set on tearing her away from the Grange to throw her back into a state of limbo for the rest of her life. Was there no escape from his war upon her?

Suddenly it seemed that for the second time her questioning thought was answered. Richard came through into the hall from the library, smiling at her as he came. Handsome, kind, strong and protective, he offered her a way of escape from Josh that would set her free for ever. From what she had observed of life, friendship gave a special quality to marriage, that survived all unions based solely on the fire of passion, which was the reason why so many arranged marriages were highly successful. She had even known a kind of happiness with Stefano.

As Richard reached her, saying that Daniel had gone out

to the stables and they were to join him there, she put her hand into the crook of his arm. That was nothing unusual, but what was different this time, and which he noticed instantly, was that briefly she rested her brow against his shoulder as if she sought some haven. But for her it was not there.

'Do you remember,' she said very quietly, drawing away again, 'that when I first found somewhere to live in Easthampton, I told you that the two places I favoured most were beyond my reach?'

'Yes, I remember. Honeybridge and the Grange. You have lived in one, albeit for a short time, and now it has been arranged that you are to live at the Grange. Are you content?'

'I should be,' she replied, her voice lacking conviction. How could she be sure when no matter what she did or where she went, Josh would continue to haunt her? And not one word of love had he ever spoken to her. Nothing but that attitude of complete assumption that eventually he would make her his own. She could not forget how near he had come to accomplishing his purpose on the night that Ben Thompson had inadvertently set the house a-creaking.

They were halfway to the stables when the running figure of Meg appeared from the direction of the drive, a little trail of dust from the gravel meeting every pounding step. She was hatless and distraught, curls flying untidily, and when they hurried forward to meet her she half-threw herself at Richard.

'You must come! The navvies have arrived to demolish Denwin Cottage, and all along Bob has said he'd never get out. Already there's been trouble, and now he's armed himself with a spike and a club. For pity's sake, do what you can to help!'

Richard shouted to Daniel, who himself took the reins of the equipage that had brought them to the Grange, whipping up the horse to take them all at a galloping pace to Denwin's Corner. There they found that quite a crowd had collected, and with Meg on her own keeping close behind them, Daniel and Richard shouldered and thrust their way through to the front, none of the spectators wanting to surrender a place of vantage in an avid curiosity to see what would happen.

A score of navvies, rough and burly fellows through the very nature of their work, were gathered at the gate of the cottage ready to launch an assault, sledgehammers in their hands, their mood impatient and unsympathetic, for time was money to each of them, and they had already wasted enough of it trying to get the fisherman out of his abode in two unsuccessful skirmishes. The windows were barricaded, and in the open doorway, looking ready to defend his home with his life if need be, Bob stood braced with feet apart. His shirt was torn and blood ran from a cut on the head from a missile thrown earlier by one of the navvies, and in his hands he gripped the weapons that Meg had described.

Richard addressed the foreman, a bearded man dressed in a battered felt hat, canvas shirt and moleskin trousers, clothes which amounted almost to a uniform among the railway navigators. 'Where's Mr Barton?'

'At the siting on t'other side o' Merrelton today. Why?' A pugnacious thrust of the bearded chin. 'There ain't nothin' 'ere that I can't deal with. It ain't the first time I've 'andled a sticker, and we'll knock t'bloody place down on top of 'im if 'ee don't move out real sharp now.'

Daniel, who had come to his son's side, glowered at the man. 'We'll have no violence here. This was Warwyck land and property until recently, and unless proper notice to quit was served on Bob Cooper by the Railway Company, he has every right to question your attempts to turn him out.'

''Ee was given notice to quit awright.' The foreman cleared his throat and spat within an inch of Daniel's shining boots, and then set calloused hands on his hips as he smirked mockingly. 'From what I 'ear, it never were your land proper, so I don't see as 'ow you've any say in what I orders to be done 'ere.' Abruptly he turned from the waist and gestured with his arm to the waiting men. 'What are you 'anging about for? Let's get it over with!'

'Wait!' Richard stepped in front, restraining his father who in spite of what he had said .about violence had clenched his fingers into fists and looked set to deal physically with the foreman as though he were back in the prize-ring. 'If Bob Cooper is harmed through no fault of his own I'll have the lot of you up before a magistrate before the hour is out!'

From the doorway of the cottage Bob's voice boomed out bitterly. 'I don't want no 'elp from a Judas!'

Richard's head snapped back and his clear skin flushed an angry crimson. He stalked through the open gate and took up a stance on the path, face to face with the young fisherman he had known since they were both children, although their lives had followed widely different paths. 'Are you crazy?' he demanded heatedly. 'What devil has got into you?'

Bob's expression was one of unremitting hatred. 'You let me down! You told me that I could 'ave this cottage and buy it later! You gave me your word on it!'

Richard gave a sigh of comprehension. 'Good Lord, man. You know it's no fault of mine that the Railway Company bought the right of way across this land. There is nothing that I or anybody else could do to prevent it. Do you honestly think I would have this happen to you and Meg?'

Bob was in no mood to be deflected. His lips drew back over his teeth and he scoffed menacingly. 'You've supported the Railway Company from the start! You could 'ave stood out against it like your Dad! Together you might 'ave at least stopped 'onest folks getting thrown out of their 'omes like common paupers!'

Richard understood how savagely the man's pride was wounded, but he had written personally to each tenant in order to ensure that nothing like this present catastrophe should occur. 'In the letter I sent to you and every other Warwyck tenant living in the path of the new railway, I stated that I would do everything I could to provide alternative accommodation. I even dealt with Radcliffe tenants who had nobody else to turn to in the present crisis. But I heard nothing from you. When you made no application, I thought you had found somewhere else through your own initiative.'

'Where could I find some place else? I sank all I 'ad into

this property. An 'ome for Meg and me. It's mine, and I ain't moving out.'

Richard tried again. 'Let me at least get the facts straight. Did you receive notice to quit from your new landlord, the Railway Company?'

'Yes, I did. A week they gave me. Seven bloody days!'

'Did you make any appeal for an extension of time?'

Bob let forth a roar as if finally goaded beyond endurance, and the raised spike shook in his grasp. 'I don't do no appealing for what's mine by rights!'

Richard took a step forward unflinchingly. 'I'll see you get compensation, and somehow or other I'll find you another cottage. Put down that spike and let's get your furniture moved out between us. There's plenty of folk in the crowd outside the garden wall who'll give us a hand, too.'

The spike tilted to a striking angle. 'You come one step more, and you'll get as good as anybody else what tries to make me leave this place.'

At the gate Meg gave a little moan of fright and ran forward to come between Richard and her maddened husband. 'Do as he says, Bob. Please do as Mr Richard says. You can't hold out against these bullies what are waiting to tear the cottage down. You'll only get hurt – and hurt others at the same time.'

'You keep outta this, Meg! I got this place for you, and – by God! – I'll see that I don't lose it now!'

It was then that the navvies made a rush, shouting and yelling as they came like fighting warriors of old. They spread out in a semi-circle, and those on the outskirts began to swing their sledgehammers to crack into the walls. Meg screamed as Bob lunged to repel the attack, but Richard seized the chance of his distracted attention to land a punch that caught him full in his ribs, following it up with a right-hander to the point of the jaw that sent him crashing back through his own doorway to lie prone on the floor, Meg rushing to him. Richard promptly snatched up the fallen spike and roared himself like a berserk warrior as he used it to beat back those who had already smashed some of the stonework and sent cracks leaping across the ancient walls, filling the air with a thick, powdery dust and causing some straw to slip from the thatch and tumble down.

'Get back! Get back! There's a woman in there! You'll kill them both if the rafters go!'

His father was with him, giving able assistance, and had been joined in turn by other bystanders who leapt over the wall and rushed forward to help prevent any further misadventure. Order was soon restored, and Richard went back to crouch down beside Bob, whose head was in Meg's lap as she dabbed the cut he had sustained earlier with a piece of clean linen, her expression showing mingled exasperation and affection. She had pushed the door to an angle.

'He's been real soft over this cottage,' she said, 'but I told him a dozen times after we received notice to go that one day we'd get a place just as good. Better, in fact,' she added cynically, 'because it's damp enough to give lung fever when it rains heavy.'

'Why didn't you come to see me, Meg? You know I would never have let things come to this pass.'

A suggestion of a smile showed about her lips, which did nothing to lift the wry look that saddened her face. 'I told you once that I'd only get you to find another place for me if I didn't have Bob around, and it's still that way.' She gave a shrug as if to throw off her troubles. 'We're going back to Ma's at Sea Cottage.' In her lap, Bob groaned and she peered down at him. 'He's coming round, I think. His eyelids is moving. We'd best get him carried out of here and get the furniture bunged on the cart that Ben has been hanging about with for the past two or three hours or more.'

Richard put his hand lightly on her wrist, making her look up sharply at him. 'You married to get away from home and that man's company,' he exclaimed. 'Surely there's somewhere else you can go.'

'Beggars can't be choosers,' she retorted with forced brightness. 'Nor can wives.' Then abruptly her face crumpled, and she leaned across to hook an arm about his neck, her quick kiss soft and moist upon his lips, her breath sweet and warm. 'Thanks for what you did today. Bob won't be grateful for it, but I will. Always.' She stroked his hair away from his face as she drew back, and with effort she tore her gaze from him to look down at Bob again with a kind of resigned tolerance as the navvy foreman kicked the door wide with the toe of his boot.

'Are you getting out of 'ere or ain't you?'

Meg tossed her chin at him with haughty contempt. 'You keep your trap shut. We're going.'

Daniel had organized some helpers to move out the furniture, but he kept them back to allow Richard to help Bob to his feet and out of the cottage before taking the fisherman's arm himself to haul it about his neck and give assistance in getting him along. Meg collected up a bundle and a basket of goods she had packed in readiness for their evacuation, having had no faith in Bob's chances of keeping the Railway Company at bay for any length of time, and she watched without emotion the carrying out of the few sticks of furniture and the rolls of bedcoverings that had made up the home in which she had found little happiness. She was glad that the wall-bed itself could not be moved and would be destroyed with the demolition of the cottage, for Bob's rough ways and basic insensitivity had made that area of their partnership something she had come to dread, whatever rare tenderness he had shown during their courting days lost in the blunt satisfaction of his own appetites now that she was merely his wife and his chattel. Only his jealousy was unchanged, and it had brought about many bitter quarrels between them.

Richard and Daniel had propped him up at the back of the cart among the furniture, where he sat groaning still and holding his head. She clambered up there with him, thankful to have an excuse not to sit beside Ben, who had done nothing to help with the removal, merely lolling a shoulder against the side of the cart, the whip in his hand, and occasionally flicking the sleeves and front of his yellow check coat to make sure no dust from the sledgehammers had settled upon it. Yet his narrow-set eyes missed nothing, and Daniel was unaware how closely he was being observed.

As the cart rolled away and the navvies began the work of demolishing the cottage with violent satisfaction, Richard returned to the wagonette where Lucy had remained seated throughout the furore. He saw that the scene had upset her

275

deeply and realized it must have resembled those she had seen in Italy and which she had described to him in argument against the power of railway companies. He had to raise his voice to make himself heard above the crashing and thumping of the sledgehammers.

'I'll do what I can for Meg and Bob,' he said to reassure her. She only nodded and lowered her gaze, not wanting to discuss it. Then Richard was seized by the shoulder and jerked about to face his father's blazing eyes.

'Now you can see what that damned railway you support can do to people! And this is only the start of it! What it has done to the Coopers it will do to Easthampton next! Have you no conscience? No shame?'

Richard, his own nerves frayed, lashed back at him. 'All credit to the man for defending his own home, but that doesn't detract from his being as stubborn and bigoted as you are! Neither of you has been able to face up to drastic change! Both of you have been like ostriches with their heads in the sand!'

Lucy leapt down hastily from the wagonette to put herself between them, never having seen two men more angry with each other, and fearful of words said that could never be retracted. 'Please! Don't let us have more trouble at this unhappy place today. Take me back to Easthampton or I shall drive myself and leave you both to walk, no matter whose wagonette it is!'

Her attitude left them in no doubt that she meant what she said, her own anger with them having a quelling if not healing effect. Daniel, still breathing furiously, made the wagonette dip under his weight as he took the driving seat, leaving Richard to assist Lucy back into it and take a place beside her. The whip cracked over the horse's head, and only Richard looked back to catch a last glimpse of Denwin Cottage. He had made up his mind never to tolerate his father's verbal abuse again. He had had enough. The rumble of collapsing walls followed them in the quiet, autumnal air.

It seemed to Lucy that from that day forth neither the countryside nor the resort were ever free of the noise of hammering and sawing, the ring of iron and the clang of spade. Blasting was frequent, making the ground shake. Josh and his assistant engineers, aided in turn by inspectors of earthworks and masonry and other areas of specialized knowledge and experience, were everywhere on horseback, their shouts of 'Whar off!' making navvies move out of their path in a hurry. There appeared to be not a minute to spare in the race to get the branch line completed in record time, the ambition of every contractor worth his salt. Horses plodded with heavy loads, many local carthorses being recruited, and as a precaution Daniel would not let his bathing-machine horses out of their stables without responsible supervision, wary of their being stolen by navvies to replace others less strong in the shafts. Almost without exception, the navvies were wild and rough and hard-drinking, and the shacks that were erected to house them blemished the landscape, for although the dwellings were white-washed frequently and Josh ordered that they be kept scrubbed and free of rubbish, all the men were accustomed to squalor and their personal habits were more fit for a pigsty than human habitation. With them came their women, camp-followers who were frequently the cause of brawls that wrecked the shacks and had any number of men fighting each other in the mud that surrounded the dwellings. By night the sounds of their roistering echoed far, the burning braziers glowing like red-gold lamps, which inevitably drew to them many local women and girls in search of excitement or monetary gain, sometimes followed by irate husbands or desperately concerned fathers, who were brutally beaten up and cast into half-dug sitings for their temerity in daring to invade the navvies' territory. Worst of all as far as the local communities were concerned were the navvies' drunken randies in Easthampton and Merrelton, as well as other neighbouring villages, when they invaded the inns and the taverns, drove out other patrons, bullied landlords, smashed glasses and mirrors and generally made a dangerous nuisance of themselves. Outside in the streets they hurled bottles at gaslamps and through windows, terrified the horses of passing trade-vans and more elegant equipages by throwing ripped-up palings into the road, and relieved themselves as openly as they copulated with their doxies in shop doorways and side-streets, heedless of passers-by.

The Easthampton Council Committee, of which Daniel was chairman, had applied at his suggestion for extra constabulary to be sent to Easthampton during the building of the railway, and this was granted, but thirty bobbies, however stalwart and burly, were ill-matched against the overwhelming numbers of those opposed to law and order. Nevertheless, discipline and training did prevail sometimes, particularly when members of the public gave assistance, and the cellars of the Assembly Rooms provided extra lockup accommodation when needed.

After one particular randy, Daniel with Kate at his side drove grimly through his cherished resort to view the damage. It was a blue-grey November morning, hazy in a mist from the sea that gave a pale glitter to everything, touching the bare branches of the trees in Ring Park as delicately as the broken bottles that littered the gutters and crunched underneath the wheels, awaiting the attention of the busy road-sweepers. Fiercely he noted the number of smashed windows of stores and homes alike, and ground his teeth at the sight of the graceful columns of the Assembly Rooms which had been daubed with paint looted from a builder's yard. He abhorred wanton damage and destruction of any kind, and it gave him no satisfaction upon reaching the site where the terminus was being built to see that on this occasion the Railway Company's own property had not escaped, and workmen were having to rebuild a new wall levelled during the night and replace window and door frames that had been ripped out and made into a bonfire on the beach. Kate had been anxious about Honeybridge, but no harm had been done there, and she kept her hand tucked into her husband's arm in silent commiseration at the scars left by the senseless vandalism. Not even the fishermen's boats had escaped. They stopped briefly to speak words of commiseration to Bob Cooper, whose beached craft had been smashed in at the side by a huge piece of rock that must have needed three men to lift it. He appeared to be enraged beyond speech, swallowing hard in his throat, and with a glint in his eyes that seemed close to madness. Meg, whose own boat had been one of the few to escape damage, came across the shingle to thank them for their concern.

'I think you've seen enough of Josh Barton's vandalism for one day,' Daniel growled to Kate as he followed a left-hand fork in the road that would take them out of town in the direction of the Grange. 'Now you shall see something to pleasure your eye instead.'

It was to be Kate's first visit to the Grange since Daniel's purchase of it, and she had not yet recovered from the joy of regaining Honeybridge after Lucy had moved into her new quarters. When Daniel had put the deeds of her dear home into her hands, her whole face had been transfigured by the love she had always felt for him, her blue eyes dewy with adoration, and he had experienced a sense of wonder that she could retain such passion for him after so many years of marriage and in spite of his short temper and his many other faults. That life would have no meaning for him without her was something he had discovered for himself years before, but then Kate with her deep, generous heart was a wife beyond rubies, and he a husband far from deserving such devotion as she had ever shown him.

'Am I forgiven?' he had asked, not able to remember ever having sought this of her before, but never had it seemed more important to know that the slate was wiped clean. She had smiled, throwing her arms about his neck, giving him such loving reassurance in whispered words that he had held her in silence, savouring his immense good fortune.

Her melodious voice broke in on the reverie that had begun to soothe his angry mood. 'You must not blame Josh for what his navvies do away from the railway sitings. When they are working he has full control over them and, so I've heard, is respected for his toughness and iron discipline. But once outside his jurisdiction they are free men, however they choose to behave.'

'He is responsible for their being here in the first place, is he not?' he demanded uncompromisingly. It irritated him that Kate should defend the fellow on all counts at every opportunity. At times it was as if she had developed some special affection for him, and although he told himself it was nonsense, he could not shake off the feeling that for some time Kate had been holding some secret to herself that she had no intention of disclosing to him. Admittedly Josh Barton had all the attributes to make him attractive to women, but Kate wouldn't start dallying at her age. The idea was preposterous! Or was it, when the fault was not her own? In their mid-forties, women often began to take the strangest fancies, and Dr Houston had said as much about her state of health after speaking to Kate at his request, recommending a tonic for her, a physic of his own concoction, saying that she ailed only from a general debility at such times. Debility? Kate? She had always enjoyed radiant health, and the bottle of tonic, followed by a second one, had had no visible effect at all. If anything, she seemed to have become slightly more wan, although she was as cheerful and obdurate as ever in speaking her mind.

'That still doesn't make him the men's moral keeper,' she countered. 'I think it's high time you buried the hatchet with the railway and made the best of things.'

He glared at her. 'You dare say that to me after the damage we've just witnessed.'

'Yes, I do,' she retaliated, head high. 'The navvies will not be here for ever, but the railway will. Jem used to say what a good loser you were in your early days as a fighter, before you began to win all your bouts and no longer knew defeat.' She tightened her clasp on his arm and leaned against him in appeal. 'Accept that this is one mill where you have been floored and treat it in good part as you did all those years ago. That in itself is a kind of victory.'

He was stony-faced. 'Has Richard suggested you put this persuasion to me?'

She straightened abruptly, arrow-backed. 'No, he did not.' Then her indignation softened away. 'But it is for his sake and yours that I ask you to concede this particular contest. Lately you've hardly spoken a civil word to him, but must upbraid him constantly for having supported the railway that has brought the navvies' unruliness as well as all else into this area. I'm afraid it will cause a permanent rift between you eventually. He no longer comes to the house as often as he did, and Donna needs to see him since he alone seems able to establish communication with her. She has not spoken to you since before she locked herself in her room, and has become almost as taciturn with me.'

She did not add that it was her attempts to heal the breach between father and daughter that had done much to turn Donna further from her. It was as if the girl felt the whole world had sided against her, and only Toby was welcome in her company. But not even for the dog would she emerge from her room, and his daily walks had been designated to a servant. To give Daniel his due, he had tried to meet Donna halfway, but her chill rejection, her averted face, and her deliberate deafness to whatever he had to say had caused him the old hurt and disappointment, out of which the familiar impatience had smouldered anew. To Kate it had never been more important that there should be no rift between Daniel and their children, and she would continue to do whatever she could to try to bring about some lasting harmony, but whether she would manage it in whatever span of time was left to her she did not know. She glanced at Daniel anxiously, trying to read his expression, for he had given her no reply, but she could tell that he was mulling over what she had said. That gave her some faint hope, and she watched the passing landscape with an effort of concentration to catch a first glimpse of the Grange through the bare branches.

Daniel's thoughts were mixed. As always Kate had spoken sound common sense. He had lost out to the railway, but that would be nothing compared with the loss of his son's respect and affection. Although it was partly Jem's training that had taught each of them in youth never to bear malice in fair combat, Richard's tolerance could not be expanded forever, and he had given him a hard time with his constant tirade against everything to do with the railway. He knew that for the first time he had soured their relationship, unable to cast out the canker of resentment that his own son should still see some kind of glory in the coming of those smoke-billowing monsters that caused such havoc and destruction in the laying of the path before them. Maybe he had forgotten how to be a good loser. It was so many years since he had suffered a knock-out or been thwarted in his plans, but no one knew, not even Kate, just how dreadful a blow it was to him to face the changing of Easthampton's tranquil character. The Grange Hotel was not going to be as he had originally pictured it, but was to be crammed with supporters of the prize-ring who were different from those who had put up purses in the old days of the Fancy. A new element had crept in, with less regard for fair play and sportsmanship, in spite of amended rules, and several times in London with the manager he had appointed for the arranging of bouts, they had been offered crossed fights or other crooked deals. Not that such tricks were not played when he was young, but he had never as much as landed a foul punch in all his years as a fighter, and he had been outraged that such offers should have been put to him. His brother, Harry, who lived in opulent luxury in a grand house in Mayfair and with whom he had stayed during the many short sojourns in London that making mill fixtures for the Grange had involved, had agreed with him that things were not as they used to be, but offered to put up a purse for the opening fight, although he could not be present as he was going back to Paris for a while. 'I'll visit you at Easthampton when I return,' he had said. 'It's a long time since I've seen Kate.'

Kate. Daniel sighed inwardly. How was he to answer Kate? Everything she had said was right. She was almost always right. He gave her a sardonic, sideways glance. 'It's quite a long time since you last petitioned me.'

Her face became vivid with hope. 'Yes?'

A grin lifted a corner of his mouth self-mockingly. 'You did right to bring me up to scratch again. I had practically forgotten how to capitulate graciously.'

Thankfulness overwhelmed her. She bit her quivering lip as if to steady her smile, her blue eyes suddenly a-swim. 'Dear Daniel. Oh, my dear Daniel.' She stretched her neck and kissed him as though they were still young lovers, and he felt no older as he held her hard about the shoulders and kissed her back.

Lucy met them at the door of the Grange, and they entered to find a log fire blazing in the huge marble fireplace. The anteroom where Lucy had waited to see Timothy for the first time had been opened into a reception area with a curved mahogany desk. After looking at the bookings with her and discussing them with the clerk who was dealing with the office work, the three of them went through to the ballroom, which had been transformed with cushioned benches and a raised ring in the middle.

'How ever many can be seated?' Kate questioned with interest.

'Six hundred on the benches, and there'll be standing room in the aisles and the minstrels' gallery,' Daniel answered. 'We're practically sold out for the opening fight next week. The Grange can only accommodate one sixth of that number, but bookings for accommodation in Easthampton have been beyond expectations.'

Lucy did not join the Warwycks where they stood together by the ring, but went across to look out of a window. 'There is only one cloud at the moment, and that is quite literally on the horizon. Work has started on Attwood land. The navvies are digging beyond those distant larches.'

'They've reached there, have they?' Daniel muttered, going to stand by her and stare in the direction in which she was pointing. Kate was struck by the similarity between father and daughter in the manner in which they both leaned their heads in exactly the same way, and she put a hand to the base of her throat, aware of a pain sharper than that which nagged daily in her side. Then she was the first to see that Josh had come into the ballroom in time to catch what Daniel had said.

'I'll do my best to ensure that there's no trouble from them on this estate,' he announced.

The others turned as Kate hurried across to him, extending her hand, her whole face radiating her pleasure in seeing him again. She had pinned such hopes on him, and never doubted that he would settle the one terrible complication that was beyond her power to unravel.

'Good day, Josh! Your coming here today is quite providential.' Her eyes conveyed the deeper message to him, which he understood. 'I've been wanting to ask you if there's anything I can do to help those unfortunate women with babies who are living in the navvies' shacks –'

Daniel's voice boomed across at her. 'Kate! You must not go near those creatures.'

'— and I have a store of baby clothes hoarded in the attic that I should like them to have. Those infants are in nothing but rags.'

Josh, who was still holding her hand, smiled at her. 'Heed your husband's advice, I beg you. Let me have those clothes and I'll see that they're delivered, but don't go there yourself. The women would resent interference, however well-meaning your intentions. They're not starving, because in most cases they cook the men's food and there's plenty of it, and should they fall ill I have arranged that they as well as their children can seek medical advice from the Easthampton doctor appointed to attend accidents and deal with any injuries.'

She withdrew her hand from his and looked across with shining eyes at her husband. 'There. You see the Railway Company has some heart, Daniel.'

Daniel snorted derisively. 'A simple safeguard against the spread of disease and pestilence in overcrowded hovels. Am I not right, Barton?'

'You are, sir. But I should like to point out that over-crowding is no fault of the Company. Shacks more than adequate for the number of men employed were not de-signed to include the womenfolk who flock after them wherever they go.'

Lucy spoke up. 'Then you should take that factor into consideration and build more.'

Josh gave her a slow look, lids narrowed. 'I did have an extra shack built in each place along the route where the navvies have their living quarters, but had I built a dozen, conditions would be the same.'

He had seen little of Lucy since the night at Honeybridge, simply because he had been working twenty hours out of every twenty-four, which was usual when work was finally launched, and from what he had heard she had been equally busy at the Grange. Yet he was starved for the sight of her and intended to remedy the matter. 'Speaking of quarters, I've a mind to move from Sea Cottage into the Grange Hotel if you've a room I can have until the spring.

It will enable me to ensure that no damage is done on this estate if I'm on the spot to keep an eye on things.'

Lucy compressed her lips. He was following her here as he had followed her to Emmie's place, and she had no illusions as to the reason. To her dismay, Kate, who should have had no voice in the matter, supported his suggestion enthusiastically.

'That's a splendid idea, is it not, Daniel? I know the hotel is fully booked for the weeks of the arranged fights, but didn't I hear it mentioned that there were some smaller rooms that had not yet been allotted to staff? I'm sure Josh would not mind one of those until a better room is available.'

'Indeed I wouldn't. I'll move my traps in the day the hotel opens.'

Daniel was puzzled and somewhat displeased by Kate's exuberance. Not only had she welcomed Josh with a warmth reserved for close friends, but she had exchanged looks and glances with him that seemed to have meanings known only to themselves. That possessive streak in Daniel, which had always been his failing, stirred again and was made more uneasy than before. Other men had made play for Kate in the past, a common enough hazard when a wife was as beautiful as she, but never since he had made her his own had he seen her face hold secrets that were not for him.

Meg was hanging out clothes on the morning that Josh moved out of Sea Cottage, and she regarded him with some envy. The day when she and Bob would be able to find another place to live was far distant, and if they could have occupied the vacated rooms life would have been a great deal easier, but already her mother had let them to a retired parson who had come to the seaside for his health. To Emmie the presence of an ecclesiastical gentleman-lodger was to give the final stamp of respectability to her boarding-house, and she positively preened as she boasted to her friends and acquaintances about his coming, considering that it more than made up for the disappointment of Mrs di Castelloni working at the theatre whilst still under her roof. At the present time Emmie was still unaware that she herself had become a topic of gossip through her friendship with Ben Thompson. What there was between them Meg did not know, for her mother still kept her own bedroom, but it sickened her to see how the odious man was waited upon hand and foot, his palate considered at every meal, and how Emmie, who delegated all chores whenever possible, ironed his shirts herself with pernickety care to make sure they were exactly how he liked them. What was far more worrying to Meg than those comparatively minor irritations was the odd friendship that had been struck up between Ben and her husband.

She had first noticed it a few weeks after they had moved in from Denwin Cottage. To find themselves cramped into a single room scarcely bigger than a cupboard had played havoc with Bob's nerves, and after being master of his own home with first right to the best chair and the fireside, it riled him beyond measure to take a back seat to Ben Thompson. He had had little liking for Emmie before his marriage to her daughter, and as a mother-in-law he found her high-handed and interfering, to say nothing of her treating his wife once more as if Meg were still a single girl with no other commitments than to be at her beck and call. Then, almost overnight, Meg noticed that he began to grumble and complain less about their present circumstances, and it appeared to date from a drinking bout he had indulged in with Ben at The Crown, when he had reeled home drunk for the first time since their marriage. She made some excuse in her own mind for him, for they had quarrelled sharply beforehand, not through his jealousy this time, but because they were both under the constant strain of never being alone except in their cramped quarters at night – and even there Emmie had no compunction in rapping on the intervening wall if they disturbed her by talking late. Their accommodation had had a frustrating effect in more ways than one, and restricted the comfort that Bob might have found in his wife's arms.

But out of that evening's immoderate sharing of bottles with Ben Thompson, Bob seemed to have gained a new purpose to lift him above the daily irritations of living in another's house where he had no authority, and he had more money to jingle in his pockets than was normal from fishing at that time of year. When she had challenged him about it he had had an answer ready.

'Good old Ben put a bit of business my way. Not much, but it could lead to other things.'

'What sort of business?'

'Carting goods on my fish-cart into Merrelton. I've a mind to go into the carrier business on a bigger scale if all goes well.'

'Don't do it!'

'Why not? It'll give me a chance to save 'ard for a 'ome of our own again, and this time we'll buy a place outright. I'm trusting nobody's word no more.'

'That's what I mean.' She spoke urgently. 'Don't have anything to do with Ben Thompson, because his word ain't worth the breath used. He's a sly-bones, out for his own ends, and shifty with it.'

'Mebbe 'ee is a bit of a sharp at the race-track and such-like,' Bob admitted, 'but 'ee's straight and on the level with me. 'Ee's talking of 'im and me being partners if we can work up enough contacts to buy a proper removal wagon.' He sketched an imaginary display in the air. 'Cooper and Thompson, Carriers of Repute. 'Ow would that strike you then?'

'You wait till you can make it Cooper and Son. You don't want nothing to do with Thompson, I'm telling you.'

He cocked a wary eye at her. 'You ain't copped it, 'ave you, Meg?'

'No, I haven't. Not much chance with you boozing out most nights with Ben Thompson to all hours.'

He released a thankful sigh. 'We'll 'ave a family later on, but I wouldn't want no nipper of mine born into your Ma's 'ouse. The way she rules the roost it'd never know I was its father. That's why it's important that we get out as soon as ever we can to live our lives to suit ourselves again. I want to make as much money as I can real quick to that end.'

'We had the chance to get out, but you wouldn't take it,' she said stonily, reminding him of the day shortly after the scene at Denwin Cottage when Richard had come to give them first chance of rooms above a shop that had become vacant. Bob had refused the offer outright with the roughest language and the threat of violence if Richard ever came near him again. Gone for ever were the days when Bob had felt honoured that the Warwyck son and heir had chosen him to be his sparring partner in the gymnasium ring. His feelings were very different now.

His face darkened. 'I thought we agreed never to mention that no more.'

She hastened to placate him. 'Those rooms have been snapped up by somebody else long since, but I wager Mr Richard has other places coming vacant now and again. If you would just let me speak to him –'

For the first time ever, he did what she had never thought him capable of towards her: he hit her hard across the side of her face, causing blood to spurt from her lip. For a moment they stared at each other as if neither was able to grasp the reality of what had happened, and then he reasserted himself aggressively, wagging a menacing finger at her.

'If ever you go crawling to Richard Warwyck on my be'alf I'll kill you for it!'

As she bathed her swollen lip afterwards, and again that morning before hanging out the clothes in the frosty air, she thought how cruelly fate had twisted their marriage. What would have been an adequate partnership with the prospect of children to bring some real joy into her life had begun to deteriorate from the time Bob knew there was a threat to his house. Orphaned at an early age, housed on sufferance by his mother's married sister in a tiny fisherman's cottage overcrowded with her own brats and she seemingly forever pregnant, he had been kicked around and bullied until he had learned to use his fists to defend himself against the older boys. Was it any wonder that he guarded jealously whatever had become his own in later life, whether it be his boat or his wife or the home that had been such a wonder to him? The loss of it had affected him more than it would have done any other man. It explained the change for the worse in him, the gradual reversion to the brutality and insensitivity of his upbringing, but Meg, putting the final wooden peg into the corner of a sheet, blamed Ben Thompson's bad influence in recent weeks as much as anything else for bringing him to the point of physical violence against her. The days when she had managed to keep the upper hand had gone. Once a man began to hit his wife, the last shreds of respect or awe had been lost forever. But that would not stop her from trying to get Bob away from Ben Thompson's evil sway before anything worse happened. She would take the risk and see Richard. Suddenly and sweetly her heart rejoiced rebelliously at the excuse to seek him out.

She saw Richard twice before an opportunity to speak to him presented itself, for she did not dare to go to the office or to the house where he had apartments in case she should be seen in the vicinity and Bob somehow happen to hear about it. On the first occasion Richard drove past her in a carriage with Mrs di Castelloni and another couple, all four of them laughing together. The second time was when she joined a small crowd that had gathered outside the gate of Honeybridge.

'What's going on?' she asked somebody with a cheerful inquisitiveness.

'Honeybridge has been broken into by thieves. It's those navvies again, without a doubt. It were a grand clock and some old silver from the vicarage last week, and two or three of the big houses around have had valuables taken.'

'Who's in Honeybridge now?' She craned her neck to try to see between the heads of those in front of her.

'Mr and Mrs Warwyck – she's real upset, I can tell you – and their son, as well as two constables. Look! Here comes a sergeant now.'

The crowd parted to let the sergeant through, and Meg, in spite of being jostled back, still managed to catch a glimpse of Richard's serious face as he came out to meet the new arrival. Later she heard that another search by the constabulary had been made of the navvies' dwellings, and although some stolen articles had come to light, mostly boots and clothes and kegs looted from shops during randies, none of the small valuables from Honeybridge and the other houses had been recovered.

Meg's chance to talk to Richard on his own came one wild, rough morning when Bob had taken his cart to

Merrelton. The tide was high and the waves were being whipped into a frenzy by a wind flecked with snow, great hills of olive-green water sweeping in against the promenade to crash and soar twenty feet or more into the air, with showers of spume and shingle sometimes spewing over the promenade into the road in a roaring torrent of water. In her sou'wester and protective coat, her skirt hitched up around high boots, she had gone to collect a half-finished lobster-pot from her tarred hut, thinking to work on it at home that day, but the force of the sea washing about the bases of the huts had kept her back, for there was a danger of being dashed off her feet and swept away by a wave. She was about to retrace her steps when she saw on the pier the wind-blown figure of Richard holding on to his hat, his coat billowing, as he came from the theatre where doubtless he had been to check that all was in order and no sea water had seeped in from the waves splashing high about the head of it.

Hastening along the road, which was deserted in a general avoidance of the high water, she dodged the crashing waves until she came level with the entrance to the pier. There she darted up the steps onto the promenade again, a carpet of wave-tossed shingle and seaweed underfoot, and reached the shelter of the entrance by the pay-box as Richard came to it from the other side.

'Why, Meg,' he exclaimed. 'What are you doing here?' His grin spread. 'The pier is closed if you've a mind to take the sea-breezes along the length of it today.'

Her eyes twinkled merrily at him, her ripe, red lips parted in a smile, and her face glistened and glowed like his with the icy dampness of the spume that they had both encountered. 'I thought I might tempt you to a boat-ride,' she quipped back, all else forgotten momentarily in the joy of being alone with him.

He chuckled, his expression showing his young male pleasure in the sight of her, for neither the unbecoming sou'wester nor the rest of her shapeless garments could detract from the bonny look of her. Then he remembered that he had not seen her since her husband had sworn at him like a madman from the steps of Sea Cottage in rejection of his offer of some other accommodation. His face took on a frown.

'How are you managing at your mother's home?'

Her cheeks hollowed. 'That's what I wanted to talk to you about.'

He took a ring of keys from his pocket and found the one that opened the door to the pay-box. 'Let's go in here out of the cold wind.'

Inside, she pulled the sou'wester from her head and shook her curls free as she looked about her. The pay-box had a desk with a chair up-ended on it as well as a high stool by the shutter where the cashier sat to take the money, but otherwise it was bare, everything having been moved into storage until the season came round again. On the wall were still pinned a couple of posters advertising last summer's attractions, which included the Asquith Company's production of *Mazeppa*. He lifted the chair off the desk and put it down for her, but she only set one knee into it with a bundling of her looped-up skirt and held the curved back with both hands as she looked up into his face.

'I would have taken those rooms above the shop.'

He leaned forward and set his hands beside hers on the chairback between them. 'I know you would, Meg. I was sorry that Bob couldn't be persuaded. Has he had a change of attitude?'

'Far from it. I was only able to see you today because he has gone to Merrelton, but I wanted to ask if you have anything else we might rent or get hold of in some way, without him or nobody else knowing you had a hand in it.'

'I wish I could help there, but at the present time there's nothing on the books. I would gladly let you have at a peppercorn rent one of the smaller villas that would otherwise only be occupied now and again by prize-ring patrons throughout the winter, but Bob knows they are all Warwyck property and if his frame of mind is still the same towards me, he'll never set foot across the threshold of any of them.'

'You're right. He has no quarrel with your father, but he knows that Mr Warwyck would never let him rent cheap one of those houses that seem real fancy to the likes of us.' Gloomily she spiralled round and sat down in the chair. 'I want to get Bob away from Ben Thompson. They're talking of going into business together.'

He moved in front of her and perched his weight on the edge of the desk. 'Getting into another abode is not necessarily going to break off whatever they're planning, Meg.'

'But it would in this case,' she said earnestly, 'because Bob's a fisherman first and foremost, and he's only considering a carrier's route to make enough blunt to buy a home quick. If we had a place of our own again there'd be no need for him to rely on Ben's co-operation, don't you see?'

He was thoughtful. 'There are a couple of other carriers in the town already, and some of the transporting of goods will be lost by them to the railway when the branch line opens, so I don't see how Bob can expect to make a big financial success out of such a venture. Is Thompson trying to get him to invest money in the scheme?'

'That's impossible. Bob has no money to invest in nothing. Every tanner he had saved was lost in the demolition of Denwin Cottage.'

'He has drawn the compensation money from the bank.'

'What!' That was something she had not known or suspected; Bob had been vehement in his declaration that he would never touch tainted railway money. She guessed immediately that Ben Thompson had persuaded him to take it, most probably for his own gain. Richard observed her consternation.

'You didn't know? Then I think you should find out if he's keeping it towards another home or using it to launch himself into business with Thompson, which I would advise against on all counts. Undoubtedly, if nothing else, Thompson is a shady character. Josh Barton told me that the fellow had the temerity to admit with full conceit to organizing the demonstration at the pier in favour of the railway, and offered to stage similar displays of support if Josh cared to grease his palm as liberally as had been done by an unnamed local person who wished to see the branch line built against Daniel Warwyck's wishes.'

'Whoever could have done that?'

'My father has an idea that an old enemy of his was behind it.' He did not intend to tell her that Daniel had suspected Olivia Radcliffe, saying the woman would not be above such a trick since her late husband had used similar devious means in the past in an attempt to bring him low. Her holding back the sale of the right of way until she judged the time right did seem as if every move she made was carefully calculated to do him the most harm. The old saying of 'Never trust a Radcliffe' appeared to hold good as much today for Daniel's interests as it had done in days gone by. Not for the first time, Richard found it hard to reconcile the mild, docile appearance of Mrs Radcliffe with the ruthless schemer that his father deemed her to be.

Meg expelled a long sigh. 'I can't ask Bob about the money, because there's no way I could have of knowing about it except by you telling me.'

'Would you like me to speak to him in this matter?'

'No!' She sprang to her feet, her concern more for the man she loved than for herself. Then, more calmly, regaining her composure, she added: 'It would not be wise. He don't take kindly to advice at the best of times, and he'd die afore he'd take it from you. I'll watch out. I'll see what I can do.' Her glance fell on the *Mazeppa* poster and she traced Lucy's name at the bottom of it against the word *pianoforte*. 'I hope things go better for you in your marriage than they have with mine.'

There was nothing self-pitying in her tone, only a loving warmth towards him, and not quite knowing why, he drew her to him and laid her head against his throat. She cuddled herself close with a yearning that was unmistakable and wrapped her arms around him, her eyes closed as if to savour to the full the exquisite joy of being moulded to him. It occurred to him then that not once had Lucy made a single, spontaneous gesture of affection towards him. Although always friendly and undoubtedly fond of him, her eyes lighting up whenever they met, she remained distant and elusive, and never once gave him the chance to hold her to him as he had Meg pressed into his arms. Yet he loved her with an all-consuming passion that had eliminated all other women for him, and apart from one indiscretion with Meg on the night he had been fired beyond endurance by kissing Lucy, he had remained faithful to that love. He realized that the time had come to ask Lucy to marry him and open the doors to a true reciprocation of feeling. He had been patient long enough. Courting a young woman of breeding and sensibility was very different from winning a fisher-girl to his pleasure. Yet that in no way lessened Meg's generous, lusty, young qualities in his eyes: he kissed the top of her head and put her gently from him.

'If I can arrange for you and Bob to get a home of your own somehow, I'll do it, but it could take time and I don't want you to raise any false hopes.'

'I won't.' She pulled on the sou'wester and shoved her curls into it. False hopes were something she had never cherished towards him, or else life would have been unbearable, and she could relegate anything he might do for her in connection with a home to the same sphere.

He opened the door for her and the cold wind whirled in. She put her head down and ran. A huge, breaking wave showered over the promenade, missing her by inches, and it thundered down in cascading foam, hiding her from his sight.

17

Lucy moved through the gaming-room, which was deserted except for the other croupiers, who chatted together while they waited for the hour of play to begin and made some last-minute check on their own tables. Christmas had come and gone, and already the New Year of 1851 was two months old. Since the day the hotel had opened, it had been crowned with nothing but success, much of it due to Richard, who had seen that it was advertised in the right quarters. At the present time he was visiting his uncle, Harry Warwyck, in Paris, at the start of an extensive venture in advertising along the Continent to encourage foreign visitors to patronize Easthampton as well as the Grange in the coming season. With his instinctive business flair, he had seized upon the unique opportunity presenting itself through the presentation of the Great Exhibition which was to open in London in May at a specially built glass hall, already known as the Crystal Palace, that was guaranteed to attract vast numbers of people from practically every country of importance overseas.

'I wish you were coming with me,' Richard had said to Lucy before his departure the previous day, an advertisement in himself for English tailoring, in his well-cut, grey-check travelling clothes. She wished it too, but she guarded any remark that he could interpret to mean more than it did.

'You don't need my poor French to help you in this venture,' she replied gaily, 'because I'm told you speak it fluently and have some German and Flemish at your command.'

The look he gave her told her clearly that he knew she was evading any kind of commitment, and his face tightened as if some new resolution had toughened in his mind. She guessed unhappily that he thought he had played the silent, waiting suitor long enough. Like many good-natured, patient people, he had without doubt come to a point at which he could be as forceful and aggressive as anybody else, and in his drawn face there was something close to a threat. He would have no more of it. When he returned he would force the issue between them. Perhaps he might have said as much to her there and then had his parents not also been present in the hall of the Grange that morning, waiting to say their own farewells to him.

'You have my uncle's address in Paris,' he said to her, 'which I shall make my base for two or three weeks at least, and after that I'll let you know where else I shall be. You will write to me, won't you? I shall miss you every day.'

As always, her affection for him surged strongly, and she nodded her promise. 'I'll write to you regularly. Take care on your journey, and may good fortune go with you all the way.'

That was yesterday. In her small sitting-room on the next floor up she had begun a letter to him after returning from a visit to the Hollands, to whom she still gave Italian lessons, using some local news they had given her as a point of interest on which to commence the correspondence. Usually something amusing or entertaining happened during the gaming sessions, and she fully expected to have enough to round off the letter the following morning as she went on a final tour of inspection and had a word with a croupier and one of the servants waiting on hand. The ornately-framed pier-glasses handed on her reflection as she passed by them. Her gown was of rich green satin, a shade that set off her creamy shoulders and burnished hair which was adorned with an inverted horseshoe-shaped arrangement of gauze flowers placed well back at the crown of her middle parting. All around her, the tables were set spaciously, eliminating any

296

crowding at play, the lights of the chandeliers supplemented by additional lamps to give brilliance to the red, white and black of some surfaces, the green baize of others, each in a waiting setting of gilded, high-back chairs. Another collection of paintings had replaced those that had been removed before the auction, and no light patches showed now on the gold and azure walls.

Although the players had yet to make an appearance, it was by no means quiet in the gaming-rooms, for from downstairs in the ballroom where a fight was in progress there arose a perpetual roar of men's voices, punctuated by thundering crescendoes of approbation or dismay according to the fortunes of the combatants concerned. The fact that the fights were held on private property without threat of disturbing the peace had resulted in no interference from the law, and in the same way Daniel's lawyers had managed to establish that the gaming-rooms constituted a club separate from the hotel, which had also put to rest Daniel's original misgivings as to how long the tables might run without intervention. Lucy had replaced three croupiers during the two and a half months that the hotel had been opened, having discovered that each of them was attempting an individual swindling of players. She had also ordered out and banished from re-admittance a number of sharps who had thought to practise tricks they had got away with often enough at other clubs. Already the Grange rooms had gained a reputation among gaming circles for scrupulously honest play, and Lucy herself had earned the reputation of being as eagle-eyed as she was virtuous, the latter quality an unusual one in such places, and a source of disappointment to any number of patrons who had thought to chance their luck in that direction.

Deciding to break the monotony of waiting by going herself to find out if the fight was nearing its close, Lucy went from the gaming-rooms, making for the head of the grand staircase. Only once had she witnessed some part of a fight, when the doors into the ballroom had been left open for a circulation of air. The sight of the two fighters, clad only in white knee-breeches, pounding each other with bloodied knuckles as they reeled and staggered together in the ring after twenty gruelling rounds, their hair dark with sweat and their bruised bodies splashed with each other's gore, was more than she could stomach. She had hated the noise made by the spectators ever since, thinking it like the roar of some ravenous animal waiting for the kill, and although Richard had tried to explain to her the finer points of the skill involved in boxing, which needed both tremendous courage and stamina, she had never been able to reconcile herself to it. Many a time she had seen the combatants the day after a fight and had been filled with pity for their battered visages and swollen, bandaged hands, making her wonder yet again what Lionel Attwood would have thought of his daughter being indirectly responsible for prize-fights held within his elegant ballroom.

Yet it had been a necessary step to recoup the great financial outlay that Daniel's purchase of it had involved, and her conscience did not trouble her. On the whole she was intensely happy to be living at the Grange, in spite of not finding herself to be as completely at home as she had expected. Coming to a standstill at the head of the staircase, she was reminded that the reason for that was known to her without the slightest shadow of doubt. The man in her thoughts was coming up the stairs.

'Is the fight over?' she asked.

He shrugged. 'I've no idea. I've only just come in.' He came level with her and rested a hand on the carved newel-post. 'You'll be glad to know that the last of the tracks were laid across the Attwood stretch today. There'll be nothing more to hear of the railway until the first train goes through.'

'When will that be?'

'The second day of April.'

'So soon?'

'Due to the comparatively mild winter, there have been no delays or hold-ups, and work is well ahead of schedule.'

'Then you'll soon be moving away.' Her clear, grey gaze mocked him.

He grinned back at her, undaunted. 'On the contrary, I intend to remain in this comfortable hotel much longer. What I hoped for has come about. The Company is to link the Easthampton branch line through Merrelton to the direct London line, which will keep me in this area far longer than I originally anticipated.' He reached out and took her by the arms, making the green satin of her sleeves tauten as he drew her one unwilling step towards him. 'Isn't it time we stopped this cat-and-mouse game that you persist in playing? Can't you at least tell me why you've never agreed to a second truce such as the one that meant so much to both of us that night at Honeybridge?'

Inwardly she had been cast down by the information of his extended stay. She wanted him out of the Grange and out of her life. He had never ceased to represent an indefinable threat to her, and it hung over her like a cloud. She felt that until he was gone she would not be able to come to terms with the remnants of her spiritual heritage that the Grange represented to her. Always he came between her and any possible adjustment that could be made. As to her feelings for him, they were equally confused and troubled, for he never failed to make the same dramatic impact upon her senses as he had done at their first meeting long ago; it was as if her body was in constant opposition to her mind. She answered him with lids lowered. 'There would be no point. Nothing could come of it.'

'In a way, I agree with you,' he said levelly, making her look up quickly at him through the shaded fans of her lashes. 'Of what use is a temporary ban? We must go beyond it to a total banishment if we are to achieve anything worth while.'

He pulled her hard against him, and his lips came down on hers with equal force, all patience flown. The latent need in her was ignited against her will, making her pulse race and her passion flare, and the two of them remained locked together in embrace at the head of the stairs until doors below burst open to let forth the stream of spectators from the ballroom. The fight was over.

He released her and she hurried back to the gaming-rooms, flustered and without her customary composure, putting to rights some soft tendrils of her hair that had slipped from place. By the time the first gaming patrons had taken their places at the tables, the air filling with cigar smoke that curled up about the chandeliers, and the spin of the roulette wheel mingled with the rattle of dice and the slap of cards, she appeared to be her usual self again, but the colour remained high in her cheeks and her concentration on the play as she sat-dealing from the Faro box was less fixed than it might have been. Out of the corner of her eye she saw Josh, who had dined and was changed into evening clothes, give her a glittering glance before taking a seat at the roulette table some distance away. She tried to forget his presence, but for her it was as if the two of them were the only people in the room and the rest had dissolved into a haze about them. He had been at the tables often enough before without disturbing her with his presence, but the unexpected kiss after such a long period of being untouched had transported her again to that state of uncontrollable sensations into which he had plunged her that night at Honeybridge. Had she been in love with him she could not have been more distracted and full of yearning. When a new player took a vacated chair to join the Faro table, she did not look at him as she would normally have done until he requested cards. He had spoken in Italian. Her head jerked round and she stared at him in shock and horror. It was Domenico! Suave, complacent, perfectly groomed, he regarded her piercingly across the table.

'*Buona sera*, Lucy. It's been a long time.'

Her one thought was to get away from him. She sprang up and signalled to an assistant croupier that he should take over from her. Seizing handfuls of her satin skirt she swirled away from the table, earrings flashing emerald sparks, and made for the door concealed by the panelling, never having dreamed that it was to be used for a different kind of escape than the one that Daniel had feared. Once beyond it, she shot the bolt and drew breath in the narrow passageway that stretched darkly to an archway of light in the distance. Her heart was pounding against her ribs and she put her hand against the wall as she went slowly along, almost faint from the unwelcome sight of him that she had suffered. For a few seconds it had been as if she were back in that Florentine room, alone with him when he had groped and grabbed and bitten and thrust in that horrific violation of her body. The very air about him at the table had seemed contaminated, and had he reached out to her she would have screamed.

Weakly she leaned against the passage wall and tried to take stock of the situation. What had brought him to Easthampton? Why had he slid insidiously back into her life? All that Timothy had done to charm her away from those black memories of Domenico's sexual abuse lay in shards about her. She had nothing to sustain her against this awful return of the past except her own will to overcome and survive.

Resolutely she straightened up and continued along the passageway, not holding on this time, but without logic or reason wishing that Josh would appear in silhouette against the distant, lighted archway that led into the rest of the house. She knew she would have run to him, but this was her own private moment of truth and she must face it with whatever courage she could summon up.

By the time she came out of the passageway and passed through a lamplit room into a wide corridor beyond, she knew she would have to endure a longer meeting with Domenico sooner or later. He would not leave the Grange without disclosing the purpose of his seeking her out again. Attack was better than defence, and she would send a note to whichever room he was occupying in the hotel, giving a time when she would be prepared to see him.

She reached her small suite of rooms, and putting a taper into the fire burning in the grate, she lighted a lamp situated on a small, round table. For the second time that evening Domenico startled her. As the rising wick dispersed the shadows, she saw he was sitting in the wing-backed chair. She gave a sharp gasp, letting the taper fall. Swiftly he moved to snatch it up from the rug, blew it out, and replaced it in its ivory holder.

'Who let you into my rooms?' she demanded hoarsely, feeling her flesh creep at his proximity. To her relief she found that she was no longer afraid of him, but then she was less vulnerable than she had been in a locked room far away in Italy, for the bell-pull was only inches from her hand. But there seemed to be no violence in him now. He set a

301

foot against the fender, leaning an arm on the mantel, and regarded her almost without expression.

'Sovereigns can loosen tongues as easily as lire. I had a suspicion that you might rush from my presence somewhat abruptly, and found out beforehand where you had your own quarters in this chill barn of a house.' He glanced about at their surroundings with undisguised contempt. 'This is no place for a di Castelloni. I must say that I never took you seriously when you taunted me with a skill at gaming that you could put to good use.'

'Why have you come here? How did you find me? I never wanted to see you again!'

'I inquired at The Warwyck first. That is where you were when your maid left you, and there I was directed to the Grange immediately. It appears you have made yourself quite well known in the area, and have added the scandal of working in a theatre to all else.' He shifted his position away from the fire. 'But I did not come here to quarrel with you. Far from it. I came to make amends. To ask your forgiveness. I have not had a moment's peace of mind since that dreadful day of my father's funeral.'

She would never have believed that Domenico, with his huge conceit and arrogance, could have humbled himself to make such a request of her. Somehow it did not ring true, and a new and different alarm went through her. 'You could have written an apology if it troubled you so much,' she said warily.

He shook his head. As always he was immaculately dressed, his evening coat of black velvet, diamond studs sparkling in his stiff shirt-front, his waistcoat of ivory brocade, but he had always had a tendency to sweat profusely at times of tension, and small beads of moisture glistened on his temples now, some already trickling down to spot the folds of the silk stock at his throat. 'I had to see you. I had to talk with you and hear from your own lips that you have forgiven me for all that took place.'

'I've tried to put the past behind me.' Revulsion was so high in her that she found it impossible to express anything more charitable.

He took a linen handkerchief from his sleeve and dabbed

at his temples. 'That does not include, I trust, the affection that many of the di Castelloni family felt for you.'

Whether he had the effrontery to include himself with that group she did not know. 'I remember those who showed kindness to me,' she said stiffly. 'I ask you again to tell me why you have come.'

'On the family's behalf. All are concerned for you. None has had a letter, and your hasty departure without a word of warning caused my wife particular grief.'

There was no comment to make on such a statement. Her eyes only widened at the man's gross insensitivity and immeasurable gall.

'You were a great comfort to my father in those last years of his life,' he continued, unabashed, 'and my wife is insistent that some recompense should be made to you. She imagines that disappointment and hurt feelings that my father should have left you out of his will were the reasons why you left Florence in such haste. Therefore it was at her persuasion I set out to find you and discover your circumstances.'

'I want nothing!' Fiercely, hands clenched, she took a pace away from him, her skirt swinging. 'Only that you be gone from here.'

'I refuse to exchange harsh words with you. Nothing could be further from my wishes. Since you have been considerate enough to relegate my much regretted action against you to the past with all else, I feel the least you can do is to give some thought to the offer I bring as head of the family whose name you bear and who are wholeheartedly behind me on this mission. I invite you to return to Italy with me –' he raised a hand quickly to silence the refusal he saw register instantly on her face, '– and there you will be welcomed back into the bosom of the family, but this time with one important difference. You shall enjoy complete independence, with your own residence in Rome or wherever else you have a mind to settle, and with an income that will be paid annually out of the estate to keep you in a manner suited to your esteemed social position as the widow of Stefano di Castelloni. Accept my goodwill and let all differences be healed. I have only your well-being at heart.'

She was undeceived. That his wife wished her well she did not doubt, for there had been respect and some mutual liking between them, and she fully believed that Signora di Castelloni had genuinely sought the rest of the family's approval to seek the prodigal's return, but that did not mean Domenico had not put the idea into his wife's mind in the first place. The blandness of his expression as he delivered the message purporting to have been put forward by others reminded her of occasions in days gone by when he had seized upon some paltry excuse to try to be alone with her. He wanted her still. Wanted her enough to try trickery of another kind to entice her back within his sphere of influence. A shudder of abhorrence went through her.

'Do you think me such a fool that I cannot see through you, Domenico? Go back to your wife and tell her whatever will spare her feelings, but the truth is that I loathe you as much in this moment of your vile hypocrisy as I did the day you forced yourself upon me!'

He stared at her as if unable to believe that he had failed. Then, to her horror, tears began to flood his eyes and course down his face. 'No!' he roared out, almost as if by the very volume of his voice he could dispel what she said. 'No! You cannot refuse! What more can I offer you?'

'Nothing! I told you! Please go. I cannot bear that this awful discussion should go on any longer.' In her desperation she reached for the bell-pull, but he snatched her hand in both of his and slobbered kisses on it as he fell to his knees at her feet.

'You must have some mercy in that temptress body of yours! I grovel before you in a plea not to condemn me once more to the fires of hell that I have suffered on your account!' Then there came from him such a stream of obscenities to express his lust for her that she, already trying vainly to free her hand from his frantic clasp, reared back as if to throw herself out of hearing. Neither had seen the door open. Josh took one look at the scene before him and seized the back of Domenico's collar to wrench him to his feet and break his grip upon her hand.

'I don't understand Italian,' Josh declared threateningly through his teeth as Domenico, recovering himself, jerked his hefty frame free, 'but I do understand enough from the tones of voice in this room that the lady wants you gone from her sight, whoever you are!' He kicked the door wider to give emphasis to his meaning.

Domenico straightened his shoulders, pulled his coat into place and would have spoken once more to Lucy, who stood stricken and huddled into herself, shuddering from head to foot, but Josh clapped a heavy hand down upon his shoulder and gave him a thrust towards the door. A second thrust sent him stumbling out into the corridor, where he recovered his balance and with some semblance of dignity went away without a backward glance. Only then did Josh close the door.

Lucy was no longer in the sitting-room. He called her name, but she did not reply. He entered the bedroom, found it deserted, and went swiftly across to the dressing-room that opened out from it. There she stood with the hand and arm that the Italian had been kissing thrust deep into the jug of water on the washstand, causing it to spill over. Her face was ashen, her whole body shuddering violently.

'He has gone, my love,' he said reassuringly, his voice low. 'Whoever he is, I'll never let him come near you again.'

She closed her eyes and opened them again as if to show that she accepted that promise, but in no way did her shuddering abate, and above her elbow the water continued to sop up her sleeve. When he would have taken her arm from the jug, she resisted him, and he spoke gently to her once more.

'I can take all trace of that man's touch from you if you will trust me.'

Her voice seemed strangled in her throat and she could only look at him with eyes still dilated, but when he took hold of her arm again she did allow him to draw it free. He poured some water from the jug into that already spilt in the basin, and holding her shaking fingers he took the soap from the rose-patterned dish and began to spread the lather over her hand and wrist and up her arm. Gradually her uncontrollable shudders began to ease, and he lifted a towel from the towel-horse and dried her skin until all dampness was gone. Then he turned her hand palm uppermost and kissed it.

'I love you, Lucy Attwood,' he said, the words vibrating with the force of his feelings for her.

Her arms folded themselves tightly about his neck and he buried her mouth in his, crushing her to him, blotting out Domenico, the Grange and the whole world for her, leaving only himself. This time no intruder was nearby to shatter their privacy, and his loving of her began as he removed her garments from her, kissing shoulders and breasts and every area of her pale form as gown and petticoats fell away into ripples about her feet. As he lifted her up to carry her across to the bed she clung to him exultantly, her mouth against his.

In the bed, shadowed by the damask hangings from the lamp's soft glow, he lay down beside her to gather her to him again in the contact of nakedness, and her hair, which he had released from its pins with a combing of his fingers through its fiery silkiness, fell about them both in a caress of its own. He made love to her tenderly and powerfully, awakening her whole body, the full flood of her desires opening to him, and she was by turn wildly passionate and rapturously submissive, giving even as she received. When he was about to enter her, some dark memory stirred in the subconscious depths of her mind, making her tauten convulsively, but he pressed his loving mouth to her and brought her to such a renewed state of bliss that through it he was able to take wonderful possession of her. For a few seconds her eyes flickered open as if she had to see the adoring fury of his face above hers, and as her lids closed again he took her with him to the summit of their ecstasy, her cry seeming to linger long after the stillness of the room had descended again.

They made love all night long. When he stirred from sleep in the glimmer of dawn, he saw that she had moved away from him and was sitting on the edge of the bed, her beautiful, white back towards him, her hair scooped forward over one shoulder. Without looking round, she seemed to sense he was awake and stretched a hand behind her in his direction. He took it and rolled over to trail his lips down her spine.

'Last night you called me by my single name,' she said softly. 'Had I not loved you already, I should have loved you then.'

'How long had you loved me?'

'I don't quite know. Since Honeybridge perhaps. Maybe before. My fear of you blotted out all else.'

'You were afraid of me? I find that hard to believe.'

She turned her head to look over her shoulder at him, eyes sweetly tired from what had passed in the night hours. 'From the start you came between this house and me. I saw you as a threat to all I was trying to do in order to establish myself, to know my own identity, to receive acknowledgement that I belonged in this place and on this land.'

He sat up and put his arms about her. 'And now?'

'In the night I forgot all else but you, and knew fulfilment for the first time in every sphere. I was totally myself, a whole person with no half-shadows of identity to make me less than the woman I have always wanted to be. Now, this morning, the truth is no longer shut out, but things have reversed and I see the Grange as the barrier between us, reminding me that I have nothing to prove who I really am in this world. I have been wondering if that has been the way of it all along.'

He took her face tenderly between his hands. 'It has, my love. More than you could possibly have realized.'

And there, in the quietness, he told her that she was Daniel Warwyck's daughter.

18

Ben Thompson mingled with the dense crowd that had gathered in the newly-completed Station Road to watch the first train arrive at Easthampton. On the platform of the terminus itself were gathered local dignitaries and many other influential people, as well as the engineer and contractor responsible for the whole successful enterprise, Josh Barton. In the train when it arrived would be the heads of the Railway Company and their specially-invited guests. Easthampton, always ready to celebrate another milestone in its history, was once more decked in flags and bunting. The woods, hidden from general view by the brick wall of the station yard, competed unseen with their own soft colours of bluebells and violets, with celandine showing yellow on mossy banks amid small clouds of primroses.

As he waited on the pavement, chewing on a thin cigar, Ben thought he might take the train on the day he departed from Easthampton, which would be soon now. He had stayed long enough, lined his pockets adequately from a number of small sidelines, and enjoyed the most comfortable lodgings that he had had in many a long day, but like all good things, his sojourn by the sea must come to an end. If he remained much longer, a number of complications could begin to gather about his ears: Cooper would begin to question when he might expect to receive profits from his 'invested' compensation money and probe again for the delivery date of a non-existent carrier's wagon; suspicion of the theft of small antique valuables in the district had already shifted from the navvies, now at work north of Merrelton, and might easily come home to roost; in addition, Emmie had been pressing for him to marry her, not knowing he had walked out on a wife and six kids years ago, and if ever he should add bigamy to his other crimes, he would look for a better bargain in age and looks and financial status than Emily Linden. There was one more killing he intended to make before his departure, though, and that was to set himself up for a spending spree and a lavish outlay at the racing tracks through exerting a little clever pressure on the Warwyck purse.

He smoothed the palm of his hand down the side of his coat and felt the hardness of the two silver buttons in a small inside pocket. He had taken to keeping them on his person after suspecting that his room had been searched. What Emmie had been looking for he did not know, but he supposed inquisitiveness about his finances more than his past had prompted her rummaging among his possessions. If she had drawn her own conclusions about the incriminating letters that he had acquired through theft and other means, she had never tried to find out more from him of his blackmailing activities.

Blackmailing was a fine art, which Ben managed exceedingly well, always waiting long enough between demands for his victims to think that he had at last passed out of their lives, before reappearing in the certainty that they had recouped their finances and were able to shell out again. Demanding too much too often was a mistake that many blackmailers made. Trying to get blood out of a stone could result in driving a victim to desperate measures, usually suicide, and that put an unnecessary end to an otherwise fairly reliable income.

Ben was a trifle disappointed that it was not Daniel Warwyck who was to be put under pressure – although indirectly the man would pay for his silence – but in spite of there being an old score to settle from the past, he could not run the risk of that very occurrence being remembered, and him as one of the smuggling band that Daniel had hounded out and forced to disperse. No matter that many years had gone by, Ben knew he could still face transportation to Australia or bring imprisonment down upon himself if anything went wrong. No, after much cogitation he had decided that Kate Warwyck was the more vulnerable and by far the safer bet, for he had overheard how desperately she wanted to keep secret the true identity of her husband's by-blow. What a scandal would break over Easthampton and what repercussions it would have if the truth were ever revealed. Warwyck would find himself ostracized on all sides and the full shame and disgrace would fall equally upon his family. As for Richard Warwyck in particular, his mother seemed to think there would be the devil to pay if he should find out that he had been courting his half-sister, quite apart from everything else.

Had Ben been a smiling man, he would have grinned openly at the satisfaction of his thoughts and the easy prospect before him of lucrative gain with such little effort, but he merely congratulated himself inwardly that without his looking for it, Lady Luck had generously dealt him a winning hand. All that remained was to find the right moment to catch Kate Warwyck on her own.

On the platform, amid the quietly talking clusters of people gathered there, the Warwycks were conspicuous by their absence. Daniel, although he had resigned himself unwillingly to the hard fact that the railway had come to stay, could not bring himself to accept Josh's invitation to see the first train arrive, and Kate naturally had no thought of going without him. Richard would have been there had not his continental advertising tour proved such a success, and although nearing the end of it, he had been reluctant to cut it short when some openings still remained. The novelty of his approach – with display drawings and actual photographs taken by one of those newly-invented cameras of Easthampton's magnificent spread of sands and its pier and other sights of interest or beauty – had resulted in his being invited to speak to innumerable gatherings. He had been fêted at social occasions, and his handsome appearance and quiet charm had had much to do with the large number of bookings that had already poured into Easthampton for hotel and villa accommodation alike.

Harry Warwyck had been a great help to him too, opening doors which might otherwise have remained closed, and securing him entrées to the homes of those best able to smooth the way for him. When Richard did return, Harry was to accompany him, and at Easthampton House Kate had had the best guest-room made ready for her husband's brother.

One who knew herself to be of Warwyck stock was on the platform at Josh's side. Torn by loyalties, Lucy had had to face the fact that her commitment to Josh came before all else, and with the spectre of the Grange and her connections to it well and truly laid, she was able to walk in freedom along the platform at his side. It was through her that some cottages on the estate, long vacant, had been repaired for the last of the families displaced by the railway to be re-housed. One cottage, a little better than the rest, occupied by a gamekeeper on the eve of retirement, was to be offered for sale to Meg and Bob Cooper as soon as the man moved out to live with his daughter in another part of the county. Daniel had suggested that Lucy should first put the proposition to the Coopers, seeing that she knew Meg quite well and was aware of the circumstances that had uprooted them beforehand, and Richard, after being written to about the matter, had endorsed that she would be the right person to handle the matter delicately. Although he could not be held responsible for what had happened to the Coopers, she knew they were on his conscience, and the cottage on the eastern boundary of the Grange estate would be ideal for their needs.

Lucy had written to Richard regularly as she had promised, and he had answered. The first of his letters had been a true love-letter, full of tender expressions and an outpouring of what it had meant to part from her, and she had known a deal of heart-searching before she had penned a reply. In it she had begged him not to write in the same strain again, and tried to warn him that she would have something of the utmost seriousness and importance to tell him when he returned, but whether she had prepared him fully she could not decipher from his letters, which still carried loving undertones although on the surface he had written nothing that could not have been written in simple friendship. She both dreaded and longed for his return, knowing that what she had to disclose to him was the hardest task she had ever had to perform in her whole life, for she knew that nothing she had said or done since the day she first saw him from the window of the Italian carriage had changed one iota his devotion to her. Had she been less bound to the Grange, less intricately involved with the past, she would have cut the bonds by disappearing out of his life, but it seemed to her that events and causes determined all things, including her own will, and no matter how she might have wished it otherwise, she had been forced to proceed inexorably towards her destiny with no turning aside.

Josh, catching her glance at him out of the corner of his eye, turned his head and smiled at her. 'Only another minute and we should see the smoke from the locomotive in the distance.'

She looked towards the brand new clock that was suspended from the domed ceiling of tinted glass, which was itself supported by columns and elaborately swagged on a mosaic frieze. It was a remarkably fine terminus, with an oak-panelled booking office, a lofty entrance hall and heavily-dentilled walls. Everywhere new paint shone glossily, and arched windows had a shine as yet unmarred by the soot and smoke that was soon to billow forth a dozen times daily. He thought that within that hard-cut, shining setting she looked like a touch of spring that had crept in from behind the wall of the yard. Her gown caught the sunlight in its primrose gathers, and her bobble-fringed jacket, hugging her narrow waist, was the same pale green as the stems of the daffodils filling the pots that encircled the columns of the platform in honour of the day.

Seeing her serene composure, her smiling conversation with those gentlemen and their wives to whom he had introduced her, Josh let his mind dwell secretly on that other Lucy, known only to him, whose sweet, unbridled passions made their union one of sheer perfection. He recalled sadly how wildly she had wept when he had told her the truth of her begetting and her birth, but gradually out of her awful sorrow had finally come a curious joy that one parent was alive and known to her, a man of flesh and blood, who had shown her innumerable kindnesses, and gone for ever were those fragmentary dreams that had been the stuff of childhood longings. He had been present when Daniel had come into the Grange the following evening and he had watched the face of the woman he loved, seeing how she shielded her emotional reaction before Daniel came across to speak to her, all unaware that his own daughter knew him for who he was. Lucy had decided that she must wait for him to tell her himself of their relationship, arguing that had he wished her to know, he would have told her long since. Josh approved her decision, but feared that she would wait in vain. Daniel Warwyck was a strange, enigmatic man. There was no way of predicting what he might do.

'Here it comes!' The shout went up on all sides. Above the distant trees the first rising of the puffing smoke was sighted. Cheers could be heard in the distance as those gathered on new-grassed embankments caught sight of the train itself. Lucy was reminded poignantly of the day she had stood on a mound far away in Italy, on the day of a funeral when her whole life had changed. Was it her imagination, or was there a more cheerful rattle to the wheels of an English train? Somehow, as it came into sight, the black-chimneyed locomotive a brighter blue than the April skies, its carriages a searing yellow, it gave an impression of bringing sunshine with it. Out of the carriage windows hands were waving and handkerchiefs fluttering, returning the greetings that had awaited the train all along the new branch line. As it slowed down, with a clanking and screeching and a demented hissing of steam, she thought what a long battle had been fought and lost and won over this moment of its arrival.

At Easthampton House, Kate saw the smoke in the distance from the window of Donna's room. 'The train has arrived on time,' she said, thinking much the same thoughts as Lucy at that moment.

'Has it?' Donna replied listlessly. She lay on the chaise-longue from which she rarely moved during the day, Toby stretched out on the floor beside her, and did not lower the book she appeared to be reading. She found that if she held an open book it was imagined she was taking an interest in something, which others found encouraging, and it was an easy way to avoid conversation.

'Richard would have liked to be there today,' Kate continued, 'but he should be home next week. Perhaps you could think of coming downstairs for a little while when he returns with Harry. You've always been fond of your uncle and it would be a gracious welcome for him.'

There was no comment from the chaise-longue and Kate fell silent. Nothing she was able to say or do could stir Donna from her lethargy. The girl ate less than a bird and had become thin and bony, her good looks quite gone, her pallor more akin to that of old age than of one in the prime of life. Kate's hand tightened about the curtain that she was holding back as she remained by the window, but her gaze had become abstracted, no longer concentrated on the direction of the railway station. She could feel her courage waning and the tell-tale beginning of one of those bouts of despair that made it so difficult to keep a normal countenance in the ordinary comings and goings of the daily routine. How was she to leave Daniel with a mere shell of a daughter for company? And leave him she must, far sooner than either of them had expected when they had always thought to live and love far into old age together. Not trusting old Dr Houston to keep what she had feared from Daniel, she had consulted a young doctor in Merrelton, who had only confirmed that an injury to lungs and ribs suffered many years before was at last taking its full toll. He had called in two older and more learned physicians than himself, but the opinions had been the same.

Suddenly she felt suffocated by the confines of the room and was filled with a longing for Honeybridge. 'I'm going out,' she said, swinging back across the room. 'Come with me. Let me drive you out in the wagonette and we'll have a picnic luncheon in the kitchen at Honeybridge. Just like we used to sometimes.'

Donna looked at her with lack-lustre eyes. 'Not today, Mamma,' she said as she always did. 'I want to rest.'

Kate turned her head sharply away to hide the dash of tears that sprang into her eyes, and she hurried from the room. Never before in her life had she felt so helpless or useless, unable to solve either her daughter's problems or her own, and like a dark cloud gathering was the prospect of Richard's return. Josh had told her that Lucy knew the truth and had decided before he had even put forward the case for keeping silent, at least for the time being, to wait until such time as Daniel should decide to confide in her. For that Kate was overwhelmingly grateful. Lucy was sensitive enough to understand what it would mean to Richard to discover their kinship in the light of loving her as he did, and Daniel would be blamed most cruelly. Better by far for Richard to accept another reason for losing Lucy, which was that she and Josh were to be married shortly. Perhaps the time would come when Richard could accept without bitterness against his father the loss of her, but that time was not yet. If nothing else was accomplished, Kate knew she must ensure that Daniel had Richard to support him when the day came for her parting from them.

She drove her dove-grey gig to Honeybridge. She had not expected to meet such a crowd of people and vehicles in Hoe Lane, but those who had come to see the first train were dispersing, and several times she had to rein in and wait as the traffic flowed past her. There were many who knew her, and she acknowledged their greetings smilingly. One who did not greet her, but who hung back on the grass verge to watch her drive the gig through the side entrance to the stables at the rear of Honeybridge, was Ben Thompson.

Kate let herself into the house through the kitchen door. Immediately her spirits were comforted as the atmosphere of the house welcomed her, and she made her usual tour from room to room, touching and adjusting, all its textures of wood and leather and cloth and stone as familiar to her as the surface of her own skin. Then, as she returned to the kitchen, thinking to make herself some tea, she saw an unknown man seated solidly at the wooden table. She gave a gasp and started back.

'Who are you? What are you doing in this house?'

Ben smiled his most ingratiating smile. 'Don't be alarmed, Mrs Warwyck. I mean you no 'arm, far from it. I just wants a little talk with you.'

'What do you mean? What about? It really is not at all convenient –'

She stopped and felt her heart thump uncomfortably. He had rolled across the table two silver buttons that she recognized instantly. They came from a set of six that had been presented to Daniel by his patron, Sir Geoffrey Edenfield, after one of his most successful fights. He still had the four, but two had been lost many years ago.

'Recognize 'em, Mrs Warwyck?'

'Yes, I do.' She sat down slowly on a chair by the table and picked them up in uncertain amazement. 'Where did you find them? My husband will be delighted to have them back.'

'I don't think 'ee will. Leastways, not as you mean.'

A dreadful apprehension filled her. There was something odd about the man and the recovery of the buttons. She thought she had glimpsed him somewhere before, but could not be sure. 'I don't understand you.'

'When I tell you the buttons was found at Denwin Cottage, would that enlighten you? I reckon they've been lying there over twenty years.'

He thought she might faint. He had never seen a woman look more stricken, a terrible awareness dilating her eyes. 'What do you want?' she demanded tonelessly.

He leaned an arm companionably on the table and cocked his head at her. 'I want to be paid for the return of them buttons. A little reward, you might say.'

She brushed trembling fingertips across her forehead. 'Yes. Yes, of course.' She rose and looked about her. 'I have my reticule with me. I think I must have left it in another room.'

'Don't bother to look for it, 'cos you wouldn't 'ave enough with you to pay me what I think would be suitable remuneration for my honesty.'

She stared at him. 'What were you expecting?'

'Two thousand pounds.'

She made no exclamation of shock or dismay, but closed her eyes as if to draw strength from some inner source in order to answer him, her face so drained of colour that even her lips were white. 'Upon what do you base such a demand?' she asked in an uneven voice.

'Upon the information I 'ave at my disposal, which you wouldn't want spread around to ruin your 'usband's good name and bring disgrace down upon you and your family.' He tapped a stubby finger on the table. 'In short, Lucy di Castelloni is your son's 'alf-sister. Wants to marry 'er, don't 'ee? Incest ain't a pretty word. Nor is adultery, if it comes to that.' He made a grand display of consideration for her, getting up to push the chair forward for her to sit down again. 'You'd best rest yourself a bit. I've given you a bit of a turn, 'ave I? Not my intention at all, madam. I only wants a right reward for returning them buttons. Then I'll be off from East'ampton and you'll never see me again.'

She knew she had no choice but to pay him. 'You shall have the two thousand, but I need a little time.'

'That's something I ain't got, madam. I need that money the evening after next.'

She nodded. 'You shall have it. Come to Easthampton House after eight o'clock when my husband will have gone to the Grange. I'll give the servants the evening off and nobody shall know that you were ever there.'

'Why East'ampton 'Ouse? You bring it 'ere.'

She straightened, her eyes flashing at him. 'That I will not do. I have my own reasons for not wanting your evil presence back in this house. Now go!'

He saw no point in arguing with her. She was going to cough up the blunt in a dignified manner without any of the pleading and hysterics and general carrying-on that he usually had to endure, and for that he would go along with her whim.

'Until Thursday evening then, Mrs Warwyck.'

She sat on at the table for some time after he had gone, looking at the silver buttons that he had left there. In themselves they meant nothing, but as soon as she had set eyes on them, rolling like dice from his opened palm, she had had a terrible sense of premonition. Of one thing she was certain: they could not be returned to Daniel, or else she would have to face questions she had no wish to answer. For Daniel's peace of mind, she must spare him her knowledge of his true relationship to Lucy. It was best that the buttons remained at Honeybridge, but where to put them?

With them in her hand, she went in search of a hiding place. In the dining-room, above the ancient hearth, was a salt-box let into the wall, left from the days when it was a place to keep salt from going damp, and at the back of it there had always been a gap in the wood. She thrust in her hand and pushed the buttons each in turn through the gap, where they might lodge forever out of sight and without risk of discovery if need be. With that task done, she went through the house opening every window, to let the April breezes banish all trace of that odious man from it. Only then did it occur to her that she had no idea what his name was.

It seemed to Meg at Sea Cottage that evening, when she and Bob came in from their boats, that Ben Thompson was in exceptionally good spirits, rubbing his hands and, with unusual generosity, inviting them to take a nip from a bottle of brandy he had brought from his room. Bob was only too pleased to sit himself down and sample it, but Meg went out to the kitchen where Emmie was preparing supper.

'What's up with him?' Meg jerked her head back over her shoulder.

Emmie stirred the thick stew gurgling in the pot on the range. ''Ee's looking forward to the Doncaster races on Friday. 'Ee says 'ee 'as a certainty for at least two of the races and expects to make some big winnings.'

'That means the races are rigged,' Meg stated contemptuously, washing her hands at the sink.

Emmie chose to ignore what she more than suspected to be a correct assumption on her daughter's part. ''Ee'll take the late train on Thursday night to make a start to 'is journey.' She said it proudly, thinking Ben a real man of the world in his travelling, and he had grumbled often enough about having to take the stage from The Crown whenever he wanted to get out of Easthampton for his racing journeyings.

'Wish he'd never come back,' Meg muttered, but not loud enough for her mother to hear.

After supper, when Bob and Ben had gone off to The Crown, Meg took her cloak from a peg and put it on.

'Where you going?' Emmie asked over her spectacles as she sat darning one of Ben's socks on a wooden mushroom.

'To the Grange. Mrs di Castelloni sent me a note saying she wanted to see me tomorrow, but I'll be fishing, so I thought I'd go along now.'

'What do she want to see you about?'

'I dunno. Perhaps she has some sewing for me.'

Meg enjoyed the walk to the Grange. The sunset had coloured the sky to the west with bands of yellow and red and orange, the whole tinting pink the few clouds that lingered overhead, and the countryside was sweet with the moistness of spring. The Grange was full of lights as she approached, carriages of every kind passing across the forecourt and filling every available waiting place. A prize-fight was in progress, and apart from those who came from far afield for these mills, the local gentry and nobility from all round the country supported them. At the reception desk she had to wait a long time while gentlemen of quality were dealt with. Finally the clerk looked at her suspiciously, taking in her humble apparel.

'What are you doing here? The servants' entrance is round the back.'

'I've an appointment to see Mrs di Castelloni,' she said haughtily.

The clerk smirked. 'Mrs Josiah Barton, you mean.'

Meg gaped at him in stunned dismay. 'Are you sure?'

'Of course I'm sure. It was a surprise to all of us. They went to St Cuthbert's in Merrelton at three o'clock this afternoon and had a quiet ceremony with only two witnesses, both railway acquaintances of Mr Barton. Nobody would have known about it if by sheer chance the manager's wife wasn't visiting the ladies of that parish in the hall there – she spotted them. You should have seen how taken aback the bride and groom were when we had champagne waiting for them when they returned, and all the staff lined up with flowers to give them a cheer.' He leaned the flat of both hands on the desk and eyed her questioningly. 'Are you sure it's today she wanted to see you? As far as I know the impromptu wedding breakfast of smoked salmon and suchlike is over, so I suppose she would see you if it's urgent.'

Meg swallowed. 'No, it's not urgent. I'll come back another time.' She was about to move away from the desk when she turned back to it. 'You don't happen to know when Mr Richard Warwyck is returning home, do you?'

'Next week, I heard.'

She nodded her thanks and hurried out. Once outside she breathed in deep draughts of the cool air. In the short time she had been indoors the sky had faded, to leave no more than a rim of rose against a dark sky already speckled with stars. Did Richard know that the woman he loved had married someone else in his absence abroad? She thought it unlikely. It did seem as if Lucy had wanted him to be the first to know, or else there was no reason why she and Josh Barton should not have made it known they were to wed. God help Richard when he returned. Loving him herself, she had plumbed the depths of his feelings, and with everything that was fine and sensitive in her she could attune to the full passion that he cherished for Lucy. Next week she would not take her boat to sea. She would keep watch and wait for Richard's return. She had to be near if he needed her.

19

By changing trains four times, Richard and Harry Warwyck
had managed the journey from Dover, after stepping ashore
from the steam-packet, in a quarter of the time that it would
have taken by horse and carriage. It was Thursday evening,
a week ahead of the time they were expected, but Richard
could wait no longer to see Lucy. The tone of her letters
had filled him with anxiety. Something was terribly amiss.
The emphasis was on their parting, with shutters finally
coming down between them. He had read each letter innumerable times, forcing himself to admit that never once
had she given him any cause to confirm hopes for the
future, but such was his love for her that from the start he
truly believed it was enough to cover any lack of reciprocation from her, and he would not and could not let her go
out of his life. He had come to the conclusion she had taken
it into her head to go back to Italy, not to her late husband's
family, but perhaps to reside near Lionel Attwood's last
resting-place. Well, he intended to talk her out of that. No,
more than that, he would do what he should have done long
ago, which had been the action he had promised himself
upon his departure from her for the Continent. He would
sweep her off her feet with such love-making that she could
not fail to respond with all the sensuality that was in her. As
the train chuffed through the last stretch of countryside before reaching Easthampton, he looked out towards the lights
of the Grange, veiled by trees blowing in the rough wind,
and thought how soon he would be with her.

'Well, we're here,' Harry observed ripely from his corner seat. He found all journeys boring unless he was driving high-bred horses himself, and he made sure that on boat or train he was well supplied with liquid refreshment in the hamper his valet carried for him. He and his nephew had been alone all the way in first class carriages, the valet travelling second class, which was munificent of Harry since most gentlemen's domestic staff usually had benches in the open wagons. But Harry liked people and cared about people, whatever their class, and with that Warwyck charm of his which could coax a bird off a tree or, more literally, any woman he fancied into his arms, he was liked in turn by folk of both sexes and all ages wherever he went. He had once boasted that he could sell anything to anybody, and it had certainly been true for him, because everything he had touched in business had reaped success; still in his early forties, he was an extremely rich man, and in spite of being overweight and somewhat bloated by the good life he led, he still retained that boyish smile and thick, soft hair that made him look younger than his years. He had married once on the rebound of losing the only woman whom he had truly loved but when his wife died a few years later, leaving him no children, he had never bothered with marriage again. He looked upon Richard as he would a son, and unbeknown to his nephew he had made him his heir, knowing full well that his many business interests would be carried on with the same astuteness and acumen that he himself had always shown.

The train came to a halt with an ear-splitting screech of wheel-brakes. Harry, a trifle uncertain of his legs after the amount of alcohol he had consumed since leaving Paris, waited until the carriage was fully at a standstill before standing up to reach for his beaver hat on the rack. He reeled, and Richard steadied him.

'Thanks, my boy,' he said with the careful articulation of the very drunk, and sat down heavily on the seat again, smiling beatifically when Richard took down the hat and handed it to him. With elaborate care he used both hands to set it upon his head, as if he feared it might fly away from him in the draught from the open door through which his nephew had alighted onto the gaslit platform. Porters had come running, and their baggage was being unloaded somewhere further down the train. Getting to his feet again, Harry managed a nonchalant saunter to the door, where he might have fallen if Richard and his valet had not helped him down onto the platform. Then he was in a cab that smelt like all hackney-cabs – of urine and leather – being bowled through the streets of Easthampton.

Ben Thompson saw them go. In the absence of the others from Sea Cottage, he had shifted out the bulk of his baggage and was checking it in, ready for his catching the late train. When he departed from the house, he would have the hand-valise he always took on short trips, and not until his return became overdue would his room be opened up and it be realized that this time he would not come back. He had actually raised his hat to Richard Warwyck, but the young man had been intent on assisting a wealthy-looking cove into a cab and had not noticed him, although he had been near enough to hear the cabby instructed to take them to the Grange. He took his watch out of his waistcoat pocket and looked at it. Everything was perfectly timed. He would return now to Sea Cottage – by which time Emmie should have come home – collect his hand-baggage, say he was going to have a few jars at The Crown before catching the last train and depart for Easthampton House. Both Meg and Bob would be out fishing, and Emmie busy getting their supper, so no awkward requests to accompany him would be made. Putting his head down against the blustery wind, he hurried back in the direction of Sea Cottage.

To his surprise, Meg's fishing-boots were in the porch, and when he entered he found her in the kitchen with her mother, setting the table for supper.

'You're 'ome early, ain't you?' he said.

She never looked at him if she could help it. 'A bad squall is blowing up,' she replied curtly.

'Bob coming in soon, is 'ee?'

'The bigger boats will keep fishing for a while longer.'

He pushed aside the knife and fork she had put ready for him. 'I've filled my belly. I 'ad 'ot pork pie and greens in the new railway restaurant.'

It was his custom to eat out when it suited him, and Meg took away the cutlery without comment, although her mother was always interested in what he had had and wanted to know more about it. He had allowed quarter of an hour for his departure from Sea Cottage and quite relished his casual air as if this going away was like any other. He made chat about the service in the restaurant and, simply for something to say, mentioned that he had seen the seven o'clock train come in just before he left the station.

'Saw several local folk get off it. That young Warwyck was among 'em –'

He broke off, for Meg had dropped a plate, which had smashed into pieces at her feet, but she ignored it and her mother's exclamation of annoyance at her carelessness and darted round the table to him.

'Are you sure it was Richard Warwyck? He's been abroad.'

''As 'ee? Well, it was 'im awright. 'Ee 'ad a rich-looking gent two sheets in the wind with 'im that 'ee was taking to the Grange.'

She gulped, and whirled about to rush for her cloak on a peg, the broken china scattering about her feet. She had the door open and was half out of it when Emmie, who could move swiftly enough for all her bulk when she chose, grabbed her by the arm and dragged her back a step.

'What's up? Where are you off to? You don't rush out of this 'ouse leaving me to cook your man's supper and do everything else without a word of what you're about.'

'Let me go, Ma!' Meg tried to prise the gripping fingers free, but Emmie, who had saved drowning people in her time, knew how to hold on when she wanted to, and the stark look of her daughter's face told her that far more was going on than met the eye.

'Not until you tell me what's up.'

Meg, frantic at the delay, would have struck at the restraining clasp, but Emmie grabbed her hand in time and bent the fingers back cruelly.

'Strike your Ma, would you, you wicked girl! Now spill it, or else I'll drag you back indoors and give you a taste of my belt, grown-up and married though you are!'

Meg's control snapped. 'All right! I'll tell you! I love Richard Warwyck and I'm going to him! Now will you let go?'

Emmie, in spite of her astonishment, did not weaken her grip. 'Are you out of your 'ead? Love?' Outrage stamped her features. 'Gentlemen don't 'ave nothing to do with the likes of you except for one reason only. You're not going nowhere or seeing nobody. Come back into the 'ouse!' She began to haul her struggling daughter back indoors, and yelled over her shoulder for assistance. 'Ben! Come and give an 'and.'

Meg, driven to desperation point, lunged and gave her mother a shove with her shoulder. Emmie stumbled. It was enough to loosen her hold, and Meg was away, racing down the garden path, the woman's abuse following her.

In the cab, Harry leaned forward, swaying with its movement. 'The cabby has taken the wrong road, my boy. There's Easthampton House over there on the hill, or else I'm much mistaken.'

'We're going straight to the Grange,' Richard replied. 'Father is usually there about this time, and since our arrival is not expected, we can dine at the Grange before I take you home.'

Harry chuckled good-humouredly. 'Want to sober me up a bit before I see Kate, do you? It wouldn't be the first time she's seen me in my cups, I can tell you.'

Richard smiled from the opposite corner seat. 'I suppose not.'

Harry wagged his head jovially. 'But you're in charge. Leave myself in your hands.'

Well pleased with this surrender of responsibility for his unsteady state, Harry sank back in his seat, his hat tipping forward onto his nose, and continued to ramble on, content to hold a one-sided conversation which lasted all the way to the Grange.

Richard assisted him out of the cab. The wind dashed at them, whirling across the forecourt, and every tree was rustling, branches creaking wildly. Harry gasped in the chilly air, which after the warmth of train compartment and hackney cab had the effect of doubling his state of inebriation. Had it not been for Richard's strong support, he would never have made the ascent up the steps and into the lamp-lit glory of the entrance hall.

'Never been here before,' Harry mumbled as he faced another ascent, crimson-carpeted this time, which led to an upper floor. 'Not 'sidered good enough in days when that nancy-boy came home from Italy and opened up the Grange. He married her, y'know. Married her, that red-headed wench. But Daniel didn't give up chasing her.'

He had forgotten that he was talking to his brother's son, but Richard was not listening to the mumbling discourse, which was half-lost in any case by Harry looking down to concentrate on setting one foot in front of the other. They reached the top at last and Richard turned his uncle in the direction of the private drawing-room, near the gaming rooms, where his father usually took a glass of brandy, talked to the manager or to Lucy, and where sometimes specially invited guests joined him.

As it happened, they found Daniel alone, reading an evening newspaper, a brandy on the table at his side. He sprang up with a laugh of pleasure at the sight of them, clapped his son on the shoulder in welcome and shook his brother vigorously by the hand.

'It's good to see you, Harry! You've passed the time well on the journey I can see. Come and sit down.'

Harry, always sweet-tempered, appreciated the joke against himself, but refused to take a chair, resting a hand on each of his older brother's broad shoulders for support, grinning into his face. 'Good to see you, Dan. You haven't changed a bit. Not a damn bit.'

'I hope not. It's only about eighteen months since we last met.'

'Is tha' all? Seems years.' He harped back to his original theme. 'Never thought you and I would be under this roof together. Remember when –'

A door from the adjoining gaming-rooms had opened and Lucy came into the room. She paused, seeing Richard before all else, and knew by the radiance of joy in his face as he came towards her that he had heard nothing of her marriage yet and that the news was still hers to break to him as best she could. She tried to tell herself that she was like a surgeon who must cut clean in order that the wound might heal the quicker, but it in no way lightened the duty ahead of her.

'Dearest Lucy!' He caught up her hand and kissed it, not taking his eyes from her and failing to see that the wedding band she had worn had been replaced by another. 'We've come straight from the railway station, and only left Paris yesterday. Is that not remarkable?'

From the other side of the room Harry spoke to her. 'You're Claudine's daughter, by God!'

They were words she had thought never to hear after the disappointments she had suffered. She looked across speechlessly at the man who had addressed her, knowing who he must be, and thinking him sent by fate to fulfil at last the long-cherished dream. Daniel, granite-faced, drew aside a pace from his brother, whose astonishment seemed to have steadied him as he went with well-judged steps to bring himself nearer her. Only Richard looked from one to the other of them in bewilderment.

'How does my uncle know your mother's name, Lucy? Was it really Claudine? But isn't that the name of the wife of the Attwood who died in Italy?'

She nodded, not taking her rapt gaze from his uncle, and his bewilderment that she had never revealed a fact of such importance was not dispelled. Harry, on the other hand, was beaming at her, apparently in full possession of all knowledge, and she dipped a graceful curtsey to him until he raised her up and took her face between his hands.

'So you have come home to your mother's house. My good brother made it possible, I believe.'

Again she gave a nod, eyes brimming with sparkling, unshed tears. 'He did,' she whispered. 'He has been wondrous kind to me.'

'And why should he not?' In Harry's befuddled mind shining scraps of information stood out like the bright pieces of a broken puzzle. He knew that she had come from Italy, although who had told him that he could not recall, and there was something about her having grown up in a convent and having been early widowed, but for the moment he in no way connected her with Richard's restrained mention of her when letters from her had reached him in Paris.

'Say no more, Harry,' Daniel's voice ordered strongly.

Harry waved a dismissing hand in his brother's direction. Gone were the days when he had had to take orders from Dan. A great wave of sentiment borne on the fumes of alcohol swept over him. 'I'm proud to acknowledge you as a Warwyck. When I heard all those years ago that your mother was to have a child I knew who the father must be –'

'Harry!' It was a despairing roar from Daniel, who rushed forward and would have pulled his brother away from her to silence him if Richard, suddenly appalled, had not stepped between them to intervene.

'Stay back, Father!' he said with painful intensity. 'I want to hear what Harry has to say.'

Harry, somewhat dazed by the confusion around him, manfully concentrated on what was of uppermost importance. 'Don't blame your mother, my dear. She should never have married half a man. I always wanted her to wed Dan, although I must admit to reasons of my own for that.' Launched on the truth, there was no stopping him. 'I loved Kate, y'see. Always had and always did and always will, if it comes to that.' He saw that tears were streaking her cheeks, and became distressed himself. 'Now, now, the time for tears is gone. Dan has brought you home to Easthampton to be his daughter for all to see, and I for one thank God for it.' Fumblingly he turned and reached out a hand to rest it on Richard's shoulder. 'A fine son and a beautiful daughter. You're a fortunate man, Dan.'

The force with which his nephew threw off his hand made him reel and half fall, half sprawl into a chair. Richard stared with hollow eyes from Daniel to Lucy and back again, neither of them knowing how to bear the stark anguish in his face. 'You knew!' he accused them both in deadly tones. 'You knew and kept silent. You let me go on loving where no loving of that kind should ever be.'

Daniel spoke in Lucy's defence. 'Don't misjudge Lucy. She knew nothing of this truth until now.'

Lucy's clasped hands moved up and down distractedly. 'I believed Lionel Attwood to be my father until after you had left for France.'

'Who told you?' Richard's voice was full of agony.

'Josh told me.'

He responded with a wild shout, throwing out his arms in torment. 'How did he learn of it? Has everyone known of this terrible thing except me?'

Daniel shook his head to and fro as if unable to accept that an outsider should have been in possession of such intimate information. 'I swear until this hour I thought none suspected what I knew to be true.'

Harry, who had managed to get to his feet again, considerably sobered, spoke in a dry and solemn tone. 'Kate would know.'

Daniel blanched anew on the pain of it, and they all looked at Lucy as if for confirmation. 'She knew,' she said, very quietly, 'but she only confided in Josh inadvertently when she was half-mad with desperation and at a complete loss as to what to do for the best. He told her to put aside her worries.' She lifted her chin bravely but unsteadily at Richard as if the weight of sadness upon her was of a physical nature. 'Josh thought he had the answer that would solve everything, and that the secret which I represented need never be known to those to whom it could cause most hurt. He loved me as I had discovered that I loved him. We were married two days ago.'

Richard stood motionless, as if he had lost the power to move in any direction, his arms stiff at his sides, only the nerve in his temples throbbing, a look of total desolation upon his face. Then he swallowed several times before he spoke, as if his vocal chords had refused to respond to speech, and his gaze travelled to each of them in turn, his eyes stony and bereft, as if all life had gone from him.

'I never want to see any of you ever again!'

He threw himself out of the room. Daniel would have followed him, but Harry caught him by the arm. 'Let him go, Dan. Nothing can be mended now. Nothing can be done yet.'

Daniel was forced to accept the wisdom of his advice and

he passed a violently shaking hand across his eyes. Feeling a touch on his sleeve, he lowered it and saw Lucy standing by him.

'Father,' she said tremulously, in solace.

He reached for her and hugged her to him.

Outside, Richard blundered in the direction of the stables, shouting for a horse and carriage. He hurled a sovereign at the ostler and took the reins. Near the gates he almost ran down a girl in the drive, the carriage lamps picking out the pale oval of her face.

'Meg!' Frantically he hauled the horse to a slithering standstill, and she clambered up beside him to throw her arms about his neck. He clung to her, not knowing why she was there, but only aware that she had come to him when he had needed her most. 'I'm going away,' he groaned. 'Right away from Easthampton and I don't intend to return. Come with me.'

'Yes, I'll come.' She kissed his forehead, his cheeks, his closed eyes, and when her lips reached his mouth his kiss was desperate in his seeking of comfort from her.

When they drove on she kept her arm tucked in his, her face against his sleeve, and it was as if all her life she had been waiting for this April night. At his apartments in Easthampton she helped him pack what he wanted to take with him, and when he went to tell his housekeeper that he was going away and would send for the rest of his possessions later, she made a vow to herself that he should never regret taking her with him. Sooner or later she would make him forget Lucy and that he had ever loved her.

At Easthampton House, Ben Thompson waited in the Green Drawing-room while Kate went to fetch the money from her bedroom. He looked about him, thinking the place was full of small treasures he could have nicked, but he never believed in carrying stolen goods on his person for any length of time, and he would content himself with the blunt on this occasion. In a couple of years he would call on Mrs Warwyck again, for he felt he could rely on her to be a regular source of income.

Upstairs, Kate, with the box containing the two thousand

pounds in her hands, paused by Donna's door. There was not a sound within and she guessed her daughter to be asleep, but when she came down to the drawing-room she did close the door after her, to make sure no sound of their voices reached the girl, for the blackmailer was one of those men who seemed unable to talk in quiet tones.

'Most obliging of you, madam.' His eyes gleamed at the sight of the box.

Kate sat down at a round table between them and put the box on it. She felt weak and exhausted. It had been no problem to get the money, because Daniel had always been generous to her and she had her own bank account, but the ordeal of dealing with this toad-like man who had penetrated the privacy of her family life was telling on her heavily. It had been a great relief to her when Josh had told her that he and Lucy were to be wed before Richard returned and that Lucy's letters had prepared her son for the news, but that in no way lessened the importance of keeping the old secret from him, for such a wound would fester for the rest of his life. She raised the box's lid to reveal the contents. 'I suppose you wish to check that it is all there.'

'A quick run through it if you don't mind,' he smirked. 'No insinuations meant and none taken, I trust, but it 'as been known for folks to try and short-change me once in a while.'

'So blackmail is your profession, is it?'

He had pulled the box greedily towards him and now paused in leafing through the large notes with a wet thumb to give her an unpleasant glance. 'I don't like to 'ear that word used, madam. Not in a business transaction like ours. You're paying me for those two silver buttons your 'usband lost when he enjoyed a bit of slap and tickle outside the marital bonds. Just that and nothing more.'

Outside in the hall, Daniel, who had let himself in with his key, jerked his head ominously as he heard what had been said as clearly as if he had been standing beside his wife and her unknown visitor. Lucy, who was with him, having begged to accompany him to see Kate, looked at him in wide-eyed dismay, guessing instantly as he had done what was taking place. She also recognized that obnoxious voice, having heard it often enough at Sea Cottage, but when she would have spoken, Daniel put a finger to his lips. She nodded, moving with him as he went to the drawing-room door and stood by it.

In the drawing-room, Kate regarded Ben with cool disgust. 'I find your insults insufferable and your wish to mince words both hypocritical and contemptible. For mercy's sake, hurry up with your counting and be gone from here.'

He pointed a stubby finger warningly at her. 'Don't you come no 'igh and mighty attitude with me. If you want plain speaking you shall 'ave it. I've been lenient with you. Two thousand pounds weren't much to ask for what you're getting. Mebbe I should've gone to your son instead. I've a feeling 'ee'd 'ave paid any sum I asked for keeping my trap shut and making it safe for 'im to wed that red-'eaded 'alf-sister of 'is with nobody being any the wiser. The bride least of all.'

Kate's abhorrence for him broke its bounds. 'You dreadful creature,' she gasped. 'I never knew such evil as I see in you.'

'Shut up!' He drew his hand back threateningly.

The double doors crashed open. Daniel stood there with feet apart, his hair wind-blown and tousled from the wild night outside, his fists clenched as if once again he had taken up a stance in the prize-ring. Ben sprang up, slamming the lid of the box and snatching it to him. He was thick-set and burly, never minding to put a boot in with a fallen victim on the ground, but stand-up fights with a powerful opponent had never been in his line and he was not starting now. Kate also rose to her feet, realizing that Daniel and Lucy must have overheard all that had been said, and seeing only too clearly what was about to happen. She clutched the back of the chair for support.

'Let this man take the money,' she cried in appeal to her enraged husband. 'He is going away and will never return. Money is not important, nothing is important except sparing Richard what he must never know.'

'It's too late,' Daniel replied harshly. 'He has come home and he does know, but even if he had not learned the truth, nothing could stop me from what I'm about to do!'

He made for Ben, such murder in his eyes that the man yelped with fright and tried to dodge past him. Daniel blocked his way, made a scything punch into his ribs and followed it up with a facer that landed above Ben's right eye, not closing it, but making the blood gush. Ben went down, dropping the box, and notes and gold went fluttering and ringing in all directions. His one thought was to get away from this dreadful punishment, and as Daniel, breathing fiercely, waited for him to get up, he used his cunning, made a show of being more stunned and winded than he had been, and then seized the leg of a small chair to hurl it upwards at Daniel as he scrambled to his feet and bolted for the hall.

He only just reached it. Daniel whirled him about and landed a blow in his mouth that broke his teeth and filled it with blood as he was rammed back against the newel-post at the foot of the stairs. Fists that had once floored the foremost fighters of a day gone by smashed into his body and his face, and the only difference was that Daniel was landing blows for the first time in his life with hatred in his heart. That such a man should threaten his Kate, frighten and offend her, was the last straw in a culmination of such desperate events that he was nigh mad with despair. His fists smashed mechanically. Ben's face had become an unrecognizable pulp, but still he stood against the post as though in terrible defiance, and Daniel saw only an enemy that had to be floored.

Kate was entreating him to stop. 'You'll kill him! Stop! Oh, please stop!'

Lucy, who had her arm around Kate as they stood together helplessly, looked around and wished that Josh were there to intervene, but he was not returning to the Grange that night, work on the Merrelton link compelling him at times to stay overnight near the site. Agitatedly she looked around for something to use against Daniel to force him to cease his battering of Ben. A heavy vase stood on a side table, similar to one that she had broken on a day long ago at the Grange, and without hesitation she darted across and picked it up. Balancing it with both hands, she raised it up and, coming behind Daniel, she smashed it down with all the force she could muster across his head. He staggered, half righted himself, and then fell face downwards full length upon the floor. Kate rushed to fall onto her knees beside him. His head was cut, but not deeply. Lucy ran to Ben, who had not moved, and then she saw why. The back of his skull was crushed in against the newel-post, and then, as she felt for his heart and found no beat, he suddenly crumpled sideways and fell in a heap at her feet.

'He's dead!' she exclaimed in a voice low with horror.

Kate, who had taken Daniel's head into her lap, clutched him closer to her as if already the law was about to descend upon him. 'No! He can't be! Daniel would never kill anybody.'

'It was an accident. He couldn't have realized he had broken the man's head.'

'Who will believe that? Look at the state of him, and Daniel hasn't a mark on him!' Her face was ashen and there was terror in her eyes. 'He'll be accused of murder! What chance will he have?'

From the top of the stairs a voice spoke. 'No chance. We'll have to get rid of the body.'

They both looked up sharply. Donna stood there in the shadows, much like a shadow herself in her darkish green dress, and Lucy, who had not seen her for many weeks, was shocked at the skeletal appearance of her, but it was no time to be thinking of that.

'How?' she demanded practically.

'Leave it to me. I know what to do.'

'I'll help you!'

'You can saddle Mamma's mare for me and have her ready at the kitchen door. I want a lantern lighted and closed for me; also find a length of rope – there's plenty in the stables – and a saddle-bag as well.'

Kate gave a soft moan. 'You told me you had made up your mind never to ride ever again.'

Donna looked at her blankly. 'It's either that or see my father go to a hangman's noose. I have no choice.'

Lucy stepped forward. 'I don't know what you're planning, but surely I could go with you in a wagonette.'

'No, you must stay with Mamma and clean up the mess.

Not a drop of blood must remain anywhere.' She addressed her mother. 'You told me earlier today that you had given the servants time off to go to the Merrelton Fair. There is no reason to expect any of them back before midnight, is there?'

Kate shook her head. 'I wanted to make sure there were no interruptions when my visitor came for his money.'

'Then we have two hours, but there's not a moment more to lose.' She turned away at the top of the stairs and Lucy rushed to do her bidding in saddling the horse and getting the rope. When she came back into the house, the silk of her gown patterned by pelting rain, she found Donna with a black coat and bonnet on, wrapping Ben's face round with a length of dark linen that looked as if it might have been a curtain. When it was fastened she took the rope from Lucy and made a loop tight about his body.

'Now we must get him through to the kitchen yard,' she said, straightening up to check her locket-watch with the clock in the hall.

The three of them took the rope together, but Ben was no light weight, and Lucy, being the strongest, bore the brunt of it, feeling her arms straining in their sockets. When they had dragged him out into the yard, Donna, heedless of the rain, fastened the end of the rope securely to the mare. Then suddenly her courage faltered. She put one foot on the mounting block, gulped, hesitated, dipped her head and then took the saddle quickly, giving herself no more time to think about it. Without a word she rode off, and as the rope tautened, the body gave a grisly leap forward, before it settled slitheringly to an erratic passage along the path she followed down through the grounds to the woods at the back of the hill, which opened out into the countryside. Lucy, going back into the house, saw that Kate had collapsed into a chair, holding her side. She rushed to her.

'You're ill! Did you strain yourself pulling on the rope?'

'I think I did, but the pain will soon pass.' Kate looked into the face of her husband's daughter and knew a kind of peace. There was strength and courage there. Daniel was not going to be as much alone as she had feared. Even Donna had rallied when all had seemed lost. How Richard had reacted to the truth of his kinship to Lucy she had yet to learn, but she hoped and prayed that with time everything would heal. Spontaneously she put her cheek against Lucy's in friendship, and response and comfort came in the midst of anxiety and sorrow.

Lucy worked hard with a bucket, cloth and scrubbing brush, and removed all trace of what had happened at Easthampton House that night. Lastly she burnt the apron she had worn until nothing of it remained. Before leaving the kitchen, she went to the window and looked out at the blustery night. Where had Donna gone on her gruesome errand? How would she dispose of the body? She shuddered and turned away.

In the drawing-room she found Daniel sitting on the sofa with Kate attending him. The money still lay scattered about the floor. He had only just recovered consciousness and was still dazed, although he had grasped the explanation that his wife had given him.

'Ben Thompson has gone,' Lucy said firmly. 'You gave him the beating of his life, and he has gone. He'll never come back.'

Donna rode grimly through the darkness. She knew every inch of the terrain and had read enough in the local newspapers as well as hearing the railways line talked about during her months as a recluse to know exactly where it was located and the route that it followed. The rain had eased again, but the wind beat into her face, made her coat and skirt flap and billow, and howled eerily amid the trees all around her, which swayed as though demented, black against a night without stars. Behind her the body of Ben Thompson trailed and bumped, but she tried to concentrate on what she must do when she reached the line.

She was making for a crossing for those on foot that spanned the track just below a siding where wagons were shunted. It was not far from the place where Denwin Cottage had stood, the siding on the sloping ground covering the very spot. The path she was following began to dip and she knew she was getting near. Coming out of the trees, she saw the crossing below her and the rails gleaming dully.

'Come on, Bonnie,' she encouraged softly, and took the mare gently down. Her mount could not have been more docile or manageable, in spite of being most surely bewildered by the late ride and the burden dragging behind, and seemed to sense the new control that the importance of Donna's mission had given over her.

When they came level with the line, Donna dismounted, checked the time on her locket-watch again with a chink of light from the lantern, and then led Bonnie beside the rails until they were some distance from the path, for she could not risk the body being seen too soon by anyone taking that route homewards. Patiently Bonnie plodded across the line under her direction until the body was resting across the rails. It would be impossible for the engine driver to see it to stop in time, for a curve in the line nearby ensured that the train would be on the place before anything could be done.

Steeling herself, Donna unfastened the rope from the body. Then she froze, the heavy thumping of her heart increasing as she strained her ears, certain that she had heard a sudden, indefinable sound above the wild rustling of the wind. Scarcely daring to breathe, she waited in an agony of fear, expecting any second to hear a voice demand to know what she was doing. But nothing happened. It must have been the creak of a wheel over in the siding. She continued her grisly task, unwrapping the linen from about the bloodied head, adding it to the coiled rope in the saddle-bag. Unscrewing a hip flask, which she had brought from her father's dressing-room, she poured brandy liberally over the body, hoping that it would be assumed that Ben had wandered from the crossing in a state of drunkenness and fallen into the path of the train. It had begun to rain once more, and her last task was to take a bunch of bracken and scrape away all sign of Bonnie's hoof-marks. Fortunately the ground was still hard from a spell of fine weather and there was no tell-tale mud of any substance to hold evidence of unusual circumstances. She tossed the bracken away into the bushes. There! It was all done. Abruptly she turned her head away and gagged in her throat. Hurrying Bonnie back to the path, she found a place just in time to vomit helplessly, and with so little in her stomach from her voluntary fasting it was a painful and wracking ordeal.

Exhausted and trembling, she wiped her mouth with a lace handkerchief and was about to remount when she heard again the same strange, metallic sound she had heard earlier. Someone *was* near! Mercy! Had she been spied upon after all? Re-looping Bonnie's reins to a branch, she went to pick her way through the trees and look down from the high ground to the siding below. Instantly she recognized Bob Cooper, who was scurrying between the loaded wagons there. What was he doing? Then, as the front wagons began almost imperceptibly to move, it came to her what he was about: he was releasing the brake levers! Through the darkness, borne on the tormented wind, came the whistle of the train.

Sweat poured from Bob under his rain-soaked coat as he darted from one wagon to another, unbraking, coupling up where he could, wanting all of them to join in a jolting, jostling caravan down to the main line in the path of the train that was almost there. On it were two people whose whereabouts he had discovered when the housekeeper at Richard Warwyck's rooms had given him the information he had failed to get at the Grange.

'Mr Warwyck has gone to catch the train,' she had informed him, seemingly much put out by such sudden notice of departure and not averse to showing her displeasure to the questioner on her doorstep.

'Was Meg Cooper with 'im?'

She looked down her nose still more disdainfully. 'There was a young person with him. I believe he did address her by that Christian name.'

Something snapped in Bob's brain. So what Emmie had told him upon his return had been true. Long harboured suspicions and doubts took full shape at last. If he made for the station he could miss them by seconds, but there was another place where he could stop them for ever. He had flung himself back into the driving seat of his cart and whipped his horse mercilessly into a constant gallop to take a short cut to a place where what stood on the former site of Denwin Cottage could be turned into a weapon of vengeance.

Meg would leave him, would she? And with Richard Warwyck? He'd see her in hell first!

As he released the last brake lever, he leaned his weight against the wagon and paused only to take a gasp of breath, knowing now that Meg had kissed her lover on the day of the navvies' attack when he had been lying on the floor of the cottage. Words he had heard spoken had not been figments of his imagination. How long had he been cuckolded? Under his shoulder the wagon shifted. It was moving! They were all moving! The steepness of the gradient was doing the work for him!

He began to run beside them, laughing and swearing and slamming his fist against the timber sides, the rumble of wheels getting faster and louder as the speed increased, racing to meet the train that was looming out of the night. He could see the sparks from the locomotive's chimney and beyond it the lighted windows of the carriages that had the look of a golden snake. Then he saw he was observed. He staggered to a halt, staring up with mouth open and saliva running at the white face of death in a black bonnet staring down at him with mutual horror. He uttered an awful cry.

Donna never knew whether it was because he knew he had been sighted and his crime witnessed or if it was in that second that one of the wagons, de-railed by too swift a speed, hit him as it was thrown sideways, causing others to crash into it. But nothing slowed the terrible chaos. The wagons in front met the locomotive head on, and Donna's own scream blended piercingly with the roar and thunder of the impact. Steam hissed and wheels were still rotating as carriages buckled and splintered and were tossed in all directions, some rearing up almost on end before tipping over against the embankment. Screams and cries began to sound dreadfully in the night air. Donna began to run as fast as she could along the ridge above the wreckage until she could scramble down the grassy slope and give what aid she could to the injured within her reach.

The ear-splitting din of the crash had echoed far. Along a road some distance away it had sounded like the rumble of a storm over the sea, but Meg, who sat beside Richard in the equipage he had taken from the Grange, did not turn her

339

head to see if any change of weather was following them. She would never look back. She had put the past behind her from the moment she had persuaded him that they should go by road instead of train for the first part of their journey: she had not wanted to risk meeting Ben Thompson on the platform in case he started a hue and cry to get Bob chasing after her.

Ben's body was lying on the track, crushed beyond recognition. Only his watch, escaping damage by some freak of chance, was later to identify him. Some of his baggage, which had been dutifully put on the train by the porter assigned to the task, was also recovered. His widow in Lancashire claimed it and the watch, but did not attend the funeral. Bob Cooper was laid to rest the same day.

20

On a warm August afternoon, Lucy paused by the rails of the pier and looked across at Easthampton basking in the sun. It was hard to realize she was about to leave it. The Merrelton line was finished and Josh's work was taking him into Kent where they would make a new home. He had been there for two weeks already, and was returning within the hour to join her for their departure together. Daniel had decided to close the gaming-rooms at the Grange, for new laws to curb gambling were going through Parliament. Fortunately, the advertising of Easthampton abroad, instigated by Richard, whose whereabouts were unknown, had been more successful than anyone could have anticipated, and many foreign visitors had already secured villas and other accommodation for several summers to come.

Mingling with the grander folk on the beach were little groups of ordinary people who had taken advantage of cheap excursions offered by the London and South Coast Railway for a day by the sea. Local traders had begun to cater for them, and hawkers with trays offered them everything from white mice to oranges and shrimping nets. Cheaper souvenirs of the seaside were taking their place on shelves in the resort, and the donkey-men on the sands had added to the number of their mounts to meet an increase in business.

The tide was flowing in as Lucy stood there. Children were paddling happily at the water's edge and digging moats for sand-castles. Every bathing-machine was in use, shrieks and squeals echoing across the lapping waves from where Emmie stood waist-deep, carrying on her seasonal work as if nothing had happened to disrupt her life since the previous year when a red-haired stranger had arrived in an Italian carriage and taken accommodation at Sea Cottage. No communication had been received from Meg either.

With a sigh, Lucy left the rails and snapped up her parasol, the lacy shade falling across her face. Reaching the promenade, she turned her steps in the direction of Easthampton House. She was going to say her farewells.

'Lucy!'

She spun about joyously as Josh overtook her in his cabriolet, and as they rode the rest of the way together he told her the news he had to tell.

At Easthampton House, Kate received them and led them through to the veranda where a table had been laid for tea. She had taken on a frail look, delicate and wraith-like, but her beauty was unimpaired and her welcome generous and warm.

'Daniel will join us with Donna for tea very shortly,' she said. 'He has been invited to stand as the Whig candidate for the forthcoming elections, and Donna is helping him with his correspondence and in planning his campaign.'

The invitation for Daniel to stand for Parliament had come during Josh's short absence, and he expressed his good wishes. Then he said, 'I've seen Richard.'

Kate sank down in the nearest chair, a silk shawl slipping from her shoulders in a blending of pastel hues. 'Where?' she breathed.

'In London. I happened to meet a mutual acquaintance who knew where he was staying. I sought him out.'

'How is he?' Eagerly.

'In good health. Much thinner, but perfectly well. He and Meg are married.'

She showed no surprise. 'I thought they might be. Did they seem happy?'

How could he answer her? Meg, handsomely dressed, had appeared frightened by his intrusion, jealously protective towards Richard, who looked as though happiness were something he had lost forever. Josh chose another reply. 'Meg is expecting his baby.'

'Daniel's first grandchild.' She was not thinking of her own claim. Always Daniel before herself. She asked Josh the next question with eloquent eyes, not daring to voice it. He inclined his head in sympathetic understanding.

'Richard said nothing about coming home.'

She looked down quickly at her lap, twisting her rings. 'At least he is well. That's all that matters.' Her composure regained, she raised her head again. 'Let me tell Daniel what you have told me, Josh. When I'm alone with him. He sorrows deeply over the loss of all contact with his son.'

Josh could see it in Daniel's face when he came with Donna out onto the shady veranda; over the past months his features had set in a deeper mould and he looked older, the wings of grey wider in his hair. As for Donna, she had recovered completely since the night she had assisted with the injured at the scene of the railway accident, although Josh recognized a subjugating of her femininity in her new political interests, a resigned acceptance of spinsterhood reflected in the severity of her hair-style, all ringlets gone, and in the lack of ornament on her prim clothes. She was full of enthusiasm for her father's electioneering plans and could talk of nothing else. There was a new quality in their relationship, no resentments on either side, almost as if Donna felt she had proved herself to him at last, whether he realized it or not, and could show him the filial loyalty and affection that he had long desired.

'You shall see the posters after tea,' she promised, sipping at her rose-patterned tea-cup, her dimple twinkling. 'They display an excellent likeness of the future new Member of Parliament for this constituency.'

The time came for Lucy and Josh to take their leave; Lucy embraced Kate and Donna before moving on to Daniel. 'Goodbye, Father,' she said fondly.

He held her by the shoulders, looking searchingly into her face. 'Come back soon, my child.'

'I will. Often.' She moved forward and pressed her cheek against his.

Josh drove her away from Easthampton House, down the

343

loops of the drive and out through the gates. As they drew level with Ring Park she caught his arm. 'Look!'

Richard was coming from the direction of the railway station, gazing about him as if hungry for the sight of the resort that was his birthplace. Then he saw her and came to a halt, following her with anguished eyes as she was driven past him. He was alone.

On impulse, Lucy raised her hand and waved. Some of the tension seemed to ease from him, and after a few moments he gave her an answering wave. Across the distance lengthening between them they continued to wave to each other until he was lost from her sight.